A NOVEL

BY MEG KERR

BEING THE CONTINUATION OF
PRIDE & PREJUDICE BY JANE AUSTEN

ISBN: 0986778907
ISBN-13: 9780986778902

Cover art by Gloria Blatt
Image of inkpot: Tetra Images

Prologue

[Pride and Prejudice, Chapter 61]

Happy for all her maternal feelings was the day on which Mrs. Bennet got rid of her two most deserving daughters. With what delighted pride she afterwards visited Mrs. Bingley, and talked of Mrs. Darcy, may be guessed. I wish I could say, for the sake of her family, that the accomplishment of her earnest desire in the establishment of so many of her children produced so happy an effect as to make her a sensible, amiable, well-informed woman for the rest of her life; though perhaps it was lucky for her husband, who might not have relished domestic felicity in so unusual a form, that she still was occasionally nervous and invariably silly.

Mr. Bennet missed his second daughter exceedingly; his affection for her drew him oftener from home than anything else could do. He delighted in going to Pemberley, especially when he was least expected.

Mr. Bingley and Jane remained at Netherfield only a twelvemonth. So near a vicinity to her mother and Meryton relations was not desirable even to his easy temper, or her affectionate heart. The darling wish of his sisters was then gratified; he bought an estate in a neighbouring county to Derbyshire, and Jane and Elizabeth, in addition to every other source of happiness, were within thirty miles of each other.

Kitty, to her very material advantage, spent the chief of her time with her two elder sisters. In society so superior to what she had generally known, her improvement was great. She was not of so ungovernable a temper as Lydia; and, removed from the influence of Lydia's example, she became, by proper attention and management, less irritable, less ignorant, and less insipid. From the further disadvantage of Lydia's society she was of course carefully kept, and though Mrs. Wickham frequently invited her to come and stay with her, with the promise of balls and young men, her father would never consent to her going.

Mary was the only daughter who remained at home; and she was necessarily drawn from the pursuit of accomplishments by Mrs. Bennet's being quite unable to sit alone. Mary was obliged to mix more with the world, but she could still moralize over every morning visit; and as she was no longer mortified by comparisons between her sisters' beauty and her own, it was suspected by her father that she submitted to the change without much reluctance.

As for Wickham and Lydia, their characters suffered no revolution from the marriage of her sisters. He bore with philosophy the conviction that Elizabeth must now become acquainted with whatever of his ingratitude and falsehood had before been unknown to her; and in spite of every thing, was not wholly without hope that Darcy might yet be prevailed on to make his fortune. The congratulatory letter which Elizabeth received from Lydia on her marriage, explained to her that, by his wife at least, if not by himself, such a hope was cherished. The letter was to this effect:

> *"MY DEAR LIZZY,*
> *"I wish you joy. If you love Mr. Darcy half as well as I do my dear Wickham, you must be very happy. It is a great comfort to have you so rich, and when you have nothing else to do, I hope you will think of us. I am sure Wickham would like a place at court very much, and I do not think we shall have quite money enough to live upon without some help. Any place would do, of about three or four hundred a year; but however, do not speak to Mr. Darcy about it, if you had rather not.*
> *"Yours, etc."*

As it happened that Elizabeth had <u>much</u> rather not, she endeavoured in her answer to put an end to every entreaty and expectation of the kind. Such relief, however, as it was in her power to afford, by the practice of what might be called economy in her own private expences, she frequently sent them. It had always been evident to her that such an income as theirs, under the direction of two persons so extravagant in their wants, and heedless of the future, must be very insufficient to their support; and whenever they changed their quarters, either Jane or herself were sure of being applied to for some little assistance towards discharging their bills. Their manner of living, even when the restoration of peace dismissed them to a home, was unsettled in the extreme. They were always moving from place to place in quest of a cheap situation, and always spending more than they ought. His affection for her soon sunk into indifference; hers lasted a little longer; and in spite of her youth and her manners, she retained all the claims to reputation which her marriage had given her.

~ *Prologue* ~

Though Darcy could never receive him at Pemberley, yet, for Elizabeth's sake, he assisted him further in his profession. Lydia was occasionally a visitor there, when her husband was gone to enjoy himself in London or Bath; and with the Bingleys they both of them frequently staid so long, that even Bingley's good humour was overcome, and he proceeded so far as to talk of giving them a hint to be gone.

Miss Bingley was very deeply mortified by Darcy's marriage; but as she thought it advisable to retain the right of visiting at Pemberley, she dropt all her resentment; was fonder than ever of Georgiana, almost as attentive to Darcy as heretofore, and paid off every arrear of civility to Elizabeth.

Pemberley was now Georgiana's home; and the attachment of the sisters was exactly what Darcy had hoped to see. They were able to love each other even as well as they intended. Georgiana had the highest opinion in the world of Elizabeth; though at first she often listened with an astonishment bordering on alarm at her lively, sportive, manner of talking to her brother. He, who had always inspired in herself a respect which almost overcame her affection, she now saw the object of open pleasantry. Her mind received knowledge which had never before fallen in her way. By Elizabeth's instructions, she began to comprehend that a woman may take liberties with her husband which a brother will not always allow in a sister more than ten years younger than himself.

Lady Catherine was extremely indignant on the marriage of her nephew; and as she gave way to all the genuine frankness of her character in her reply to the letter which announced its arrangement, she sent him language so very abusive, especially of Elizabeth, that for some time all intercourse was at an end. But at length, by Elizabeth's persuasion, he was prevailed on to overlook the offence, and seek a reconciliation; and, after a little further resistance on the part of his aunt, her resentment gave way, either to her affection for him, or her curiosity to see how his wife conducted herself; and she condescended to wait on them at Pemberley, in spite of that pollution which its woods had received, not merely from the presence of such a mistress, but the visits of her uncle and aunt from the city.

With the Gardiners, they were always on the most intimate terms. Darcy, as well as Elizabeth, really loved them; and they were both ever sensible of the warmest gratitude towards the persons who, by bringing her into Derbyshire, had been the means of uniting them.

Chapter One

[December 1812, Pemberley]

It is a suspicion generally entertained, that a honeymoon too sweet may bode ill for the marriage. It was well, therefore, that Mr. Fitzwilliam Darcy had a source of vexation, and that it did not derive, at least directly, from his new wife.

"Shall I ask you the reason of your grave and troubled look this morning?" inquired Mrs. Darcy as their coach conveyed them out of the innyard onto the North road. "I am inclined to attribute it to the breakfast ham, though it might equally have been the cold damp toast."

Darcy hesitated for a moment, and then withdrew from his inner pocket a letter and handed it to her. Elizabeth Darcy unfolded it, glanced at the signature "C. de Bourgh", and began to read.

> Rosings, Kent
> October –, 1812
>
> Darcy,
> You can scarcely imagine my astonishment at your announcement of impending marriage to Miss Elizabeth Bennet. You no doubt wrote in the hope of receiving my congratulations. However my character is celebrated for its sincerity and frankness, and I shall certainly not depart from it in this moment. When I first became aware of a report that Miss Bennet might be united to you, I knew it must be a scandalous falsehood, and I did not injure you in my mind by supposing the truth of it. When I called upon you in London following my interview with her I emphasized every expression of hers which peculiarly denoted her perverseness and assurance, in the belief that

such a relation must undeceive you as to her true character. But it now appears contrariwise that, in a moment of infatuation, you allowed her arts and allurements to draw you in and make you forget what you owe to yourself and your family. But consider what she is! A young woman of inferior birth, of no importance in the world, and wholly unallied to us! Who is her mother? Who are her aunts and uncles? Her sister is infamous for her elopement with the son of your father's steward! Is such a man to be your brother! She has refused to obey the claims of duty, honour and gratitude. She is lost to every feeling of propriety and delicacy. She will be censured, slighted and despised by everyone connected with you, and you will be ruined in the opinion of all your friends, and subject to the contempt of the world.

Are the shades of Pemberley to be thus polluted?

Honor, decorum and prudence forbade this alliance. So ought to have forethought for your estate, for the young woman's mother bore five daughters and never an heir. Of what were you thinking? Do you no longer retain your reason? You and my daughter were destined for each other by common voice of every member of our respective houses, but now are divided by the upstart pretensions of a young woman without family, connections or fortune. Her name will henceforth never be mentioned by me.

C. de Bourgh

"Lady Catherine expresses herself with uncommon energy," observed Elizabeth, returning the letter to her husband. She was herself tolerably indifferent to Lady Catherine's spleen, and was the less astonished by the sentiments contained in the letter from having heard something very similar from Lady Catherine's own lips. She knew that Lady Catherine and her sister Lady Anne Darcy had long ago planned an union of their two children to unite the family estates. Lady Anne, dead more than fifteen years, was capable of no distress at her son's marriage to Elizabeth Bennet rather than to her niece, but Lady Catherine appeared to feel displeasure more than sufficient for both.

"You see that she wrote when I informed her of our engagement. I have not replied."

"Yet you carry it with you, and you dwell on it."

"It is so offensive that my recollection of her words cannot be repelled. I am sorry to make you privy to a communication that must give you distress; however I thought you ought to see it so that you are not taken unaware by reports you may hear in the future."

Elizabeth laid her hand on her husband's. "Do you intend answering her soon?"

"I do not intend answering at all."

Elizabeth was silent for a moment. Although she found Lady Catherine insolent, arrogant, interfering and disagreeable, she did not wish to be the cause of a permanent separation between her and her nephew. "Have you read the letter more than once?"

"Several times. It does not grow less inflammatory on subsequent readings."

Elizabeth smiled. "Rather the opposite, I suspect. Put it away and do not let us think any more about it at the present. When shall we be at Pemberley? In four hours?"

"A little less. We shall be able to eat a late breakfast, and put behind us the memory of our early breakfast."

Elizabeth leaned against Darcy's arm and the coach rolled on.

Mr. Fitzwilliam Darcy was a young gentleman of eight-and-twenty, clever, well-informed, and the possessor of an income of ten thousand pounds a year, the estate of Pemberley in Derbyshire, and a townhouse on a fashionable street in London. He was also handsome, which a young man ought to be, if he possibly can. Mrs. Darcy, formerly Miss Elizabeth Bennet, was a young lady of one-and-twenty, with a pretty face rendered uncommonly intelligent by the beautiful expression of her fine dark eyes, a figure that was light and pleasing, and a sweet smile; and easy playful manners that had captivated Darcy, who himself had been denied the talent that some possess of conversing effortlessly with strangers. To the marriage she had brought, however, a mere one thousand pounds in the four per cents, together with relations decidedly lacking high connections, and some of them of questionable gentility.

Miss Elizabeth Bennet had wed Mr. Darcy in the parish church at Longbourn, on the same day that Miss Jane Bennet, her elder sister, had been united with Darcy's close friend Mr. Charles Bingley. The courtship of the Bennet sisters had not been without incident, indeed had threatened to come to naught on a number of occasions; and the rejoicing at its successful conclusion within the Bennet family, and by Mr. Darcy and Mr. Bingley themselves, had been commensurate with the discomposure of spirits that had not infrequently attended its pursuit. The rejoicing had not been universal, however, for Lady Catherine had been exceedingly agitated by Darcy's choice of wife, as had Bingley's sisters Miss Caroline Bingley and Mrs. Louisa Hurst; all of whom had marked Darcy out for a different nuptial partner: Miss Anne de Bourgh in the first case, and Miss Bingley in the second. The newly-wed couple bore up under these disappointed wishes as best they might, and were able for comparatively long periods to put them entirely out of mind, having, as Elizabeth remarked, extraordinary sources of happiness necessarily attached to their situation, that upon the whole left them no cause to repine.

"I have never before managed a household myself you know," said Elizabeth thoughtfully from her place on Darcy's arm. "And Pemberley is such a large house. I hope you will not be inconvenienced if I some times misplace a footman or a soup tureen."

"I assure you, Elizabeth, that Mrs. Reynolds has been a most competent housekeeper at Pemberley for many years, and that you will not be called upon to do more than issue occasional instructions."

"What if I should have a notion to inventory the linens or count the turnips or teaspoons?"

"I shall make clear to Mrs. Reynolds that you are to be humoured should you have an outburst of domestic feeling. But it is my hope that you will not be enticed away too frequently from the more civilized parts of the house by the charm of the root cellars and linen presses."

As the morning passed and they drew nearer to Pemberley, Elizabeth began to watch eagerly for the first sight of the Pemberley Woods. The hills of the estate, their trees a sere brown now rather than the lush green of the summer, were visible for some distance before the carriage turned into the park at the lodge.

"We are home," said Darcy with satisfaction.

The lodge keeper and his wife appeared at the side of the drive, and Darcy tapped for the coachman to stop. He leaned across Elizabeth and lowered the glass. "Good morning, Walters, is all well?"

"We heard as how you were bringing your lady home today and wanted to be the first to give you good wishes," said Walters.

"We receive them with thanks," said Darcy. "This is your new mistress."

"I am very glad to see you," said Elizabeth with her sweet smile, "and I am certain that such punctual good wishes on arriving home must bring good fortune."

"Ah," said Mrs. Walters, "I believe the master has already brought his good fortune with him, madam. We have been waiting these five years or more for him to choose his lady, and now we see he has chosen properly."

Darcy laughed and signaled the coachman to drive on. "The endorsement of the servants is a strong antidote to Lady Catherine's choler," he said as he pulled up the glass.

They drove for some distance through the park until the road gradually rose and the woods ended on the top of a hill. From this height they had their first sight of Pemberley House across the valley, with its ridge of high woody hills behind it. "It is as beautiful as I remembered it," said Elizabeth to Darcy. To herself she said in wonder, "And now I am mistress of Pemberley!"

They descended the hill, crossed the bridge and drove up to the house. At the door Miss Georgiana Darcy, Darcy's younger sister, greeted them. She had, at sixteen, a handsome face marked with sense and good humour, a womanly and graceful appearance, and gentle and unassuming manners. She had not seen Elizabeth since the summer, when the latter with her aunt and uncle had come into Derbyshire, and had been disappointed at Elizabeth's sudden departure, when news from home summoned her away peremptorily. When she had received tidings from her brother of his engagement, four sides of paper had not been sufficient to contain her happiness, and her earnest desire of being loved by her new sister. The reserve characteristic of the family, that had often been taken in Darcy for conceit or arrogance, in her exhibited itself as exceeding shyness, but her delight overcame it on this occasion, and the sincerity of her joy at claiming her relationship with Elizabeth could not be doubted.

Mrs. Reynolds and the butler Mr. Spurgeon waited discreetly behind Miss Darcy. "Welcome home sir and madam," said the butler. "There is a good fire in the breakfast parlour, and a hot meal." The family repaired to the parlour, where Darcy and Elizabeth warmed themselves, and took refreshment more palatable than they had yet had that day.

"Now," said Elizabeth after they had finished their repast, "will you give me leave to see Lady Catherine's letter again?"

"Why do you wish to read it a second time?" asked Darcy. "You cannot find more gratification in it than do I."

Elizabeth could hardly help smiling as she assured him that she had no desire to read it. "You need not be under any alarm! I only wish to advise you how to deal with it."

Somewhat reluctantly Darcy produced the letter. Elizabeth took it from him and then went to the fire. She held the paper by the tips of her fingers above the blazing coals. "This is my advice," she said. "Will you take it? I should not like you to have the power of reading it again."

After a moment Darcy said, "If you believe it essential to the preservation of any remaining regard for my aunt."

Elizabeth let the letter fall and it slowly scorched and then burned. "And now," she said, "we must hope that you had not committed too much of it to memory!"

Chapter Two

[December 1812, Longbourn]

At Longbourn, the home of the Bennet family, the Christmas was far from cheerful, for the absence of Elizabeth and the youngest daughter Lydia from the family circle was acutely felt. Jane was living only three miles away at the nearby estate of Netherfield; but Elizabeth was in Derbyshire and Lydia was in Newcastle with her husband George Wickham, an ensign in the regular army. Mrs. Bennet's brother and his wife, Mr. and Mrs. Gardiner, together with their children made their customary visit and did all in their power to raise the spirits of the remaining family members; however they were unable entirely to console Mr. Bennet for the loss of Elizabeth, or Mrs. Bennet and the second youngest daughter Kitty for the loss of Lydia.

Kitty was rendered even more than ordinarily fretful by the receipt of a letter from Lydia at the new year, inviting her for a visit.

> Newcastle
> December 31, 1812
>
> Dear Kitty,
> I have been too busy to find time to write letters but I did not want you to think I have forgotten you! You cannot imagine how many officers there are here, all in their red coats. Of course my Wickham is the handsomest, but there are several who are almost as handsome, <u>and I have seen one or two of them giving me a look</u>! If I did not have my Wickham I think I would have given them a look back! One of them, a captain who is next handsomest to Wickham, danced with me twice at the Christmas ball and begged to dance with me again but I told him he was impertinent to act the way he did with

me, a married woman, and I turned my back on him. Then what do you think he did! Oh Kitty! He came up very close behind me and whispered in my ear that he wanted to give me a gift that only a married woman could appreciate! I would have boxed his ears, but when I turned around he had such a smile on his face that I could only laugh! I ran away and found my Wickham but he did not want to dance because he was winning at cards. I almost told him what Rawdon said, but then I thought it was better not. The next time I see Rawdon I will give him such a set-down! But Kitty you must persuade our father to let you come for a visit because we have a ball at least once a fortnight, and there are such a lot of private parties, and there are many more gentlemen than ladies. You would be able to flirt with at least three or four officers at once, and I am certain that within two or three months you would find a husband. Then we would be able to live in the same town and go about together. Kitty what fun we would have! Perhaps you would like Rawdon—but no that would not do, I wish him to go on liking me! Do talk to our father and mother and let me know what papa says, but do not show him this letter, he probably would not like to hear about Rawdon, or about Wickham playing cards for money.

Your affectionate sister,
Lydia Wickham

Kitty simpered at the thought of a flirtation with several officers, and hoped that her turn would come soon to find a husband, now that three of her sisters were married; but she refrained from showing the letter to anyone, as she was certain that neither her father nor her mother, nor her aunt and uncle, would wish to hear either about Rawdon or about Wickham's gambling, and she did not even dare broach the subject of visiting Newcastle. She grew quite dejected at the thought of Lydia's abundant felicity, thereby increasing the langour of the family party.

Mrs. Bennet was unable to contain her melancholic ill-humour and would from time to time fall to scolding Kitty or Mary, her other daughter still at home, for minor or imaginary trespasses.

"Kitty, for Heaven's sake, do not sit there so idle, and staring me out of countenance."

"I am not looking at you at all, mama."

"Do not contradict me. It tears my nerves to pieces to be contradicted so by everyone in my own house."

"I am not contradicting you, mama, any more than I am staring at you."

It had been agreed between Jane and Elizabeth before their weddings, that after they had establishments of their own Kitty would spend the chief of her time with one or the other of them. It was her elder sisters' hope that she would gain material advantage from society superior to that provided by Lydia, for Kitty had been comprehended in the same danger that had consumed her younger sister. From ignorance, vanity, idleness and emptiness of mind, she like Lydia would be unable to ward off any portion of the universal contempt that a rage for admiration excites. Jane, on a morning call from Netherfield, perceived that her mother's querulousness might furnish an opportunity to forward their plan. "Dear madam, Kitty *is* idle here. Let her come to me and Bingley at Netherfield for a little while."

"What would I do at Netherfield?" said Kitty peevishly.

"We should find something for you. You can scarcely do less at Netherfield than you do here."

"There is nothing to do in this neighbourhood, now that Lydia has gone, and the regiment has left Meryton; and Lydia is having such fun in Newcastle. I do not even ask my father if I may go and visit her, for I know what his answer would be. It is very unfair."

"Yes, Jane, take her," cried Mrs. Bennet, "and perhaps we shall have some peace in this house for my nerves at last."

Accordingly it was agreed that Kitty should remove to Netherfield immediately.

Chapter Three

[January 1813, Pemberley]

Elizabeth's father Mr. Bennet, captivated by the youth and beauty of a certain Miss Gardiner, the daughter of an attorney in Meryton, and by the appearance of good humour which youth and beauty may give, had married beneath his station in life. Mrs. Bennet was a woman of mean understanding, little information, and uncertain temper, and Mr. Bennet had early in their marriage lost all real affection for her. She had a sister, Mrs. Phillips, a vulgar woman married to their father's former clerk who had succeeded him in his business. Elizabeth however was fortunate enough to have relations on her mother's side for whom she did not need to blush, for her mother also had a brother who, though in trade in London, was a sensible and well-bred man, greatly superior to his sisters by nature as well as education. He was married to an amiable, intelligent and elegant woman who was a great favourite with her nieces. Mr. and Mrs. Gardiner had been instrumental in bringing together Elizabeth and Darcy; and on informing her aunt and uncle of her engagement to Darcy, Elizabeth had invited them to Pemberley for Christmas.

The Gardiners would have been delighted to join their niece and new nephew, but upon reflection Mrs. Gardiner had written to Elizabeth, "We are sensible of our obligation to our sister and brother who are also expecting us for the Christmas visit at Longbourn and who are already deprived of two daughters (Jane of course is still near by). I would not add to their loss by decamping so promptly to Pemberley. But dear Lizzy do not take this refusal as anything other than it is, and we are looking forward most eagerly to visiting you and Darcy as soon as may be thereafter. My heart is still set on the drive all around the park with the phaeton and ponies."

Elizabeth had been excessively disappointed by her aunt's letter, but as it was not her nature to fret over unavoidable evils, she had written in reply as cheerfully as she could that the Gardiners were to come to them in June, and that from Pemberley they could make together the trip to the Lake District that had been planned for the previous year. "Of course we shall go around the Park with the ponies, every day if you wish it. You know that I do not regret the Lakes last year, as something much better came of it, but I should still like to go there with you."

Darcy too had been regretful that the Gardiners could not come, but he had consoled Elizabeth with the prospect of another guest at the beginning of the new year, his cousin Colonel Fitzwilliam. Darcy and Fitzwilliam were connected not merely by their family relationship but also by a warm affection between them. The preceding spring they had been staying together with their aunt Lady Catherine at Rosings Park in Hunsford, Kent, where they had encountered Elizabeth on a visit to her friend Charlotte Collins, the wife of the rector of Hunsford parish. Darcy had been violently in love with Elizabeth at that time, and Colonel Fitzwilliam's fancy had also been caught very much by the pretty Miss Bennet. She had enjoyed Fitzwilliam's company and had never been half so well entertained at Rosings as when talking with him. She had even indeed been reminded, by his evident admiration of her and by her own satisfaction in being with him, of George Wickham, who had for a time engaged her affections. Darcy she had disliked; however it had been Darcy who had made an offer to her in Kent, and not his cousin.

Elizabeth expressed her pleasure at seeing Colonel Fitzwilliam again, and Georgiana too was exceedingly satisfied at the news of his coming, for as well as being, together with Darcy, her guardian, he was a particular favourite of hers.

Colonel Fitzwilliam was about one-and-thirty, not handsome, but in person and address most truly the gentleman. As befit a military officer, he arrived at Pemberley punctual to his time. He was greeted by the butler as an *habitué* of the house and shown up to a sitting room where Elizabeth was in solitary but earnest contemplation of some new fabrics. At his entrance she turned with a smile. "Colonel Fitzwilliam!"

Looking at Elizabeth, Fitzwilliam felt that he had not been recollecting since their last meeting her pretty face and captivating smile, with the slightest degree of unreasonable admiration. He bowed and said, "Mrs. Darcy, how very agreeable to see you again."

"Welcome to Pemberley. Darcy and I are most happy to have you here, and I am certain that he will tell you so himself once he appears. But presently I have no idea where he is or what is detaining him."

"For my part, I know that if you were my wife I would never leave your side," said Colonel Fitzwilliam gravely.

Elizabeth replied with an arch smile, "How fortunate then that I fell to Darcy's lot instead of yours, or you would have a great deal of difficulty earning your living as a soldier. Will you walk with me in the gallery while we wait for him? He has just had restored a portrait of your and his great-grandfather. I think you will like to see it."

Fitzwilliam assented and they left the sitting room and proceeded through the upper lobby to the gallery, through which they walked slowly, pausing from time to time in front of a portrait that caught the eye of one or the other, and chatting cordially about Colonel Fitzwilliam's journey down from London. He had made an excellent ten miles an hour on the North road, with fine weather and good horses. At length they stopped before a portrait of James Fitzwilliam, 5th Earl of Tyrconnell.*

"Good Lord!" exclaimed Fitzwilliam. "Old Earl James would not have much difficulty recognizing his descendants, would he? There is a picture of him at the Castle, but he is older and the resemblance is not so marked. Less hair, more nose."

"Certainly not in recognizing *you* as a descendant," agreed Elizabeth, for the portrait was as like the young man standing at her side as it was possible to be, allowing for the passage of a hundred years and changing fashions.

"Has Darcy told you about the old reprobate?' asked Fitzwilliam. "He drank his bottle of port every day, and loved his dogs and horses far better than his wife and sons. And not all of his sons had any connection with his wife. Altogether, he was a fine example of the old school."

"I am afraid that all Darcy thought fit for my ears was that he published a pamphlet about the treatment of leg injuries in horses," laughed Elizabeth.

"He does not want you to think less of him for being descended from a line of coarse and lusty—and rather wicked—peers. He would prefer that you appreciate the refinement of the present generation. And yet," said Fitzwilliam, pausing a moment and looking closely at Elizabeth, "and yet I'd be willing to lay a wager that you could have managed the old boy and never turned a hair at his bottle and dogs and horses."

"I might have objected to all of the unconnected sons."

"It seems possible to me," said Fitzwilliam thoughtfully, "that if you had been his wife, all of his sons would have been connected."

Elizabeth blushed a little at the turn of the conversation, but reminded herself that she was a married woman. She exerted herself to appear quite composed and said lightly, "I am not persuaded that amounts to a compliment, but if it does, I thank you for it."

"Most definitely a compliment," said Fitzwilliam gazing at her attentively.

"Fitzwilliam!"

They turned at the sound of Darcy's voice from the entrance to the gallery.

---

* The title of Earl of Tyrconnell was created in 1661 by King Charles II for Oliver FitzWilliam, 2nd Viscount FitzWilliam. –Editor.

"Well," said Fitzwilliam as Darcy came nearer, "this must be my host. Better late than never, although perhaps it would have been better *much* later, for you are interrupting my tour of the family skeletons with your wife. But I am at your disposal, as ever."

"My apologies, cousin, business with my steward occasioned the postponement of my welcome. But I am certain that Elizabeth has taken as good care of you as I could have."

"Far better, I assure you. I was not intending to remark on your absence until tomorrow morning at the earliest."

"Elizabeth brought you to look at Earl James, I see."

"Yes. I wish I had his land and income, instead of his looks. I speak feelingly."

"How goes your search for an heiress?" inquired Elizabeth as they turned and retraced their steps along the gallery. "Your friends will rejoice when you have met the one who will accept you."

"Badly, I fear," said Fitzwilliam. "I was introduced to a lady whose most remarkable charm was her fortune of thirty thousand pounds. However I could not reconcile myself to the countenance attached to it. My brother is quite irritated with me, asked me whether I thought properties of thirty thousand pounds littered the roadside like stones."

"We cannot consider your situation with much compassion," said Elizabeth with a smile.

Georgiana appeared at the entrance to the gallery and welcomed her Cousin James with excitement, and the party returned to the sitting room where refreshment was soon provided for the traveller. At five o'clock the ladies retired to dress for dinner, and Darcy and Fitzwilliam in their absence spoke together of matters of family business.

Chapter Four

[January 1813, letters]

At some time in the distant past, an owner of Longbourn had placed the property in fee tail male. Whether or not, as Mrs. Bennet asserted, such things are all chance in this world and there is no knowing how estates will go when once they come to be entailed, the heir of Longbourn was a distant cousin of Mr. Bennet's, the Reverend William Collins, rector of Hunsford Parish and client of the great patroness Lady Catherine de Bourgh of Rosings Park. Very soon after his installation, Lady Catherine had given Mr. Collins her particular advice and recommendation that he ought to marry—for Lady Catherine's sake a gentlewoman, and for Mr. Collins' sake an active, useful sort of person, not brought up too high but able to make a small income go a good way. "Find such a woman as soon as you can, bring her to Hunsford, and I will visit her," Lady Catherine had said with great condescension. Such encouragement had fortified Mr. Collins' resolve to find a wife, and he had promptly set out to do so.

Mr. Collins' first intention had been to make amends to his female cousins for the hardship that he was causing them by being heir to the estate, by choosing a wife from among them. Jane, his first choice as eldest and most beautiful, he was warned away from by Mrs. Bennett, who supposed at the time that she would very soon be engaged to Mr. Bingley of Netherfield Hall, and Elizabeth, next to Jane in birth and beauty, refused him. Not wishing after these two defeats to essay his fortune with the three younger sisters, he instead turned his attention to the Bennets' neighbour, Miss Lucas, and within a wonderfully short time the two of them concluded the matrimonial business to their mutual satisfaction. Charlotte now resided at Hunsford Parsonage, on the edge of Rosings Park, where she and her husband performed valuable service to Lady Catherine by dining with her and her daughter when more eligible guests were not available and making up a table on evenings when extra players were required for quadrille or whist.

Mr. Collins had been married to his dear Charlotte less than a year when he wrote to inform Mr. Bennet of his expectation of a young olive-branch. Charlotte in due course was delivered and Elizabeth received the following communication from her father, containing an enclosure.

Longbourn House
January –, 1813

My dearest Lizzy,
As you will see from the enclosed, the young olive branch has sprouted. I advised Mr. Collins to stand by the nephew, as he has more to give, but he appears determined to remain with the aunt, and although he has about as much sense as would fit into a thimble, I am compelled to admire his loyalty.

The Gardiners have returned to town, and Kitty has been farmed out to Jane and Bingley for improvement, so Longbourn is quiet, or quiet at least when Mary is not practising the pianoforte or Mrs. Bennet is not bemoaning the loss of her daughters. My dear child your absence is felt and you may depend upon a visit from me in the early spring, or sooner if Mary does not desist from tormenting the Klavier into Ill Temper.
Yours,
Etc.

The enclosure was a letter to Mr. Bennet from Mr. Collins.

Hunsford Parsonage
January –, 1813

My Dear Sir,
I am called upon by our relationship to inform you that my dear Charlotte has been delivered of a young olive branch. I must ask for your congratulations on this happy event, and hope that it constitutes some amends for any injury I may have caused my amiable cousins. She will be christened Catherine Anne Collins, and I trust that you and your family will take no offence at the choice of these names, for I conceive myself bound to pay these little delicate attentions, and to take every opportunity to display my humble gratitude to my patroness. Lady Catherine was most pleased by this compliment to herself and her daughter. Recent events have much irritated her, and

she does not turn a friendly eye upon your family; indeed she has frequently opined that my cousin Elizabeth will bring disgrace upon her nephew. I urge you to warn your daughter to govern her conduct with the greatest care, as those high in the realm are no doubt watching her.

I am, dear sir, etc. etc.

Elizabeth also received, a short time thereafter, a letter directly from Mrs. Collins.

Hunsford Parsonage
January –, 1813

Dearest Eliza,

Have no fear for me for I am come safe through the event, and my little daughter is as pink and healthy as could be hoped. Mr. Collins looks at her with awe from a distance but has not yet summoned the courage to hold her as she is so small, and of course liable to sudden squawking outbursts that startle.

I dearly wished to have you at the christening as godmother, but even if we were not separated by such a distance now it would have been most inadvisable! Lady Catherine is as unreconciled to your marriage today as she was on the day she first received news of it. I almost welcomed my confinement simply as an escape from taking tea and eating dinner at Rosings, for the conversation inevitably would turn to Darcy's imprudence and your numerous imperfections. Mr. Collins does not dare speak to her of Christian forgiveness or charity, and finds the only way to calm the tempest is to agree with her remarks, so I fear that there is no one at hand who can or will lead her to a *rapprochement*. I am not likely to leave Kent for some time, and I therefore depend on receiving your letters here very often.

Yours affectionately,
C. Collins

Elizabeth responded immediately to Charlotte's letter with warmest expressions of regard and a promise of faithful correspondence. Mr. Bennet after the passage of a fortnight replied to Mr. Collins' letter with the requested congratulations and an assurance that the Bennet family was not in the least discommoded by the choice of names bestowed on the young olive branch.

Chapter Five

[January 1813, Pemberley]

"Darcy, you have set yourself an hopeless endeavour!" said Elizabeth, pulling on the reins in an unavailing effort to slow her horse's prancing walk. "I am no horsewoman and nothing that has happened this past hour suggests to me that I will ever become one."

"You have had a remarkable effect on that mare," observed Darcy. "I have mounted you on the quietest horse in the stable, one that would prefer to amble along at a walk and not bestir herself to a trot much less a canter, and you have kept her on the verge of running off at a gallop for our entire ride."

"The effect has been completely unwished-for, I assure you!"

"The mare understands your intentions only through your actions, and your actions are telling her that you desire her to run. That is why I have continually repeated that you must sit back instead of forward, and you must lengthen the reins instead of shortening them."

"It runs so contrary to my natural inclinations that I cannot seem to do it."

"There is something of the swan about you on horseback, Elizabeth," laughed Colonel Fitzwilliam, who was riding on her other side. "A swan out of water, that is!"

Elizabeth laughed heartily at this picture of herself. "I do not need you to tell me that I look like a goose! I may be able to delude others into thinking that I have some slight claim to grace or elegance when I am sitting at an instrument or standing up in a ballroom, but no one who could see me now would give it any credence!"

"Elizabeth, I ought to beg your pardon, whatever you are doing, it is not possible for you to look anything other than lovely," said Fitzwilliam with great sincerity.

His words seemed to strike Darcy forcibly, and the latter's eyes were directed with a very serious expression towards his cousin; yet he said nothing.

When the party was seated at dinner that evening Fitzwilliam said to Georgiana, "You should have come riding with us today. You would have seen a superb display of horsemanship on your sister's part. When I saw the groom lead out that old mare Sorrel for her to ride I thought we were going to have a very dull time of it. But she had the mare chewing the bit and set to run a race from the moment she mounted. I think Elizabeth is almost ready for a steeplechase,* don't you Darcy?"

Darcy looked at Elizabeth. "It would be wise in you not to teaze Elizabeth, Fitzwilliam, or she will give as good as she gets."

"Colonel Fitzwilliam has little to fear from me on the subject of horses," said Elizabeth ruefully.

"Cousin James, have you been steeplechasing?" Georgiana asked anxiously. "You will break your neck."

"Not since last year in Ireland, although to tell the truth of it I very nearly did break my neck, one fellow broke his leg, and we had to put down a horse after it took a tumble into a ditch. It was an unpleasant thing."

"I suppose you are telling this to Georgiana in order to soothe her concern for your neck," said Darcy.

"I think he is telling it to show himself off," said Georgiana.

"Now if I were showing myself off I would mention the six-foot hedge I cleared clean as a whistle."

"I should think such a performance reflected credit rather on the horse than you," said Darcy.

"You are rather lessening the honour of my triumph, are you not? But I will not speak of my own arts. Father keeps some fine animals, and there is really not much to do at the Castle save ride or drink." Elizabeth suddenly remembered Earl James and the unconnected sons, and coloured a little in spite of herself. "If I had to live there I daresay I'd go steeplechasing as often as possible in the very hope of finishing myself off."

"I think you need a wife, Cousin James," said Georgiana.

"Everyone agrees with you," said Fitzwilliam, "and I will be happy to oblige the world when Darcy conveniently dies and leaves Elizabeth a rich widow."

"'Like Niobe, all tears,'" said Darcy. But his brow was contracted with doubt as he looked at his cousin.

"Come," said Elizabeth, "let us find something to talk of besides broken necks and widows."

---

* A steeplechase, also known as a point-to-point (a church steeple being a particularly visible point) is a cross-country horse race, with obstacles taken as they occur. It first became popular in the mid-18th century, in Ireland. –Ed.

"Fitzwilliam, will you visit our aunt this spring?" asked Darcy.

It occurred to Elizabeth that Lady Catherine was a subject no happier than broken necks and widows, but she could see no immediate way to turn the conversation.

"I have been invited for Easter, as usual, but I have given no definite answer as yet. Even allowing for it being a penitential season, I am hard put to find a reason to go there without you and Elizabeth to provide relief. But would I not be declaring for her side if I went to her?"

"No more than you are declaring for our side by being at Pemberley," said Darcy.

"I thought that was what I was doing here. I have declared for you and Elizabeth."

When the family was assembled in the drawing room after dinner, Fitzwilliam applied for some music. "Elizabeth, will you sing for us?"

"Let Georgiana perform first," said Darcy. "She is in need of practice before an audience."

"I do not mind performing for you and Elizabeth and Cousin James," said Georgiana. "I am not afraid of *you*."

"Then we must all look very fierce," said Fitzwilliam, "and exclaim in loud voices if you miss a note, so as to give you an audience that you *are* afraid of."

Georgiana laughed. "I do not think you can intimidate me, Cousin James, however hard you try. What do you wish to hear?"

"Let us have some of Moore's Irish Melodies,"* said Fitzwilliam at once.

"Georgiana, do you give us 'Silent, oh Moyle'," said Elizabeth. "I heard you singing it the other day and thought how pretty your voice sounded."

Georgiana took her place at the instrument and began:

> Silent, oh Moyle, be the roar of thy water,
> Break not, ye breezes, your chain of repose,
> While, murmuring mournfully, Lir's lonely daughter
> Tells to the night-star her tale of woes.
> When shall the swan, her death-note singing,
> Sleep, with wings in darkness furl'd?
> When will heaven, its sweet bell ringing,
> Call my spirit from this stormy world?
>
> Sadly, oh Moyle, to thy winter-wave weeping,
> Fate bids me languish long ages away;
> Yet still in her darkness doth Erin lie sleeping,

---

* Compiled by Thomas Moore (1779-1852), and released in ten volumes between 1808 and 1834. –Ed.

Still doth the pure light its dawning delay.
When will that day-star, mildly springing,
Warm our isle with peace and love?
When will heaven, its sweet bell ringing,
Call my spirit to the fields above?

"It's a pretty song," said Fitzwilliam, "and no doubt the prettier for being completely unintelligible."

"It is about Fionnuala, who was turned into a swan," said Georgiana, "and she wandered for hundreds of years until Christianity came to Ireland and she heard the mass-bell."

"Thank you, Georgiana, for making the completely unintelligible entirely incomprehensible. Elizabeth, will you take your turn now?"

Elizabeth seated herself in Georgiana's place. "I await your command, Colonel Fitzwilliam."

"Then my command is that you shall play and I shall sing." Fitzwilliam came to Elizabeth's side and leafed through the music book. "This one," he said, setting the open book in front of her.

"This is one of my favourites," said Elizabeth, and she straight away played a short introduction. "Now, Colonel Fitzwilliam, please begin."

Fitzwilliam placed himself so as to command a full view of her countenance, and commenced the song. He was possessed of a pleasing baritone voice and sang with an affecting air of candour, with his eyes fixed on Elizabeth.

Believe me, if all those endearing young charms
Which I gaze on so fondly to-day,
Were to change by to-morrow and fleet in my arms,
Like fairy gifts fading away.
Thou wouldst still be adored as this moment thou art,
Let thy loveliness fade as it will,
And around the dear ruin each wish of my heart,
Would entwine itself verdantly still.

It is not while beauty and youth are thine own
And thy cheeks unprofaned by a tear,
That the fervor and faith of a soul can be known,
To which time will but make thee more dear:
No, the heart that has truly loved never forgets,
But as truly loves on to the close,
As the sun-flower turns on her god when he sets
The same look which she turn'd when he rose.

There was a silence when the last notes had died away. After a moment Elizabeth closed the instrument. "I think that is enough music for this evening," she said, striving to speak lightly.

Fitzwilliam's eyes remained fixed on her. "If music be the food of love, play on," he said softly.

"No one will wish to try to match your performance, Colonel Fitzwilliam," she said with a smile that cost her no small effort. She had been far from suspecting that she might be still an object of interest in the eyes of her husband's cousin. However she now recollected a remark she had once made, that while one good sonnet will starve away entirely a slight inclination, everything nourishes what is strong already.

Chapter Six

[January 1813, Pemberley]

Colonel Fitzwilliam had not been a man much given to romantic entanglements in the course of his life, and as a result when the partiality towards Elizabeth that he had first felt at Rosings had developed into a deeper attachment he had not taken it very seriously, presuming that such feelings are easily regulated or, if they prove recalcitrant, run their course swiftly, in the manner of a bad cold. It was for that reason that he had been able to tell Elizabeth without much concern, before they parted in Kent, that a younger son of an Earl cannot marry where he likes. He had been quite unprepared for the increase of his feelings towards her after he had left Kent; and he had been utterly astonished when Darcy's announcement that he had engaged himself to marry Elizabeth struck him like a sword thrust. The few days he had spent at Pemberley convinced him that she was the most entrancing woman of his acquaintance, and he sought out opportunities to be in her society.

Although Elizabeth was no horsewoman she was fond of walking, and often went out by herself in the morning, coming in to breakfast with her face glowing with the warmth of exercise. When on the fifth morning of his visit she came out of the house through a terrace door she was greeted by Fitzwilliam.

"Good morning, Elizabeth, you are looking exceeding pretty this morning," he said.

"Fitzwilliam! You surprised me. I did not expect to see you, especially here, at this hour."

"I have observed that you usually take a walk in the morning—I admire the brilliancy of your complexion on your return— and I thought I would offer to escort you."

Elizabeth hesitated.

"Unless of course you do not wish for my company," added Fitzwilliam with sudden reserve.

Elizabeth relented. "Of course you may join me. But all praise of me will be unnecessary. You must not make any more improper compliments."

"Improper? How so? Would you forbid me also to praise the sun for its warmth on my face or the breeze for its cooling touch?"

"No, you are quite at liberty to compliment the sun, the moon, the wind and the rain, and all other forces of nature."

"Now, you see," said Fitzwilliam reproachfully, "you have given with one hand and taken away with the other, and then you will claim you have absolutely forbidden me to admire you aloud."

"What do you mean by this?"

"Surely a beautiful woman is a force of nature?"

"Fitzwilliam, you must not say such things to me, indeed," said Elizabeth, in genuine distress.

Fitzwilliam was instantly contrite. "I apologize, my dear cousin, for displeasing you." He took her hand and lightly kissed her fingers. "Am I forgiven?"

She paused uncertainly, her feelings still perturbed, but no other idea befriended her; and she said with civility that was a little strained, "Of course, Fitzwilliam. Let us go on. Oh! Here is Samson, he has appointed himself my guide." A large black dog ambled out of the shrubbery and stood regarding Elizabeth in anticipation.

"Hello, Samson," said Fitzwilliam cordially. "You never demonstrated any interest in going for a walk with me in the past."

"Darcy says he is a breed called a Newfoundland. I had never seen a dog the size of a pony. But he is quite gentle."

The dog strolled towards the path and then turned and stood looking at them.

"We must not keep him waiting," said Elizabeth, and started off.

"May I offer you my arm?"

"Thank you, but I am quite used to long walks and I am wearing my stout shoes."

"Onward then," said Fitzwilliam. "Samson, I trust you not to lead us into a bog, or a pit of vipers, or any form of temptation."

Samson gave his tail a brief wag and walked on ahead of them.

"Mistress of Pemberley," said Fitzwilliam after they had proceeded for a few moments in silence. "It seems to suit you."

"Do you believe so? Some times I find myself wondering if I am deceived that I have a right to be here, and whether a footman will appear to put me out of the house."

"If you are an impostor, you carry it off very well. I am entirely certain there is no one here who suspects you at all. Darcy is treating you well I trust?"

"He has given me a bloodstained key to a secret chamber and made me promise never to open the door, on pain of death," said Elizabeth solemnly. "Other than that, I am perfectly happy with his treatment of me."

"I always suspected that he must have a Bluebeard side, no one could act with such propriety as he does at all times and not have some dark blemish on his character."

"Fitzwilliam, I spoke in jest, but I should not have, Darcy does not have any dark blemish and I am very happy with him. He and I both hope, that you and your wife will someday be as happy as we."

"I am expected to marry with discretion," he replied mordantly, "and to be happy not with a wife but with her fortune and connections. A man in my circumstances does not have leisure to observe the more elegant conventions of society."

Elizabeth responded with the liveliest solicitude, "Fitzwilliam, have you truly ever known of dependence or self-denial, or been prevented by want of money from procuring whatever you chose? I do not quarrel with you for your wish of independence, but where does discretion end and the mercenary motive begin? You must have something to live on, that is only prudent, but when does prudence become avarice? Do you not consider there may be some deficiency in feeling for you to pursue this course? Oh Fitzwilliam do anything rather than marry without affection. Darcy and I would be very grieved to see you unhappy with your wife."

"We all love to instruct, do we not," said Fitzwilliam with a faint smile. "I have already found the lady to whom my affections are given, and I do not find myself deficient in feeling. But it is not possible for me to gain *her* regard, for she is the wife of another." He looked at Elizabeth, whose cheeks immediately became suffused with a deep blush. She instinctively turned away from him a little, feeling an embarrassment that was almost impossible to overcome, and a confusion that rendered her almost incapable of speech. But at length she forced herself to say, "I cannot express a sense of gratitude for the sentiments you express, for of course it is impossible for me to return them, and it is wrong of you to utter them. But I am very sorry to occasion any pain to you, for Darcy's sake, and for the sake of my regard for you as my cousin."

"The pain you cause me with your words is small in comparison with the pain occasioned by my own emotions."

"I implore you, Fitzwilliam, do not give way to such feelings as these, for they will ruin your happiness," said Elizabeth in acute misery. There was silence between them for a time. Then with an effort she said, "I pray you, let us henceforth be silent on this matter. Let us talk of other things. In the past we were able to speak of books and music and travel."

"As you wish."

After many pauses and many awkward trials of different subjects their walk brought them back within sight of Pemberley House. There Elizabeth stopped on the path, contemplating its ascent.

"Elizabeth, you are rather white, do you feel unwell?" asked Fitzwilliam.

"I am quite well," said Elizabeth. "But—I believe I must sit down for a moment." She suited the action to the word and seated herself on the stone wall by the edge of the path.

"Elizabeth, I fear you are *not* well," said Fitzwilliam in alarm as he watched her head droop.

"It is exceedingly odd, but I am a little faint."

Without saying another word, Fitzwilliam swept her up into his arms.

"Oh Fitzwilliam, put me down," she protested. But in fact she felt very unwell and had not the strength to pursue her objection.

Fitzwilliam wasted no time but carried her straight to the house. A footman ran out as they approached. "Fetch your master," commanded Fitzwilliam. "And Mrs. Reynolds. Hurry, man."

Mrs. Reynolds met them as they reached the hall. "Madam, what is the matter?" she exclaimed.

"She is ill. Send for a physician."

"Fitzwilliam, I am not ill, I simply require a few moments' repose. Mrs. Reynolds will assist me to my room. Put me down now I pray you."

"Elizabeth! Good God, what is wrong?" cried Darcy hurrying into the hall.

"Darcy, it is nothing," said Elizabeth plaintively. "I turned a little faint, that is all."

"Give her to me," said Darcy. Reluctantly Fitzwilliam delivered Elizabeth into Darcy's waiting arms. "Mrs. Reynolds, come with us," Darcy ordered, and he led the way up the staircase, with Elizabeth continuing to protest that she was not ill, could walk, did not wish to be carried about like a sack of grain.

Fitzwilliam stood at the foot of the stairs and watched them move out of sight. The expression on his face was gravely anxious.

Elizabeth's indisposition was, as she had said, not serious, but she did not join her husband and Fitzwilliam for breakfast and kept her room for the chief part of the morning. Fitzwilliam, in concern, however, remained in the house, and two or three times summoned Mrs. Reynolds to inquire after her mistress. Her lack of apprehension on the subject finally made him seek out his cousin. "Darcy, have you sent for a physician?"

"There is no need," he replied. "Elizabeth will most likely take dinner with us."

"Darcy, do not take any chances with Elizabeth's health," urged Fitzwilliam.

"Fitzwilliam, if I thought it a matter to raise alarm I would of course send for a physician. Elizabeth is *my wife*, and I take the greatest possible care of her."

"Yes of course," said Fitzwilliam slowly. "She is *your* wife."

He left the house and rode out into the Park, where he could dwell without interruption on the situation in which he now found himself. As he walked his horse along, without knowing in what direction, there was a powerful feeling in his breast towards Elizabeth, that he knew was wrong and reprehensible, which he could neither banish nor overlook. He understood that his feelings towards her, and also his recent behaviour, merited the severest rebuke.

"This will not do," he said aloud. He had never felt so strongly as now the dangers which must attend the pursuit of a wife for her fortune and connections instead of for the esteem and regard that he felt for her.

Finally the recollection that his long and unexplained absence might arouse his cousins' concern made him return to the house. His reluctance to see Elizabeth determined him not to dine with the family, and he sent a message by a servant that he would not join them but that he wished to speak to Darcy alone later in the evening.

Darcy met him in the library after dinner, and Fitzwilliam came immediately to his point. "I must make a confession to you, which I believe I ought to have made some time ago. I fell in love with Elizabeth at Rosings last Easter, when, although knowing she was an object of your interest, I was unaware of the degree of your attachment to her. Since coming to Pemberley I have been unguarded in my conversation with her, and have caused her distress. Do not make yourself uneasy," he added quickly, "for she of course reproved me, and I shall not repeat such remarks. My purpose now must be to show you both that those reproofs have been heeded, and to lessen Elizabeth's ill opinion of me. This and other inducements have decided me not to remain longer at Pemberley."

Darcy listened at first in anger; but his affection for Fitzwilliam almost immediately procured his pardon, and he replied in a tone of regret, "I am exceedingly sorry that this should have arisen, and I assure you that my regard for you, and Elizabeth's also, is unchanged. But if you feel it necessary to leave Pemberley in order to restrain and command your feelings, we will understand and will not press you to stay."

"I cannot be so easily reconciled to my conduct as you are, Darcy," said Fitzwilliam; but his mind was now relieved from a heavy weight. The cousins remained together for a space of time, speaking affectionately, until

Darcy said that he must inform Elizabeth of Fitzwilliam's resolve, and they parted for the night.

Chapter Seven

[January 1813, Pemberley]

Neither Darcy nor Elizabeth thought it wise to deter Fitzwilliam from carrying out his resolution of quitting Pemberley without delay, and although Georgiana was astonished and distressed by the sudden leave-taking, he made his preparations on the following morning.

"We are very sorry to lose you, Fitzwilliam," said Elizabeth as she walked with him in front of the house prior to his departure. "You know my affection for you, as a cousin, and I think you are more important than ever to Darcy now that he has cut off communication with Lady Catherine."

"It is not yet a year since we were all together at Rosings, yet what changes there have been," mused Fitzwilliam. "I certainly never thought to see you married to Darcy at that time. Indeed," he faltered briefly, "indeed it almost seemed more likely that you would be married to *me*."

"Fitzwilliam, please let us not speak on that subject again. And I assure you, it no more entered my mind then that I might be married to you than it did that I might be married to Darcy, which is to say, not at all."

"But it did enter *my* mind, Elizabeth. Do I have no right to suppose it?"

"Well, it is past now, and you and I are both saved from the infamy and penury that would have resulted," said Elizabeth with all the lightness she could summon.

"Yes, it is past; but it is not done with for me. Elizabeth, tell me truly, if I had made an offer to you last April, would you have accepted it?"

"Fitzwilliam, how can it profit either of us to talk about what might have been? You did not offer, and a multitude of things has happened since that time. We cannot return there."

"Elizabeth, last April I made a mistake. At the time it did not seem like a matter of great weight, but I have come to see that it was. I loved you and

I did not value that love above wealth and the narrow principles of my family. Perhaps if I had never seen or heard of you again less damage would have been done. But I have watched you become the wife of my cousin, the companion of his heart and the capable mistress of a great house, and I look upon you and think, 'She could have been mine, she might now have been greeting *my* guests, her smiles might have been for *me*, and when we walked it might have been *my* arm she took. She might have been the mother of *my* sons and daughters.' My family point out this or that wealthy or noble woman to me and wonder why I do not rejoice in the income attached to her or her exalted lineage. I did not comprehend last April, but I do now, the difference between gold and dross. So I ask you to tell me, what would have been your answer? I want to know if possible the extent of my folly."

"Fitzwilliam, you are being very unjust to me. You are asking me to wound you. There is no benefit to be gained, whether I answer yes or no."

"The benefit is to allow me to see clearly the consequences of my education and actions."

"I cannot."

"I know your honesty and generosity. If you do have regard for me you will grant this request."

She was silent.

"Please, Elizabeth, pray let me hear what you would have said," said Fitzwilliam quietly. "This is a matter of the greatest importance to me."

Elizabeth was wretchedly uncomfortable, but her sense of justice urged her to accede to his request. She reflected for a moment, and then replied. "Very well. I will answer because I believe you already know what I will say. When I made your acquaintance at Rosings I found you very amiable and I had a great deal of pleasure in your society and conversation. You would have been a much better match for me than I could have expected, being without fortune or connections. If you had offered, I would have told you that you could come to me again if you obtained the consent of your family to our marriage. And then," she concluded, "we know what storms would have descended on our heads—I would have been sent back to Hertfordshire without a moment's grace."

"Your answer would have been yes. That is what I wished to know. Thank you, Elizabeth."

"Fitzwilliam, it takes a great deal of wilful self-deception to twist my answer into yes."

"I am satisfied."

After breakfast the separation took place, and Colonel Fitzwilliam left Pemberley in low spirits and with a mind much occupied.

Chapter Eight

[February 1813, London]

The Bingleys were of a respectable, wealthy family in the north of England, the respectability being more deeply impressed upon them than the fact that the wealth had been acquired by trade. Charles Bingley was a good-looking and gentlemanlike man, with easy, unaffected manners. His sisters Louisa and Caroline were very fine ladies who were rather handsome, had been educated in one of the first private seminaries in London, had each a fortune of twenty thousand pounds, and were in the habit of associating with people of rank. They were therefore inclined to think much better of themselves than of others, and were proud and conceited, although they were not deficient in good humour when pleased, or lacking power to make themselves agreeable when they chose.

Caroline Bingley had been mortified by Darcy's marriage to Elizabeth, for until the actual announcement of their engagement she had not abandoned hope of securing him to herself; she maintained that she could never see any beauty in Elizabeth, and that she had an intolerably self-sufficient air about her coupled with a complete absence of accomplishments. She had for a considerable time hugged to herself Darcy's early comment about Elizabeth, "She a beauty! I should as soon call her mother a wit," while dismissing all evidence of her own senses that Darcy increasingly admired Elizabeth. The playful manners that had bewitched him she had looked on as bordering on conceit and impertinence. Altogether, she was unable to comprehend how Darcy could prefer Elizabeth to herself, and had waited impatiently for him to arrive at the same conclusion. His engagement to Elizabeth had put an end to her attentions to him; but it had not as instantly ended her attachment. Although to the fashionable world she presented the same countenance, and was still able to relate an anecdote with humour, and laugh heartily at her acquaintance, within the bosom of her family she did not endeavour to conceal that her spirits were disturbed.

After the passage of several months, with no serendipitous event producing either a substitute for Darcy or an alteration in Miss Bingley's disposition, Mrs. Hurst took it upon herself to seek out a partner for her sister. She first hinted at the possibility of a match with Darcy's cousin Colonel Fitzwilliam, who like any younger son must certainly be seeking a rich wife. Miss Bingley received this suggestion with a little interest, but when rumours shortly thereafter went abroad that another match was being arranged for him, Mrs. Hurst discarded the scheme. However a prospect too enticing to ignore soon presented itself, and she adopted a plan.

"Mr. Hurst, tell Caroline whom you met last week when you were at your club." Thus Mrs. Hurst as the three of them gathered around the coffee service following dinner in the Hursts' London townhouse.

"Some bounder who took fifty pounds off me at cards," said Mr. Hurst laconically.

"No," said Mrs. Hurst tolerantly. "Sir Hugh's nephew."

"Oh, that fellow. Mallinger. Been in Rome or somewhere."

"Sir Hugh Mallinger's nephew, Henry," said Mrs. Hurst, clearly perceiving that she would be forced to take the narrative into her own hands. "He is heir to the baronetcy. The family is very distinguished. He has been out of the country for several years I believe, but Sir Hugh asked him to return."

"What of him?" said Miss Bingley without curiosity.

"Sir Hugh must be seventy or more, his health is not good, and he has no sons of his own. Henry Mallinger is past five-and-thirty and not yet married. It is surely time he thought about his own heirs, for the family property is quite extensive. From what I hear, however, the income has not kept pace with the expenses. Damson Hall is theirs you know."

"I know of Damson Hall," said Miss Bingley carelessly.

"He would be very suitable," said Mrs. Hurst.

There was silence for several minutes as they sipped their coffee.

"And you know there is a cousin who is a baron. There is a chance that the title would come to Henry Mallinger—one or two deaths, one can never be sure what may happen—and then he would be a peer."

Miss Bingley gave a yawn.

"Lady Grandcourt knows the family well," said Mrs. Hurst.

A further pause succeeded.

"She is a very good friend of mine."

Miss Bingley made no answer.

"I was intending to write to her on the morrow to tell her about that affair of the Harleths'," said Mrs. Hurst.

"I am sure you may write to her or not as you like."

"I was thinking that Charles and Jane might invite him to Netherfield."

"Oh! that is of no consequence to me."

"If Henry Mallinger accepted an invitation, it might be prudent for you to be of the party."

"It would doubtless be insufferably tedious."

"I shall write to Lady Grandcourt, then," said Mrs. Hurst, pleased that the matter was settled.

Chapter Nine

[February 1813, letter from Netherfield]

Upon Kitty's arrival at Netherfield, Jane had immediately set her to work acquiring some of those accomplishments that had not been instilled in her under Mrs. Bennet's maternal guidance. After she had been in residence for a little more than six weeks, Jane wrote to Elizabeth the following letter.

> Netherfield, Herts
> February –, 1813
>
> My dearest Lizzy,
> This evening is the monthly ball at Meryton, and Bingley and I attend with Kitty—Caroline will not join us—but I have a little time before I must go and dress, and so I write to you. Be assured that we are all well, and much engaged. You received my earlier letter, laying out the designs I have formed for Kitty, and now you shall hear what has passed so far. I have taken stock of the depth of her knowledge—or ignorance rather, for I do not believe that a single word of any of our masters ever penetrated her head! I have always had a value for Kitty, and never thought she had anything bad at heart (even though she was always affronted by any advice that you and I sought to give her) or that she was as light-minded as Lydia, and I do not throw any blame on her, for many causes or circumstances may have prevented her from benefiting from the means of education that our parents provided us. She was always slight and delicate, and if she was idle it may surely rather be imputed to a want of robust health than to a desire to learn. I have encouraged her to spend each morning in improvement of her mind, and she has submitted

to do so, in a manner most creditable to her, and from this I am inclined to hope that in time she may learn to behave like a perfectly rational being. The continuing shock of Lydia's example, and even more to the loss of the society which Lydia always provided her, will I believe account for her willingness to apply herself now. (And perhaps something is owed to Caroline, whose look of scorn when she found that Kitty did not play, sing, draw, speak any languages or have any idea where Russia is could have frozen over the Thames.) A French master comes daily, and a music master and a drawing master twice a week. In the evening Bingley and I encourage her to read. Bingley offered her Gibbon's History of the Decline and Fall of the Roman Empire but after looking into it she said she would as soon read Fordyce's Sermons, and as Bingley's library is not large we are making do with poetry for the time being. We have heard so much about Childe Harold's Pilgrimage that Kitty and I were anxious to read it, but Caroline and Louisa think that Lord Byron is not suitable for young girls (Louisa wrote to me what is being said in London about him and Lady Caroline Lamb—and the countess of Oxford—and Lady Webster as well! and I wish she had not, for I do not know when I have been more shocked; but I am quite in agreement with her that we should avoid Childe Harolde, if even a quarter of what she told me about the author is true) so we are reading Scott mixed with some Wordsworth and Grey. In the afternoon when it is not wet we ride out, frequently just the two of us, with a servant. I conjecture that Kitty is more likely to make her mark as a horsewoman than a musician or linguist, for she has a naturally good seat and, I confess myself a little surprised, a good deal of courage. (She quite scandalized Caroline at dinner last night by saying that she thought she would like to go hunting!) So dear Lizzy I believe I have made a respectable beginning with her, and that her disposition is improving and becoming less irritable, but you shall judge for yourself when we come to you in the spring. Our mother and father are well, but <u>she</u> misses Lydia prodigiously and <u>he</u> misses you at least as much! I must conclude now, for Kitty tells me I must dress instantly or we shall miss the first set. I look forward to hearing from you without delay.

Your affectionate sister,

J. Bingley

Chapter Ten

[April 1813, Pemberley]

Darcy and Elizabeth both did Fitzwilliam such justice that when they spoke between themselves about his attachment to Elizabeth, it was only to feel compassion. They frequently discussed the possibility of Fitzwilliam marrying, and both hoped for a speedy conclusion to his search for a suitable heiress.

In response to intelligence conveyed to him by one of his correspondents, who had been among a party that included Fitzwilliam and a very eligible young lady, Darcy wrote, somewhat in exasperation, the following letter:

> Pemberley, Derby
> April --, 1813
>
> Dear Fitzwilliam,
> I have been made acquainted by accidental information that your attentions while in Somerset to Miss Cholmondeley, which she received with pleasure, and her affection for you, which she believes you return with equal regard, have given rise to a general expectation of your marriage among her family and connection. A suspicion of the nature of the sentiments which you feel—indeed I have no apprehension of your feeling a serious attachment—shall not prevent me from encouraging you to consider the advantages of making such a choice. I readily engage in the office of pointing out to you that your immediate prospects would be greatly enhanced by what I esteem a most happy alliance. I do not scruple to assert that the charms of nature, which have been so liberally bestowed upon the lady, combined with her fortune of twenty-five thousand pounds, would secure

you in the future from want of amiable society, as well as from the reputation you risk acquiring of a man who cannot be satisfied; and I urge you to be sensible that there is little time to be lost.

However this admonition may affect your determination, I do not suppose at any rate that it would ultimately prevent or delay a marriage, and therefore I have not hesitated to write to you. I hope that the effort of the formation and perusal of this letter has not been wasted; and what I do, I do for the best. I do not, nor would I ever, remonstrate with you concerning your attachment to Elizabeth, but it is imperative for the sake of all that you seek your happiness elsewhere. I write without the intention of paining you, and if I have injured your feelings, I beg your pardon; but you are aware that the motives which govern me do not originate in jealousy but in sincere regard for your welfare. On this subject I shall say nothing more.

Yours,
F. Darcy

As Fitzwilliam's response was to thank his cousin for confirmation of an uneasiness that had been excited in him, by the young lady's conduct, and to assure him of his complete indifference to her, it may be supposed that Darcy's advice, however valuable, was not heeded.

The arrival of letters at Pemberley was the object of every morning's anticipation, but none had reached Darcy from Lady Catherine de Bourgh since her missive abusing Elizabeth. It had been Darcy's custom for a number of years to visit Lady Catherine de Bourgh in Kent at Easter-time, where he had frequently been joined by Colonel Fitzwilliam, and as the season approached, Elizabeth could not fail to remark that her husband seemed a little out of spirits. Attributing this to its proper cause, one evening when he was at his writing-table, she urged him very mildly to write to Lady Catherine to see if a reconciliation could be brought about. He resisted for a time; "I cannot forget the follies and vices of others so soon as I ought," he said, "nor their offenses against myself. My temper is too little yielding." "Surely," said Elizabeth in the gentlest of accents, "Lady Catherine has not lost your good opinion forever?" At last he took up his pen and wrote a short note.

Pemberley, Derby
April 18, 1813

Madam,

> I write without any intention of humbling myself, or of referring to your last letter, which cannot be too soon forgotten. However I regret that any difference has arisen between us, and my character requires that I do not suspend communication with you, however unwillingly you may bestow your attention upon this letter. I am mindful of the relationship in which we stand to each other, and would not see it erode further. My wife Elizabeth and I send you our respectful duty.
> Fitzwilliam Darcy

Almost immediately he received the following reply.

> Rosings, Kent
> April 20, 1813
>
> Darcy,
> I am gratified that your broken wrist, or whatever physical impediment has prevented you from writing for six months, has mended. Dear Anne has not been well, for reasons to which I hardly need allude, but I trust this half-year has passed without untoward incident for you, as you have not heretofore communicated any news or sought my advice on any matter. I have received reports that you have scarcely left Pemberley in this time, but I will not remark on what might be the reason for your seclusion. No doubt my warning to you in my last letter, to which you did not vouchsafe a reply, had some salutary effect. However you cannot conceal yourself from society forever.
> C. de Bourgh

"May I?" asked Elizabeth. Darcy nodded, and she dropped the letter on the fire.

Chapter Eleven

[April 1813, Pemberley]

It had been agreed between Jane and Elizabeth for some time, that she and Bingley should come to Pemberley after Easter and bring Kitty with them, who would afterward remain there. Accordingly a few days after Easter Sunday the Bingleys' carriage rolled up the drive, and their party was greeted with affection by the Darcy family. All was delight and kindness. The meeting between Elizabeth and Jane after their separation of several months was marked by their joy, and they embraced each other with alternate smiles and tears. Looking into Jane's face, Elizabeth was reassured to see that it was as healthful and lovely as ever.

Darcy took Georgiana's hand to draw her forward, and Bingley expressed his delight at seeing her again and Jane hers to meet her for the first time. "And here is Kitty," said Jane.

"Kitty, it is very agreeable to see you, and we hope that you will like to stay with us," said Darcy with great cordiality. Kitty had before Darcy's engagement to Elizabeth been too much afraid of him to talk, but afterwards he had treated her kindly, and she now returned his greeting a little shyly but with warmth.

"I am sure she will be very comfortable here," said Jane.

"Kitty, I think you have grown an inch since I last saw you," said Elizabeth. "You are taller than I now. I believe you are of a height with Georgiana."

"I am much mistaken if the two of you would be taken for anything but sisters," said Jane looking from one to the other. "I never thought before that you resembled each other greatly, but today when I see you together I think you look remarkably alike."

"Oh," cried Kitty, "I am sure you mean by that that I am much improved, Jane, since Lizzy last saw me!"

"And so you are. Anyone might take you for an accomplished young lady now."

"Jane thinks great doses of French and music and drawing have improved my complexion and deportment," confided Kitty to Elizabeth, "and she wishes to take credit for that."

"Well something has improved your complexion and deportment, but I hope that the French and music and drawing have also improved and informed your mind," said Elizabeth.

"I have not found Racine improving no matter how many times the French master has told me what a great dramatist he was. Rhyming couplets make me sleepy. But I persuaded him to tell me how the French swear," added Kitty. "It is a great relief to be able to say *sacrebleu* or *mordieu* when I am not allowed to swear in English."

"I hope you will not swear in any language while you are living here!" exclaimed Elizabeth.

Georgiana looked at Kitty with wide eyes. She still found rather alarming the light and sportive manner with which Elizabeth sometimes treated Darcy, although she was becoming accustomed to it, but here now was her new sister who was intending to swear in French!

The party entered the house, and Elizabeth ordered refreshment for the travellers to be brought to the saloon. They gathered around the table and while engaged in eating cold meat and preserves and cake exchanged news of Derbyshire and Hertfordshire.

When they had finished the meal Kitty said, "May I go to the stables now? I should like to see Darcy's horses."

"Kitty, do consider in what a light it places you, to go darting off to look at the horses when you have been in the house scarcely an hour," exclaimed Jane. "Can you not defer your visit until tomorrow? You do not wish it to appear that you have already tired of the people here!"

"There is no need to defer the visit; I have not the smallest objection to show her the stables," said Darcy.

"I will come with you," cried Bingley with alacrity. Jane exchanged a glance with Elizabeth. Gentlemen cannot always be indoors.

"There you see," said Kitty.

"At least you had better change your clothes."

"I am sure that Darcy's stables are quite clean. Are they not, Darcy?"

"Perfectly clean. My head groom does not permit dirt or disorder that even I might overlook."

The Pemberley stables were as carefully kept as the house, and the oakwork of the stalls gleamed. As the three walked through the centre aisle, a horse's head immediately thrust over the half-door of any stall that was tenanted. One of the horses whickered at Darcy and he paused to stroke its nose.

"I thought you might like this mare to ride," said Darcy, stopping in front of another stall. A chestnut horse pulled her face out of the hayrack and looked at them alertly. "This is Sorrel."

"Oh!" said Kitty. She and the horse regarded each other. "How old is she?" asked Kitty at length.

"Nineteen or twenty I think. I used to ride her when I was a boy. She is a good steady quiet animal now."

"Oh!" said Kitty again.

Bingley laughed. "Come, Darcy, do not make the mistake of thinking you can fob a steady quiet animal off on Kitty. She likes something with a bit of spark. There is a black hunter over there that I dare say would suit her."

"Kitty might have difficulty in managing Zanzibar."

"Do let her take him out; if she falls off and breaks her arm you may perhaps persuade her that she really belongs on Sorrel. But I should think it more possible that they will get on admirably. Kitty wants a horse that wants to run."

"She may take him out tomorrow, then. But Bingley, Kitty—you must assure me of your secrecy, for I would not intentionally give Elizabeth uneasiness; and *she* could not manage Sorrel."

"Lizzy was never a horsewoman," said Kitty disparagingly.

Elizabeth and Jane had experienced no regret at being left alone by the gentlemen, for they had a great deal to say, that would have been of little interest to their husbands. They seated themselves on a sopha a little apart from Georgiana and Kitty and gazed at one another.

"Jane, I am so happy to see you!" exclaimed Elizabeth.

"I can well believe it, for you have said so three times in the last hour," replied Jane with a countenance no less smiling than her sister's. "But shall I own how much I have longed to see *you*? You are the only one in the world who immediately comprehends what I feel."

"Dearest Jane! There are few people whom I really love, and when we were parted I felt as if I had never loved you as you deserve."

Jane, however, laughingly disclaimed any extraordinary right of praise and extolled her sister's regard. "It is only your sisterly partiality and no merit of my own that makes you speak so."

"Jane," said Elizabeth after a pause during which they looked at each other with affection, "I have news to tell you."

"I believe I can make a conjecture," said Jane, "for I have never before seen you look as you do now—there is a sort of rosy glow diffused over your features, as if you are lit from within."

Elizabeth blushed. "I thought it was my secret, and Darcy's, to keep or to tell as we chose. But it seems it is written all over me!"

"I could not be happier for you and Darcy. When do you expect the child?"

"In September."

Jane was silent a moment and then said quietly, "Bingley and I thought—perhaps—that there would be a child for us in the autumn as well, however—."

"Oh! Jane, I am grieved to hear it." Elizabeth pressed her hand in sympathy.

"Darcy must be pleased," said Jane, struggling to regain her composure and speak with her usual cheerfulness, "you have certainly wasted no time."

"It did not seem wasted even if I had not conceived," said Elizabeth slyly, drawing a smile from Jane.

"I believe I now better comprehend Lydia's conduct when she was staying with our aunt and uncle in London, and when she came home to Longbourn with Wickham! Although she was very wrong to act so, her behaviour is now accountable to me," said Jane, still smiling. "And yet we were so shocked then, and we could form no idea of it. I wonder what other circumstances we may see in a different light as we gain experience?"

Elizabeth was amused but not astonished that Jane found in the married state a reason to defend Lydia, for she always was anxious to think well of everyone, and quick to defend anyone who appeared to be at fault.

"I am afraid that we will have more shocks with Lydia's behaviour yet," said Elizabeth, growing serious. "We could justly have expected neither rational happiness nor worldly prosperity for her; even at best her situation must have been bad enough. But now I cannot help thinking that perhaps Wickham is—returning to his former ways. In almost every letter she mentions that Wickham is away somewhere—gone to Bath with some of the officers, or to London to visit some friend or other."

"Oh Lizzy, you cannot believe that? Wickham's character must surely have altered when he married Lydia. He cannot have been immune to any sense of gratitude for the assistance he received on his marriage, when his debts were settled and a commission purchased for him, or to repentance for his former ways. He must have determined to start his life anew."

"My dear Jane! You are too good. You never see a failing in anybody, and indeed you see goodness, where anyone else might be excused for seeing nothing but wickedness. If *you* do not change, Jane, and if Lydia does not change, why do you suppose that Wickham would?"

"You know how painful it is to me to censure anyone. I pity those who act wrong, for they must feel that they have been acting so, and we cannot always know the cause of their actions, whether there may be circumstances that justify them."

"You are a great deal too apt, you know, to excuse the faults of others. Wickham is not the good and agreeable man that you wish him to be, and Lydia is not much better."

Jane looked a little uneasy. "Kitty showed me a letter she had from Lydia. It almost seemed, reading it in a certain light, that Lydia may be flirting with other officers."

"If Wickham bestows no attention on her she will seek it elsewhere. She cannot bear not to be the centre of interest."

"If indeed she is flirting with other men, she is at fault, to be sure, but is there truly a great deal of harm in it?"

"Jane, you are truly angelic. But the more I see of the world the more my belief is confirmed that little dependence can be placed on the possibility of goodness, or even of good sense. I love Lydia as my sister, but I do not think well of her. I fear we should be prepared for something worse. If she cannot find conjugal intimacy with Wickham, she may look for it with another."

Jane was instantly afflicted by astonishment and horror. "Lizzy, you cannot believe that!" But when Elizabeth assured her that she could, Jane continued, "Surely if we make a representation to her, her regard for us will make her curb her unguarded and imprudent manner. Will not the influence of our friendship and affection combat her natural desires?"

"I think it unlikely that any consideration that we might present will influence her."

"But would she not be grieved at our disapprobation? She must acquire some right principles as she grows older. She is still very young, not yet seventeen; it may be that she will listen to us."

"I doubt she is ready to listen to sermons yet. I recollect our father saying that she would never be easy until she had exposed herself publicly. Marriage to a man like Wickham, who would not have been capable himself of teaching her proper behaviour and who now appears to be losing interest in her, will, I fear, furnish her with yet more opportunities for public exposure and disgrace."

"She never really believed she was disgraced by eloping with Wickham and living with him before they married," said Jane in distress. "To her it seemed no more than an adventure, the consequences of which were very slight. Indeed, she was rewarded, if marriage to Wickham can be deemed a reward."

"It may be that it is beyond her sensibility to feel disgrace. If that is so, there is little or nothing standing between her and conduct of any kind, however shocking."

Jane was struck with another idea, and with a look of apprehension said, "Lydia did harm enough to our family when we were only the Miss Bennets of Longbourn, and no one knew of our existence beyond the village of Meryton.

I will be very grieved indeed, if Lydia and Wickham behave in such a way as to bring shame or contempt upon Darcy."

Elizabeth immediately replied, "Oh Jane, you make me laugh! Lady Catherine already thinks that Darcy's reputation has been injured beyond restoration by his marriage to me. What depths will she have to plumb if Darcy's sister and brother-in-law behave as we fear! She will have an apoplectic attack. We have burned her last two letters to Darcy, but if she is given occasion to write to us about Lydia and Wickham her letter will catch fire itself through spontaneous combustion."

Their conversation then turned to lighter thoughts and hopes for future happiness, and continued until it was time to dress for dinner.

When the party was seated in the drawing room following the evening meal, discussion turned to the plans projected by Bingley and Jane. They intended taking a tour of the neighbouring counties when they left Pemberley. "Is it safe to travel in this part of the country now?" asked Jane. "Lydia wrote me that Wickham is away in Lancashire with his regiment pursuing the Luddites. But they are close by here as well, are they not?"*

"It is quite safe at Pemberley, and I think in all Derbyshire," said Elizabeth. "There are no mills or factories near us. Indeed there really has not been any machine breaking in this county."

"The Luddites have been suppressed in Nottinghamshire and Yorkshire," said Darcy, "and I can readily believe that the army will soon deal with those in Lancashire."

"I wish they may, with all my heart," said Bingley.

Darcy turned a cold eye on his friend. "What is there so very laudable in this? What is the argument in favour of it? Last year in the House of Lords, Byron said 'As the sword is the worst argument that can be used, so should it be the last'."**

"Darcy does not believe that the army should be sent against hungry men," said Elizabeth by way of explanation.

---

* The Luddite movement was a product of the Industrial Revolution in England. It opposed mechanisation in textile mills, believing (correctly) that it would reduce employment for skilled textile workers. It began in Nottingham in 1811 and spread rapidly throughout England in 1811 and 1812—the West Riding of Yorkshire in early 1812 and Lancashire from March 1813. The Luddites destroyed many wool and cotton mills until they were suppressed by the British government. "Machine breaking" was made a capital crime by the Frame Breaking Act of 1812 and 17 men were executed after an 1813 trial in York. Many others were transported to Australia. –Ed.

** Lord Byron after taking his seat in the House of Lords was an advocate of social reform. He defended the actions of the Luddites (one of the few in parliament to do so), and in 1812 he spoke against the passage of the Frame Breaking Bill. See also his poems *Song for the Luddites* (1816) and *The Landlords' Interest* (1823). –Ed.

"I do not believe that the sword and the noose are the *only* arguments to make to hungry men," said Darcy. "There must be order kept, but where there is want, it must be addressed, and reduced if possible."

"I am sure those men are not to blame if they cannot find work and cannot feed their families," agreed Jane. "But still they frighten me, and now we are much closer to them than we were in Hertfordshire. Are you quite certain that there is no danger?"

"Upon my word," Bingley cried, "I have heard there are more English soldiers in Lancashire fighting the Luddites, than there are on the Continent fighting the French."

"Oh!" said Jane, with restored confidence. "With so many of our soldiers about we shall be perfectly safe." She was blissfully unaware of the Duke of Wellington's comment, that he did not know what effect English soldiers would have on the enemy, but by God, they terrified *him.*[*]

"Now let us tell you our news," said Elizabeth. "This is an evening of wonders, indeed! Darcy is going to become a Member of Parliament."

This announcement threw Jane into a new flutter of anxiety. "Oh Darcy, are you not placing yourself at risk to go into politics? What of the killing of the Prime Minister last year?"[**]

"There are six hundred members of Parliament and more, and *they* are all alive. I foresee no peculiar danger to myself, Jane."

"Congratulations, then, Darcy," said Bingley. "But do you not have to wait for an election, and then do you not have to win the vote?"

"There is no doubt that he will win!" exclaimed Jane with loyal prejudice.

"Jane gives me more credit than can be," said Darcy laughing, "and I make no such pretension. However at Pemberley we can dispense with both a general election and a contested vote, for we have a pocket borough[***], Lambton Close. A friend of my father's, John Chamberlain, has been the member for some time, holding the seat until I was of an age to take it. He will resign within the year."

"*That* is exceedingly convenient," cried Bingley. "How many voters are you obliged to impress?"

"There are some forty of them, and as far as I recall only half a dozen ever troubled to vote against the Pemberley candidate. Indeed I am not sure

* Arthur Wellesley, 1st Duke of Wellington (1769-1852), became a prominent general during the Napoleonic Wars, and then a field marshal, and received a dukedom in 1814. It was under his command that the allied army defeated the French army at the Battle of Waterloo in 1815. – Ed.

** Spencer Perceval (1762-1812), who became the British Prime Minister in 1809, was assassinated in May 1812 in the lobby of the House of Commons by a disgruntled merchant. –Ed.

*** So called because it had a very small electorate and so was "in the pocket" of an individual. Also known as a "rotten" borough. Pocket boroughs ceased to exist after the Great Reform Act of 1832. –Ed.

that I remember any other candidates coming forward when my father was the Member."

While the Darcys and the Bingleys spoke together of the Luddites and Darcy's political calling, Kitty and Georgiana sat together on a sofa and listened. After a time Georgiana turned shyly to Kitty. "I have so been looking forward to your coming here. It was very dull when I was living in London with Mrs. Annesley, but it is much better here at Pemberley with my brother and Elizabeth, and now I will have two sisters."

"Georgiana, let us be great friends," said Kitty impulsively. "My sister Lydia was my best friend, but she is gone now and I am not allowed to see her. Everyone is afraid that I will behave as badly as she did if I am not kept away from her."

Georgiana turned a little pale at the mention of Wickham's wife, but she was more afraid of offending Kitty than of hearing of Wickham at the moment, or of having it found out that she herself had already behaved almost as badly as Lydia, and so she forced herself to stay and speak instead of running away. "I will like it very much if we can be friends," she said awkwardly.

When affection and compatibility of mind are present, time spent together seems short in the same proportion that a longer time is desired. The Bingleys were positively resolved, however, against postponing the start of their tour of the neighbouring counties more than a se'nnight, but when the day arrived and they took their leave everyone was most regretful at the parting.

Chapter Twelve

[June 1813, Netherfield]

Charles Bingley, being an affectionate brother and a sociable neighbour, made no objection when his sister Mrs. Hurst petitioned him to entertain at Netherfield, and further to ask Henry Mallinger to be their guest for several days. The invitations were sent around and accepted, immediately by the Bingleys' neighbours, to whom the prospect was extremely agreeable, and rather more deliberately by Mr. Mallinger. The entertainment was to include not only a ball and a supper, but also an archery contest and a dinner on the day preceding, and the young ladies of the neighbourhood at once set about honing their skills with bow and arrow. Miss Bingley was an excellent archer, as might be supposed of a lady of her accomplishments, but she did not disdain to practise also, for the idea that a country girl might best her in a competition was intolerable. As for Mallinger, she reflected upon him as little as possible, and was not in the least grateful to her sister for her endeavours to make up a match. She had determined that she would meet Mallinger and consider his suitability, but she would not allow herself to be influenced into a marriage.

The day of the archery party arrived, and to the astonishment of all dawned clear and warm. Alternate plans involving shawls, tents and indoor activities were happily put aside, and the Netherfield servants busied themselves setting up targets and tables and chairs on the lawn.

Charles and Jane Bingley greeted the guests on the terrace, and when Mr. Mallinger arrived Bingley, by previous arrangement with Mrs. Hurst, invited him to walk down to the archery butts where Miss Bingley was practising with the other young ladies. As they approached she was taking up her position to shoot.

Caroline Bingley was entirely conscious of the elegant figure she made as she drew her bow, took aim and loosed her arrow at the target. A good hit, just outside the bullseye. She lowered her bow.

"Caroline, well shot," said Bingley, coming up behind her. She turned to meet him unhurriedly, and with perfect posture. At Bingley's side she saw a man of about five-and-thirty, a little taller than herself, with a fringe of reddish-blond hair surrounding a balding head, a face that was very handsome although somewhat lacking in animation, fair skin, and long narrow grey eyes that expressed, if anything, indifference. There was no trace of a smile on his features as he looked at her. She thought that she had never seen a more aristocratic-looking man. "May I introduce to you Mr. Henry Mallinger? Mallinger, my sister Miss Bingley."

Mallinger bowed slightly. Caroline curtsied slightly. There was a pause.

"Mr. Mallinger has been abroad and has recently returned to England," said Bingley. "Some time we shall be very happy to hear you tell us of your travels." Mallinger bowed again, noncommittally. He glanced around the garden with the expression of one who had found himself cast away on an island inhabited by painted savages. There was another pause, uncomfortable as such pauses always are.

"Oh!" said Bingley, looking up at the terrace with relief. "I see the Gouldings have arrived, I must go and welcome them. Pray excuse me."

Miss Bingley and Mallinger watched Bingley walk away.

"I have always thought archery a great bore," said Mallinger after a moment, in a drawling voice.

Miss Bingley turned to look at him. "But now that you have seen me shoot you have changed your mind," she said coolly.

"I am not in the habit of changing my mind." He gazed around the garden once more. "It rather surprises me to find *you* enjoying provincial society."

"I am quite of your opinion, but one cannot be always with people of rank and fashion. The society is insupportable but I do not flee Netherfield each time my brother gives a dinner." She nocked another arrow, turned towards the target and shot again. This time the arrow landed squarely in the centre of the bulls-eye.

Mallinger looked at the target and then at Miss Bingley. "If one must engage in shooting arrows, one ought to strive for mastery," he said with a mocking glint.

"It is a rule with me, to strive for mastery in all fields of endeavour," she said, lifting her chin up and looking him in the eyes.

There was a silence while they studied each other. Then Mallinger raised his eyebrows very slightly. "Now that you have demonstrated your mastery, perhaps I can persuade you to abandon the hay bales and walk with me. We may need protection from the rustic populace, you had better bring your bow."

Miss Bingley deliberately leaned the bow against a tree. "For my own part, I do not require protection."

"Very well, it shall be on your head." He offered his arm and she took it.

"If archery bores you, what does not bore you?" inquired Miss Bingley as they began to walk.

"Cards. Horses. Beautiful women."

"Shocking! You no doubt find it costly to assuage your boredom."

"As yet I have not pledged my entire inheritance. In any event, I would put a bullet into my head if I had to lead a life of complete safety."

"I comprehend the risks of gambling and hunting. What is the risk of beautiful women?"

"The risks of beautiful women are myriad. Have you not just demonstrated that yourself with your bow and arrow?"

"There was no risk to you. My object was the target."

"Ah," said Mallinger. "That is where we differ in opinion."

Miss Bingley could not repress a slight smile.

After they had strolled without speaking for a time Mallinger said, "I think your brother does not own Netherfield?"

"No, he is a tenant only."

"That is fortunate, it is an undistinguished property."

"He intends to purchase an estate, in Derbyshire perhaps, or one of the neighbouring counties."

"It will be a drain upon his income. Damson Hall certainly is on my uncle's."

"One cannot well avoid the expense, when it is a family property."

"It is entailed, I am not likely to be able to rid myself of it any time soon. But when it is mine the temptation to leave it to molder will be great."

"Where will you reside, if not at Damson Hall?"

"I shall go abroad again. I have travelled a great deal and never found a climate to rival the wretchedness of England's. I would keep my uncle's town house, perhaps live in London for a few months each year, during the season."

"And what attractions do you contrive to find abroad, Mr. Mallinger? Apart from the climate."

"Freedom, principally."

"And risk?"

"Sometimes."

"Are there no considerations that would detain you in England?"

"Dynastic considerations, perhaps. I would raise my sons here. I would not want them to be foreigners in this country."

"Then I conjecture that you desire an English wife?"

"I would not marry a foreign woman."

"However beautiful?"

"However beautiful."

They walked about the garden, speaking to no one they met. Nor did anyone endeavour to speak to them, other than Sir William Lucas, who conceived it to be his peculiar duty to speak courteously to everyone he encountered, for both had manners that were not inviting.

"And you?" inquired Mallinger. "You are now acquainted with my plans, what of your own?"

"Oh! I shall marry, I dare say. What other plan does a lady have occasion to make?"

"If you were free to make any plan you wished, what would it be?"

"I am talking of possibilities. You can scarcely expect me to reply that I would sail the seven seas or own a tea plantation in China."

"Those would be interesting answers, but I cannot envision you doing either. Your place is in England. Have you chosen your future husband yet?"

Miss Bingley glanced at Mallinger. "On the contrary, I do not know whether I have even made his acquaintance."

"Or perhaps you have and you are struggling against your feelings for him."

In the evening Mallinger took Miss Bingley in to dinner. Across the table from them were Mrs. Long and Mr. Philips; on Mallinger's left was Mrs. Bennet and on Miss Bingley's right was Sir William Lucas. Miss Bingley simply ignored Sir William's worn out courtesies. Mallinger responded with a slight nod of the head to Mrs. Bennet's civil bow. She took this as sufficient encouragement to begin a conversation with him, and commented on the weather. After waiting a short while for him to introduce a subject of conversation in turn, and when he instead turned deliberately to Miss Bingley to speak, she directed her attention to Mr. Philips across the table.

"Brother," she cried, "You must own that Sir William Lucas, who always has a civil word to say to everybody, has the right disposition." She continued, with more perseverance than politeness, "It is a pity that more great persons are not more like him. You know my ideas of good breeding, that those who fancy themselves very important and never open their mouths, quite mistake the matter. But they care no more for us than if we were at York. By the bye, I recollect that I meant to tell you that, I have had news from dear Lydia. Wickham has returned from York or wherever he was, for he has quite subdued the machine breakers, and I don't doubt there will be some hangings. I am sure it must be the only way to deal with such heathens. Sometimes my nerves are quite torn to pieces worrying about Lydia away in those foreign places. But she is such a favourite with the officers that I suppose she must be quite safe." Mr. Philips gave his opinion that his niece was perfectly safe in Newcastle, and the conversation between them continued.

Mallinger ate in silence for a time, giving no more attention to Mrs. Bennet than to the salt cellars, and then said to Miss Bingley, "Your brother has been unable to entice a decent cook to Netherfield."

"He does not consult my wishes but his wife's when hiring the servants."

There was another pause and Mallinger spoke again. "Your brother's guests strike one as typical of English country gentry—well-fed, complaisant and vacuous."

"I pay them as little attention as possible, but he cannot well avoid including them in his invitations. He married into one of the families. The Bennets. Mrs. Bennet is next to you."

"*That* is Mrs. Bingley's mother?" said Mallinger in a low voice. "*She* seems perfectly rational as well as beautiful as a Titian Madonna—but with such a mother? She is perhaps a changeling. I believe it was her sister who married Darcy of Pemberley?"

"Yes," said Miss Bingley shortly.

Mallinger cast a look at her, but said nothing. After a moment he remarked, "Altogether great deal of dreary domesticity."

"Why dreary?"

"Should I have instead said domestic felicity?"

"Are you inclined to consider them the same?"

"Surely even the happiest couples find it fatiguing to stare at one another over the joint each night for their entire lives."

"And how, pray, would you remedy this evil?"

"Argument; variety; absence. One must endeavour to remain alive, rather than be buried under a mass of convention."

"Is this then your design for domestic concord?"

"Perhaps. I would not always be settled in one place, or constantly at my wife's side."

"And your wife, if I may raise so delicate a question—would she too be at liberty?"

"The days of immuring one's wife in a keep while one goes to war or on pilgrimage are surely over. A discreet wife could have as much freedom as she chose, once an heir had been produced."

"You have always been much abroad—you would continue so?"

"Certainly. I would return to England more frequently with a wife and family here, that is all."

"And if a wife's preference were to be at her husband's side?"

"Then she would be wiser to marry one of these stout red-faced gentlemen that this country seems to produce in such abundance. I daresay it has something to do with the abominable climate."

Miss Bingley considered. She had been engrossed by Darcy. When he was in the same town she wished to be in the same house with him, when in the same house, in the same room, when in the same room, close by him. A marriage with Darcy of the sort proposed by Mallinger would have been torment to her. But Mallinger was not Darcy. And yet—he was not devoid of attractions, although income was not among them. Although *her* first recommendation to *him* must be her fortune, she would receive a benefit in return. She would be the wife of an aristocrat, and soon the wife of a baronet.

"Surely you cannot wish to continue living with such neighbours? And such a cook?" inquired Mallinger.

"I am indeed contemplating a change," acknowledged Miss Bingley.

"Ah, then we are both open to change in our lives at this time."

The following evening the ball and supper took place.

"Caroline, how many dances are you engaged to Mr. Mallinger for?" asked Mrs. Hurst coming up to her sister as the dancing was about to begin. "I think two sets would be the proper number."

"I am not engaged to him for any dances," said Miss Bingley with an expression of disdain.

"Upon my word, why not?"

"Because he has not asked."

"Not asked? Whyever not?"

"Mr. Mallinger it would appear does not dance. He has a *penchant* for freedom and risk and takes pleasure in nothing but gaming."

Mrs. Hurst frowned slightly. "How many dances have you kept for him?"

"Not one."

"None! Caroline, he is certain to ask. It could ruin our plans if you refuse to dance with him."

"*I* have no plans," she cried proudly. "If he has any, let him carry them out. I shall not anticipate them."

"I hope you know what you are doing," said Mrs. Hurst a little anxiously. "He is not a man to be trifled with."

"Nor am I a woman to be trifled with." She surveyed the room with asperity. "He appears to be in need of money. *I* am not swooning over his glances *or* his title. To be Lady Mallinger is scarcely the highest ambition a woman can form."

"I see him coming this way," said Mrs. Hurst.

"I wonder how he could presume to address me now. The first set is about to begin."

Mallinger reached Miss Bingley only a few steps ahead of the partner arriving to claim her for the first set. He bowed to her and Mrs. Hurst. Miss Bingley noticed him only by a curtsey.

"Miss Bingley, may I request the honour of dancing with you this evening?" His tone was perfectly composed and confident.

"Mr. Mallinger," she replied with cool civility, "it is the gravest misfortune that I have already engaged myself for every dance." She was pleased to see that for a moment, exceedingly brief however, he looked disconcerted.

"I believe we must take our places now, the set is forming," said her partner coming up to her, with a polite bow to Mallinger. She took his offered arm and moved away with him.

Miss Bingley was not surprised to see that Mallinger did not stand up with any other lady. Indeed she did not see him in the room at all, and she supposed he had taken himself out of the way. However immediately before the two fourth her brother came up to her.

"Caroline, I have a message for you from Colonel Glasher. I did not apprehend all the details, but he asked me to bring you his apologies for being unable to dance with you."

Miss Bingley was infinitely vexed but too well bred to show it. She would have to sit out these dances as there was not an excess of gentlemen, and it offended her pride.

"Miss Bingley," said a voice behind her.

She turned to find Mallinger, with a sort of smile on his face which she fancied she understood.

"May I ask for your hand for this set? I could not avoid overhearing your brother's message."

She fixed her eyes on his countenance. "Yes," she said at length.

Mallinger bowed. "One way or another I usually get what I want," he murmured. "You might as well know that about me now."

Chapter Thirteen

[June 1813, Pemberley]

The steady friendship between Darcy and Fitzwilliam was not one that could sustain a long period of separation, and the cousins anticipated with pleasure Fitzwilliam's return to Pemberley in the second week of June. It was understood, however, that, there must be no repetition of those sentiments that he had expressed to Elizabeth previously, and which for the happiness of both must be forgotten. His object during this visit must be to show by restraint and civility that his feelings for her if not vanquished were under his firm regulation.

On the appointed day Colonel Fitzwilliam passed through the gates of the Park, and rode up to Pemberley House. As he trotted along, dwelling on Elizabeth, he caught sight of her ahead of him, alone and mounted on a black horse.

"Mrs. Darcy!" called Colonel Fitzwilliam. "Elizabeth!"

The rider looked back over her shoulder.

"Elizabeth, please wait a moment."

She turned her horse to face him. "You are looking for my sister," said Kitty. "She is in the house."

Fitzwilliam reined his horse to a stop, and then nudged it to a walk and came slowly towards her. "I mistook you for Mrs. Darcy," he said. "You resemble her greatly. May I have the honour of introducing myself?"

"Oh, I already know who you are," said Kitty.

"And then—who are you?"

"I am Catherine Bennet, Mrs. Darcy's sister."

"Are you the one they call Kitty?"

"Yes."

Her horse danced a little and gave an annoyed tug on the reins and she patted his neck to quiet him. "I must go," she said. "We always have a gallop on the path just ahead, so he does not want to stop here."

Fitzwilliam looked around. "Are you alone? Do you have no companion?"

"None," said Kitty. "If I promise them I will stay close to the house they have stopped making a fuss about taking a servant with me."

"And do you always keep your promise?" asked Fitzwilliam with interest. From his extremely short acquaintance with Kitty he already suspected that such a promise had but a small chance of remaining unbroken.

"Sometimes I have a little difficulty with my horse," she said consideringly. "If he *will* run away with me, what am I to do? But we cannot stop here longer."

"May I come with you? I am on my way to the stables."

"Yes of course," said Kitty, instantly turning the horse and picking up the trot. Colonel Fitzwilliam's horse was a little weary from travelling but was not at all pleased to see another horse take precedence, and Fitzwilliam came up beside her before she had gone two strides.

"Darcy wrote me that you are living here at Pemberley now."

"Yes, for a time. I was with my brother and sister Mr. and Mrs. Bingley for a few months before. They are sharing me."

"And where do you like it best?"

"Darcy has the better horses," said Kitty. "Here is the path." She turned to the left and tapped her mount into a canter. Kitty's slight weight and light hands made her almost a phantom rider to her mount, and the canter quickly turned into a gallop.

Fitzwilliam held back his mare for a moment to watch. Miss Kitty Bennet certainly made a pretty picture in her riding habit, with her straight back and neat hands, as the horse raced along. She turned her head. "Are not you coming?" she called without slowing down.

"You are going to break your neck!" he called back, more, however, with admiration than concern. Kitty's only answer was a laugh that receded from him between the trees. Fitzwilliam gave his mare her head and followed—first at a sedate canter, and then seeing that his horse was determined to catch up to the other if at all possible, at a gallop to rival Kitty's. The path wound uphill through the woods, and Fitzwilliam caught flashes of Kitty's habit as she dashed ahead of him. Several times he thought he had caught her up, only to find that he was still separated from her by a turn of the path. Towards the top of the hill the path straightened out and he came out into more open ground several strides behind her. She was still galloping very fast. Suddenly he saw that the path ended in a four-barred gate that was closed. "Miss Bennet! Kitty!" he called in alarm. "Stop!" He urged his horse ahead more quickly. She had probably expected to find it open, and she would crash directly into it at the pace she was going. But she did not stop, or even slow down, and just when he expected her horse to strike the gate, he rose up and leapt it cleanly. On the other side of the gate was a paddock, and the stables were just beyond. Kitty turned her horse in a circle to slow him and then cantered back to the gate, where Fitzwilliam had pulled his mare to a halt. "What is the matter?" she cried, slightly out of breath from the run. "Why did you call to me to stop?"

"I thought you had not seen that the gate was shut." Fitzwilliam leaned down and opened it, and walked his horse through. Kitty closed it behind him with the stock of her whip and refastened it.

"That gate?" said Kitty. "It is always shut, there are often horses in this paddock."

"I was afraid you would run into it and be hurt."

"Why would I run into it? I could see it as well as you."

"I did not know you could leap it," said Fitzwilliam.

"That little gate?" said Kitty incredulously.

Fitzwilliam smiled. "Well, it was all conjecture, and I will not make the same mistake again about you and gates. Are you finished your ride?"

"Oh no, if I stop now I will not be able to get on him tomorrow, he will be so anxious to run. Goodbye, Colonel Fitzwilliam, your mare is all lathered up, make sure the groom cools her down properly."

"Goodbye, Miss Bennet, I hope to see you at dinner," said Fitzwilliam, but Kitty was already some distance away.

Fitzwilliam gazed at her retreating figure and reflected that his past arrivals at Pemberley had comparatively been rather dull.

Fitzwilliam was alone in the drawing room that evening, waiting for the others to join him before dinner was announced, when Darcy entered the room with a young lady whom, once more, for a moment he mistook for Elizabeth. "Fitzwilliam, I would like to introduce you to my sister Miss Catherine Bennet," said Darcy. "Kitty, this is my cousin Colonel Fitzwilliam."

Fitzwilliam smiled at Kitty. "Miss Bennet, it is a great pleasure to make your acquaintance. Yet you remind strangely of a centauress I met in the woods today. Indeed I am rather surprised to come upon you unaccompanied by a horse."

"Do you already claim an acquaintance then?" inquired Darcy in surprise.

"We have met, one might say, in passing," said Fitzwilliam, "or perhaps in being passed. Miss Bennet has no missish reservations about leaving a riding companion behind in the dust."

"We were just having a little canter up the hill to the paddock," said Kitty demurely. "Colonel Fitzwilliam's horse was fatigued from the road. I hope the groom cared for her properly?"

"You may set your mind at rest, the horse is in excellent health and spirits. Perhaps you are now going to inquire after *my* health following the journey, not to mention the little canter?"

"You look perfectly well to me," said Kitty. "I hope dinner is announced very soon, for I am practically starved."

"Now there is something one does not often hear in company, Darcy, a young lady admitting to an appetite."

"I would admit to almost anything right now if it meant getting something to eat. Why do you suppose it is unladylike to be hungry?"

"A lady is supposed to be above human needs and wants."

"I think that is silly," observed Kitty. "Do you esteem a lady more highly for not being human?"

"This is a home question. I do not, particularly. But then, I am known to be eccentric."

"I do not suppose you have anything to eat in your pockets do you? Do not soldiers carry food with them always?"

Fitzwilliam felt in his pockets and produced a handkerchief. "I am afraid I only carry food in my pockets when I am on campaign."

"Cousin James!" called Georgiana, entering the drawing room with Elizabeth behind her. "I am so glad to see you again. You have met Kitty?" She kissed Fitzwilliam on the cheek. Elizabeth held out her hand to Fitzwilliam, unaffectedly glad to welcome him back to Pemberley, and he bowed over it in silence.

"Yes I have met her," he said, grateful to be obliged to respond to Georgiana at that moment, "and having proven conclusively that I have nothing to feed her, I was just retreating. Your arrival is providential, if Miss Bennet grows any hungrier I shall be able to give *you* to her to eat, and so save myself."

"Oh Cousin James, you talk greater nonsense every time I see you. I am so glad Kitty is come to live with us, for now I have two sisters, when only a few months ago I had none. Kitty, shall we sing a duet after dinner?"

"Yes, if you like, Georgiana. Oh! There is Spurgeon at last. Thank heaven."

The butler announced that dinner was served.

"Thank heaven indeed," said Fitzwilliam. "We are short one gentleman, may I take you both in?" he inquired, neatly avoiding the duty to escort his hostess. Each of the girls took one of his arms and they followed Darcy and Elizabeth to the family dining parlour.

As the fish course followed the soup, Fitzwilliam, who had been unobtrusively studying Elizabeth and Kitty, said, "Georgiana, do you not think that Miss Bennet looks remarkably like Elizabeth?"

Georgiana looked from one to the other. "Yes, I suppose they do look quite alike. But that is not very surprising when they are sisters, is it?"

"That is a not unnatural surmise. There is good sense in what you say. I shall feel compelled to take advantage of your sound judgement in the future. What do you and Miss Bennet do with yourselves all day? When you are not riding, that is?"

"Oh Kitty is the one who rides mostly. I am not specially fond of it. We have masters several days a week – you know that Cousin James."

"I do not mind the music master," said Kitty in a low voice, "but the rest is piffle really. I am desperately tired of sketching pitchers and flowers, are not you Georgiana?"

"I am going to paint a tea set, I shall like doing that."

"But would you rather not sketch a cow—?"

"Or a horse," interjected Fitzwilliam.

"—or a face?"

"Flowers are pretty," said Georgiana doubtfully. "I think I would be too nervous to sketch someone's face. To keep staring at the person!—and all the while he is thinking how ugly one is making him in the drawing."

"And how do you get along with your languages?"

"Georgiana looks very pretty when she speaks French," volunteered Kitty, "but I am afraid her German lessons make her look very plain. She has to twist up her face so in order to pronounce everything as the master wants."

"Are you learning German too, Miss Bennet? You do not look especially plain this evening."

"Oh Kitty is only learning French," said Georgiana. "Her French is very bad."

"Miss Bennet, you must explain yourself. You stand accused of bad French. What do you have to say?"

"What do I need to know French for?" asked Kitty irritably. "I do not know any French people and no one will allow me to read French novels."

"That is perfectly reasonable, Miss Bennet, and I for one believe that a day devoted to riding and to drawing cows would be entirely well spent."

"Kitty's masters are not quite basking in her achievements," said Elizabeth, who had been listening to this interchange with amusement, "although she is doing nicely with her music. She has several years of inattention to pay for."

"What of the bovine portraiture?" asked Fitzwilliam sternly. "Are her artistic talents being recognized and encouraged?"

"We are endeavouring to encourage her to acquire the *usual* talents of a young lady."

"You certainly appear to have your work cut out for you," said Fitzwilliam.

Chapter Fourteen

[June 1813, Pemberley]

Colonel Fitzwilliam, though not sufficiently wealthy to maintain his own stable, had had from his boyhood in Ireland a keen interest in horses and much admired his cousin's. At Pemberley, when they were not actually on horseback, the two frequently passed their time looking at the horses and poring over the General Stud Book, discussing matters of pedigree and plans for breeding. On a warm afternoon they had been watching a groom longe a young horse in a paddock and now returned through the stables.

Near the entrance Fitzwilliam was struck with the appearance of a dark bay. "Darcy, that's a very handsome hunter. Did you have him out this season past?"

"Just once. He is still green, and requires work before next season. Take him out if you wish."

"I shall."

"Come back to the house now and we will have a game of billiards."

As Fitzwilliam was well aware, that there was less chance of meeting Elizabeth in the stables than in the house, he replied to his cousin's entreaty, "To confess the truth, I would prefer to remain here a little longer. I will join you later."

"As you wish." Darcy walked away and Fitzwilliam turned back, nearly colliding with Kitty and the stable's two Dalmatian dogs who were at her heels.

"Is he gone?" whispered Kitty.

"Yes," whispered Fitzwilliam. "Why are we whispering?"

"They do not like me to be in the stables so much," said Kitty in an ordinary voice. "I ought to be practising my music or my French or drawing flowers."

"But what are you doing instead?"

"Helping Orley. Today he has a stone bruise, a cut knee and bowed tendons."

Fitzwilliam noted that Kitty was wearing over her muslin gown a faded old linen coat that swept the ground, with sleeves rolled up to her elbows, and on her feet riding boots.

"Miss Bennet, does Darcy not employ grooms enough to care for his horses?"

"I suppose he does, but I want to know for myself how to care for them." She turned and led the way past several stalls to a side aisle, where a groom was bringing out a chestnut mare, limping on her off-foreleg.

"Now Miss," said the head groom Orley from behind them.

Fitzwilliam turned. "Look here, Orley, do you really believe Miss Bennet should be congregating in the stables without your master's permission?"

"No indeed, Colonel," replied Orley. "Now Miss, do you recollect how to make the poultice?"

"Yes, is there hot water?"

"On the hob." Kitty proceeded up a side aisle to the tack room at the end. The Dalmatians pattered after her, in the hope of a tidbit.

"Orley, I am surprised at you. Is this any occupation for a young lady?"

"Not for young ladies in a general way, sir, but this young lady is different. She wants to know a farrier's business, and I won't say her nay. It's a sight more useful to know how to poultice a horse's foot than to speak French, if you ask me to speak my mind."

"Well I do not recall that I did."

"And if Miss Bennet is going to tear around the countryside, it behooves her to know what she may be doing to a horse's legs."

Kitty reappeared carrying a small bucket and a knife.

"Let me have a look, Miss," said Orley. He gazed into the bucket and stirred its contents with a finger. "Go ahead then."

Kitty stood by the mare and lifting up her foot cleaned it out with a pick which Orley provided to her. Then she packed the poultice into the sole of the hoof, securing it with a heavy woollen sock pulled up over the fetlock. The mare watched attentively. Kitty let down the foot and Orley handed her a roll of linen bandage, which she wound carefully around the leg from hoof to knee.

"Neatly done, Miss," said Orley. "Now the other."

Kitty bandaged the other leg in the same fashion.

"I couldn't have done it better myself, Miss," said Orley approvingly.

Kitty gave the mare a pat on the neck. "There you go, Vixen, does not that feel better? You can put her away now Bob." The groom returned her to her stall. "Give her a carrot, she has been a good girl," said Kitty. "Who is next, Orley? Octavian with the cut knee?"

"Yes, we'll look at Octavian, and then I think you'll want to see Pandora. She's off her feed, and it is likely her teeth. Have you ever seen a horse's teeth floated?"

"No," said Kitty with great interest, following Orley off.

"Miss Bennet," called Fitzwilliam to her retreating back.

"Yes?" said Kitty turning around.

"Are you by the remotest chance contemplating writing a pamphlet on leg injuries in horses?"

When a gentleman and a young lady are staying in the same house and share a common interest, it is natural for a measure of intimacy to develop between them, and also for that intimacy to be detected by others.

"Elizabeth," said Georgiana at dinner one night after Colonel Fitzwilliam had been a week at Pemberley, "have you noticed that Cousin James keeps calling Kitty Kitty?"

"I am afraid I do not understand you. Do you mean he is calling a cat? The only cats are in the kitchen and the stables."

"No I mean he is calling Kitty by her Christian name rather than calling her Miss Bennet."

"How can I continue to call her Miss Bennet when I call you Georgiana and Elizabeth Elizabeth?" inquired Fitzwilliam.

"I do not mind if he calls me Kitty," said Kitty, "but should I have to go on calling him Colonel Fitzwilliam? It takes so long to say. What if I wish to warn him that a servant is about to spill a sauceboat of gravy on him? By the time I reached the third syllable all the damage would be done."

"You could call him Cousin James as I do," suggested Georgiana.

"But he is not my cousin, is he?"

"No, I suppose not."

"Then it is not fair if I must call him Colonel Fitzwilliam when he calls me Kitty."

"Well," said Colonel Fitzwilliam. "Kitty shall be Miss Bennet and I shall be Colonel Fitzwilliam. We shall go to our graves, white-haired and crabbed, still addressing each other in this manner. We have but one mind and one way of thinking on this point, is it not so, Miss Bennet?"

"Cousin James, you know it will not be a quarter of an hour before you are calling her Kitty again," said Georgiana.

"Then Miss Bennet must correct me very sternly when I commit such a *faux pas*. I shall be shocked if my manners are allowed to be so very appalling under Darcy's roof."

That evening Kitty could not be prevailed upon to retire until she had assured herself of the well-being of one of the horses that she and Orley had treated during the day, and when all of Elizabeth's attempts to dissuade her from going out had proven unsuccessful, a servant with a lantern was dispatched with her to the stables. Darcy and Fitzwilliam returning from the billiard room discovered Elizabeth in a state of unease over her sister's nocturnal activities, and Fitzwilliam immediately offered to go himself and ensure Kitty's safe return to the house. Elizabeth expressed her gratitude, and Fitzwilliam departed on his errand. He found Kitty and Orley conferring earnestly over an ailing mare. Dismissing the waiting servant, he remained at a little distance from them, attending to their conversation without them perceiving him, until they had finished their consultation.

"Good evening, Miss Bennet," he said as Kitty drew near to him on her way out.

"Good evening, Colonel Fitzwilliam," she replied, smiling to see him.

"There, we have done our duty. I am to escort you back to the house, but first I will tell you a secret. I call you Kitty because I like it. It is a pleasing name. And it *is* rather like calling a cat, for you come or go as you will, just like a cat."

"I like you to call me Kitty," said Kitty complacently. "It is a much nicer name than Miss Bennet. I still think Miss Bennet is my sister Jane."

"Then we must arrange the business according to our own wishes, but without distressing the delicate sensibilities of the Darcy family."

"What arrangement do you have in mind, Colonel Fitzwilliam?"

"Simply this: when we are undisturbed by the presence of Darcys I shall call you Kitty and you shall call me James."

"But will not my sister and brother be uneasy to hear you calling me Kitty and me calling you James?"

"Ah but you see they will not know. It is private between us."

"Is it not improper for me to call you James?"

"No, not at all."

"I do not think I believe you. But I shall like to call you James when we are alone, and so I do not care. Will you come out riding tomorrow?"

"Yes, but we must have a design to prevent the others coming with us or we shall have to creep along sedately."

"If someone insists on accompanying us, my horse can run away and you shall have to give chase to rescue me," said Kitty. "Then we can lose our way in the wood."

"Or we can do it the other way round, for it is just as plausible that *my* horse would run away and that you would give chase to rescue *me*."

When they reached the house they parted for the night in the liveliest of spirits, having settled their plans to elude anyone who might presume to join them on the morrow.

Chapter Fifteen

[June 1813, Pemberley]

If the shades of Pemberley had been polluted by the advent of Elizabeth as its mistress they must have been wholly defiled by the arrival of a guest who was in trade, and lived within sight of his own warehouses in Cheapside. But however violently perturbed the shades, Elizabeth and Darcy were to all appearance tranquilly unaffected, and they welcomed Mr. and Mrs. Gardiner to Pemberley with delight.

As soon as possible Elizabeth and her aunt drove around the Park in a low phaeton with a pair of ponies. "Darcy has been forced to admit defeat in teaching me to ride, but he has taught me to drive," said Elizabeth as she took up the reins. The ponies tossed their heads and trotted along smartly.

The road through the park was ten miles around, and the two ladies devoted the morning to making the full circuit of it. They spoke of many things—Lady Catherine's continuing ill-humour, the love that had grown up between Georgiana and Elizabeth and Kitty, Kitty's general improvement, Colonel Fitzwilliam's search for a wife; and of Elizabeth's and Darcy's joyful and anxious anticipation of their first child. "But Aunt Gardiner, I am heartily sorry that we have had to postpone the tour of the Lakes again!" said Elizabeth. "The phaeton ride goes a long way to making up the loss," replied her aunt affectionately.

The Gardiners found themselves most comfortably settled at Pemberley, and they were treated very attentively by their niece and nephew. After the passage of a few days Mrs. Gardiner had leisure to observe the rest of the party with increased interest, and grew curious about the relationship between Colonel Fitzwilliam and her niece Catherine. Their preference for each other's society was plain, but she was uncertain whether they were in love with each other. What she did see however, both the preference and the Darcys' apparent inattention to it, caused her to be sufficiently troubled that she resolved to make Elizabeth aware of the situation, and soon she found an opportunity of speaking to her alone. "Lizzy, do you know what is going forward between Kitty and Colonel Fitzwilliam? Do you have reason to believe they are in love?"

Elizabeth almost stared at her. "That had not occurred to me."

"Why do you find the idea so extraordinary? Kitty is a very pretty young lady, and Colonel Fitzwilliam is a single gentleman."

Elizabeth was silent for a moment. At length she said, "Aunt Gardiner, I will tell you why I had no reason to think them in love. It is because Colonel Fitzwilliam earlier this year gave me to understand that *I* had secured his affections."

Mrs. Gardiner looked at her with a coolly inquiring gaze, and Elizabeth blushed consciously. "There has been nothing improper, aunt, you must know that. He simply told me that he had fallen in love with me last spring in Kent but said nothing because he could not marry where he chose, for he suffered from want of money; and that he now regretted his decision."

"If it were not allowable for him to gain *your* affections because you had no money, what occasions could there be for him to gain Kitty's, when she is equally poor?"

"I am sure Kitty is not thinking of such a thing. Fitzwilliam treats her much as he does Georgiana, like a younger sister. He teazes her as much as anything."

"A child might not be justified in thinking anything of the attentions that a man such as Colonel Fitzwilliam was paying her beyond the playful affection of a relative, but Kitty is no longer a child. Nor is she his sister, or his ward. If his attentions to her are thoughtlessly given, they may not be received in a like way. She may have the notion that when there has been one intermarriage, a second may be achieved. It would be very imprudent for Kitty to become attached to him, if she has not done so already. She must be warned against developing such an attachment."

"Dear aunt, you are treating this very seriously."

"Yes, I am. I would not see Kitty injured. Does Colonel Fitzwilliam conclude his visit soon?"

"Within a few days."

"And does he visit here often?"

"There is constant intimacy between him and Darcy, and he is welcome at Pemberley whenever he chooses to come. I could not ask Darcy to deny him."

"Then I would counsel that you speak to Kitty as soon as possible and put her on her guard, and that you send her away the next time Fitzwilliam visits. Send her to Jane, or to Longbourn."

Elizabeth took her aunt's advice and shortly thereafter spoke privately to Kitty.

"Kitty, I would like to discuss with you a matter of importance."

"If it is about the new hunter, I already know that Darcy does not wish me to ride him until he has been worked more. He has asked Captain Boyce to come and give him some training."

"No, it is not about the new hunter, or, to forestall you on the subject, about any horse. It is about Colonel Fitzwilliam."

"What of him?"

"You find him a very agreeable man, do you not?"

"Yes, of course. So you do, Lizzy. So do Darcy and Georgiana."

"He is without pretension when he is here with us."

"Does he have pretension when he is elsewhere?"

"No—that is, not precisely. He has rank."

"He is the son of an earl. I know that."

"He is the younger son of an earl, which means that although he has a place in society that he must keep up, he does not himself have the means to do so. He has habits of expense that must make him dependent on others for money, and therefore he cannot afford to marry without attention to the fortune of his wife."

"Are you trying to say that he cannot marry *me* because I have no fortune?"

"Yes, that is it exactly. He treats you affectionately, and I wish to warn you against feeling a regard for him, a partiality, that is stronger than his for you."

"I do not think that I have a greater partiality for him than he has for me," said Kitty slowly.

"Whatever degree of partiality exists, it is impossible that he could ever marry you. It is not only that you have no fortune, you also have no noble connections. Lady Catherine is not the only member of the Earl's family who strives to preserve the distinctions of rank."

"Darcy married you, and you have no more money or connections than I."

"It was a great struggle for him to overlook such imperfections. I have not told you this before, but Darcy made an offer to me when I was visiting the Collinses last year in Kent. I was astonished, I was quite unprepared for his declaration, and he made it in a form that that was almost intended to offend and insult me. He dwelt as much on the subject of his pride and consequence as on his tender feelings towards me, and was exceedingly eloquent on his sense of my inferiority and the obstacles that our family threw up against his inclination. My feelings towards him then were very much different from what they became thereafter, and as you can imagine were not improved by the manner of his suit, and I rejected him. However the sentiments he expressed were simply what all members of Lady Catherine's family must feel."

"But you are now Darcy's wife. He must have overcome them."

"He did, because he is a man of good principles."

"And because he loved you."

"Yes, because he loved me well enough to get the better of himself. His father was, Darcy has told me, all that was benevolent and amiable, but his parents—and I conjecture this must have been due in large part to his mother Lady Anne's influence—allowed and even encouraged him to care for none beyond his family circle and to think meanly of the rest of the world. Darcy was able to overcome his pride and vanity, but he had no close relatives to buttress those qualities in him. His parents are both dead, and Georgiana of course was too young to influence him. Lady Catherine, it turned out, has less power over him than she would like to think. But Fitzwilliam has, as well as a higher rank than Darcy's, Lady Catherine, a father and an elder brother. *He* will not be able to escape his instruction in the superiority of his family, and the inferiority of ours."

"But Colonel Fitzwilliam never seems proud and superior, as Darcy did when we first knew him in Hertfordshire."

"Kitty, I must counsel you very strongly against believing yourself his first object, even for a moment. Could he ignore the family sentiment about rank and connections, he would still need money. Certainly he is not poor as ordinary people see it, but his officer's pay and whatever inheritance he may also have are not sufficient to give him independence. He must have wealth."

"What do you wish me to do?" asked Kitty with a look of doubt.

"I would not have you conduct yourself differently towards him. He leaves Pemberley in a few days' time, and I do not want him to conceive that there has been any change in your or anyone's regard for him. But you ought not to encourage further any regard that you may feel for him. When next you see him he is likely be engaged or married to a woman of fortune and rank."

Kitty offered no further argument to Elizabeth, and was unusually quiet and thoughtful in the following days. Colonel Fitzwilliam could not fail to notice the change in her demeanour, and when they took a last ride together prior to his departure he determined to ascertain the cause.

"Kitty, you have been out of spirits these past few days. Have I vexed you in some way?"

"No, James."

"Then what is it? Will you tell me?"

"Oh! It is nothing. I am sorry that you are leaving tomorrow, that is all."

"I am sorry as well. I have never enjoyed myself at Pemberley as much as I have on this visit."

"Will you come back again?"

"Yes, but not before autumn. I have duties to attend to."

"You must find a wealthy wife."

Fitzwilliam turned inquiring eyes on her. "I was speaking of my military duties. What have people been saying to you about me, Kitty?"

"Nothing more than everyone says of you all the time, James, that you must marry a woman of fortune and rank."

"There has been a great deal of such talk, it is true." He reined in his horse.

"What is the matter? Why are you stopping?"

"I think my horse has come up a little lame. He may have picked up a stone." Fitzwilliam dismounted and lifted up the horse's near hind foot. "Yes, a pebble. I wish I had thought to carry a pick with me."

"Here is one," said Kitty, producing a hoofpick from the pocket of her habit, and leaning across Fitzwilliam's horse to hand it to him.

"Do you carry a pick with you everywhere? If I required one at dinner tonight would you produce it as conveniently?"

"Only if I were to dine in my habit."

Fitzwilliam cleaned out the horse's hoof, and returned the pick to Kitty. "I think I will walk him a little distance to make sure he is sound. Will you come down and walk with me?"

"Yes, if you like."

Fitzwilliam lifted her from the saddle, and they walked side by side leading their horses. He glanced down at her from time to time, and finally said, "Kitty, I have never met a young lady who was quite like you."

"Have you not? You have met so many ladies there must have been some like me."

"Do you mean the ladies that I am supposed to consider for marriage?"

"There have been a great many of them, have there not?"

"Well, a considerable number, although their name is not yet legion."

"Why have you not married one of them?"

"I did not like any of them well enough to marry."

"But you must marry one of them soon, is that not so?"

In answer Fitzwilliam halted, put his arm around Kitty's waist and kissed her gently on the lips. After a long moment he released her and they stood very close together, looking at each other.

"I did not like to mention it earlier, James," said Kitty at last, "but your horse did not look lame to me at all."

When on the following day Colonel Fitzwilliam bade farewell to the Darcys, he did not distinguish Kitty by any particular attention, and she appeared perfectly composed when she offered him her hand and said goodbye. Elizabeth and Mrs. Gardiner were contented with the success of their interference, and by Kitty's good sense in heeding Elizabeth's admonition.

Chapter Sixteen

[July 1813, Pemberley]

Elizabeth's father Mr. Bennet had been prodigiously apprehensive about her future when Darcy had requested her hand in marriage, believing that Darcy was a proud and unpleasant man and that Elizabeth hated him; and he had dreaded the grief of seeing his favourite daughter united, solely because he was rich, to one whom she did not respect and esteem. Elizabeth's repeated assurances that she loved him, and that he was a perfectly amiable man with no improper pride, drew her father's consent; and her revelation that Darcy had arranged Lydia's marriage to Wickham, paid Wickham's debts and bought his commission in the regular army, astonished him. Thereafter he had taken pains to get to know Darcy, and was wont to say that although Wickham was his favourite son-in-law, he admired Elizabeth's husband quite as much as he did Jane's.

Mr. Bennet was an odd a mixture of quick parts, sarcastic humour, reserve, and caprice. He missed Elizabeth exceedingly after her marriage, for she of all his family was the one who best understood him and appreciated his character, and his affection for her prompted him to visit Pemberley frequently. Although he was indolent, when he had business to transact he was as quick in its execution as he was dilatory in undertaking it, and the result was that he almost invariably arrived to visit his daughter when least expected.

"Whose carriage is that?" inquired Georgiana looking out the sitting room window at the sound of a conveyance on the gravel.

"We are not expecting anyone," said Elizabeth, coming to look. As she watched the coach stopped at the door and a man emerged. "It is my father!" said Elizabeth, and she and Kitty immediately ran down to greet him.

"Ah, Lizzy, I am very glad to see you," said Mr. Bennet as his daughters embraced him. "You as well Kitty. Have you been behaving yourself?"

"I think so," said Kitty after a brief pause for thought.

"An ominous reply, but whatever it portends I believe I will leave Darcy to deal with. Where *is* Darcy, Lizzy? I hope I have not missed him."

"No you have not, he is here—but if you will not write to us and let us know you are coming you may arrive one day and find us all departed."

"I did write. If you have not received my letter yet I am sure you will tomorrow."

"I do not see how you could have travelled faster than the mail."

"Perhaps it is still sitting in the mail bag at Longbourn then," he said unconcernedly. "How is the fishing in the stream? Has Darcy caught anything lately?"

After Mr. Bennet had been brought into the house, and offered and taken refreshment, he turned his attention to his younger daughter. "Well, Kitty," he said, "your sisters seem to think that you are coming along. To all appearances you spend some part of each day in a rational manner, you attend no balls, and there are no officers within several miles."

"There is Colonel Fitzwilliam."

"Oh yes, I had forgotten. I have never seen him in a red coat."

"He does not come to Pemberley in his regimentals."

"That is sufficient for me. I believe we may not need to wait the entire ten years before I take you to a review as your reward for being a good girl. And now I have some diverting news for the two of you. I have had a letter from Mr. Collins. (I would not give up my correspondence with Mr. Collins for any consideration.) Lady Catherine is beginning to recover from the loss of Darcy as a son-in-law and has a new design for her daughter. Can you guess whom she has now chosen?"

"If she could not have Darcy, I suppose she would not settle for anything less than a duke," replied Elizabeth.

"No, not a duke, only a younger son of an earl. Colonel Fitzwilliam, you see!"

"Fitzwilliam!" said Elizabeth in astonishment not a little mingled with alarm for the gentleman. "How can that be, sir?"

"I merely report what Mr. Collins has written."

"Fitzwilliam has neither money nor a title," objected Elizabeth after a moment's reflection. "What does he have to offer to Miss de Bourgh?"

"You are underestimating Lady Catherine's pride in and attachment to her family, and also without doubt her wish to prevent Sir Lewis de Bourgh's fortune from moving about the country in an unregulated manner. In addition, Miss de Bourgh is not growing younger. She is the same age as Darcy, Mr. Collins says."

"But what does Fitzwilliam say of this scheme?"

"I have not heard; indeed I do not know whether he has as yet received intelligence of his future domestic comfort from Lady Catherine, Mr. Collins does not specify. However from what you and Darcy have told me, he must marry a lady with money and connections. If he cannot afford to be particular as to the lady's character or appearance, or his own inclination towards her, then what could give him less of trouble and inconvenience than marrying his cousin?"

Elizabeth was silent. What her father said of Fitzwilliam she certainly knew to be true. Lady Catherine generally carried all before her when she had made up her mind, and she would probably be more than usually determined in this case, having lost Darcy, despite her best efforts, to a young woman of inferior birth, no importance in the world, and having no connection to the family. But to see Fitzwilliam the husband of Anne de Bourgh, and the son-in-law of Lady Catherine! No doubt Lady Catherine would expect him to live at Rosings—Fitzwilliam, who found a month there a trial to his patience! Elizabeth's lively imagination saw him leaving his wife and Lady Catherine at Rosings, to rusticate in all their splendour while he visited Pemberley, lived in London, and produced unconnected sons—like James, the 5th Earl.

"I should be sorry to see it," said Elizabeth after a pause for this contemplation, "but it seems very possible."

"What is Miss de Bourgh like?" inquired Kitty.

"In appearance she is quite a little creature, thin and pale, with insignificant features; she is of a sickly constitution. She rarely speaks, except to her mother or to the lady who is her companion."

"Oh!" cried Kitty, sounding quite astonished. After a moment she added, "Does she ride?"

"I am doubtful of it. When I was at Rosings I heard nothing of her being a horsewoman, although she was often driving a pair of ponies."

"Is Colonel Fitzwilliam much attached to her?" said Kitty in amazement.

"When we were all together I cannot say that I ever saw him pay her any attention at all. I suppose he may feel cousinly regard for her."

"Oh! You think he will like her money."

"You know that it has always been understood in Fitzwilliam's family that he must marry an heiress; and although he is somewhat behind hand in the execution, he has never disputed the principle, to my knowledge."

Kitty looked very reflective.

"Come, Kitty, I trust you had no designs on Colonel Fitzwilliam yourself?" said Mr. Bennet. "It is a miracle on the order of the loaves and fishes that Darcy escaped Lady Catherine and her matrimonial schemes, you cannot expect the laws of nature to be so suspended a second time."

"I like to ride with Colonel Fitzwilliam," said Kitty with a graceful shrug of her shoulders. "I suppose when he is married and visits Pemberley with his wife we shall not be able to ride out together."

"Miss de Bourgh—or rather the Honourable Mrs. Fitzwilliam as she will then be—probably would not care to see the two of you racing around together on horseback. I think you may take it that you have had your last ride with Colonel Fitzwilliam."

Mr. Bennet stayed with his daughters and son-in-law a fortnight, increased his acquaintance with Darcy to the pleasure of both, and took his leave of Pemberley as suddenly and unexpectedly as he had arrived. Upon his departure he remarked to Darcy, "When you asked for my consent to marry Lizzy I gave it without delay, for you are the kind of man to whom I should never dare refuse anything, that you condescended to ask. But now I am convinced that you deserve my Lizzy, and that I could not have parted with her to anyone less worthy."

Chapter Seventeen

[July 1813, Netherfield]

Lydia Bennet's elopement at the age of sixteen with George Wickham had been a great scandal in the vicinity of Longbourn, although their subsequent union had disappointed the neighbours, who would have found more matter for discussion if Lydia had come upon the town or been secluded from the world in a distant farmhouse. The event of her marriage had been borne with philosophy, however, since everyone considered her eventual misery certain with such an husband. News of the arrival of Mr. and Mrs. Wickham at Netherfield spread quickly through the district, and the malicious old ladies looked forward to hearing that Lydia's repentance had been swift. They were destined to be disappointed once more, for Lydia when she appeared was as assured and untamed as she had ever been.

Lydia was a tall, well-grown young woman of seventeen, with a fine complexion and a good-humoured countenance. She had high animal spirits and natural self-consequence. Wickham was an exceedingly handsome man, with an easy address and manners that were always pleasing.

Jane heard their voices in the hall, and almost immediately the door to the drawing room was thrown open and Lydia bounced in. Jane came forward and embraced her with an affectionate smile, and gave her hand to Wickham. The young couple had lost nothing of their easy assurance that had so struck the Bennet family on their reception at Longbourn following their wedding.

"Good Lord, Jane," said Lydia, hardly pausing to receive her sister's embrace, "you have been married these eight or nine months and still you have not got rid of that ugly footman! If you must keep such a fright, can not you send him out to work in the garden?"

"Hush, Lydia!".

"Oh, are you still worrying what the servants will hear and what the servants will think! Your formality and discretion—being a married woman has not changed you a particle. This is a pretty vase, was it a wedding present? Do you know that you never sent me and Wickham a wedding present? Now that you are rich I hope you are going to remember us." Lydia flung herself into the corner of a sopha with a great sigh, and then immediately rose again to examine a porcelain dish sitting on the mantelpiece.

Wickham smiled benevolently at his wife's liveliness.

"Well, then," continued Lydia, turning from the mantel, "what has happened in the neighbourhood since I left? How are the Lucases, and the Gouldings? Mamma wrote that Harriet Harrington is going to marry one of Mrs. Long's nephews. What about Pen? Has she not found a husband yet?"

"I have not heard that Penelope Harrington is either married or engaged. The Lucases and Gouldings are well."

"They may be well but they are *very* dull. By the bye, did I tell you that Mrs. Forster had a baby? Colonel Forster was so pleased that it was a boy, I cannot think why. But perhaps he will like him to become a soldier. Harriet Forster used to say when I was staying with them at Brighton how much she would like a girl, but now she says she is glad it is a boy."

"No doubt they will try to please you and produce a girl the next time," said Wickham.

"Oh, it is nothing to me whether they have a boy or a girl. But Jane what does anyone do here now that the regiment has left Meryton? It must be very thin."

"We still have the monthly ball at Meryton, and dine with our neighbours."

"I should die of boredom if I lived here. You can't think what fun we have in Newcastle, with the parties and balls. I am a great favourite of some of the officers, which is well, for Wickham does not like to dance, he is always in the card room. However none of the officers are as handsome as Wickham. Are they, dear Wickham?"

"I leave it to you to decide, dearest Lydia."

"Well, perhaps Captain Rawdon. Ah Jane, I have told mamma that she must get papa to let Kitty to come to me and Wickham, for I shall certainly be able to get her a husband. Mary as well. There are so many officers and not enough ladies, there would even be someone who would like Mary. Wickham, what do you think of Lieutenant MacMurdo for Mary? I am sure he likes books for I have seen him reading when I have been at the circulating library."

"I daresay they would get along," said Wickham equably. "You may feel free to propose an union to either, or both, of them."

When tea had been served, Lydia remarked, "I wrote to mamma that we were coming to see you and that she could come to visit me here. Perhaps she will come tomorrow."

"Lydia, why do you not go to her, you have nothing in particular to do here. You can have the carriage if you wish it."

"Oh I cannot always be running about after my relations and acquaintance. Anyone who wishes to see me must come here. Anyway, now that the regiment has gone there is no one in the vicinity worth calling on."

"I think you might make an exception for your mother and father and sister."

"Papa does not care if he sees me, and Mary would rather read a book. That only leaves mamma, and it will give her something to do to come here to visit me. It is too bad that Kitty has gone away, she would be in raptures at all my stories about the officers. It takes too long to write them down in a letter."

Although Jane deplored Lydia`s unfilial resolve not to go to their mother but to make her come to Netherfield, Lydia perhaps had a better understanding of her mother`s character. Mrs. Bennet drove to Netherfield at the earliest opportunity and met her youngest daughter with great delight. "How I have missed you, Lydia!" she cried. "A letter is nothing in comparison to a visit. Let me see you! You have grown taller. And you are as much in looks as ever. I am sure everyone in Newcastle must admire you very much!"

"Madam, she is a married woman now," cried Jane. "Surely she should not be seeking the admiration of men other than her husband?"

"There is no harm in a little admiration!" said Mrs. Bennet. "Really, Jane, there is no need to bring me up so sharp. You and Lizzy always set yourselves against innocent little amusements, and I think to this day that if I had been able to persuade your father to take us to Brighton—well, no mind, for all has turned out as pleasant as can be. Is that not so Wickham?"

"I cannot conjecture in what way my mother-in-law could be improved upon," said Wickham with a smirk, and Mrs. Bennet bestowed a smile on him.

Wickham indeed had little to say to anyone, after inquiring of Mrs. Bennet after his acquaintance in the neighbourhood, but Lydia and her mother were ready enough to talk and there was no want of conversation. When they parted, Mrs. Bennet said, "Lydia, why do you not come and stay at Longbourn? We can go visiting together. The Lucases and the Gouldings will be very glad to see you, and Mrs. Long and the Harringtons."

"Good Lord, mamma, I cannot think of anything duller than going home to Longbourn. Papa will look as though he is thinking of giving me a lecture about something, and Mary will quote her extracts at me. And I shall not visit the Lucases or the Gouldings or anyone else, and if they visit here I shall run away and let the servant tell them I am not in. Well, Pen and Harriet may come to me. Anyway, Wickham and I are very happy here at Netherfield, are we not, my dear Wickham?"

"Paradise itself could not be more blissful, dearest Lydia."

Jane, watching her sister and brother, concluded unwillingly and with sorrow that Elizabeth had been correct, and that Wickham's affection for Lydia was not equal to Lydia's for him. Lydia was exceedingly fond of him, and he received her attentions with good humoured ease; but his manners were always so agreeable, and his smiles and easy address so delightful, that the inequality of regard was not susceptible of immediate detection to a casual observer.

Lydia's good spirits increased during dinner, and when she and Jane went to the drawing room to await the arrival of the gentlemen, she found it difficult to contain them until he entered the room. "Oh Wickham, there you are!" she exclaimed when he and Bingley appeared, "I thought you should never come. Lord, how dreary it was here alone with Jane! What have you and Bingley been talking of this great while?"

"We have been talking about the beauty of our respective wives," said Wickham genially.

Lydia wound her arm through his. "La! Why would you want to *talk* about our beauty when you could see it? Come and sit with me." She drew him to the sopha, and would nearly have sat in his lap if Wickham with a patient smile had not made her sit at a remove from him.

She pouted. "Wickham, I have not seen you this last hour."

"No, my dearest Lydia, but you saw me for a full two hours before that."

"You were on the other side of the table."

"So much the better for looking at me."

"But I do not want to *look* at you."

"Well then I shall go and play billiards."

"Wickham! You know very well what I mean."

"Dearest Lydia, do you think you took a little too much wine at dinner?"

"I think I did not take enough if you are going to treat me this way." She jumped to her feet.

The servant entered with the coffee and tea. Jane and Bingley looked at each other. "That is all, thank you," said Jane in haste to the servant.

Wickham rose lazily from the sopha. "Shall I bring you coffee?"

Lydia stamped her foot. "I do not want you to bring me coffee. Or tea either."

"As you wish, my dear. Jane, I will take coffee, please."

Jane poured his coffee and handed it to him. He remained standing, with his back to Lydia, who began to give indications of extreme impatience.

"What do you think of my husband?" she cried to the room at large. "Is he not a charming man?"

"Upon my honour, it has been rather a wet spring has it not?" exclaimed Bingley.

"Yes, exceedingly damp," agreed Jane with energy.

"Good Lord, are we going to talk about the weather all evening?" cried Lydia. "Jane, I do wish you could play, then we could have a reel or a Scottish air. Wickham and I want to dance."

"If you insist on dancing, you will have to dance by yourself," said Wickham coolly. "I want to drink my coffee."

Lydia began to move restlessly about the room. "Come, Wickham, and dance with me. We will do without music. It is too stupid to sit here doing nothing and saying nothing."

"Dearest Lydia, not everyone is as full of activity as you after dinner. See if you cannot find a way to amuse yourself that does not involve disturbing everyone else."

"Jane, shall we play cards?" said Lydia.

"Yes, we could have a game of whist."

"Oh, whist, I would as soon have you read a sermon to me."

"Vingt-un then, or Commerce."

"Let us play lottery tickets."

"Lydia, no one but you has the slightest desire to play lottery tickets," said Wickham.

"Then one of *you* think of something to do."

"For my part, I think I will seek a little peace and quiet. Bingley, will you join me in a game of billiards?"

"Thank you, no, Wickham."

"Then I shall say goodnight to all of you."

"Wickham, you are not going to leave me here?" protested Lydia.

"You are not alone, you can talk to your sister and brother."

"Wickham!" Lydia took his arm as if to hold him back. He gently detached himself and walked to the drawing room door. Lydia kept her eyes on him for a moment, and then flew after him. Jane and Bingley watched as she wrapped her arms around her husband's waist. He endeavoured to free himself but this time she would not be separated from him. She looked up pertly into his face and spoke, still holding him tightly, but Jane and Bingley were too far away to hear what she said. However after a moment Wickham put his arm about her and they went along the hall towards the bedrooms.

A look passed between Bingley and Jane. "If we no are no longer obliged to entertain our guests, we too could retire," said Bingley after a pause.

"Bingley! What would the servants think if we retired now?"

"Perhaps Lydia makes a point when she says that you worry excessively about what the servants think."

"But if Lydia and Wickham go and then we go it will look so—so—."

"You are right," conceded Bingley. "If you will pour me some coffee, I shall be exceedingly gratified."

When Lydia and Wickham had been at Netherfield for a fortnight, and showed no signs of ending their visit, Bingley began to turn over in his mind the possibility of asking them to leave. When he finally unfolded the idea to Jane, she was not horrified, somewhat to his surprise. Nevertheless she said, "Surely we need not speak so very directly. I would not want them to think they are not welcome here."

"Jane, upon my word, they are *not* welcome here. They have deserved much less attention from us than they have received."

"Wickham must return to duty some time. Let us not say anything yet."

"Very well. But if they are still here tomorrow se'nnight I will not defer speaking to them."

Fortunately Bingley was not called upon to fulfill this desperate resolution, for the very next day Wickham announced that he was going to London.

"Is Lydia to accompany you?"

"She would have a tedious time of it there with no friends, and I will be much engaged. She is better to stay here, or go back to Newcastle."

Lydia sulked at Wickham's desertion, but after a short while announced that she would return to Newcastle if Wickham would arrange an escort for her. "Did you not tell me that Rawdon is in London but must return to the regiment shortly?"

"You would like Rawdon to escort you, would you?"

"He will do as well as any other, I suppose," said Lydia unconcernedly.

The young couple, who only the day before had seemed likely to the Bingleys to be in permanent residence at Netherfield, with celerity packed up their belongings and departed for London. Wickham smiled, and said many pretty things when they made their adieus, while Lydia, exhibiting less of grief at leaving than her husband, expressed the hope that London would not be as tedious as Netherfield.

"So you see," said Jane with relief as the Wickhams' post-chaise drove away from the door, "there was no need to say anything to them."

"I find their precipitate departure as laudable as it was unexpected," replied Bingley.

Chapter Eighteen

[August 1813, letters]

Whatever the salutary effect of Mr. Bennet's announcement of Colonel Fitzwilliam's impending marriage, it did not extend as far as putting an end to Kitty's private correspondence with that gentleman, which had begun as soon as Fitzwilliam left Pemberley in June and continued through the summer.

Pemberley, Derby
August –, 1813

Dear James,
The weather continues wet, so the footing has been poor and I have not been able to take Zanzibar out as often or for as long as he would like. He wants to take his revenge by running away, but he is afraid of puddles and has to tiptoe through them, so his progress is much impeded. I do not like what you tell me of Jezebel's lameness for what you describe could be navicular disease. Please send me more particulars of her condition. Orley and I were afraid last Tuesday that Vixen had foundered, but she seems to have recovered with no ill effects.

I fear that I am dreadfully ignorant of geography and history (Caroline Bingley would say that I am ignorant of everything) and I have been asking Darcy questions about our army and what it is doing on the Continent. He has explained to me about the killing of the king in France five-and-twenty years ago and why the French are fighting with everyone. I know that armies are in Saxony now

preparing for a battle,* and I am very thankful that our army is not there, and that you are not there. Now that I understand—or am beginning to understand, for it is all very complicated—I am going to take a great interest in the war, so that I will know what you are doing and when I ought to be frightened for your safety.
Kitty

Lydiard House, Wilts
August –, 1813

Dear Kitty,
I am very much indebted to your diagnostic skills for we did conclude that Jezebel had navicular and I had to shoot her for as you know the lameness does not improve and she was in pain. Do not be too distressed Kitty for she had a good life and I hope I did not let her suffer for too long. Perhaps you will be the person who finds a way to treat it and you will write about it in your work on horses' legs.

You are quite right that the situation on the Continent is complicated, and there are many men who do not understand it, even great men who are directing their countries and soldiers. However I have faith in the Duke of Wellington, and you are not to worry about me at all. I have been visiting in Wiltshire as you see, and the ladies in the party are all very accomplished, but the society is much better in Derbyshire!
James

London
August –, 1813

Dear Kitty,
Thank you for your sketch of Zanzibar. You have caught the head and the expression of the eye, and I would only counsel that you work a little on the hind legs, although to speak frankly I have seen painters who exhibited at the Royal Academy who were somewhat deficient with respect to hind legs. When I was visiting my brother recently, I came upon a copy of my great grandfather's little pamphlet on leg injuries in horses, which I enclose under cover of this letter. You may find it interesting, and there is a poultice receipt that is worth looking at.
James

* The Battle of Dresden was fought on August 26-27 1813, involving the French, Austrian, Prussian and Russian armies. The French were victorious. –Ed.

Kitty kept Colonel Fitzwilliam's letters in a packet tied up with a pretty ribbon, in a drawer, underneath her handkerchiefs, and occasionally took them out and re-read them, especially on evenings when there had been even more discussion than usual in the dining room or drawing room concerning his matrimonial affairs. Fitzwilliam likewise kept Kitty's letters, though they were strewn carelessly about his rooms, intermingled with other letters and bills, for he had few apprehensions of his servants or visitors reading his correspondence.

Chapter Nineteen

[September 1813, Damson Hall]

Henry Mallinger's visit to Netherfield in June had concluded on an indefinite note. He and Miss Bingley had been in each other's company for a week and had been invariably civil to each other. Jane and Bingley told each other that they made a handsome couple, and Mr. Hurst told Mrs. Hurst, who told Miss Bingley, that Mallinger was known to have debts of honour that he might have some difficulty paying unless his uncle soon died and passed on the estate to him. Nevertheless Mallinger had not approached the subject of marriage with Miss Bingley, and Miss Bingley had not made any show of regard for him that might have encouraged him to do so.

At the end of July Miss Bingley and Mallinger met for two days at a house party, and again the meeting proved inconclusive, although by now there was a general expectation among their acquaintance and in fashionable society that it was only a matter of time until they should marry. In the middle of August Sir Hugh Mallinger invited Charles Bingley to Damson Hall for shooting on the first of September, together with his wife and his sister. The invitation was accepted, and Mrs. Hurst strongly advised Miss Bingley to take the opportunity to bring the matter to a close, since it was clear that the match now had the approval of Sir Hugh.

"Caroline, Mallinger's vanity will not allow him to show a preference for you if you show none for him. He is not a man to make a proposal in form unless he is tolerably certain of being accepted. If you do not assist him he will never ask you to marry him."

"Would you have me show a preference that I do not feel?"

"I pray you do not vex me. I am not asking you to love him, I do not care if you love him. He is a man who will have wealth, position and a title and will therefore make a very suitable husband for you. I have gone to some trouble to make up this match."

Miss Bingley was silent.

After a short time Mrs. Hurst ventured, "I know that we planned that you would marry Darcy, and that Charles would marry Georgiana. However that is all gone by now. I trust that you are not foolish enough to allow some lingering feelings for Darcy to distract you."

"Naturally I have no feelings for Darcy."

"That is what people are saying, that you are putting off Mallinger out of partiality for Darcy."

"I never heard anything so abominable."

"You know how people will talk.'

"Let them. I shall do as I wish."

Mrs. Hurst sighed. There were occasions when she found her sister exceedingly fatiguing.

The Bingleys departed from Netherfield for Somerset and arrived at Damson Hall, a large Jacobean house set in a park with ancient oak trees, on the last day of August. Sir Hugh's health did not permit him to greet them on their arrival, but Henry Mallinger met their party and welcomed them with his usual collected manner. No symptom of love was detected by Mr. and Mrs. Bingley on either side when he and Miss Bingley greeted each other.

The following day, the first of September, a large party of men went out for shooting on the manor, Bingley and Mallinger among them, while the ladies followed the usual employments of sitting and talking or doing needlework, or walking about the grounds, until the gentlemen returned for dinner.

On the second of September another shooting party was arranged. Sir Hugh, having been so nettled at missing the first day's shooting that he had agitated himself into improved health, was able to join it. However when Mallinger met Miss Bingley at breakfast he was not dressed for sport.

"Miss Bingley, will you join me for a ride today?"

"Do you not intend shooting with the others?"

"Even killing innocent and defenceless birds can become a bore after a short time. I shall leave it to my uncle and his guests to decimate the creatures on the manor."

She understood that Mallinger intended to forward his suit by bringing them together alone. "Yes, I will ride with you."

"Good. You shall have Criterion, he is my favourite horse."

"Do not you wish to ride him?"

"I will take another. I had the groom put a side saddle on him last week and take him through his paces. I think you will like him. We shall endeavour to keep our distance from the carnage."

Accordingly Miss Bingley and Mallinger rode out together in the late morning. She made no effort to show him that he had engaged her feelings, or even to converse with him. His self-regard was disturbed by her excessive composure. She had received him as a suitor at Netherfield, and had accepted the invitation to Damson Hall. He was not in doubt about her intentions, yet she gave him as little encouragement as possible when they were together.

As they trotted along, a bird flew up under Criterion's feet and startled him, and he bolted. Mallinger followed at the gallop, caught the horse's bridle and pulled him to a walk. Miss Bingley expressed no gratitude for these attentions. She could have controlled the horse soon herself if he had not interfered, and she was unmoved by his display of gallantry. They walked on side by side for a little time. At length Mallinger said intrepidly, "Caroline, it pleases me to take care of you, and I should like to have the right to take care of you always."

"Do you propose that to me as a punishment or a pleasure?" she inquired coolly. This was not the best method of recommending herself; and Mallinger did not say anything but checked his horse angrily. Then he rode on, leaving a space of several feet between them.

Miss Bingley was aware that she was risking Mallinger's suit, on the chance of being asked a second time; and she was not certain that she wished to do so. She halted her horse. Mallinger glanced back, and then turned his own. "Is something amiss, ma'am?"

"I was uncivil to you. I beg your pardon."

"It is given."

"And I thank you for stopping Criterion."

"You are welcome," he replied coldly. "Shall we return to the house?"

"For my part, I desire to ride a little further, should I have the power to persuade you to accompany me."

"Willingly."

They rode on in silence, each in thought.

"Did Mallinger say anything while you were out?" asked Mrs. Hurst anxiously when she saw her sister. She had been waiting in sight of the hall door for her return.

"What of it, if he has?"

"Oh Caroline, you did not give him a teazing answer?"

"I have not answered him at all."

"Why not? How do you expect him to persevere? It would be abhorrent to his feelings to make a second proposal to the same woman!"

"That is as he chooses."

"Caroline, do not act with caprice. If you wish to marry him, give him the proper encouragement. If you do not wish to marry him, then have done with it. But unless there is a particular reason that you have not imparted to me, it would be folly to refuse him."

"I know I must be married—sometime."

"Before it is too late."

"My fortune will not grow old," said Miss Bingley with a slight sneer. "I assure you that it will be as eligible in two years, or ten, as it is now."

"I really do not see how you could do better than Henry Mallinger."

Miss Bingley turned away without replying.

On the following afternoon Lady Mallinger proposed a walk with some of her guests, to show them the gardens. Miss Bingley and Henry Mallinger were of the party. He spoke to no one other than her, but to her said nothing that could not be heard without impropriety by the rest of the party, and he looked at her neither more nor less than usual, and then with no particular expression in his eyes. She expected that he might seek some opportunity of a private audience with her, since he himself was leaving Damson on the morrow, but they made the tour of nearly the whole grounds without any suggestion from him that they leave the party. At last as they passed the entrance to a path that ran up a little hill, Mallinger said, "Shall we go this way?"

"If you wish."

They stopped at the top of the hill and gazed over the park. He looked at her. "You said when we were at Netherfield that if you were free to make any plan, it would be to marry."

She did not reply

"You *can* marry, if you are not determined against it."

"Is that your belief that I have done so?"

"Or perhaps that you feel no regard for me."

She said nothing.

"Do you wish me to understand, then, that you have no regard?"

"I have not said that."

"Does that mean that you have?"

Miss Bingley was ready to allow that to all appearances Mallinger had as few faults as it was possible for a husband to have. Was her only objection to him that he was not Darcy? She could not secure Darcy by dismissing Mallinger. Ought she to demonstrate to the watching multitude that Darcy meant nothing to her, by marrying, and marrying well? Mallinger had good looks, impeccable manners, an excellent lineage, and an imminent baronetcy; he had been everywhere in the world, seen everything, done everything; and with such attractions and experience he wished to make *her* his wife. She could not avoid being a little flattered by his proposal, even knowing that her first attraction must surely be her fortune.

"That may be," said Miss Bingley in a collected voice.

Chapter Twenty

[September 1813, Pemberley]

One afternoon Georgiana, looking for her book she thought to have left in Kitty's room and not finding Kitty within, picked up a volume lying on a table there. It opened of its own accord to a page marked by a piece of paper. The paper was a letter. Georgiana instantly recognized the handwriting as her Cousin James's, and she had absorbed the first few words before she was even conscious of reading. "Dear Kitty" the letter began. She had not known that Kitty and Cousin James were writing to each other; Kitty had never mentioned it; but here was Cousin James writing to her very familiarly as "Dear Kitty"! Georgiana felt her face grow warm with embarrassment, and she hastily put the letter back and closed the book. But astonishment and apprehension oppressed her, and in half a minute she took it out again. She held it in her fingers, considering, and then she began to read.

London
August –, 1813

Dear Kitty,
Thank you for your sketch of Zanzibar. You have caught the head and the expression of the eye, and I would only counsel that you work a little on the hind legs, although to speak frankly I have seen painters who exhibited at the Royal Academy who were somewhat deficient with respect to hind legs. When I was visiting my brother recently, I came upon a copy of my great grandfather's little pamphlet on leg injuries in horses, which I enclose under cover of this

letter. You may find it interesting, and there is a poultice receipt that is worth looking at.
James

Everyone said that Cousin James was going to marry her cousin Anne, yet he and Kitty were writing to each other—without telling anyone! And he was calling her Kitty and signing himself James. She thought of her own adventure with George Wickham: the secret letters, the secret meetings. Cousin James could not be thinking of marrying her. Did Kitty not realize this correspondence was wrong and wicked? It could only harm her, and perhaps harm Cousin James' chance of a suitable marriage. With her mind painfully engaged, she considered what she ought to do; and at last she carried the letter away and sought out Elizabeth.

Elizabeth read the letter and grew very uneasy. She thanked Georgiana for bringing it to her and assured her that she found no fault with her. Then she summoned Mrs. Reynolds and asked her to send Kitty to her in her room. The interview between the sisters was short. Although Kitty was surprised and vexed when Elizabeth showed her the letter, she listened quietly when Elizabeth told her that she must immediately suspend all correspondence with Fitzwilliam. Then she went to her own room to reflect on what had passed.

Georgiana found her there a little later, tapping softly on the door for admittance. Kitty bade her visitor enter, but upon seeing who it was gave her a look of deep resentment.

"You are angry with me, Kitty," said Georgiana in distress. "Please do not be, I cannot bear it if we cannot be friends."

"You read my letter."

"I did not mean to, indeed I did not. I went into your room to look for *Udolpho* and picked up your book without thinking. It opened it to the page marked by the letter. I had looked at it before I knew what it was."

"But then you took it to Elizabeth."

"Oh Kitty, I know you think that was very wrong of me."

Kitty turned away in silence. Georgiana followed her with her eyes, pressing her hands together anxiously.

"Kitty, perhaps if I tell you why I did it you will understand and forgive me."

Kitty made no answer, and Georgiana followed her into the room.

"I—I have never told anyone, except my brother. It is very hard for me to speak of it. You will probably laugh to think it, for I must seem exceedingly proper to you, but when I was fifteen I did a very wicked thing, and was going to do worse."

Kitty's attention was caught in spite of her anger, for the idea of Georgiana being wicked in any way seemed most unlikely. "What did you do?"

"I made an agreement to elope with a man."

"You, Georgiana! I do not believe it!"

Georgiana was almost overcome with confusion and was hardly able to lift up her eyes after making this confession, but after a moment she forced herself to speak. "It is true." She was silent for a few moments while Kitty continued to look at her in amazement, and then she added, "And there is much worse."

"What worse?"

"The man—was George Wickham."

"Wickham! Georgiana, how can that be? I do not understand you at all."

"Kitty, I will tell you everything; but it is very difficult for me. Please, be kind to me."

Kitty's antagonism was almost entirely subsumed in astonishment and curiosity, and she moved closer to Georgiana and took her hand.

After a moment, encouraged, Georgiana began. "Wickham was the son of my father's steward, you know that of course? He and my brother are of an age, and when I was born they were twelve years old and had already been sent away to school. Not the same school, of course; my brother was at Eton. When they were home I was almost their plaything, I was so much younger than they, but Wickham was always much fonder of me than my brother. I respected my brother, indeed, but I did not feel for him the affection that I did for Wickham. Wickham was often with me, playing with me, teasing me, making me little toys, taking me with him on his horse. I used to say that one day I would marry him, you know as children do. I loved him with all my heart, and was always very sad when he went away. I used to go into my father's room and look at his picture there. The miniature. You have seen it?"

"Yes," said Kitty.

"I knew even as a young child that although my father was attached to Wickham, my brother disliked him; but I did not know precisely why. Then of course he—he began to behave badly, and he and my brother quarrelled, and I did not see him any more. I often thought of him, though there was no one at Pemberley to whom I could speak of him—his name was never mentioned. I did not forget him, however. Then I went away to school, and after a few years my brother set up my own household for me, and I lived in London with my governess Mrs. Younge. It was two years ago that we went to Ramsgate for the summer, and there I met Wickham again. He came to see me. Oh Kitty, he was so handsome! Much more handsome than I had remembered, for by then I really only recalled his features from the miniature. And his manners were so gentle and charming, and his conversation so pleasing—I could talk to him though I find it difficult to talk to most people. We spoke about so many things! I had never stopped loving him, you must understand, Kitty, but at that time the love I felt changed from the love of a child to the love of a young woman. I knew that my brother and Mrs. Reynolds thought that he had turned out bad and wild, but I did not see it in him. I did not want him to go away. I admitted him, and Mrs. Younge did not object, so I thought it no harm." She paused, and then resumed slowly, "No, Kitty, that is not true. I knew it was wrong for him to visit me every day when my brother did not know. And—and I allowed him to kiss me." She stopped a moment. "Oh Kitty, his kisses were so wonderful! I would have died for them. So when he asked me to go away with him to Scotland, to be married at Gretna Green, I said yes. And I would have gone. Yes, I would have." Her tone was defiant. "But then my brother came unexpectedly to see me, two days before we intended to elope." She bowed her head.

"Then what happened?" said Kitty impatiently.

"It was very terrible. I loved Wickham and wanted to go with him more than anything in the world. But I could not support the idea of grieving and offending my brother. I acknowledged the plan to him, and he wrote to Wickham, who immediately left Ramsgate. And I have never seen or heard from him since."

Kitty was too much overpowered by Georgiana's story to say a word, and after a moment Georgiana continued, "But I have heard things. That he eloped with your sister, that he—he—seduced—tradesmen's daughters, that he was idle and dissipated; that he gambled and had debts of honour. I have heard people say that he is not a good man, and my brother believes that he wanted to elope with me only to take revenge, and not because he loved me. And he thinks that I only imagined that I loved Wickham. He does not understand what my feelings are." Georgiana collected herself as well as she could and added, "So you see, Kitty, when I saw that letter from Cousin James to you, I could not help but think of Wickham, for we exchanged secret letters too. I know you and Cousin James should not be writing to each other in secret, for it is wrong."

Kitty's anger was now entirely done away with, and instead of taking offence at Georgiana's words she pressed her hand.

"Kitty, promise me that you will not tell anyone what I have told you."

"You have my promise, Georgiana."

"Then I will tell you something even worse now." She paused, and then burst out, "I envy your sister so, that she is married to him! And—and— I know that it is very wrong to say so, but I regret that I told my brother about Wickham before we eloped. Each time I hear his name it is like a stab through the heart because I long so to see him, and—and—for him to kiss me and hold me to his bosom. I think I will always love him! Do you know that I still go into my father's room sometimes, when there is no one near, and gaze at his picture? If there were a fire at Pemberley and I could save only one object before I fled, it would be that picture. It may be that for some women there is only ever one man. Perhaps I am one of those women."

With affectionate solicitude Kitty did what was in her power to comfort Georgiana, and promised that they would always be friends.

That evening Elizabeth related to Darcy the story of Kitty's letter, and then asked him, "Darcy, what can it mean that Fitzwilliam is writing in such an intimate way to Kitty? There is no possibility of them marrying. Surely he cannot be thinking—."

"I am certain you need not be under any apprehension, but I admit that I am as much in perplexity as you. You have told Kitty that it must stop, and I will write to him with the same injunction. I can only think this is some innocent misjudgment, and not a disgraceful scheme on the part of either of them."

Elizabeth was in concurrence with this opinion. Nevertheless before she retired that night she made her way to the portrait gallery with her candle, where she stood for a time gazing at the portrait of James, 5th Earl of Tyrconnell, and thinking about the Earl's unconnected sons.

Chapter Twenty-One

[September 1813, Pemberley]

It is possible for a woman to be settled too near her family, although the far and the near must be relative, and depend on many circumstances. While Elizabeth at Pemberley found herself too far from her eldest sister and her father, Jane and Bingley at Netherfield found themselves within too easy a distance of Mrs. Bennet and her relations in Meryton, even for Bingley's easy temper or Jane's affectionate heart. Bingley one day declared that although he was an idle fellow, and had thought himself quite fixed at Netherfield, he had received an eligible offer for Netherfield and now resolved to buy his own estate outside Hertfordshire. Whatever Bingley undertook to do, was generally done in a hurry, and the entire business was conducted rapidly. Jane soon wrote to Elizabeth with tidings.

Netherfield Park, Herts
September –, 1813

Dearest Lizzy,
We have <u>talked</u> of being closer to each other than we are at present, perhaps within easy distance for visiting; and now I have good news to tell you, for Bingley has bought an estate in Nottinghamshire. One of the reasons for our tour last June was to look about for the purpose, but as we had no settled plans we were reluctant to mention it and raise expectations. But now we will live at Clifford Priory, which Bingley says is no more than thirty miles from Pemberley.

I must tell you about Clifford, at least until you can see it for yourself. It stands on a wooded escarpment overlooking the river, and is approached by a long avenue running between two double rows of ancient elms, that is known as Clifford Wood. There are seventeen bedrooms, so we shall have no trouble accommodating a large party from Pemberley. Charles I stayed in one of them, and while visiting played bowls with the first Baron Clifford. Below the house is a series of grassy terraces, the first with two sleeping stone lions, the second with a summer house. (We are uncertain on which terrace the game of bowls took place, but will treat all of them with suitable respect.) Georgiana will be delighted to hear that Clifford even has its own ghost. The daughter of the fourth Baron was killed in an accident while riding in the Wood; at the time her portrait was being painted, and when she died her father ordered that it be turned into one of his sister. We have been unable to ascertain, whether he was prompted by grief, or merely economy. The portrait is still at Clifford, in one of the parlours. By day if one looks at it, one sees the Baron's sister; however it is said that if one looks at in the moonlight, it is the daughter's face that appears. Clifford is not quite Udolpho, but I hope we may be able to hold up our heads if our guests demand a disquieting atmosphere and occasional alarming noises in the middle of the night. We intend to go there from Netherfield at the beginning of October, and will stop at Pemberley on our way.

Dearest Lizzy, I have said little of this in my letters to you, but to be closer to you and Darcy is but one of our objects in leaving Hertfordshire. You know how little I like to think ill of anyone, and indeed there are always extenuating circumstances that require allowances to be made for any person's conduct; however our residence at Netherfield has not always been pleasant. My mother, now that only Mary remains, finds little comfort in staying at home and is a frequent visitor here, often bringing with her aunt Phillips. They are very welcome to me, but my aunt is eager to retail to her neighbours all the particulars of our house and our doings, and speaks very familiarly to Bingley. Uncle Phillips has made overtures to Bingley that he place some of his affairs into his hands; I believe that his business may have suffered from the departure of the regiment. All mean well, but they cannot know how their visits at times distress me. Although Bingley is always unaffectedly civil to my mother, and endeavours to make his sisters civil also, Caroline scarcely opens her mouth when my mother is here, indeed avoids her as much as possible, and shows candidly how she wishes her out of the house. When Louisa is present, she and Caroline are supercilious, and make derisive signs to each other, and then remarks upon my mother when she has left. The two of them, as you know, were no friends to Bingley's acquaintance with me, which I did not wonder at for he might have chosen more advantageously in some respects, but I had hoped that they would learn to be contented with me and civil to my family when they saw their brother happy. The anxiety that they felt on his behalf was natural, for he is dear to them, but we have never really come to be on good terms again. It is difficult at times to take the situation in the best light, and although I have striven to bear them with tranquillity, I am glad that *you* have been spared these disagreeable scenes.

My mother's spirits are greatly shaken by the news that we are leaving Netherfield, and Bingley's sisters are vexed that we are removing so far from London, for they have both gone back and forth between Netherfield and the Hursts' townhouse with tolerable regularity. I am grieved for my mother, and for Bingley that he will lose the constant society of his sisters, for whom he feels affection. But I will endeavour to banish these injurious thoughts, and think only of what will make me happy—to be close to you once more.

Nothing has come yet of Louisa's plan to marry Caroline to Henry Mallinger, and Caroline seems not to like to hear mention of his name. If she does not marry, she will make her home in London with the Hursts, though of course Bingley and I will be happy to receive her at Clifford whenever she wishes to visit.

Be assured, dear Lizzy, that despite what I have written, I am perfectly well. Let me hear from you very soon. Adieu!

Your affectionate sister,

J. Bingley

Elizabeth felt an anxiety upon reading this letter, that her sister's spirits had been so much affected by the behaviour of her own family and Bingley's, and longed to have been with her to alleviate the cares that had fallen upon her. That Jane had not alluded to this situation before did not surprise her, for she was ever desirous of concealing what was painful. But Elizabeth shortly determined that she, like Jane, would think only of what made her happy and, rejoicing, she showed the letter to Darcy. "They will be not much more than a half a day's journey from us. It will give me so much delight to see Jane more often!" Darcy responded that he had had a letter from Bingley, that he conjectured contained the same news, but which because of Bingley's careless writing style, with half the words left out and the rest blotted, he could scarcely make out. "The power of doing anything with quickness is always prized much by the possessor," he remarked, "and often without any attention to the imperfection of the performance—and therefore I very much hope that Bingley has not purchased a property that is falling into ruin!"

Nevertheless the prospect of having the Bingleys so close was very cheering, and they spoke of it with mutual pleasure. They further agreed that with the Bingleys' consent Kitty should go to Clifford when Fitzwilliam next visited Pemberley.

Chapter Twenty-Two

[September 1813, Pemberley]

It is universally acknowledged that a man in possession of an estate must be in want of an inheritor. And it is further acknowledged that, if the estate be entailed only God can make the heir—that omnipotent Being, however, requiring in such case the assistance of the lawful wife of the estate's owner. The present owner of Pemberley also, and much to the credit of his more tender feelings, was deeply desirous of a child of his union with a wife for whom his affections were almost boundless. Very great was Darcy's delight, therefore, on being informed that Elizabeth had been delivered of a son, and that mother and child were both well. When he was admitted to Elizabeth's room, with an expression of heartfelt joy diffused over his features, he expressed his contentment so warmly that she could not but find his affection for her more valuable with every word that he spoke.

The nurse brought the child in and placed him in Elizabeth's arms, and together the new parents looked at him, with a mixture of pride at their achievement and anxiety at handling such a fragile creature.

"I believe he will look very much like his father," said Elizabeth, gazing at the baby. "And bear his father's names of course."

"I am relieved that you have no objection to Fitzwilliam."

"None at all. But it seems a great deal of name for such a small individual. Can we not be a little less formal with him, in private discourse?"

"My own baby name was Will. Would that suit?"

"Yes, very well, I think. Will you write to Lady Catherine and tell her she has a grandnephew?"

"It is a duty I cannot neglect, and it must be done directly."

"She will not be pleased by the adulteration of the noble line—but we may hope that she will look upon it more happily as an ennobling of the baser blood."

"That is unlikely."

"Then perhaps when little Will grows up to resemble her, she may relent and acknowledge the relationship."

When the nurse had taken the baby away Darcy said, "I wish to give you a surprise. There will soon be a new portrait in the gallery."

"Whose?"

"Yours. I have commissioned Sir Henry Raeburn to paint you."

"Darcy! Is this to be my reward for producing an heir for Pemberley?"

"Not a reward, Elizabeth. There is no reward great enough to thank you for becoming my wife and the mother of my son. If I must give an explanation it is that I wish to capture you as you are now, so that you will be always here at Pemberley, for our children and grandchildren and great-grandchildren." Elizabeth was exceedingly moved by her husband's speech, but finding it impossible to express her feelings in words, she could respond only with her eyes, and the touch of her hand.

Upon leaving Elizabeth, Darcy immediately sat down to write to his aunt.

> Pemberley House, Derby
> September –, 1813
>
> Madam,
> I wish to inform you that my wife Elizabeth has been safely delivered of a son and that he will be christened Fitzwilliam Oliver Darcy.
> Fitzwilliam Darcy

To this letter he received the following reply.

> Rosings Park, Kent
> September --, 1813
>
> Dear Darcy,
> It was uncommonly kind of you to inform me of the birth of my great-nephew. It would have been natural to ask me to stand as godmother to your first child, however I can readily understand the diffidence that prevented you making such a request, the child having, as it does, on one side of its family, inferior birth and no connections. I sincerely hope that you have not asked the son of your late father's steward to stand as godfather, or the attorney's wife to stand as godmother.
> C. de Bourgh

Darcy dropped this letter into the fire himself and did not trouble to show it to Elizabeth.

Elizabeth also received a letter from Hunsford, which brought her considerably more pleasure than Darcy's.

Hunsford Parsonage, Kent
September –, 1813

Dearest Eliza,
I rejoiced with all my heart to hear your news. I am so happy for you and Darcy, and I trust that you will love your little Will as much as I love my little Catherine. Lady Catherine has condescended to visit her namesake frequently and gives me a great deal of advice. I am sure if I took half of it the poor little thing would be in her grave by now. However as *she* has experience of the raising of only one child (and one that is still sickly at that!), and *I* of several younger brothers and sisters, I take my own advice rather than hers, and the baby seems to be thriving. Lady Catherine urges me to have a boy next so that the Longbourn entail may be broken—as she says it was never considered necessary in Sir Lewis deBourgh's family, and I presume Mr. Collins and I have become by geography subject to the customs of Sir Lewis's family.
Yours affectionately,
C. Collins.

A second letter from Kent arrived for Darcy, and after perusing it, he took it to his wife. "Elizabeth, I profited from your advice on how to deal with Lady Catherine's letter; now there is another on which I wish to obtain your counsel."

Hunsford, Kent
September –, 1813

Dear Sir,
As there must be a wide difference between the established forms of ceremony amongst the laity and the clergy, and further as I consider the clerical office as equal in dignity with the highest rank in the kingdom, provided that a proper humility of behaviour is maintained, I take the liberty of writing to you to perform what I look upon a as a duty, both as your cousin by marriage and more importantly as the spiritual advisor of your esteemed aunt Lady Catherine de Bourgh, to congratulate you and my cousin Elizabeth on the ar-

rival of a son and, dare I say, the olive branch that may mend the differences between yourselves and my illustrious patroness. As a clergyman I am called upon to promote the blessings of peace in all families within the reach of my influence, and I have been much concerned by the breach within yours. I am so well convinced of Lady Catherine's discernment as to be certain that she would not quarrel with you and your wife without the best of reasons, and yet I give myself leave to hope that the present misfortune of the rupture between you may soon be alleviated. Be assured, my dear sir, that I shall do all within my power to bring comfort, and to endeavour to heal the disagreement subsisting between you.

Your humble well-wisher,
WILLIAM COLLINS

Elizabeth changed colour as soon as she saw the first words. "Good heavens!" she cried. She had done all she could to shield Darcy from the notice of those members of her family with whom he could not converse without mortification, not excluding Mr. Collins with his obsequious civility. As well as she liked follies and nonsense, Mr. Collins' no longer had the power to divert her, and Darcy they had never diverted. "Must you reply to him?"

"If I do not, what becomes of the lesson you taught me? If I do not answer a civil letter of congratulations, what is my motive other than vanity and conceit?"

"But if you do reply you will not be able to escape a correspondence with him. My father is greatly amused by his with Mr. Collins, but you do not have his predilection for the ridiculous."

"I do not, unfortunately. Yet I can see no way to avoid becoming Mr. Collins' correspondent."

"He writes to you in all humility; perhaps he will not take much advantage of a reply."

"Nothing is more deceitful than the appearance of humility."

"Darcy, I would not have had this happen, of all things," she cried. "Can you forgive me for being related to Mr. Collins?"

Darcy smiled. "If I had had any conception, before I first offered to you in Kent, that by taking you as my wife I would also receive George Wickham as my brother and Mr. Collins as my regular correspondent, I very much doubt that a single word would ever have passed my lips! And yet I will bear this, and would bear much more, for you. What do I not owe you, my dearest Elizabeth?"

"You are bound to praise extravagantly my good qualities whenever the opportunity arises. But I fear that this new connection with Mr. Collins must go a long way towards settling any debt between us."

Darcy however could not be brought to confess the truth of this assertion, and the argument was not settled until a kiss had been given and returned.

Chapter Twenty-Three

[October 1813, Pemberley]

The discovery of a private correspondence between an unmarried young lady and a gentleman who in the eyes of the world is destined to marry a different young lady must necessarily be attended on the part of the correspondents by a certain embarrassment, and Colonel Fitzwilliam was not untouched by this sensation as he journeyed towards Pemberley. However it was secondary to his anticipation of seeing Kitty after a separation of several months, and once within the Park he watched keenly for her appearance—but in vain, and he arrived at the house alone.

Georgiana was the first to greet him, and after embracing her affectionately he said, "Where is Kitty? I was not run down by a lady on horseback, so I naturally wondered whether she was aware of my arrival."

"Oh, Kitty is not here right now."

"Where is she? When will she be back?"

"I am not certain—perhaps my brother or Elizabeth can tell you—but in the meantime come and see them, and the baby."

He accompanied Georgiana to the saloon where Elizabeth was lying on a sopha before the open windows, for the day was warm and pleasant, with Darcy seated beside her. After greeting them and inquiring after the health of Elizabeth and the baby, he said, "Georgiana has been very mysterious about Kitty's whereabouts. What have you done with her? She has not run away with the gypsies I trust?"

"She is visiting Bingley and Jane for a little while, there is no great mystery in it," said Darcy.

"Was she not aware that I was coming?"

"Yes, of course."

"And yet she would go to Clifford Priory rather than remain at Pemberley?"

"We thought it best for her not to be here, Fitzwilliam," said Elizabeth. "She feels an attachment for you that it would not be wise to encourage. Like any young girl she is inclined to read more into a man's good humour and attentions than is really there."

"I must say, you are quite taking it upon yourselves to move her about like a chess piece. Did you ask her opinion or did you simply pack her up like a parcel and send her off?"

"We did not employ any threats or violence, she went willingly," said Elizabeth with a smile.

It would not be true to say that all pleasure in his visit to Pemberley was now forfeited, for Fitzwilliam was deeply attached to the entire family, but he felt Kitty's absence very strongly, and thought about her perhaps even more than he would have done had she actually been present.

Although he was frequently abstracted, Elizabeth and Darcy were in general content with him, for he was now able to treat Elizabeth as a dear cousin, in much the same way he treated Georgiana. Fitzwilliam himself, through preoccupation, scarcely noticed the difference in his own behaviour.

One evening when he and Darcy were playing billiards he began a subject that had been on his mind. "Darcy, you say that Kitty is a young girl, but she is of marriageable age. Have you and her family formed any plans for her as yet?"

"Elizabeth and I have discussed it a little between us. When we are in town next season she will have an opportunity of making the acquaintance of some eligible gentlemen. I will assist her father in providing a proper dowry so that she will not be at a disadvantage—I cannot have a penniless sister, even though my own wife came to me in more or less that state."

"I don't doubt there are gentlemen of property who would take Kitty with no more than the clothes she stands up in."

"I dare say, but there is no need to give the hypothesis a trial!"

"Darcy, I do not know what candidates you and Elizabeth may have discussed, but might I put forward one of my own?"

"Ah, you have determined to take an avuncular interest in Kitty and her prospects? I commend you highly, Fitzwilliam. Who is the young man you wish to be known to her?"

"I believe you may have met him in my company once or twice—it is Captain George Villers. He comes from a good family, and is an agreeable fellow."

Darcy stopped his shot and fixed his eyes upon Fitzwilliam. "Captain Villers is under your command, I believe?"

"Yes; he is a fine soldier."

"I am not concerned with his military ability, and I am by no means convinced that you are."

Fitzwilliam looked uncomfortable as Darcy kept his gaze on him. After a few moments he said, "If Kitty and I were both married, there would be nothing—extraordinary—in our being together. Consider Lord Nelson and Lady Hamilton.* We would not be so indiscreet as they were, naturally."

"Fitzwilliam, whatever effort it may cost you, you must relinquish Kitty. If you feel any regard for her you will not take any step, that would stain her reputation. She is my sister now, and subject to the same care that I confer upon Georgiana."

"You *do* take care of her, in those points where you believe she most wants care!"

"Would you truly compass playing Wickham's role with her?"

"It is most inequitable of you to counter Nelson with Wickham," protested Fitzwilliam. "You are tempting me to trump you with the Prince Regent. Darcy, you know how common are *liaisons* within our rank of society."

"Your conjecture is wrong. I would no more countenance His Royal Highness' pursuit of Kitty than I do yours. Now do you put Kitty out of your mind and let us finish this game."

"You like to have your own way very well," said Fitzwilliam. "But so do we all."

Nevertheless Fitzwilliam could not oppose Darcy's injunction; and from this time, he rarely spoke of Kitty to him or to Elizabeth.

---

* Horatio Nelson, 1st Viscount Nelson, 1st Duke of Bronte (1758-1805), was an English naval officer who won several famous victories during the Napoleonic Wars and was a national hero. He was killed in the sea Battle of Trafalgar. Emma, Lady Hamilton (1761-1815) was a beauty of humble birth who became a courtesan and the famous model of painter George Romney. She was first the mistress and then in 1791 the wife of Sir William Hamilton, the British Envoy to Naples. She became Lord Nelson's mistress after he arrived unwell in Naples in 1798 and she nursed him back to health in her husband's house. They lived together openly, and had a daughter in 1801. –Ed.

Chapter Twenty-Four

[October 1813, London]

At the beginning of October, Bingley and Jane vacated Netherfield and removed to Nottinghamshire. Miss Bingley did not accompany them but remained with the Hursts at Grosvenor Street in London, and shortly after her arrival there, Henry Mallinger called upon her.

"Mr. Mallinger, I did not know that you intended coming up to town," she said when he was shown into the drawing room.

"I came up from Damson on purpose to see you. I heard that you had left Hertfordshire."

"My brother and his wife have gone to their estate, and I am staying in town."

"Will you go to them soon?"

"I join them in November."

"Caroline, I would like matters settled between us before then."

"What is your meaning? To what matters do you refer?"

"You know quite well what I mean. I do not wish to importune you, however. If there is no hope I do not intend making myself a bore. I would ask you to tell me so, here, tonight, if there is no hope. Then I shall leave England."

"Leave? Where will you go?"

"That will be of no concern to you."

Miss Bingley heard this with unease. It had rather pleased her to know that he was waiting for her answer, for the past three months. Now it seemed he would not wait longer. Her feelings towards Mallinger were difficult of definition, and even now she felt a contrariety of emotion; she did not wish to accept his proposal of marriage, nor did she wish to send him away with a clear refusal. She sought for a way to put the decision off, at least for a few moments.

"Surely you do not intend me to believe that you will quit England and drown yourself if you cannot have me for your wife?" she asked mockingly.

"I certainly shall not drown myself, or cast myself off a cliff, or even take to drink. Your grip on my heart is somewhat more tenuous than that. But do you intend to go on tormenting me this evening? Shall I take my departure immediately?"

She now grew serious. "It is not my intention to torment you."

"Then will you order me to go, and not return?"

After a short pause she said, "No; I do not want you to go."

"Caroline, look at me." She obeyed. "Will you marry me?"

"Yes," she said slowly. "I will marry you."

Mallinger took her hand, raised it, pressed his lips to it; and then released it. "How soon shall we be married?" he asked. "I would prefer not to delay. Waiting for anything is fatiguing. Before Christmas."

Miss Bingley wondered briefly if he feared tiring of her company even before the wedding. However now that she had made the decision, she did not care how soon the ceremony occurred. "Yes, if that is what you like."

"In this world things are always turning up that one does not like. The end of November then, here in London. I will have my solicitors communicate with yours about the settlements."

Chapter Twenty-Five

[November 1813, Longbourn]

Slight as the sympathy was between Jane and Elizabeth and their mother, the two young women were attentive to their filial duty. While Jane was mistress of Netherfield she had frequently been seeing Mrs. Bennet, but now that the Bingleys had moved to Nottinghamshire such intercourse had been cut off. Mrs. Bennet had more than once declined to make the journey to Pemberley, with or without her husband, as she considered it too arduous. Deeming the regular exchange of letters insufficient, after some discussion Jane and Elizabeth arranged to return to Longbourn for a few days' visit, bringing Kitty with them as well. When Elizabeth wrote to Charlotte Collins to inform her, the latter replied almost by return of post, that she and Mr. Collins would take the opportunity to visit her own family at Lucas Lodge so that the two friends might see each other for the first time in more than a year and a half. The addition of Charlotte greatly improved the plan and Elizabeth began to look forward, rather than be resigned, to the visit.

After stopping overnight in London with their aunt and uncle Gardiner, the young women arrived at Longbourn House in the late morning. They found Mrs. Bennet and Mary sitting in the dining parlour.

"Well, well," said Mrs. Bennet, "you have finally come. We have been expecting you these last two hours and my nerves are nearly torn to pieces from wondering whether you were overturned in a ditch. But no one has compassion on my poor nerves!"

Jane and Elizabeth exclaimed at Mrs. Bennet's fears and assured her that the journey had been without incident. However their mother was not disposed to be comforted and indeed seemed to wish to agitate herself further.

"I have made myself quite a slave to finding husbands for you girls, and I suppose this is all the thanks I can expect. Jane was established very comfortably—I do not know a place in the country that is equal to Netherfield!—but it was not good enough for her and Bingley, they had to go to some foreign part of the country where I would never be able to see her again. Lydia has been taken such a way from me and is to stay there I do not know how long—that is very hard. I say nothing of Lizzy, for she had no choice but to live in a wild place if she would marry Darcy, but Jane might have given me some consideration. Nobody can tell what I suffer! But as I do not complain no one pays any attention to me. Those who do not complain are never pitied."

Jane, Elizabeth and Kitty glanced at each other, but listened in silence to this effusion, for they were well aware that any attempt to soothe their mother would only increase her irritation. She talked on in a similar vein, therefore, without interruption from either them or Mary until Mr. Bennet entered the room.

So overjoyed had Mr. Bennet been by the arrival of his three daughters, and particularly of Elizabeth, that he left his library no more than half an hour after being informed by a servant that they were in the house. He had intensely felt the loss of his two eldest children, for without them evening conversation in the family circle had lost not only its animation but almost all of its sense. As he came into the dining parlour he said, "Ah, girls, I see that your mother is exerting herself to make you feel quite at home. It must be a great comfort to all of your children, Mrs. Bennet, that they may depend upon you not to alter in any particular no matter how long they may have been away."

"I hope that at my time of life I am not flighty and changeable like a young girl, Mr. Bennet."

"No indeed, Mrs. Bennet, you have changed scarcely a jot since the day we married. Girls, I am very glad to see you, and I hope you will consent to stay to dinner."

"What nonsense, Mr. Bennet, they are here for a week, as you very well know."

"Indeed, my dear? From all that I can collect from your manner of talking, it must be an exceedingly short visit, for you appear anxious to unburden yourself as quickly as possible. If the girls remain beyond tomorrow you will have nothing left to say to them."

Mr. Bennet's speech would have been unlikely to have any effect on his wife other than to cause a temporary break in the flow of her words, however as his coming led his daughters to rise and greet and embrace him affectionately, the interruption turned the tide of the conversation, or rather of the monologue. They now exchanged news with each other, and Mr. and Mrs. Bennet were especially desirous of hearing all that Elizabeth could tell them of their first grandchild. Kitty had brought a sketch of the sleeping baby that she had made, and it excited such interest as can be aroused only in the near relations of the subject. Mrs. Bennet was certain she could identify little Will's ear as one passed down from her maternal grandfather, while Mary solemnly opined that as an infant is *tabula rasa* it was unreasonable to endeavour to trace any sort of resemblance between it and other family members.

Mary was the plain daughter in the family and, being vain and conceited, had always been mortified by comparisons to her sisters' beauty. The same vanity had given her application, however, and she had worked hard for knowledge and accomplishments, and was always impatient to display them. But she had neither genius nor taste; when she spoke her manner was pedantic, and when she exhibited her air was affected. Her conversation generally consisted of moralizing over events and retailing extracts from the books she had read. She and her sisters had had little interest in each other, and their absence from Longbourn had not distressed her.

For her part, Elizabeth had not missed Mary's presence, and had not intended inviting her to visit the Darcys. Nevertheless the few hours she, Jane and Kitty had spent in Mrs. Bennet's company moved her to some sympathy for her sister, that she should be left alone with their uncompanionable mother. Therefore she said to her when the females of the family were sitting together after dinner, "Mary, should you like to come to Darcy and me in London this winter for a month? We will go there at the end of January. Darcy takes his seat in the House of Commons you know."

Mary's vanity was immediately pricked, that she might possibly be considered an object of pity; and although the prospect of a visit was in fact an appealing one, she replied, "Far be it from me, my dear sister, to depreciate the pleasures of life in town, for I know they are congenial to many. But the activities and exertions attendant on residence there would interfere with my studies, and so I must decline." Elizabeth assured her she would be left to her own devices as much as she wished, and would not be required to join in any entertainments that were objectionable to her, and reminded her that the library in Darcy's townhouse was an extensive one. With a little more resistance on Mary's side and a little more persuasion on Elizabeth's and Jane's, Mary was at last brought to agree. "If I may have my mornings to myself," she said, "then I will not object to participate in occasional evening engagements with the rest of the family."

"While she is there," said Mrs. Bennet, "you must take care to see if you can find her a husband, for there is a vast variety of people in town, and there may be gentlemen who have no objection to a wife who has her nose buried in a book all day long."

Mary was offended by so direct a reference to her unmarried state and present lack of prospects. She responded in an affronted tone, "Everything I have read leads me to believe that when we are unable to find tranquillity in ourselves, it is useless to seek it elsewhere. Only one of no virtue or ability is afraid of solitude."

"Aye, if you go on in that way," said Mrs. Bennet, "you will never get a husband at all, and then I should like to know who will maintain you when your father is dead and we are turned out of this house. I shall not be able to keep you, I warn you of that. You have no care for my nerves, they are nothing to you compared to one of your books."

As Mrs. Bennet's ill humour had not abated on the morrow, all four of the girls thought it not only healthful but expedient to walk to Lucas Lodge to see if Charlotte and Mr. Collins had arrived. They found that the Collinses had been there since the previous evening, and upon greeting Mr. Collins, Lady Lucas and her daughters in the parlour, they learned that Charlotte had declared herself slightly indisposed and would receive her friend in her dressing room.

Mr. Collins, a tall, heavy-looking young man of seven-and twenty with a grave air and very formal manners, accompanied his cousin Elizabeth to his amiable Charlotte, whom they discovered sitting in a small room with but little light and a somewhat smoky fire. The two young women greeted each other most affectionately, for they felt the sincerest pleasure at being reunited after such a long separation. Mr. Collins was delighted to be able to give Elizabeth all the recent news of the family at Rosings for, as he said, owing to the estrangement between Lady Catherine and her nephew and niece, it was doubtful that the Darcys had the intelligence of Rosings, that he was able to furnish, from any other source. He at once produced all the information in his possession, not neglecting to include many of Lady Catherine's comments on the misfortune of one nephew's marriage and the happy prospect of the other nephew's impending marriage, until Charlotte stirred the fire and lamentably increased to a considerable extent the amount of smoke wafting into the room.

"My dear Charlotte!" he cried. "Would you not be more comfortable in the parlour with your mother and sisters?"

Charlotte assured him that at present the dressing room suited her exactly, as it was warm and had no drafts, and was close by the nurse and baby should she be required. Then she added with the same command of countenance that Elizabeth had admired when visiting her at Hunsford, "But Mr. Collins, I fear you find it rather close in here. Did you not say you intended walking to the vicarage? The weather is fine and I am sure the exercise would benefit you after yesterday's travel."

Mr. Collins owned that he had planned to visit the vicar of Meryton, and that a walk would perhaps be refreshing, and so he took leave of his cousin Elizabeth with many civil apologies for abandoning her before he had been able to satisfy her fully with the news of Rosings, and she had been able to answer in detail his inquiries after her family at Longbourn and Pemberley. Elizabeth and Charlotte were then able to pursue their own conversation in comfort, after Charlotte had opened the window and let out some of the smoke.

On the following day the Collinses and Maria Lucas returned the call, and were warmly welcomed at Longbourn by Mrs. Bennet's daughters. Mrs. Bennet herself had never, since Charlotte's marriage, been able to see or hear of the Collinses without feeling thoroughly annoyed by their treacherous behaviour in being next in line for the entailed property, and some of her remarks were rather biting, although Charlotte with great civility and Mr. Collins with inattention to anything but his own flow of words paid them no heed. After sitting with the ladies for half an hour Mr. Collins sought out Mr. Bennet in his library and was pleased to wander about the room examining the bookshelves and talking of his doings in Hunsford Parish until Mr. Bennet was enabled, by the serving of tea in the dining parlour, to evict his guest without resorting to the necessity of violence.

The Collinses' departure did not restore Mrs. Bennet's spirits, and at dinner she was acerbic about Charlotte's interest in the drawing room furniture that she claimed to have observed, "For," she said, "I make no doubt that she was calculating the cost of replacing the upholstery on the sopha and side chairs that is a little worn, when they move into the house. I could see that the Collinses looked upon Longbourn quite as their own when they came in."

"Mrs. Bennet, I have the greatest confidence that the task of reupholstering the drawing room furniture will fall to you and not to the Collinses."

"Ah, Mr. Bennet, you are always disposed to make light of the business, but I have never understood how you could in conscience have entailed the estate away from your own family. And then to have the Lucases artfully step in and take the estate from under our noses, when Lizzy might have married Mr. Collins and I would not have been turned out when you are lying dead. I do think it the hardest thing in the world."

"My dear, how many times have I comforted you that *I* may be the survivor?"

Jane, seeing that their father's caprice was only increasing their mother's irritation, assured Mrs. Bennet that if she would never be left homeless, and would always find a place with her and Bingley, whatever became of Longbourn.

"Yes," said Mrs. Bennet, "you would drag me away from my family and friends to those foreign places where you and Lizzy have gone, and who knows what heathenish people live there." Elizabeth, for the sake of saying something that would turn her mother's thoughts, reminded her that she would be closer to Lydia. Mrs. Bennet was pleasantly distracted by this idea, and the meal concluded in a less querulous atmosphere.

With visits to the Philipses, the Gouldings and Mrs. Long and the other families in the neighbourhood, and with a dinner party at Longbourn every night when they had not been invited to a neighbour's house (for Mrs. Bennet had firm ideas as to the need of constant company for visitors), Elizabeth, Jane and Kitty found that the week passed quickly. The entertainments seemed to put their mother in a more cheerful frame of mind, for she was flattered by the curiosity with which their acquaintance examined her two married daughters, their clothing and their jewelry, as though they were travellers returned from exotic lands, and by the degree of respect they accorded Elizabeth for her newly exalted position in the world.

The young women parted from their father with real regret and warm invitations for him to visit them whenever he wished, and from their mother with civil regard and promises to write frequently. Mary had a platitude for them, and a promise to meet Elizabeth and Darcy in London in three months' time.

Chapter Twenty-Six

[November 1813, London]

Having at last agreed to wed Mallinger, and to do so within a short space of time, Miss Bingley found that she was too much employed in nuptial arrangements to travel to Clifford Priory. Bingley came up to London, leaving Jane to direct activities at Clifford, to instruct the family solicitors about the marriage settlements. It now wanted but a fortnight until the wedding.

Miss Bingley had received a steady stream of callers from amongst her acquaintance since the announcement of her engagement. The proper time for morning calls was quite at an end when the servant appeared and inquired whether she would receive a visitor.

"Who is it?" She numbered only one or two among her acquaintance whom she would admit at this hour. The servant proffered a card on a salver. Miss Bingley took it and read, 'Signora Leonora Giovanese.' "It is a dress-maker or milliner seeking custom. I am not in."

"Madam, if you will permit me, she does not appear to be a tradeswoman, and seemed very anxious to speak to you. She asked me to say that it was a matter of extreme urgence—to you."

"To *me*? How excessively intriguing. Show her in; inform her however that I will give her no more than five minutes."

"Yes, Madam." The servant departed, and returned shortly to announce Signora Giovanese. A beautiful woman of about forty, dark-haired, dark eyed, olive-skinned, and elegantly dressed, entered the room. She advanced straight to Miss Bingley with as much composure as if the house had been hers rather than the Hursts'.

"I thank you for receiving me." She spoke English perfectly but with a slight and charming accent.

"I am much engaged at the moment. To what occasion do I owe this visit?"

"I can see that my name means nothing to you."

"Nothing at all."

"Perhaps then this name means something to you: Henry Mallinger."

"It does," said Miss Bingley, drawing herself up. "I am engaged to marry Mr. Mallinger."

"He has never spoken to you of me?"

"Certainly not. Why should he?"

"Why indeed," said Signora Giovanese. She turned away from Miss Bingley for a moment. Then over her shoulder she asked, "Has he told you about his children?"

"Mr. Mallinger has no children," said Miss Bingley in a cold voice.

"He has four children, two sons and two daughters. They are my children also."

"Do you claim to be his wife?"

"I am his companion of many years. I am the mother of his children. In Venice we live together."

"I do not know why you have come here, to me, but it would be insupportable to continue this conversation." Miss Bingley turned to ring for the servant.

"I came to tell you that if Henry Mallinger marries anyone, it is me he should marry."

Miss Bingley looked at her with disdain. "I am much mistaken if he would unite himself to a woman who has borne him four children without benefit of marriage. What possible inducement could he have?"

"I was married when I met him, but my husband and I had separated. It has been agreed between us for many years that if my husband should die, we would marry. My husband died in September."

"And Mr. Mallinger engaged himself to marry me in October. Assuredly he does not consider himself bound to such an agreement with you, if indeed there was any."

"Miss Bingley, do you believe that marrying him will put an end to all of his ties with me and our children?"

"That is certainly my expectation," she responded haughtily. "He will have a wife and legitimate children to engage his affections. He will have no need of recourse to a foreign woman and her bastards."

"Miss Bingley," said Signora Giovanese slowly, "I and our children will not disappear simply because he marries you. You deceive yourself if you think this. We have a claim on him that cannot be altered. I counsel you to think with care about your future with a man who already has a wife and a family."

"Impertinent woman! Mallinger would never marry a foreigner. It is his wish to marry an English lady who will present him with English heirs."

"I see that you will not listen to me. Yet I speak to you for your benefit as much as for my own. What happiness will you find with a man who is husband to another?"

Miss Bingley walked to the bell and pulled it firmly. When the servant entered the room she said, "Show this woman out. If she returns she is not to be admitted."

Signora Giovanese bowed her head gracefully at this uncourteous dismissal. "It sufficed for me to be admitted to you once. I shall not return, however I think you will find it difficult to make yourself rid of me." With that she glided from the room.

Miss Bingley went about her tasks set for the day, and in the evening wrote a brief note to Mallinger asking him to come to her. Upon his arrival she came to her point without any ceremonious delay. "Mallinger," she said, "a foreign woman, very dark and coarse-looking, was here today. A Signora Giovanese."

"Leonora is certainly foreign and she certainly has dark hair, however I would contest your description of her as coarse-looking. She is one of the most beautiful women I have ever seen."

"I confess I could see no beauty in her. However you acknowledge an acquaintance with her?"

"Yes, I know her, she has been my mistress for some fifteen years."

Miss Bingley was astonished by this careless admission, but with an effort kept her countenance and rejoined as coolly, "Her coming to me was a most insolent thing."

"I dare say she hoped to dissuade you from marrying me."

"She did, indeed."

"I shall ensure she does not trouble you again."

"When we marry you will put her aside, of course."

Mallinger looked at her quizzically. "My dear Caroline, what an odd assumption. I love her and I love our children. I have no intention of putting them aside. I intend to continue living with them in Venice when I am not in England."

"It is then your plan to marry *me* yet live with another woman?" exclaimed Miss Bingley.

"When I am in England I will live with you—no doubt at that damp and dreary Damson Hall."

In the desperation of her feelings Miss Bingley cried, "Would you use me so ill—make such a joke of me? I would be a wife with half a husband, the other half belonging to some foreign courtesan!"

Mallinger came very close to her, and Miss Bingley had to exert herself not to take a step backwards. "You will be Lady Mallinger of Damson Hall, with a somewhat unconventional husband who spends part of the year outside England, as he has always done." He added more lightly, "Have a care, Caroline, perhaps you do not know what you are wishing for if you would have me at your side a twelvemonth of every year. The time may come after we are married when you would prefer that I spent the entire year abroad."

"Mallinger, are you serious in meditating our alliance still?"

"Certainly. I fail to see that Leonora's visit to you, although ill-conceived on her part, alters the arrangements we have made. It is not as though you have discovered that I intend to commit bigamy. I am free to marry, and I am far from the only man in England who has a mistress, or even a mistress and children, and yet wishes to take a wife. I have behaved discreetly, and there is no reason to believe that you will become an object of derision."

"I must have time to think."

"What is there to think about? You now know the whole situation. I am not a different man from the one you agreed to marry a little more than a month since."

"Not different? Then you were an unmarried man, now you are a man with a wife and children!"

"I am still an unmarried man; she is not my wife."

"She considers herself so."

"She may think as she chooses; she is not my wife in my eyes, or the eyes of the law. Caroline, I went to some trouble to obtain your consent, I do not intend to give you up over such a trifling thing."

"Do you call this trifling?"

"I do."

"Upon my honour, I do not. I cannot marry you in two weeks' time," said Miss Bingley.

"In four weeks, then or six weeks. I am already weary of the English rain. I have not been in this country in November in many years, and would not willingly be here now. It was my intention to bring you to Italy or Greece for the winter."

"To Venice perhaps?"

"There are other places in Italy than Venice."

"I cannot marry you in four or six weeks' time either."

"Name a time then. I have told you that I will not release you from your engagement."

"I cannot tell you at this very moment when, or if, I will marry you. You are treating me in a most infamous manner."

"It is when, it is not if. And I am not prepared to wait any great length of time."

"Do you propose carrying me to the altar by force?" she cried.

"If necessary. I am willing to sacrifice myself to this weather only briefly."

"Go then if you cannot tolerate the rain."

"I shall go, if that is what you wish. When I return in the spring we shall marry."

Miss Bingley turned aside angrily and did not reply.

Chapter Twenty-Seven

[December 1813, Pemberley]

Elizabeth had continued to urge Darcy most gently to seek reconciliation with Lady Catherine de Bourgh, and in November had proposed that he invite her to Pemberley for the Christmas celebration. Privately Elizabeth thought that Lady Catherine would decline, for she would hardly think a month's ablution enough to cleanse her from its pollution, were she once to enter the house with its upstart and unconnected mistress; however Darcy wrote the letter and to the astonishment of both the invitation was accepted.

Lady Catherine de Bourgh was not, as she herself said, in the habit of brooking disappointment, and this circumstance had rendered her situation the more pitiable when Darcy had thwarted her longstanding expectations and given preference to Elizabeth Bennet over her own daughter. In her extreme indignation she had given way to all the genuine frankness of her character in the abusive letter to Darcy, that he had shown to Elizabeth on their honeymoon, thus for some time ending all intercourse between them; but she had soon found that this self-imposed exclusion from her nephew's affairs was not to her taste, as it deprived her not only of his society, of which she was fond, but also of an opportunity of attempting to dictate to him—as well as of indulging her curiosity to see how Elizabeth conducted herself. Therefore after a little resistance, exhibited in her subsequent letters to Darcy, she finally allowed her resentment to be overcome, and condescended to agree to wait on her nephew and his wife at Pemberley.

Lady Catherine and her daughter duly arrived and were shown at once into the drawing room where the females of the family were sitting. Lady Catherine was a tall, large woman, with strongly-marked features, in which might be traced some resemblance to her nephew Darcy, and which might once have been handsome. She entered the room with an exceedingly ungracious air. Elizabeth immediately rose to greet her, but Lady Catherine responded to her salutation with only a slight inclination of her head, and seated herself without saying a word. Miss de Bourgh made a perfunctory curtesy, and then allowed herself to be guided by her companion Mrs. Jenkinson to a seat as close as possible to the fireplace. Elizabeth asked the servant to find his master and inform him and Colonel Fitzwilliam that Lady Catherine and her daughter were within, and to bring refreshment to her ladyship and her party, and then resumed her own seat.

Georgiana approached her aunt and made her curtesy.

"Well, Georgiana," said Lady Catherine. "How do you do?"

"I am well, Lady Catherine."

Her aunt nodded, and Georgiana too went back to her seat. She took up her work in her hands, but looked at Elizabeth as if to ask what they should do now with their guest. Elizabeth merely raised her eyebrows, for although she was prepared to welcome Darcy's aunt with civility, she was determined to make no effort to thaw her out first, as it was clear that she had arrived with the intention of making herself disagreeable.

Colonel Fitzwilliam soon appeared; Lady Catherine was exceedingly pleased to see him, and greeted him with almost effusive warmth. "And now Fitzwilliam, go and greet your cousin Anne," she said. "She has been most eager to see you, indeed she has hardly spoken of anything else these two or three weeks. She is rather chilled from the journey, so I rely upon you to look to her needs."

Anne DeBourgh exerted herself so far to hold out her hand to Fitzwilliam and to make some token response to his inquiry after her health. Her eagerness to see her cousin Fitzwilliam was not by any means apparent to the ladies of Pemberley, who watched the meeting with varying degrees of interest. In truth, Mrs. Jenkinson appeared to respond to Fitzwilliam's polite salutation with greater enthusiasm than her charge. After sitting with Miss de Bourgh for a few minutes and attempting to converse with her, and receiving replies of one or two syllables, Fitzwilliam retired from battle and returned to the other ladies, seating himself near Georgiana and Kitty. Lady Catherine's attention, which had followed her nephew, was now turned towards the girls. After observing Kitty in silence for a moment Lady Catherine said very stiffly to Elizabeth, "*That* is your sister, I suppose."

"Yes," said Elizabeth concisely.

"I believe I recall seeing her at your home in Hertfordshire. She resembles you a great deal."

"The resemblance has been remarked upon, ma'am."

"Indeed?" Lady Catherine paused portentously. "Her features are undistinguished. In point of true beauty my daughter Anne is far superior, because her features are marked by her noble ancestry." Lady Catherine said to Kitty, "Come here and let me look at you."

Kitty glanced with some apprehension at Elizabeth, but stood and approached their guest, who after looking Kitty up and down said, "Turn around." Kitty revolved slowly until she stood facing Lady Catherine again. "You have no style at all," said Lady Catherine authoritatively. "Do you play and sing?"

"I play, Lady Catherine, and I sing a little."

"What languages do you speak?"

"A little French."

"Is that all? No German?"

"No, Lady Catherine."

"Do you draw?"

"A little."

"Your accomplishments by your own telling seem minimal. It is clear that your education was neglected as much as your sister's."

Kitty, dismissed, returned with an offended step to the sopha beside Georgiana.Her ladyship continued, "My daughter Anne's education was not neglected. She had the benefit of a governess and London masters. Her French accent has been favourably compared to that of France's royal family—that is, before those unfortunate events occurred in that country. Fitzwilliam, you would agree would you not?"

"I am afraid I have never had the pleasure of hearing my cousin Anne speak French, ma'am." Colonel Fitzwilliam had exceedingly rarely had the pleasure of hearing her speak English, or any other language either.

"Well, you must speak French with her while we are here, so that you may hear and appreciate her accent. Her German is not as good, unfortunately, for her health was delicate and that prevented her from becoming proficient. Have you seen her drawings of woodland flowers?"

"I believe they are framed in the summer breakfast parlour at Rosings, are they not, ma'am?"

"Yes, quite so. I am pleased you remember them so precisely. They are exquisitely executed, are they not?"

"They are very pretty."

"Her taste, like mine, is naturally excellent. Her dressmaker said to me the last time she was at Rosings, 'Lady Catherine, your daughter's taste is quite superb. She understands the importance of line and draping without my saying the least word.'"

"You and my cousin are always elegantly dressed," said Fitzwilliam politely.

"Of course you would notice, Fitzwilliam, for such things are important to you. I am sure you would rather live in a tent on campaign surrounded by soldiers, than be in the company of females who do not know how to dress."

"No doubt, Lady Catherine."

Lady Catherine turned her basilisk gaze upon Kitty once more. "Miss Bennet, do you have any other accomplishments?"

"I do not think so, Lady Catherine. However I like to ride."

"Indeed? Anne would have been an adept horsewoman, if her health had allowed it. She is an excellent driver. Is she not Fitzwilliam?"

"Yes, ma'am, she drives very well."

"Do you ride, Mrs. Darcy?"

"No, Lady Catherine, I am afraid I am not a horsewoman."

"Then with whom do you ride out, Miss Bennet?"

"I often go out by myself, Lady Catherine."

"What, out by yourself? Without even a servant? It is highly improper, and I have the greatest dislike in the world to that sort of thing. Young women should always be properly guarded and attended. I am excessively attentive to such things. If Anne rode I would never permit her to go out by herself. Mrs. Darcy, you must always send a servant out with Miss Bennet when she is not riding in a party."

Darcy then entering the room, he went to his aunt and welcomed her very courteously.

"So there you are, Darcy. I thought I might sit here all day before you appeared."

"I came immediately I received intelligence that you had arrived. I am pleased, exceedingly pleased, that you have joined us at Pemberley for Christmas."

"Allow me to say, Darcy, that when I arrived I was astonished. I did not think to see Pemberley looking so dilapidated," said Lady Catherine caustically.

"Madam," said Darcy, "Pemberley looks precisely as it did when you were last here."

"It does not, Darcy. It looks frowsy and unkempt. The servants are evidently taking advantage of a new and inexperienced mistress."

"Elizabeth does not direct the servants. Mrs. Reynolds manages the household, as she has for years."

"There!" said Lady Catherine triumphantly. "Your housekeeper is growing old and complacent, and her sight is declining. Your wife must no longer evade her duties, she must take more responsibility."

"I do not desire my wife to be my housekeeper, and Mrs. Reynolds can see perfectly well." With strained civility Darcy then asked her leave to greet his cousin, and walked away to Miss De Bourgh.

Lady Catherine could not win Darcy to any further conversation, and soon finding that none of the party present exhibited an inclination to listen to her abuse Elizabeth even indirectly, and she was forced to turn to the usual subjects of travelers—the weather, the roads, and the indigestible fare of inns.

The interval of waiting to dress for dinner appeared very long to Elizabeth, Kitty and Georgiana, but at last it was over and they obtained a brief respite before coming again under Lady Catherine's artillery. At dinner Lady Catherine, as she was accustomed to do, dominated the conversation, for when she was not talking about her own concerns to Darcy, she was attempting to follow conversations out of her hearing and demanding to know what was being said. She was particularly engrossed this evening by Colonel Fitzwilliam, however as she was seated on Darcy's right, and Colonel Fitzwilliam on Elizabeth's right, there was an expanse of table between her and Fitzwilliam that prevented her from hearing many of his words. Fitzwilliam spoke chiefly with Elizabeth, and Georgiana, but made little effort to converse with his cousin, who spoke only to Mrs. Jenkinson beside her. Lady Catherine had no compunction about calling out from time to time, "What is that you are saying, Fitzwilliam? What are you talking of? Let me hear what it is."

"We were conversing about travel, Lady Catherine," said Fitzwilliam when he found he could not avoid answering her.

"Then speak up, for I must have my share in the conversation. I much desired to see Paris, however the circumstances have prevented it since I was young. Where are you speaking of?"

"Darcy and Elizabeth are projecting a tour of the Lakes in the summer."

"Ah, the Lakes. That would be delightful. Anne would be pleased to join you, Darcy, if her health permits it. Fitzwilliam, you would accompany them."

"We have invited Elizabeth's aunt and uncle to accompany us," said Darcy.

"Her aunt and uncle? Her aunt and uncle in—Cheapside I believe it is? The uncle who is in trade?"

"Yes."

"Well, Darcy," said Lady Catherine heavily, "you may associate with whom you wish, I suppose." Affronted by this rebuff she was silent for a short time.

The meat course was served; the servant placed the joint before Darcy for carving. Lady Catherine examined it with a critical eye and then said loudly to Elizabeth. "Mrs. Darcy, the joints you are serving are too large, unless you also intend feeding the servants from them. I hope that is not the case, for the servants do not need to eat their master's meat. A large income does not justify wasteful practices in domestic economy. I am most particular about domestic economy, and I have often spoken to my daughter Anne about it. She will not permit such practices in her own household, when it is established. You must speak to the housekeeper immediately and let her know that you will not suffer her to order larger joints than the family needs and eat what is left herself or send it to the servants' hall. The servants require only an inferior cut of meat." Elizabeth restrained her indignation and only nodded in acknowledgement of these remarks.

When dessert was served, Lady Catherine commenced a new topic. "As I was passing through the upper lobby I noticed that one of the sitting rooms has been altered. It is no longer in keeping with the character of the house. What is this frippery, Darcy? Are you allowing your wife to refurnish Pemberley according to her own ideas?"

Georgiana catching this observation glanced at her brother. Their aunt was clearly referring to the room that had been fitted up by Darcy himself for her particular use, with greater lightness and elegance than the formal rooms below. She looked as if she would like to speak, but Darcy anticipated her and said, "Madam, the fault if there is any must imputed to me. I had that room repainted and refurnished last spring, before I became engaged to Elizabeth, in order to give pleasure to Georgiana, who had expressed a liking for the apartment. She was delighted with it, and indeed she and Elizabeth and Kitty frequently sit there during the day."

"Well, Georgiana, I hope that *you* are not going to cultivate a low taste."

"It is a lovely room, Lady Catherine," said Georgiana with unaccustomed spirit. "It is as pretty as anything I have seen in London."

"London! London is full of people in trade nowadays. Their taste cannot be equal to that of people of distinguished birth. Anne and I, if we had been consulted, would have advised most vehemently against meddling with the character of Pemberley's rooms."

"Pemberley is our home, not a mausoleum, Lady Catherine," said Georgiana.

"Well, whatever else you have learned in London, miss, you have certainly learned to be insolent. Darcy, I look to be treated with the respect due to my rank and my position within the family, when in your house."

"I apologize, Lady Catherine, and so does Georgiana." Georgiana looked distinctly unapologetic. "How did you leave Mr. and Mrs. Collins? Are they well?" This question plainly spoke Darcy's desire to escape from the subject, for his interest in Mr. Collins was non-existent, and in Mrs. Collins only slightly greater.

"The Collinses are in good health, although I am concerned for their child, for I strongly suspect that Mrs. Collins does not take my advice about her. Your wife's father's estate is entailed on Mr. Collins, I know. For the sake of Mrs. Collins I am glad of it, but entailing estates from the female line was not thought necessary in Sir Lewis de Bourgh's family, and I see no occasion for it. Sir Lewis's fortune descended directly to his daughter upon his death. She is one of the greatest heiresses in the country. However with the entail your wife's father could scarcely have much disposable property. I suppose he has hardly been able to provide his daughters with proper dowries. Indeed I understand from Mr. Collins that each daughter is entitled to no more than a thousand pounds. When I heard that the son of your father's steward had married one of the Miss Bennets I at first thought it must be a great love match, for he was not believed to have a penny, from what I heard, and indeed was thought to be quite in debt. And so to marry Miss Bennet would have been a great sacrifice on his part if he had not been deeply attached to her. However I later heard other details. Her marriage was a patched-up affair, I know all about it. Are they together still?" She looked at Kitty.

"Yes, Lady Catherine. They are living at Newcastle."

"Well, I am pleased for your sister's sake that they are living in a place where there are a great many officers."

Darcy was relieved that Elizabeth had been unable to hear, or at least had not listened to, most of his aunt's remarks; however Georgiana appeared desirous of making a retort. He quickly introduced another subject. "Lady Catherine, we are expecting others to join our party shortly—after Christmas."

"May one inquire whom one is expected to meet in this house?"

"Elizabeth's sister and her husband will join us."

"Her sister! Not I hope her *youngest* sister!"

"Her eldest sister, Jane Bingley."

"Thank heaven that you have the delicacy and propriety not to bring that girl— and certainly not her husband—to this house, at least while I am here. Whom else have you invited?"

"Bingley's sister Caroline, and his sister and brother the Hursts."

"I have heard something of Mr. Bingley and his sisters. I believe the family was in trade recently."

"The Bingleys are particular friends of mine, Lady Catherine," said Darcy pointedly.

"Is that the entire party?"

"No, there are also some political gentlemen and their wives. I intend to sit in Parliament as a Tory, you know."

"The way we live now, one must be broadminded in one's acquaintance, I suppose. At least you have not so far taken leave of your senses as to become a Whig. Will the Prime Minister come here?"

"No, he is not able to join us."

"That is a pity. We are connected to his wife, you know, Lady Louisa Hervey as she was.* The Herveys are a handsome family, however somewhat eccentric."

"Was not her sister Lady Elizabeth** the mistress of the Duke of Devonshire for years and years?" said Georgiana unexpectedly.

"Georgiana! What a thing to say! She is the Duchess now."

"I did not know it was a secret."

"It is not a thing to be discussed by young girls."

"It does not seem so very different from discussing—Lydia—and—and Wickham, and you do not mind talking about that in front of me and Kitty."

"Upon my word, you give your opinion very decidedly to me, Georgiana," said Lady Catherine in unaffected astonishment. Everyone stared at Georgiana, for this was a very noticeable departure from her usual self-effacing behaviour.

Georgiana coloured and looked at her plate. She was a little revived when general conversation resumed, but had not the courage to speak again before the ladies rose.

In the drawing-room after dinner, there was little to do until the tea and coffee and the gentlemen came in but listen to Lady Catherine talk—principally of her nephews, and their attachment to her and hers to them—or to sit oppressed under her majestic silence when she did not wish to speak. Elizabeth did not trouble herself to carry on any conversation in opposition to her guest.

When the gentlemen joined them Darcy asked Elizabeth to play, and she sat down directly to the instrument. Before she had finished the piece, however, Lady Catherine remarked in a loud voice, "I told Mrs. Darcy when she was visiting at Hunsford that she will never play really well unless she practises more. Indeed I even invited her to practise on the pianoforte in Mrs. Jenkinson's room; however she did not. I can see that she has neglected my advice entirely, in this matter as well as others. A musician cannot expect to excel if she does not practise a great deal, it cannot be done too much. My daughter Anne has natural application, and if her health had allowed her to learn to play she should have practised very constantly. She inherited my taste as well—there are few people in England who have a better natural taste in music than I do—and she should have been far more skilled a performer than Mrs. Darcy. Well, let us hear Miss Bennet now."

---

* Lady Louisa Hervey (1767-1821), daughter of the 4th Earl of Bristol; married Robert Banks Jenkinson, Lord Hawkesbury and 2nd Earl of Liverpool. Lord Liverpool was Prime Minister from 1812-1827. –Ed.

** Lady Elizabeth Hervey (1759-1824), married John Thomas Foster in 1776, and William Cavendish, 5th Duke of Devonshire in 1809. Lady Elizabeth Foster lived with the Duke and his Duchess (Lady Georgiana Spencer) for some 25 years and had two children by him, and married the Duke after the death of his first Duchess. –Ed.

Darcy looked cross at this interruption of Elizabeth's performance, but she smiled pacifically at him and ceded her place to Kitty, who although less than pleased to be put to the examination in this way seated herself gracefully at the instrument and began to play and sing an English air. Lady Catherine listened to half of it. "That will do," she announced. "Miss Bennet would improve with practice and a London master, although her taste will never be as good as Anne's. Georgiana, we will hear you now."

Georgiana took her turn at the pianoforte. Lady Catherine permitted her to play several songs, although not without interruption, for she gave constant instruction on execution and on taste in phrasing, which Georgiana received with the forbearance of a performer too shy to protest. However her proficiency as a musician was proven for she was able to continue her recital under Lady Catherine's assault and give pleasure to those listeners who were sufficiently far removed from the sound of her ladyship's voice to be able to listen to the music.

After she had been adequately entertained by the young ladies' performance and her own comments, Lady Catherine called for card-tables to be placed. She wished to play quadrille and appointed Darcy, Kitty and Elizabeth to join her. "Fitzwilliam, you and Anne must form a table, with Georgiana and Mrs. Jenkinson. It will give you and Anne an opportunity to talk to each other.

When Lady Catherine had played as long as she chose, fatigued by the day's journey she announced the end of the games at both tables. She then gathered the party around her to hear her instructions on the morrow's weather. "In all likelihood it will be clear. Fitzwilliam will drive around the park with Anne. Darcy and Georgiana, I shall take a short walk after breakfast and you shall accompany me." As she did not countenance leaving the rest of the party behind when she withdrew, the others soon discovered that they were expected to retire as well, and somewhat to their astonishment found themselves leaving the drawing room considerably earlier than they had intended.

Chapter Twenty-Eight

[December 1813, Pemberley]

Lady Catherine was in her own parish at Hunsford a most active magistrate, taking interest in the minutest concerns carried to her, and sallying forth to investigate the deeds and misdeeds of her fellow parishioners, to settle differences and silence complaints, and to scold into conformity with her desires anyone who appeared to have set out on a diverging course. She perceived no necessity to temper her activities merely because she was not in Hunsford, and nothing escaped her observation that was passing at Pemberley, that could furnish her with an opportunity of exercising authority. She found fault with the arrangement of the furniture, detected the housemaids in negligence and suspected the footmen of idleness. When the females of the family sat together in the morning she examined the books that they were reading and pronounced them unsuitable, and she looked at their work and advised them to do it differently. She had, in addition, many questions to ask, of which the young ladies felt all the impertinence, and although she answered many of the questions herself, it was necessary for them to pay attention to her, for she did not answer all. When Darcy joined them, she interrogated him about the electoral proceedings in Lambton Close, and endeavoured to insist on accompanying him there to speak to the voters. When Darcy declined this assistance she was severe upon him.

"Would to Heaven," said Darcy to Elizabeth after Lady Catherine had been two days at Pemberley, "that anything could be said or done on my part that might give you relief from this affliction. If I am punished by your connection with Mr. Collins, you are doubly so by mine with Lady Catherine."

It was not Elizabeth's disposition to increase her vexations by dwelling on them, and as she was confident of performing her duty as the mistress of Pemberley, she had already determined not to fix her mind on Lady

Catherine's conduct. "There is a stubbornness about me that never can bear to be intimidated at the will of others," said Elizabeth with a smile. "I have courage enough to endure her for a few days more."

"I am not persuaded that I have."

"Take comfort, then, that she may choose to leave soon because of the ruinous state of the house and the unrefined taste of its inhabitants."

"I must confess that I have at no time attempted to direct Lady Catherine and I do not depend on my own judgement now in undertaking such a task. What might you suggest to be advisable?"

"I am afraid I can think of nothing, beyond running away. But she has not yet seen Will. He may draw out the more benevolent aspects of her character. Do *you* take her to him, Darcy. She may be kinder to the child if she is not reminded who his mother is." Darcy undertook to carry out this mission, without delay or enthusiasm.

Lady Catherine had failed in the paramount duty to produce an heir for her husband's title and property, and although Sir Lewis de Bourgh had never reproached her she could not escape the self-censure which, although perfectly concealed from the rest of the world, gnawed in her bosom. Her niece Lady Fitzwilliam was also failing in this regard, and Lady Catherine had a secret fear that her daughter's delicate health might prevent her from producing a child at all.

Upon entering the nursery she gazed at the infant in his nurse's arms for some time without speaking. At last she said to Darcy, "He resembles you a good deal, when you were a baby. I remember my sister Anne showing you off to me very proudly, and saying, 'He has turned out quite Fitzwilliam, and very little Darcy.' The Fitzwilliams are considerably handsomer than the Darcys you know."

"Yes, I have heard it said—by the Fitzwilliams, principally. But I think the dash of Bennet has not injured him."

"Perhaps not," said Lady Catherine with great condescension. "Perhaps not, Darcy. I have not changed my opinion of the suitability of your marriage, for as undoubtedly you know I am celebrated for the firmness of my opinions once formed, but your wife has done her duty by you and Pemberley, with admirable promptness."

From that time forward she treated Elizabeth with noticeably increased respect. "Do you think it possible that Mr. Collins was correct, and that Will is indeed a young olive branch?" Elizabeth said to Darcy that evening.

"It would appear so. We may hope that the effect is lasting."

The following day Jane and Charles and Caroline Bingley, having passed the Christmas at Clifford Priory, joined the family party at Pemberley, where they were greeted by the Darcys and Kitty with thankfulness. Lady Catherine pronounced Jane to be a pretty, genteel young woman, and she allowed herself to be taken with Bingley's easy manners and perfect good breeding.

Caroline Bingley was quite alive to the advantages of numbering Lady Catherine de Bourgh among her acquaintance and had arrived at Pemberley prepared, within reason, to cultivate her ladyship. However Miss Bingley's haughty demeanour when they were introduced by Elizabeth failed to please Lady Catherine. Her ladyship looked down at her and said remotely, "Ah, Miss Bingley. Darcy has spoken of you. Your family is from the North, I believe?" The she turned to speak to her nephews.

"Insolent woman!" said Miss Bingley in a low voice, also turning away. She knew quite well, that the family fortune was connected to trade, but they had been at pains to leave their origins in the North, and had set about becoming ladies and gentlemen of fashion. Her grandfather had been a wealthy manufacturer, an educated man, and had had all the appearance of a gentleman. Her father had been a gentleman, with no connection to trade. Her brother was a gentleman, who had found his way into superior society and had brought his sisters with him. She was engaged to marry a man of impeccable aristocratic lineage. Yet there would always be some nobleman or noblewoman who would look down the nose at the Bingleys—like this daughter of an Irish bog-earl.

Elizabeth observed the encounter between Lady Catherine and Miss Bingley with a barely repressed smile. Caroline Bingley had always held in contempt Elizabeth Bennet, and jealousy over Darcy's affections had not infrequently made her uncivil both behind her back and to her face. However upon the announcement of Darcy's engagement Miss Bingley had taken the pragmatic view that she wished to retain the privilege of visiting Darcy's homes, and she had promptly paid off every arrear of civility to Elizabeth. She therefore was a visitor from time to time at the Darcys' town-house in London and at Pemberley, but it could not be said that the two ladies were intimate friends.

"Lady Catherine is in form today," Elizabeth remarked. "You may take it as a kind of compliment that she was offensive to you immediately upon being introduced. I believe it means she went to the trouble of finding something out about you beforehand."

"Such nothingness, yet the self importance!" replied Miss Bingley with a sneer. "Perhaps considering her descent one could not expect better. Her family has some little Irish title, does it not?"

"The Earldom of Tyrconnell. Let me introduce you to Colonel Fitzwilliam. He is the son of the Earl—and Lady Catherine's nephew, but you would never know it by his manners."

On Boxing Day the gentlemen of the party were to join a hunt, which would meet at the inn in Lambton. The ladies accompanied them there to see the start of the hunt, Kitty, Jane and Miss Bingley on horseback, and Elizabeth, Georgiana, Lady Catherine and Anne De Bourgh in a chaise. In the general milling of horses and dogs before the inn, the ladies became separated, and when the members of the hunt set off, Kitty was found to be missing. "She has just gone to watch the beginning of the hunt, I am sure," said Jane. "She will be back shortly." The ladies then went into the inn to warm and refresh themselves before they returned to Pemberley.

In a copse a quarter of a mile from the inn, one of the riders lost, stolen or strayed from the hunt came upon a young lady sitting pensively upon a black horse. Looking about, he saw no other person. "Ma'am, are you by yourself, without a companion? Not even a servant? What are your family about? I have the greatest dislike to seeing a young lady not properly guarded and attended."

The young lady smiled. "Hello James."

"Hello, Kitty. I also have the greatest possible dislike for duplicity and deceit but I seem to have discovered an aptitude for them. Perhaps I should turn spy—I fear my talents are being wasted as a cavalry officer. Shall I beat the bushes to find out if we are being watched?"

"I think we are alone."

"How long has it been since we could see each other privately?"

"A very long time. Half a year."

"It seems longer."

By common accord they turned onto a path leading out of the copse and walked their horses along side by side. They spoke little, but their hearts and minds were so full that they scarcely noticed their own silence.

"Do you think we will ever be alone together again?" asked Kitty after they had walked perhaps half a mile and exchanged hardly a word.

"I do not know," said Fitzwilliam.

The huntsman's horn sounded at a distance, and then began to draw nearer to them. Soon they could hear the hounds baying. Zanzibar grew restive, and Kitty had to hold him to a walk. "He is very vexed that he has not been asked to join the hunt. Do you suppose he could run away with me for a little while?"

"No. You must go back to the inn, and I must take this opportunity to rejoin the hunt discreetly." He held out his hand to her and she took it.

"Goodbye, James."

"Goodbye, Kitty."

As Fitzwilliam had scarcely spoken ten words to Kitty since his arrival at Pemberley, and as Kitty would not even look at *him*, Darcy and Elizabeth were satisfied that their attachment was at an end, and Kitty's explanation of her absence, upon returning to the inn, that Zanzibar had bolted when he had seen the other horses following the hounds, was accepted without remark.

That evening. Lady Catherine, content after an excellent dinner, and feeling expansive towards Darcy and his wife, invited them and Georgiana to Rosings for Easter, where Fitzwilliam would be one of the family party. Darcy glanced his eye at Elizabeth and then civilly accepted the invitation. "Your sister Miss Bennet may come too," said Lady Catherine. "She seems to be a quiet, well-behaved girl, and she will not be in anyone's way."

Chapter Twenty-Nine

[January 1814, Pemberley]

Elizabeth had not been much tested as a hostess until the coming of Lady Catherine, and now another challenge lay before her with the arrival of Darcy's political guests. Her confidence giving way a little, she confided her anxiety to her husband privately; but he said with much affection, "My dearest, loveliest Elizabeth, anyone to whom you wish to make yourself agreeable is prepossessed in your favour, and you will be sure of success. You need have no concern upon that score, for I have none. You have already worked a charm on Lady Catherine, and I am certain that was a more difficult ordeal than the one you next face."

"I believe it was Will who charmed her. But Darcy, how will we manage Lady Catherine with the politicians? We do not want her to offend men who will be important to you in your career."

"We ought, I suppose, to attempt to keep her away from certain of them with whom she is bound to disagree. Mr. Wilberforce, for example."[*]

"He is working for the abolition of slavery, is he not? I do not wonder that she disapproves."

"It is more that she does not approve the emancipation of Catholics, and he has recently spoken out in favour of it.[**] But if we have brought together the powder and the spark, we must deal with the consequences as they arise."

---

* William Wilberforce (1759-1833), philanthropist, social conservative and social reformer, evangelical Christian, member of Parliament (independent). An abolitionist, his (and others') anti-slavery campaigns led to the Slave Trade Act (1807), which abolished the British slave trade, and the Slavery Abolition Act (1833) which ended slavery in most of the British empire. –Ed.

** Following the Protestant Reformation in England in the 16th century, successive British monarchs imposed restrictions on the rights of Catholics, for example prohibitions against being elected to Parliament, holding public office or serving in the army. –Ed.

The following day the politicians began to arrive, and Darcy and Elizabeth welcomed them and saw to their comfort. Mr. William Wilberforce and his wife had not long been in the house before the Darcys saw Lady Catherine conversing with him; and although their exchange of opinions appeared to be vigorous, neither appeared to be in great peril at the hands of the other, so they refrained from any interference.

Caroline Bingley while in hopes of winning Darcy's heart had doted on Georgiana as one who might thereafter become her sister, and had often expressed to Darcy, and those around him, her delight with her and her admiration for her beauty, elegance and accomplishments. Her performance on the pianoforte and harp was exquisite, her taste in design sent Miss Bingley into raptures. This degree of affection was resolutely maintained in the face of Darcy's indifference to Miss Bingley, and in a wonderful instance of resentment being vanquished she became fonder than ever of Georgiana upon Darcy's marriage. The day after her arrival at Pemberley, quite exhausted by the attempt to amuse herself before it was time to dress for dinner, other than reading a book, for most of the gentlemen were engaged outdoors and most of the ladies were under Lady Catherine's thrall, she drew Georgiana aside and proposed a *tête-à-tête*. Georgiana was no longer deceived by Miss Bingley's pretended regard, now that she had experience of her two sisters, Elizabeth and Kitty, who really loved her, but she was too polite to refuse the invitation. "Let us go to the saloon, for I know there is a good fire there," said Georgiana.

As they entered the room, a stranger rose from a chair by the windows. Miss Bingley and Georgiana, not expecting to find the room occupied, stopped in the doorway.

"I beg your pardon," said the man. "I am waiting for Mr. Darcy, he told me that he would attend me here as soon as he could." There was a strong trace of the North in his accent.

Miss Bingley, hearing his voice and concluding that he was one of Darcy's political guests from Manchester, dismissed him from her thoughts without acknowledging his existence. She seated herself on a sopha at a sufficient distance from him that his presence would not interfere with her conversation with Georgiana, but not so distant as to make it appear that he had influenced her decision where to place herself.

To her surprise Georgiana did not immediately follow her but shyly moved towards the man. "I am Mr. Darcy's sister," she said.

The man bowed rather awkwardly. "John Thorn."

"I hope my brother will not make you wait too much longer. May I offer you some refreshment?"

"No, thank you."

To Miss Bingley's further surprise, Georgiana did not then retreat to her side, but sat down near the man, gestured for him to take his seat again and commenced a stilted conversation about the weather and the roads. Miss Bingley recalled that Elizabeth was endeavouring to instruct her sister in her role as a hostess in the family of a MP; Miss Bingley was quite certain, however, that the man would have preferred to sit in silence and that Georgiana would better have spent her time and resources on herself. Now she was abandoned in a corner of the room with nothing to do but play with her bracelets. She began to have an uncomfortable feeling that she looked slightly silly, and she certainly felt bored and impatient. She gave a great yawn, and cast her eyes around the room for some distraction. Perhaps she would not be lowering herself to speak with a Northern politician as long as Georgiana thought it proper to do so. After a few more minutes' reflection and a corresponding increase in boredom and impatience, she got up and walked across the room. Her figure was pleasing to the eye and she walked well, and she necessarily drew the notice of the man. As she approached, he rose once more. She could not avoid making a comparison of the abrupt and powerful way in which he came to his feet and the languid aristocratic grace of Henry Mallinger.

"Caroline, may I introduce Mr. Thorn to you?" asked Georgiana. Miss Bingley graciously nodded her assent. "This is Mr. John Thorn of Manchester. Mr. Thorn, Miss Bingley."

Thorn made another choppy bow, and Miss Bingley responded with a curtsey that was exquisitely crafted to be perfectly elegant but not too low, and thus to convey the social abyss between one who associated with people of rank and one to whom superior society was closed. However Thorn did not appear to acknowledge the abyss; instead he looked at her very frankly, almost, she thought, as if she were a horse at a country fair. She was aware that he was seeing a handsome young woman of above average height with an elegant figure, dressed in the latest London fashion, and after a moment she determined to subject him to a similar examination. She saw a tall, dark, broad-shouldered man, about thirty years of age, with a face that was neither exactly plain nor exactly handsome. He was not a gentleman; and yet there was an expression in his face of resolution and power that contradicted any suggestion of the vulgar or common about him, and a look of not simply intelligence but penetration that made Miss Bingley reconsider whether it was quite safe to despise him for having a Northern accent, and exhibiting manners that were not polished. He looked like a strong man who was used to commanding respect and obedience, whatever the cut of his waistcoat.

"Miss Bingley," he said. "You bear a name that is still held in high regard in my part of the country. It would have been your grandfather, I believe, who was in the cotton trade?"

Miss Bingley's astonishment at being so addressed was extreme. "Sir—you are impertinent. My family is not in trade."

Thorn smiled at her with keen and honest enjoyment, his smile rendered uncommonly attractive by his white and perfect teeth. "You imagine, Miss Bingley, that I recall your grandfather in order to offend or embarrass you, whereas in fact I do it out of genuine esteem for a man of great ability. My admiration, perhaps unlike yours, is not given to those who know how to dress fashionably or speak elegantly—or bow or curtsey with grace—but to those who use their intelligence, energy and courage to undertake a difficult enterprise and see it to the end."

Miss Bingley's astonishment increased. That he would not only show himself indifferent to her reprimand, but turn it back on her—and do so with good humour— seemed to show abominable sort of indifference to decorum. After a moment she said in a cold tone, "You are candid."

"And you also. Candour is another valuable quality. It saves a great deal of time and prevents misunderstanding."

Miss Bingley replied with civil disdain, "Pray, on what subject are we likely to misunderstand each other, and to what end must we save time?"

"It was a general observation. But I hope we shall have no reason to misunderstand one another. As for time, it is always lacking to one in the thick of business affairs."

"Business! How odious!" But then, feeling an involuntary curiosity, she said, "I find I often have too much time rather than too little."

"Then you are doing the wrong things with it. You are clearly an intelligent and active woman—how do you spend your time?"

"In the usual employments of a lady."

"In other words, you are wasting your mind as well as your time. But that is like the South. In the North we behave differently."

"You may depend upon it that the difference is apparent."

"You mean to be supercilious. You would elevate meaningless tasks and activities above honest hard work. But I ask you, what would England be if everyone disdained every form of labour and indulged instead in frivolous amusement? Do you suppose that London is built on perfectly tied cravats? No, it is built on trade and industry. England is the greatest trading nation in the world and the greatest industrial nation also. There is nothing superior in one who looks down his nose at the source of wealth and power of the greatest country this world has seen since the time of the Romans. Only a fool would disparage it. And you, Miss Bingley, are not a fool."

"I thank you for the compliment, Mr. Thorn! Do you seek to recommend yourself to me?"

"You would prefer that I remark on your beauty instead of your intelligence?"

"There is no necessity for you to remark upon anything about me at all!"

Thorn smiled once more. "Then perhaps *you* would like to choose a subject for conversation?"

Miss Bingley hesitated. She wanted in part to collect her dignity about her and depart from the room; but this man was exercising a kind of fascination over her. No one had ever addressed her in this way—at once disparaging her manner of living and admiring her person and mind. It in some way opened to her new possibilities of freedom, yet it was a freedom which she had never suspected she was in want of. And she quite suddenly made the embarrassing discovery that she did not wish to leave his presence. His height and broad shoulders formed a striking contrast with Mallinger's aristocratic slenderness, and his eyes had all the animation that Mallinger's lacked.

"I believe I should like to hear about the line of trade that you are in."

"I am not a trader, madam, I am a manufacturer."

"And what is it that you manufacture?"

"Cotton cloth, for domestic consumption and for export."

Miss Bingley seated herself across from him and motioned him to be seated as well, and she set about making herself agreeable. When the passage of a quarter of an hour brought Darcy into the saloon, with apologies to Thorn for his delay in joining him, Miss Bingley to her amazement found herself irritated by his entrance, and she would willingly have seen him delayed by yet another hour. When she and Georgiana took their leave of the gentlemen, Thorn smiled at her and said, "I hope we may often meet again."

She left the room with her mind much engaged, and greatly surprised her dear friend Georgiana by expressing a disinclination for the *tête-à-tête* that she had proposed only a half-hour previously.

Chapter Thirty

[January-February 1814, Pemberley and London]

With such tender regard do the British people look upon their members of Parliament that once elected they are not suffered to resign, and if unwilling to wait until death or a general election overtakes them must disqualify themselves from serving their constituents by accepting a paid appointment to serve their King. Thus it was that John Chamberlain, Tory member for Lambton Close, accepted the Office of Steward and Bailiff of Her Majesty's Three Chiltern Hundreds of Stoke, Desborough and Burnham in the County of Buckingham, and a writ was made out for the electing of a new member to serve for Lambton Close in the present Parliament.

Darcy in the company of Chamberlain had previously visited Lambton Close and been introduced to all forty of the voters there, most of whom had been gratified to meet him, and some of whom had detained him to reminisce about his father and grandfather. On the day of the election he had given a speech in the yard of the local inn which, if not rousing, was at least short. The voting then proceeded, with little suspense as no other candidate besides Darcy had come forward. At the end of an hour Darcy was formally declared the duly elected member for Lambton Close, and the residents of the Close were treated to a round of ale.

Darcy assumed his seat in the House of Commons as a Tory, and was welcomed as courteously by the other members as might be expected—in brief, after he had taken the oath, his introduction into the House furnished a Whig with the grounds to rise to his feet and declaim against the evils of a Government that permitted rotten boroughs to exist beside ridings in which candidates underwent the true democratic process of contest and election. As Darcy had no wish to make his maiden speech in the House as a defender of rotten boroughs, however greatly he himself had benefited from one of them, he sat and listened with an indifferent air, his indifference apparently being shared by the vast majority of the members present upon the benches, who variously read their newspapers, looked off into the distance or chatted with their neighbours until the honourable member's remarks—which in any case were scarcely to be heard above the ordinary din of the House—were concluded. Elizabeth, Georgiana, Jane and Bingley, and Mary Bennet, watching from the gallery, were excessively disappointed that Darcy's entry into political life had occurred with so little éclat, but comforted themselves that even a great journey must begin with one step. The Prime Minister not being in the House that evening, the opposition was only half-hearted in its attacks on the Government; no new legislation was introduced; and the session ended early. The family party returned to the Darcys' townhouse before nine o'clock, with more time at their disposal than was quite requisite to discuss the events of the evening. However Darcy was able to acquaint them with a request made that day by the Prime Minister's secretary, that he provide the venue for a political meeting the following week, a request that he had, naturally, acceded to at once.

Mary Bennet upon her arrival in town to visit her sister had taken possession of Darcy's library and emerged from it only for infrequent morning visits and for dinner, but even she expressed no disinclination for joining the meeting. "Surely it will be instructive for the females of the family to observe those who govern our country, and the members of the House may in turn see that the weaker sex has no aversion to sharing political discourse with the sterner," she said. She looked forward to the opportunity of exhibiting her intellectual powers, and hoped to have an occasion to demonstrate to the Prime Minister himself that some females, or at least she, had the capacity to comprehend and make valuable comment upon the political issues of the day.

On the appointed evening the MPs and other political gentlemen, Mr. Wilberforce among them, entered the drawing room, some with their assistants and friends, a few with their wives, already in conversation or, in some cases, dispute, with one another, and proceeded to make themselves entirely at home. They were pleased with their new member, as Darcy had as yet done nothing to alarm or provoke the Party, delighted with his house as a meeting place, happy with the excellent supper provided, and charmed by his lovely wife and sister who acted as hostesses.

Mary was disappointed that the Prime Minister did not remain long enough to benefit from any conversation with her, and indeed she found in general that the politicians were more interested in talking to one another than in being engaged by her in discourse. Her attempts to instruct certain of them in the moral foundation of one or two of the bills currently before the House were met with polite, or surprised, silence or a bow. After a time her vanity grew a little sore, and she retreated to an empty sopha on one side of the room. Taking a book out of her pocket she ostentatiously began to read. If these undeserving men did not care to receive the benefit of her study and reflections, let them see that she did not retreat in confusion or defeat but rather calmly ascended above them to the realm of the intellect.

Some time later, a young man entered the drawing room, and looked around it rather awkwardly. He was about four-and-twenty years of age, slightly built, with fair hair that was somewhat disordered. After a moment's search he perceived Mr. Wilberforce, approached him quietly and spoke to him in a low voice. Wilberforce turned to the young man, and received his message; laughed and made an observation to him; and then with a motion of his hand dismissed him to wait. The young man withdrew to the dimmest corner of the room, which chanced to be near Mary's sopha. Mary looked up from her book as he approached, but immediately returned to the page she had been reading. Presently Elizabeth came up to him and asked if he would take tea or coffee. Mary looked up once more, feeling some vexation at being disturbed a second time. At Elizabeth's approach the young man retreated further into the corner.

"Thank you, no, Ma'am," he said, stammering a little. "I am just waiting for Mr. Wilberforce to let me know what he desires to be done."

"You are his secretary, are you not?" asked Elizabeth with a smile. "I am sure you will carry out his instructions all the better if you take some refreshment while you wait."

"No, indeed, Ma'am, I do not require anything." He moved backward until his further retreat was stopped by the wall.

"I will not press you, then," said Elizabeth. "But if you change your mind my sister Miss Darcy or one of the other ladies will serve you." She turned and looked for the next guest who might need her attention.

The young man watched Elizabeth depart, and then became aware that Mary was looking at him from the sopha. When he met her gaze her she immediately bent her eyes to her book so that he would see that she had better employment than examining *him*. For a few moments they stayed in their positions, the young man in the dark corner and Mary on her sopha, not looking at each other but each now unable to disregard the other's presence. After a time it occurred to Mary that the young man might wonder why she was not with the other guests; he would be unaware that she had chosen to read rather than to converse and might think that she had been sent to wait in a corner—as he had been. Her vanity aroused, she turned her head to him. "Such an entertainment is doubtless congenial to most minds," she remarked, gesturing towards the room, "but I confess it holds few charms for me. I prefer to read a book."

He seemed startled to hear her speak, and took some time to reply. "Meetings with political men usually are rather noisy, I find," he said at length.

"I do not object to the clamor. It necessarily accompanies such an interval of recreation."

The young man bowed slightly in lieu of replying.

Mary coloured a little. He perhaps thought that she had been forward in speaking to him, since he did not know that she was a member of Darcy's family and had really done so merely out of duty. "I am Mrs. Darcy's sister. I have been assisting her in her obligations as hostess."

"I am Mr. Wilberforce's secretary. I came to deliver him a message."

After a moment Mary commented, "Doubtless he keeps you much occupied."

"Yes, at times." The young man paused and then added, "I was delayed on my way here." Mary was undecided whether to encourage continuance of the conversation by acknowledging the remark. But the young man seemed to need no additional encouragement, for he burst out, "There was a carter with a heavy load, flogging his horse up a hill. If he had got out to lighten the load, and had led the horse, I think it would have been able to pull the wagon. But with the load, and the hill, and the beating it was hardly able to move. I told him to stop, and he hit me with the whip."

Mary gasped. The young man moved forward out of the shadows, and Mary could see that there was a red welt on his cheek. Mary wished to say something extremely sensible, but she knew not what, and her heart was beating faster with excitement. "Have you suffered an injury?" she cried out.

"No, at least nothing of moment," said the young man. "I pulled him out of the wagon and knocked him down and threw away his whip." He smiled slightly. "I boxed a good deal at Cambridge."

"What then occurred?" asked Mary breathlessly.

"I made him walk the horse up the hill. And I told him that if I ever heard of him flogging a horse again I would beat him until he was bloody."

"Oh!" exclaimed Mary.

"I beg pardon, ma'am," he said quickly. "I did not mean to offend you with my language. I am very angry and I was not thinking."

In the light Mary could see that he had intense dark eyes, and that they were glittering with strong emotion.

"You displayed most commendable courage," said Mary. She added, "Courage is one of the four natural virtues, while cowardice is a mortal sin. Courage is not the lack of fear, it is acting in spite of fear. A coward turns away but a courageous man goes forward."

The young man looked at her with a small frown of puzzlement.

She wished he would speak again, and when he did not, after a moment she said, "I might have been at a loss to know what course of action to take had I been there."

"But would you have done anything for the horse?" he asked.

"Every impulse of feeling should be guided by reason. By all that I have ever read, I believe that the purpose for which men enter into society is for the preservation of their property. So great is the law's regard for private property, that it will not authorize the least violation of it, not even for the general good of the community."

The young man seemed rather astonished. "I would not have taken you for one devoid of Christian feeling, who would elevate ownership of property above every other principle of conduct."

Mary was very disconcerted, and turned scarlet. "I—I did not mean to say that private property holds supremacy," she cried. "I meant—that—that I should have been too afraid of the carter. The horse is his, after all. In what manner would I address him?"

"What to say is easy," said the young man. "'Do not harm that animal, you have a right to its labour, not to its suffering. Animals are created for our use, but not for our abuse.' They were created by God, just as man was. He took the same care to provide, just as he did for man himself, organs and feelings for their own enjoyment and happiness. Just as man does they see, hear, feel, think, sense pain and pleasure, love and anger. They are sensible to kindness, and to unkindness and neglect."

"But I am quite ignorant of the art of boxing," said Mary, imagining the carter's reaction if she had been the one to interfere.

"A lady's injunction to spare an animal may perhaps do as much as a man's fist."

After this there was silence between them. Mary was desirous of prolonging the conversation but was prevented by the thought that she had no experience of accosting carters and would be little able to show herself to advantage. She pondered over her extracts but could not recall any concerning the protection of beasts. The young man seemed disinclined for further speech and stepped back a little into his corner; and after a few minutes Mr. Wilberforce beckoned to him. He turned to Mary, made a slight bow and said politely, "Perhaps we will meet again," made his way back to Wilberforce's side and soon, after listening to his employer's instructions, left the room.

When the meeting had concluded and the guests had departed, Mary said to her sister, "Elizabeth, are you acquainted with the name of that young man? Mr. Wilberforce's secretary."

"The one who would not come out of the corner?" smiled Elizabeth. "I believe I heard it. I think it was—Kenshall. No, Kendall. He seemed rather timid."

"I do not think he is timid at all, rather he was suffering from discomfiture to be seen in refined company. He bore a mark on his countenance, where a carter had assaulted him with a whip."

"With a whip!" said Elizabeth in amazement.

"He was interfering in his maltreatment of a horse. He subdued the carter," added Mary, a little proudly.

"Oh, then I am not surprised. I believe Mr. Wilberforce's concerns extend to domestic animals. I suppose he is in agreement with Lord Erskine, who Darcy says keeps bringing a bill in the House of Lords every year to stop their abuse.* Mr. Wilberforce perhaps expects his secretary to take an interest in such matters as well, although I think it rather hard if Mr. Kendall must get into fights with carters as part of his duties."

"I believe his actions were voluntary," said Mary.

The following morning she returned to her books in the library but experienced some difficulty in giving them her full attention. She was dwelling instead upon the notice that the world must take of one who would knock down a carter in the street, and then force him to walk his horse and wagon up a hill. She imagined herself reprimanding a carter—who would not be astounded and full of admiration to see a young woman undertaking such a task! But then she thought of the whip, and she turned her attention back to making extracts from her books.

When several days had passed and Mary had declined to accompany Elizabeth and Georgiana on any morning visits or errands, Elizabeth inquired if she were expecting someone to call on her.

"Most assuredly not," said Mary stiffly. "I do not have any acquaintance in London."

---

* Thomas Erskine, 1st Baron Erskine, lawyer, politician and animal rights activist. He was a Whig (Liberal) member of the House of Commons from 1783-4 and from 1790 until 1806 at which time he was elevated to the peerage and so entered the House of Lords. –Ed.

Chapter Thirty-One

[February 1814, London]

Caroline Bingley was not long in encountering John Thorn again after her visit to Pemberley. In town in February at a dinner at the house of Lord Castlereagh, they were seated at a distance from each other. She followed him with his eyes and envied everyone to whom he spoke, and scarcely had patience to talk to those seated next to her. But when the gentlemen removed from the table and joined the ladies Thorn sought her out as soon as he entered the drawing room.

"Miss Bingley, it is my pleasure to see you once more. I trust you have been in good health since our last meeting?"

She received him very politely, invited him to take the seat beside her, and inquired what had brought him to London.

"I am here to discuss with government ministers and investors a railway."

"A railway? I am not familiar with this word. Pray, what is a railway?"

"It is a kind of road, made of two tracks or rails, of timber or iron, on which a conveyance may run. A carriage drawn by a horse, or a steam carriage."

"I am quite dying to know—you must tell me—what is a steam carriage?"

"An engine powered by steam, that can draw heavy loads."

"And what is the purpose of this railway and this steam carriage? Do not horses draw heavy loads? Do the roads and canals that we have not suffice to permit their transport?"

"The load that a horse can draw is light compared to what a steam carriage may draw. Last year a steam carriage was built that is equal in power to ten horses all pulling at once. There is no reason that a steam carriage may not equal the power of twenty or even fifty horses."

"How I long to see one! But it must be the size of twenty or fifty horses, must it not?"

"Not at all. A steam carriage is large, but weighs no more than a *few* horses. At the moment railroads are used only to transport coal over relatively short distances, but in the future they will be used to ship all raw materials and all manufactured goods. They will replace rivers and canals for shipping. I believe that we will live to see the day when railways and steam carriages supersede not only horses but all other modes of conveyance in England. The railroad will become the King's Highway."

"Why do rivers and canals need replacing? I do not suppose they are not running dry?" she said with an expressive smile.

"You speak facetiously, Miss Bingley, but I do not. Up to this time it has been the owners of collieries who have been interested in constructing, and have constructed, railways; but now there is need for improved means of shipping cotton, between the seaports and the manufacturing towns. I am here in London to promote interest in a railway between Manchester and Liverpool. At the moment it may take longer to ship raw cotton from Liverpool to Manchester by river and canal, than it takes for the cotton to arrive in England from the United States. And when the canals freeze, the factories are idle. We have a like difficulty in conveying manufactured goods from Manchester to Liverpool for export. The traders and the manufacturers both are eager to find a more efficient method of transport."

"I would be quite in raptures if a more *comfortable* method of transport could be found, for I have recently travelled over some shocking roads."

"That will come to pass sooner than the railroads. There is a Scot named MacAdam who has published plans for improved roads, that I am certain will soon be put into practice."*

"Oh! It cannot be too soon for me."

"But it will not be long before roads will be superseded by railroads. The time will come when it will be more comfortable to travel on a railroad than in the most luxurious coach, and cheaper than to travel by foot. And far faster than any mode of transportation we have now. I am told that there will be nothing to hinder a steam carriage moving on a railway at a velocity of one hundred miles an hour."

"One hundred miles an hour! How pray can I give confidence to such an assertion? It must be false."

"It would be impossible for a horse, or a barge or a ship. But not for a steam carriage. They are in their infancy as far as technical development, but

---

* John Loudon MacAdam (1756-1836) designed a roadbed with a foundation of raised earth for drainage, covered by several layers of stones. He was appointed Surveyor General for Bristol roads in 1815 and began to implement his design, which quickly spread throughout England. –Ed.

only a few short years ago one made fifteen miles an hour on a circular track here in London.* What I tell you will come to pass, and in our lifetimes."

As Thorn spoke, Miss Bingley listened very attentively, and thought how handsome he looked. They continued talking together with mutual satisfaction until the party broke up.

After the passage of a fortnight Miss Bingley had dined in company with Thorn three times, danced two dances with him at a ball—to her surprise discovering him to be a remarkably good dancer, and at morning visits had seen him once at the Darcys' and twice at the houses of other acquaintance. He was continually in her thoughts.

They next met at a dinner at Mr. Canning's, and Miss Bingley found the interval between the ladies leaving the dining room and the gentlemen entering the drawing room almost excruciatingly tedious. When the gentlemen did make their appearance, her eyes were instantly turned towards Thorn, and his to her. He approached and sat down beside her.

After the trial of a few subjects, during which Thorn spoke in such a way as plainly showed some distraction of his thoughts, he said, "I must return to Manchester the day after tomorrow."

Miss Bingley instantly felt herself fill with disquiet, but with an effort she controlled her countenance and voice. "I shall be sorry to see you go," she said with assumed composure.

"And I to leave London and the opportunity of your society."

Striving to sound indifferent, she replied, "I have been diverted by our conversations—I assure you they have been very refreshing. I have gained an infinite knowledge from you about the state of English trade and commerce."

"Have you learned no more than that?"

"That the future will be exceedingly different from the present."

"As could your future."

"Surely everyone's future will be different."

"I speak only of yours."

Miss Bingley's heart beat a little faster. "I do not have the pleasure of apprehending your meaning, Mr. Thorn."

"I believe you do." He paused briefly. "I will not speak more clearly now lest you take offence at my presumption." He paused once more but Miss Bingley said nothing. "However, if you do not find it presumptuous, I ask that you be direct with me and tell me so."

A confusion overtook Miss Bingley's mind, that prevented her from forming a clear thought. After a delay she replied, "I cannot tell you anything at this moment."

---

* Torrington Square, 1808. –Ed.

"As a man of business, I know how to wait until the right time when I see an opportunity that I wish to—seize. With your leave, however, I shall wait upon you at your earliest convenience."

Thorn's offer, for as such it must be understood, caused a perturbation of Miss Bingley's feelings, which increased by the moment after she and the Hursts had returned to Grosvenor Street. She walked up and down the drawing room, endeavouring to compose herself, while Mrs. Hurst threw her looks of inquiry that did nothing to restore her self-possession.

"Caroline, what ails you this evening?" Miss Bingley did not respond, for she was in no humour for conversation this evening with anyone but Thorn. Mrs.Hurst continued. "I believe I can make a conjecture. Miss Hale told me, that everyone was talking about you and Mr. Thorn at Mr. Canning's. Your preference for each other is becoming very evident. People are asking whether your engagement to Mr. Mallinger has been ended. He has not been seen in England these three months, and you are certainly giving the appearance of a woman who is at liberty. Caroline, you have not been very forthcoming with me about Mallinger. Did you send him away?"

"No. That is, I am not certain."

"Do you not expect him to return to you?"

"When he left he said that he would not release me from our engagement, and that we would marry in the spring."

"Then you asked him to release you?"

"No—that is, not exactly."

Mrs. Hurst threw up her hands. "Really, Caroline, you are quite impossible. You say you are engaged to one man while you are about to engage yourself to another."

"I am not—Thorn has not made an offer to me, at least not in so many words."

"What if he did? Surely you would not entertain an offer from such a man!"

"And why not?" demanded Miss Bingley with heat. "He is wealthy, he is clever, he is handsome, he is honest."

"He is not a gentleman."

"I daresay he is as much a gentleman as Hurst," cried Miss Bingley, perhaps unwisely. Miss Bingley was not always wise when she was angry.

"Hurst and I are received in superior society," retorted Mrs. Hurst. "You and Thorn would not be."

There was a constrained silence for some moments. Mrs. Hurst, however, had not concluded what she wished to say to her sister, and she soon re-commenced, "I have heard—." She stopped, a little afraid of stoking Miss Bingley's wrath.

"What have you heard?"

"A rumour concerning Mallinger. That he—that his affections may previously have been engaged elsewhere."

"That is very delicately put, Louisa. The fact is that he has a mistress with whom he has lived in Venice for many years, and they have four children. He says that if he marries me he will not give her up."

As this was precisely what Mrs. Hurst had heard, she exhibited no surprise. "Caroline, I hope you would not send Mallinger away simply because he has a mistress. He is five-and-thirty and never married. It is only to be expected. Surely you would not give up a man of consequence for such a reason. Your fancy for John Thorn cannot be so strong that you would throw away the chance to become Lady Mallinger. His accent alone—!"

"He has a Northern accent," said Miss Bingley impatiently. "Do you suppose our grandfather's was any more euphonious?"

"We have risen above our grandfather's station. Do you wish to discard all the work we have done to reach our present position?"

"A position that would entitle me to marry a man who is already in possession of a wife and family, and who desires me only for my fortune!"

"Really, Caroline, you are talking like a silly love-struck girl. I suggest that you think what you are about. If you do not take Mallinger, another woman will, and the world will call you a simpleton." Mrs. Hurst, greatly irritated, departed from the room.

Miss Bingley remained, standing in the same attitude for some time. She was not so entirely convinced by her sister's remarks as to cease her ruminations upon John Thorn, and she considered for an hour or more, before retiring for the night, how far it would be for her happiness that she should encourage his addresses.

Chapter Thirty-Two

[March 1814, London]

Henry Mallinger had not been altogether displeased by Miss Bingley's quarrelling with him over Leonora Giovanese; he was a man who valued the more anything that was difficult to obtain; and also one who was exceedingly sure of his abilities. Upon returning to London in March he called upon Miss Bingley at the Hursts' townhouse. When he sent up his card, however, he was shortly informed by the servant that Miss Bingley was not in.

It was not Miss Bingley's intention to dismiss Mallinger, but she needed time to ascertain her feelings concerning him and John Thorn, and it was for this reason that she had turned him away. When two days had passed and she had still not been successful in this endeavour she dared not put him off longer and wrote a note asking him to call on her again. She was in part annoyed by Mallinger's return, for her anger with him had scarcely abated, but she also felt a certain relief, for she had a dizzying sense of falling towards Thorn in a way she was incapable of halting—if she wished to do so. The agitation of her feelings required her to exercise a great deal of self control when she received Mallinger, and when he arrived she concentrated all of her energy into walking into the drawing room with composure and giving him her hand.

"You are looking very well," he said in his cool, languid voice, gazing at her with his usual lack of expression. "Evidently my absence has not caused you to repine. On the contrary it would appear to have made you bloom."

Mallinger's unruffled demeanour immediately assisted the restoration of Miss Bingley's poise, and when she spoke she was able with comparatively little effort to match his tone. "I did not expect you to return so soon. It is not yet spring. I was about to remark on *your* appearance, how exceedingly Venice agrees with you. It is the climate there I presume."

"You would not receive me when I called the other day."

"I was not in."

Mallinger ignore this falsehood. "Why did you refuse to see me, and then send for me? Are you quite reckless about me, to bait me in this way?"

"I am not baiting you."

"Perhaps there is someone standing between us now?"

Miss Bingley experienced a strong temptation to say, "There are two standing between us, a woman and a man." But she kept silence.

Mallinger continued. "I have been told, warned rather, that you have formed an attraction for another man. Is this true?" Miss Bingley turned her gaze from him and did not respond. "Do you wish me to understand that *he* is now your favourite?"

Although Miss Bingley had been unable to find out her feelings prior to Mallinger's entrance, she now began to comprehend them. Mallinger's habitual composure called forth the same in her. With Thorn there was a continual perturbation of her emotions, and a sense of his power over her. But Mallinger had no power over her, except what she gave him freely. For a moment her thoughts turned to Thorn's height and the strength that he exuded, his teeth flashing white when he smiled—all so different from Mallinger's languid manner. But at last she replied coolly, "He is not my favourite."

"Do not lie to me," said Mallinger in a low voice. "It answers no purpose. I have been told about this Northern manufacturer who holds your attention."

"I am not lying to you. There is no other man to whom I would engage myself." She thought with pleasure that Mallinger now understood there to be a man who had captured *her* affections as Leonora held *his*.

"The talk then is without foundation?"

"What does it matter what people say? Unless you wish to break our engagement, upon which you insisted before you left England, then I am ready to marry you."

"When?"

"As soon as may be. Within a month if you wish."

When Mallinger had departed Caroline took a sheet of her elegant hot-pressed paper and in her fair flowing hand wrote a brief note to John Thorn, informing him that her wedding to Henry Mallinger would take place before the end of April.

Chapter Thirty-Three

[April 1814, Rosings Park]

Elizabeth's previous visit to Kent, now two years past, had perfectly prepared her for the Easter visit to Rosings. When the Darcys' carriage left the high road for Hunsford Lane, the Parsonage soon came into view, and there was Mr. Collins walking within view of the park lodges that opened into the lane, in order to have the earliest intelligence of their arrival. He bowed to them as the carriage passed and turned into the Park, and then hurried home to Charlotte with the news. Darcy, Elizabeth and Kitty (Georgiana having declined to join the party) were received at Rosings with majestic civility by Lady Catherine, and Anne de Bourgh offered each of them her hand. Colonel Fitzwilliam, whose arrival had preceded the Darcys' by only two or three hours nevertheless looked grateful to see them.

Lady Catherine could speak of little that evening but her daughter's impending marriage to Fitzwilliam. She congratulated herself on the strengthening of the family connection, on Anne's fortune that would allow Fitzwilliam to live in his proper sphere, and on Anne's distinguished birth that was sure to result in children of noble mien. "The late Countess, your mother, would have entirely approved of the arrangement. She used to speak with approbation of the union of her own mother and father, who were first cousins and united a title with a large property through the match, and she supported your brother's marriage to your second cousin."

The morning after their arrival, Elizabeth, Kitty, Darcy and Fitzwilliam walked to the Parsonage. Mr. Collins welcomed them formally to his humble abode, and great was Charlotte's and Elizabeth's delight to meet again after their separation. There was much to see, for the baby had to be admired, and the improvements in the house pointed out, and the garden visited; but the entire party was finally seated in the parlour. Elizabeth could not help glancing at Darcy to conjecture if he were recalling the last time they had met there, when he had made an offer to her and she had refused it most uncivilly; his answering look told her that it is in his mind as well. But each made an effort to put behind that event and take part in the general conversation.

After the Collinses had made offers of refreshment, and everyone had inquired about the others' families and exchanged news, Mr. Collins after presenting a few pompous nothings turned to Colonel Fitzwilliam and said, "We believe you are to be congratulated upon your approaching connection with the very noble lady whom I have the honour of calling patroness? That is to say, of course, with her daughter. I have observed to Lady Catherine, that Miss de Bourgh's marriage to Colonel Fitzwilliam will elevate the rank of wife of a younger son of an earl to equality with that of a duchess, and she was most pleased." Colonel Fitzwilliam thanked him a little distantly for the delicacy of the thought, and managed to maintain a perfect absence of expression on his features when Mr. Collins added that he and his dear Charlotte were much looking forward to having him as a neighbour after his marriage, and of taking every occasion of testifying their respect towards him as Lady Catherine's son-in-law. Mr. Collins added with humility, "Our situation with regard to Lady Catherine's family is indeed the sort of extraordinary advantage and blessing which few can boast, and we cannot regard its members with too much deference."

When Lady Catherine's guests parted from their host and hostess they assured one another of the pleasure it would give them to see each other either at Rosings or the Parsonage during the course of the Easter visit, and Elizabeth and Charlotte embraced most affectionately.

Each day at Rosings was similar to the one before. After breakfast, during which Lady Catherine revised, as necessary, the weather forecast she had given before everyone had retired the previous night, and had inquired closely of her visitors what plans they had formed for the day, each individual sought his own amusement. Anne de Bourgh drove out in her little phaeton, almost invariably unaccompanied by Colonel Fitzwilliam despite Lady Catherine's repeated and increasingly forceful invitations. The others walked in the park and called at the Parsonage daily. Only desperation could have made Darcy seek the company of Mr. Collins, but he had acquired an esteem for Mrs. Collins and with a concentration denied to Elizabeth seemed able to emulate Charlotte in not hearing the majority of what Mr. Collins said. Fortunately the weather was fine enough for outdoor exercise and visiting, although it would have taken a particularly heavy rain to keep the visitors in the drawing room with Lady Catherine for an entire morning.

Elizabeth's favourite walk at Rosings, and one where she frequently went alone when the others were engaged in their own pursuits, was a path along the open grove which edged the side of Rosings Park, far enough distant from the house to be quite out of the way, and sheltered by a line of trees and shrubs so that a walker could find undisturbed privacy. Neither Lady

Catherine nor her daughter was given to walking, and when she attained it Elizabeth felt herself beyond the reach of her ladyship's curiosity. During her previous visit no one had seemed to value the path but herself—therefore she was a little surprised to see others on it from time to time. At a distance one day she thought she caught a glimpse of Colonel Fitzwilliam, who had never walked there except the day when he made a tour of the park before leaving. He disappeared from sight before she was close enough to call his name. Twice she ran into Kitty. The first time she said to her, "Kitty, I asked you if you wished to walk and you said not." "Oh, I changed my mind. I was going to read a book, but the day looked so fine. It is a pity that Lady Catherine does not keep any riding horses. Are you turning back to the house now?" Elizabeth nodded affirmatively. "I will go with you then." The second time Kitty merely greeted her and walked on in the opposite direction.

In the evenings the family party was often increased by the presence of the Collinses—perhaps more often than Lady Catherine would have liked, for she desired to have her nephews to herself as much as possible. Colonel Fitzwilliam however had expressed a wish for their company and Lady Catherine was intent on pleasing him. When Lady Catherine could not get better company the Collinses joined her for dinner twice a week, and Mr. Collins sat at the bottom of the table and carved. He could not of course be so distinguished while Lady Catherine's nephews were her guests, but he took his demotion in rank with humility and set himself to please Lady Catherine by agreeing with her every statement and paying her and her daughter little compliments throughout the meal. After dinner, when the gentlemen had left the table and come to the drawing room, Elizabeth and Kitty took turns playing the piano, and Colonel Fitzwilliam would join them in singing sometimes, or else the card tables would be set up for whist or quadrille. If they were not playing cards, Lady Catherine would lead the conversation and would shepherd back any who strayed into a private conversation. Each evening ended with Lady Catherine's directions concerning the next day's weather.

The resemblance of one day to the next was interrupted the day before Easter when an express arrived for Colonel Fitzwilliam.

"Well, Darcy, here's news," he said upon reading it.

"Why? What has happened?"

"It seems that my services will not be required on the Continent after all. Buonaparte has abdicated his throne. It would appear that the war is over."*

* On March 31, 1814 the Coalition forces (Austria, Great Britain, Portugal, Prussia, Russia, Spain, Sweden) took Paris, and on April 4 Napoleon Buonaparte's highest ranking officers mutinied against him. Napoleon abdicated on April 6 in favour of his son, but the Coalition refused to accept this and he was forced to abdicate unconditionally on April 11. He was exiled to the island of Elba off the coast of Italy. Louis XVIII, the brother of Louis XVI who had been executed in 1793 during the French Revolution, took the throne. –Ed.

The rest of the party was quickly informed, and everyone gathered together and exclaimed over the news. The following day, Easter Sunday, the entire party attended church, where Mr. Collins presided, and a Te Deum was sung for the end of the war.

The eruption of peace after twenty-five years of hostilities was an event of significance, but it did not long distract Lady Catherine from matters of greater consequence. The more she spoke to Colonel Fitzwilliam of his union with her daughter, the less he seemed to heed, and she was growing increasingly irritated by his failure to conclude arrangements for his and Anne de Bourgh's earliest felicity. On Easter Monday, when the ladies rose from the dinner table, Lady Catherine requested that her nephew wait upon her in the library after he and Darcy had finished their port.

"Fitzwilliam," she began immediately upon his entrance into that room, "you can be at no loss to understand why I wish to speak to you."

"Quite on the contrary, Lady Catherine."

"It is about your marriage to Anne. It has been agreed within the family for many months now that you and Anne will wed, but you as yet have failed to perform your part. I have not been used to submitting to any person's whims, and now that the war is over and you will not be posted to the Continent it is time that the matter was settled. The first week of June will be a suitable time for the wedding. You will be married by special licence—publication of the banns I have always found somewhat vulgar. If Anne's health were not delicate, you would be married in London at St. George's. However I think it best that Anne not travel, so the ceremony will be performed in Hunsford parish church. For the same reason you will dispense with a wedding tour. I will notify the family solicitors to draw up the marriage settlements. Now as to where you will live, of course Rosings will be your home. But you will need a residence in London for the season. I shall look into it. I recently heard of a suitable house in Audley Square that is for lease. How soon will you resign your commission?"

"Resign my commission, Lady Catherine?"

"As the husband of a great heiress you would not expect to remain in the army. In any event your services will be dispensed with, now that Buonaparte has been removed."

"Ah. I suppose I would expect to retire to Rosings and lead the life of a country gentleman?"

"Naturally. You are not thinking of standing for Parliament I trust?"

"No, the thought had not crossed my mind. Neither frankly had the thought of resigning my commission."

"It would look most peculiar if Anne's husband were taking orders from men below his station."

"I confess I never thought of the Duke of Wellington as being below my station. Lady Catherine, I am exceedingly obliged to you for putting my affairs and my cousin's to rights, however do you not think of consulting us in making these arrangements?"

"My dear Fitzwilliam, whatever for? I know what is suitable and proper for the marriage of my daughter, a young lady of distinguished birth and splendid fortune. Surely neither you nor Anne would propose anything different? Have you spoken to Anne?"

"I have not."

"I thought not. She told me not. You must speak to her immediately—requesting her consent is purely a matter of form but forms are not to be neglected. She is in the drawing room, go to her now."

"Now, Lady Catherine?"

"Yes, what is the purpose of delay? Surely you do not think she will refuse you. She is greatly attached to you, I assure you, and she will not make the least objection to any arrangements that you and I have agreed upon."

Colonel Fitzwilliam looked very sober. "I must decline. I have business that I must transact this evening."

"Surely whatever business you have can wait. I particularly wish you to speak to Anne tonight."

"Unfortunately, Lady Catherine, my business *cannot* wait. With your permission, I will go and attend to it."

"You refuse to oblige me, Fitzwilliam?"

"In this matter I must."

"I am displeased with you. Most displeased. Accomplish your business then. But you must speak to Anne after breakfast tomorrow. I will tell her to expect you."

Fitzwilliam was grave as he went to his room and seated himself at the writing desk. He now faced his duty, to bring to culmination an evil that he had created himself. He took up his pen, and after the passage of some time wrote the following letter:

> Rosings Park,
> April 11, 1814
>
> My dearest Kitty,
> I have spent nearly a quarter of an hour endeavouring to determine whether to begin this letter, or to end it, by telling you that I love you. But why may I not do both, for it is the lines between that will cause me great pain to write and you to read. Dearest Kitty, I love you; but I have engaged myself to marry my cousin Anne. We will wed in June. She has a splendid fortune and is of noble birth—God

knows, Kitty, that you have heard these things until they are engraved on your heart—and by marrying her I will satisfy the expectations of my family and my own need for money. If you believe I write these last words without the greatest shame, you mistake my character. But I could not blame you, could I, however ill you thought of me. I know there is no means of atoning for my conduct, and I do not ask for your forgiveness or your understanding. I am worthy of neither. I love you, Kitty.

God bless you,
James Fitzwilliam

After he had finished writing he sealed the paper in an envelope, and sat unmoving at the desk for several minutes. Then he rose and rang for his manservant. When he appeared Fitzwilliam put the envelope into his hand. The servant waited for further instruction, and when it did not come he asked what he was intended to do with the letter.

"There is no direction on the envelope, sir," he pointed out.

"Is there not?" said Fitzwilliam. He took the letter back and stood looking into the distance for a moment. The servant waited patiently. After dinner gentlemen often thought and moved rather slowly.

Quite suddenly Colonel Fitzwilliam seemed to make a decision. He strode back to the desk, inscribed a few lines on another piece of paper, sealed it in an envelope, and presented this document to the servant. "Take this to Miss Bennet's room."

"Yes, sir." The servant departed. It was nothing to him, other than a report to entertain the servants' hall, if Miss de Bourgh's betrothed husband wished to write letters to another, and very pretty, young lady.

The following morning Fitzwilliam was walking on the sheltered path at the edge of Rosings Park when he caught sight of a lady moving towards him. When she had advanced near enough for him to see her clearly he pronounced her name. "Kitty."

"Hello, James."

"Kitty, you received my note."

"Yes. I thought it must be something very important for you to send it to me under Lady Catherine's nose."

"It is important, very important. Kitty, I have a letter here that I want you to read."

Kitty took the letter from his hand. As she read it she turned a little pale but remained composed, for the contents were scarcely unexpected.

"You did not need to ask me to meet you here to tell me about your marriage to your cousin Anne."

"I did, because I have something to say to you, and it cannot be put into a letter." Fitzwilliam hesitated a moment, and then resumed. "Two years ago when I was visiting Rosings, I fell in love with a young lady. She was without fortune, and instead of telling her that I loved her and making her an offer, I told her that in my rank of life one could not afford to marry without some attention to money. It humiliates me to think of my words now, although at the time I thought no ill of them. She married another, one who might also reasonably have been expected to reject her for want of money and connections, but who had the wisdom to listen to his heart. I was very envious of him, indeed jealous, and I bitterly regretted what I had thrown away. If I had asked her before he did, I believe she would have accepted me."

Kitty fixed her eyes on his countenance. "James, are you speaking of Elizabeth?"

"I am. Did you know?"

"I suspected perhaps, but I did not know until you told me now."

"I repented my actions, but repentance did no good. I could not have her for my wife. And then, Kitty, a wonderful thing happened. I made the acquaintance of another young lady, and fell in love again."

The two of them gazed at each other in silence for a moment; but then Kitty said sadly, "And that story must end the same way."

"No, Kitty, that is just it. It must *not* end the same way. I threw away one chance for happiness with a wife, and I shall not do it again."

Kitty looked at him in astonishment. "But you wrote that letter to me."

Fitzwilliam took the letter from her and tore it into two pieces. "Lady Catherine has ordered me to ask Anne de Bourgh to marry me. It is my intention to put that quite out of my power, by engaging myself now to another lady. Will you take me, Kitty? We will not have a great deal of money, and Lady Catherine and my father and brother will be fit to be tied, but we will be with each other."

"James," said Kitty, smiling with tears in her eyes, "of course I will have you, even if we must live under a hedge. Shall I tell you something? It is a most terrible secret I have been keeping, and you will be shocked to hear it. But if you had married your cousin, and if you had wanted it, I would have become your mistress."

"Kitty, that is an appalling thing for a young girl to say. Anyone would think you had been raised on a steady diet of French novels. What would you know of becoming a mistress?"

"I found a book in the library at Pemberley. I believe they thought it was locked away, *Manon Lescaut*, it is called. It is much more interesting than Racine's plays."

"Well, if you are determined to read French novels, you had best do it now, for once we are married I intend to forbid them to you, if reading a single one of them can put such reprehensible thoughts into your head."

Fitzwilliam then took Kitty into his arms and kissed first her forehead and afterward her lips. They stood together for several moments, her head resting on his breast, until she raised her eyes to his.

"James, you know that I am not a coward, at any rate when I am riding at a gate I am not, but I am afraid of your telling Lady Catherine that you are going to marry me instead of her daughter."

"I am not a coward either, at any rate not when I am facing the guns of the French, but I quite agree with you that this is not the place or time to inform Lady Catherine of our engagement. I am going to leave Rosings this morning, before breakfast, and I have already prepared a note for my aunt. I will come to you in town. Then we will talk to Darcy and Elizabeth, but until then I think it best that our engagement remain undisclosed."

Lady Catherine was thrown into an agony of ill-humour when she received in the breakfast parlour a brief note from her nephew telling her that he was called away upon urgent matters with such suddenness that he had not time to take leave of her and his cousin Anne. As she made her resentment felt throughout the house and it showed no signs of decreasing after a day or two, the Darcys determined to get away; and after an affectionate parting between Elizabeth and Charlotte Collins, they returned with Kitty to London.

Chapter Thirty-Four

[April 1814, London]

Where there is affection, people are seldom withheld by immediate want of fortune from entering into engagements with each other. Nevertheless, very great was the astonishment and dismay of Elizabeth and Darcy when upon their return to London Kitty and Fitzwilliam communicated their news.

"Darcy," said Fitzwilliam reasonably, after listening to their remarks, "if you would not marry our cousin Anne, I fail to see why you should take umbrage if I do not either."

"This is exceedingly imprudent on your part."

"Do you expect me to be wiser than other men? Yet I have come to the conclusion that there is no wisdom in resisting this course of action."

"And how will you live?"

"As other officers and their wives do, on my own income. Come, Darcy, Elizabeth, will you not wish us joy?"

"Of course, we wish you both very happy," said Elizabeth warmly.

"Many thanks, and you may expect us to be your frequent guests at Pemberley," smiled Fitzwilliam. "Now all that is left is to know what Lady Catherine's reaction will be."

"I admire your intrepidity in announcing to her what is to befall," said Darcy. "Will you do so directly?" Fitzwilliam acknowledged that he must, and the conversation was then turned playfully by Elizabeth to the slyness of the couple in evading her ladyship's, and everyone else's, detection in their courtship.

Within a day or two, her mind full of the event, Elizabeth wrote to Charlotte Collins with the news. It was not a week later that she got Charlotte's reply.

The Parsonage
Hunsford, Kent

April –, 1814

Dearest Eliza,
I must tell you that I have never in my life seen anything like Lady Catherine when she received the news of your sister's engagement to Colonel Fitzwilliam. You must know that I told Mr. Collins as soon as I read your letter this morning, and he, assuming that Lady Catherine must also be aware of the report, wished immediately to hasten to her side to provide her comfort, and asked me to accompany him. I could not refuse, either as his wife, or Lady Catherine's neighbour, and did not wish to as your friend, for I was tolerably curious to know how she was bearing up under this news. Accordingly we walked to Rosings and were admitted to an audience with her. To my amazement she seemed much as ever, and I could scarcely credit her composure in the face of a second marital calamity. When Mr. Collins began to express his sympathy for the situation in which she and Miss De Bourgh now found themselves, she demanded to know of what he was speaking. Now the explanation for her equanimity became clear, for she had not yet received the information. No doubt Colonel Fitzwilliam and Darcy are more leisurely in their correspondence with their aunt than you are with me. Mr. Collins and I now found ourselves in a delicate position, for we could no longer be guarded, but to tell her all was indeed to beard the dragon in its den! After stumbling in his words to begin with, Mr. Collins told her that Colonel Fitzwilliam had engaged himself to marry Miss Catherine Bennet. "Nonsense!" she said at first, and loudly. "If such a report is abroad I insist upon it being universally contradicted, for Fitzwilliam is engaged to my daughter and they are to be married in June, here in Hunsford. By special licence." Mr. Collins and I would gladly have retreated, and left her to learn the truth from another, but unfortunately she then began to inquire whence we had heard this rumour, and Mr. Collins was forced to acknowledge that you, Eliza, were the source. Even then she was not prepared to believe in its truth, suspecting some scheme on your part, probably, to separate Miss De Bourgh from her bridegroom. However at last she asked me to read from your letter, which I had unluckily brought with me, and I did so, and the particulars were so precise that she could no longer doubt. "Upon my word!" she said. "Upon my word!" and she sat down very heavy upon a chair and did

not say *another single word for a good quarter of an hour*. I rang for the servant to find Miss De Bourgh and Mrs. Jenkinson, for I feared that this blow might have brought on an apopleptic attack, and they came and were just as shocked as Mr. Collins and I by her utter silence. Mrs. Jenkinson sent for the apothecary. However before he could arrive she began to recover, repeating "Upon my word" several times, and then "Bennet". Finally she rose with great dignity and thanked Mr. Collins for bringing her this intelligence, and walked from the room—rather like the ghost stalking about the battlements of Elsinore, with a countenance "more in sorrow than in anger"! We four remaining behind looked at one another, wondering if one of us ought to follow her, and after a moment Miss de Bourgh did so. This was a great relief to Mr. Collins and me, as we now realized that if Lady Catherine was in the dark, Miss de Bourgh was equally so, and we had no desire to be the bearers of the news to a second hearer, as you may easily conjecture. We are even now packing our trunks for a visit to Hertfordshire, for we have not yet forgotten the storm that raged here when news of your engagement to Darcy arrived!
Yours affectionately,
C. Collins

Chapter Thirty-Five

[April 1814, London]

Henry Mallinger married Caroline Bingley in London. Everyone present at the wedding breakfast agreed that the bride, with her handsome countenance and elegant figure, was worthy to become Lady Mallinger one day. The bride's face was pale, but she was perfectly composed.

"I am sure he will treat you well," said Mrs. Hurst, a little anxiously, as she said goodbye to her sister.

"I, at any rate, intend to treat *him* well, unless he deserves otherwise," replied Mrs. Mallinger.

"I do not wonder that I never married before," said Mallinger as he handed his wife into their coach to begin the journey to Damson Hall. "I had forgotten what a bore weddings are."

"Do you intend finding marriage a bore as well?" inquired Mrs. Mallinger.

"I hope you will give me no reason to."

"Nor you me?"

"You have taken me as I am, Caroline. If I bore you now I am certain to do so in the future."

"You do not bore me particularly," said Mrs. Mallinger, turning to gaze out the window.

Mallinger looked at his new wife with complacency. Her behaviour that morning, her first appearance in the role of the future Lady Mallinger, had been impeccable. She carried herself as though she had been born to be a duchess, and her fortune would allow them to live comfortably until he came into his uncle's title and property. He felt certain that she would never blemish his honour by word or deed. The stories about John Thorn's admiration for her did not cause him concern, indeed they provided a *frisson* of self-congratulation that he had openly won his wife in a contest with a man who, although not a gentleman, was to be reckoned with. He felt his approbation ripening into something more tender, and he took her hand. She did not draw it away from him, although neither did she make any sign of acknowledgement. She continued to look out the window of the carriage.

It was late afternoon when they entered the park gates. "We have arrived now," remarked Mallinger. He drew Caroline to him and for the first time kissed her on the lips. Although she did not respond, neither did she recoil.

They were greeted at the door by Lady Mallinger, who welcomed her nephew and new niece very civilly and informed them that Sir Hugh was too unwell to join them at dinner or see them that evening. Then Mallinger led his wife upstairs. "Here is your sitting room, and your dressing room and bedroom are next to it. Shall I have your maid sent to you?"

"No, I will ring for her when I am ready."

Mallinger bowed and left her, and Mrs. Mallinger took off her hat and cloak and sat down by the fire. The housekeeper appeared and asked if there were anything she wanted. "Tell my maid to put out my dress," said Mrs. Mallinger.

"Yes, Madam." Instead of leaving the housekeeper drew nearer. "I have a letter for you," she said. "I was told to give it to you and no one else, when you were alone."

"A letter? From whom?"

The housekeeper held out a square of paper silently, and Mrs. Mallinger took it. "Thank you, you may go." After sitting for a few moments with the letter in her hand she opened it. There was no salutation or signature. She read:

> Do you think you will be happy with him, as I once was? Do you think you will have beautiful children with him, as I did? No—you will not. I gave you a warning, and you did not heed it. He was to have married me. His love is mine, and he will make you miserable. But you have taken him with open eyes, and you will have no right to complain. The wrong you do *me* will curse *you.*

Mrs. Mallinger remained in her chair for a long time with the letter on her lap. Then there came a light tap at the door, and her husband entered, dressed for dinner. He raised his eyebrows a little to see her still in her travelling clothes. "I had thought you would be ready to go down," he said. "What have you been doing?"

"Reading a letter."

"It must have been a long and important one to delay you so."

"No," said Mrs. Mallinger calmly. "It was neither."

Chapter Thirty-Six

[April 1814, Longbourn]

"Mary, you not have forgotten that we are dining with the Lucases tonight," said Mrs. Bennet.

"What necessity is there that I attend?" inquired Mary. "Although I am not unwilling to forfeit my evenings occasionally for engagements, it is just two nights past that we dined with the Lucases at the Gouldings'. I have come to an important passage in the book I am reading and I wish to make some extracts."

"You have had your nose in that book all day long, and the Lucases will be offended if you do not come."

"Though I admit to the claims of society as a whole, I refute the premise that I must be guided in my activities by the feelings of its individual members. '*Il est plus aisé de connoître l'homme en général que de connoître un homme en particulier*'."

"I do not know why your father allows you to fill your head with that flimflammery," said Mrs. Bennet impatiently, "but you are coming to the Lucases' tonight and I'll thank you not to carry on in such a way while we are there. You are considered peculiar enough as it is. And you have been more peculiar since you stayed with Lizzy in London, there is hardly any pleasing you of late. I suppose you think you are above the Lucases and the Gouldings and the other families we dine with, after meeting those busybodies and radicals that Mr. Darcy entertains. It may be well enough for him and Lizzy to associate with those who want to end slavery and who knows what other notions they may have, and I will not be surprised when I hear that they have had actual black slaves in their house as well, and I have no idea how I will explain that to Mrs. Goulding, but I am sure they have nothing to do with you."

The Lucases had a larger party to dinner than the Bennets had expected. The vicar of Meryton had been invited, to provide some ecclesiastical company for a guest, Dr. Cramer, the rector of a parish in Cambridgeshire, who had that day arrived to stay at Lucas Lodge. Mary was pleased to see the two gentlemen, as it meant that the Lucas boys would be required to behave more respectfully and would most likely refrain from teazing her about Latin grammar.

Dr. Cramer was a tall and handsome man in late middle age. When he was introduced to Mary he remarked with civility that he had heard about the lovely Miss Bennets and was gratified to meet one of them. Mary was not used to being complimented on her appearance, and Dr. Cramer's words were pleasant indeed to her ears.

"Ah, you should see my eldest daughter Jane," said Mrs. Bennet. "She is as beautiful as an angel, and married just a year ago to a gentleman who had taken Netherfield Hall. Do you know Netherfield? You do not? It's of little consequence, for he has recently purchased an estate in Nottinghamshire and they have moved away. How I miss her! I have three daughters married and Mary is the only one at home at present. But it is all I can do to get her away from her books."

Mary bore these comments with the fortitude of long experience. However Dr. Cramer smiled at her kindly and said, "Miss Bennet I hear has a reputation as a scholar."

Mary blushed deeply. She could not recall that anyone had ever referred to her accomplishments in such a very flattering fashion, and here was a learned man taking notice of them! She was preparing to observe that the business of the scholar is to talk in public and to think in solitude, but hardly had he spoken before he turned his attention away from her to Sir William Lucas.

Dinner proceeded much as usual, and Mary, seated between her mother and the eldest Lucas son, had leisure in plenty to follow her own reflections without interruption from her neighbours. Mrs. Bennet rarely had anything to say to Mary that was of the slightest interest to her, and the Lucas boy confined his waking thoughts to the affairs of the home farm—for somewhat to the mortification of Lady Lucas, he was at heart a farmer. When the ladies withdrew from the table, Mary contrived not to see her mother's signals that she was to join them in the drawing room, and she slipped off to the library. Sir William's library was devoid of works that fitted in with her present interests, but there were some ancient volumes of Bracton* and she took one down and was soon deep in puzzling out the jurist's discussion of what law is and what custom is. She thought it likely that her mother would

* Henry de Bracton, *De legibus et consuetudinibus Angliae* (On the laws and customs of England), written primarily before c. 1235. –Ed.

send for her when the gentlemen joined the ladies for coffee, and perhaps a game of whist, at which time she would have to obey the summons, but that she would probably remain undisturbed until then, Sir William's library not by any means being the most frequented room in the house.

However when the door opened it was not a servant sent to bid her to the drawing room, but Sir William himself with Dr. Cramer and the vicar.

"Miss Bennet, pray do not be disturbed by us," said Sir William with his usual courtesy. "We are just looking for a little book on the history of the county that I believe I have in here." The vicar bowed to her and moved past with Sir William. But Dr. Cramer paused and glanced at her book. "*De legibus et consuetudinibus*. England's finest jurist. It does you both credit. I half thought to find you with a novel or play."

"I find little enjoyment in novels. They can scarcely be said to improve the mind. I have of course read the works of Mr. William Shakespeare."

"I am uncertain that I would call Shakespeare's works improving to the mind," said Dr. Cramer with a smile. "I would not allow my young daughters to read *Othello*, or *Romeo and Juliet* or *A Midsummer Night's Dream*, they like many of his works are full of corrupting passions, and so rather unsuitable for a young lady's mind."

"Yet think how often we learn from Shakespeare that a female cannot too closely guard her virtue!" cried Mary. "We are shown the tide of the passions and where they must lead. Perhaps more rather than fewer young women should read these plays and take instruction from them. Female virtue is more precious than rubies, and the loss is irretrievable."

A slight frown crossed Dr. Cramer's face.

Mary suspected he was recalling a story he may have heard about Lydia. She looked back down at the book, expecting him to rejoin his companions. Lydia's shameful behaviour, even patched over as it was by her marriage, continued to grate on Mary's sensibilities—the disgrace of eloping, and living with a man before the wedding took place!

Dr. Cramer did not leave her. Instead he said gently, "Miss Bennet, can I persuade you to leave your tome and accompany me to the drawing room? I will take my own advice and postpone my researches if you will honour me with your company."

Mary hardly knew how to respond to this request, but seeing her hesitation, Dr. Cramer closed the book and stood behind her chair to draw it back. She nodded and rose, and took his offered arm. "I will see you in the drawing room," said Dr. Cramer to Sir William and the vicar. "Pray excuse me for this evening."

As a rule no one took any notice of Mary's comings or goings, but there was a pause in the general conversation when Mary entered the room on Dr. Cramer's arm. Even Mrs. Bennet was startled into silence as Dr. Cramer settled Mary on a sopha and brought her a cup of tea. Mary found it very congenial to be the centre of attention for such an unaccustomed reason.

"As you have an inclination for history, you would perhaps like to hear about the work I am doing right now," said Dr. Cramer as he seated himself by her side.

"Most willingly," said Mary. "I profess myself to be a student of history, and have been studying it for a considerable length of time. The learned man may draw from history many useful lessons."

"I am writing about the martyrs of the reign of Queen Mary. I am in Hertfordshire to examine some records of the period. I have nearly finished collecting my source material, and soon I will have to confront its organization—and then of course the writing of the book!"

"It must involve much labour, and require much application."

"Yes, I often feel daunted in the face of it," laughed Dr. Cramer good humouredly. "I have written fifteen books, and each appears an unconquerable mountain when I first face the task."

"Fifteen books!" exclaimed Mary. "Do you do all yourself?"

"Some times I have had one of the students from the University assist me," he replied. "I live very close to Cambridge, you know."

"How fortunate you are to reside in the vicinity of a great university and its library, and to have the opportunity to communicate with so many scholarly men."

"Yes, I suppose it is," said Dr. Cramer. He fell silent a moment, his face shadowed.

"Is aught amiss? Have I spoken words of a nature to give offence?"

"No, no," he replied, smiling at her again. "It is simply that my dear wife passed away a twelvemonth ago. It seems strange to hear you envy me the company of scholars when it is *her* dear company that I miss."

"I regret that I have created reflections distressing to your mind. I have read that there is no more lovely, friendly and charming relationship, communion or company than a good marriage, and that that marriage halves our griefs and doubles our joys."

"Miss Bennet, on the contrary you have done me a great deal of good, sitting and conversing with me."

Across the room Mrs. Bennet, her eyes sparkling, watched her daughter. Lady Lucas followed her gaze. "Dr. Cramer's wife died last year, and they say he was quite devoted to her. He has two daughters, both grown up and married, with families of their own. However he is very well looking for a man of his age, is he not?"

"Does he have a good living?" inquired Mrs. Bennet.

"He is the rector of St. --- close by Cambridge. I believe the living is worth about eight hundred pounds a year, but he also has independent means,

I understand. Perhaps his capital is not entirely settled on his daughters at his death." The two ladies entered into earnest conversation.

The following afternoon Dr. Cramer paid a call on Mr. Bennet. After entertaining his visitor for half an hour, Mr. Bennet solicitously proposed that he pay his respects to Mrs. and Miss Bennet, and thus regained sole possession of his room.

Mrs. Bennet was more than willing to receive such a guest, and sent a hasty message to the housekeeper to find Mary and order her to attend her mother instantly, with no excuses admitted.

"Mary will join us directly," said Mrs. Bennet, smiles decking her face, "and will be very pleased to see you again. She has such an excellent temper! And she is clever, although perhaps Mr. Bennet has allowed her to indulge in reading books a little too much, and she needs to be drawn more into company. Of course, her studies will fit her to manage a household, accounts and such things, so I daresay it is not as though her time has been wasted. And she plays and sings—of all my girls she was the one who never minded practising. She could play scales all day. Not that she does now, of course," added Mrs. Bennet hurriedly, remembering periods when Mary *had* played scales all day. "Oh, Mary, come in. Here is a most agreeable surprise, Dr. Cramer has called on us."

Mary stopped in the doorway, a little discomposed to see the gentleman.

He rose and bowed to her, his pleasure at seeing her again clearly expressed on his countenance. Mary made her courtesy, and he said, "Miss Bennet, I see that you are even lovelier in the full light of day than by candlelight." She blushed with gratification. "Your mother has been telling me that you are an accomplished musician. Will you do me the favour of playing for me?"

Mary was delighted to have such an occasion of exhibiting her powers, and she immediately went to the instrument and began to play a concerto. Although she had little natural talent for music or natural taste, by applying herself she had acquired a certain degree of excellence. Dr. Cramer, having some knowledge of music, recognized her skill; and as he preferred to listen with his eyes closed or fastened on a distant corner of the room he was most happily unaware that her performance was injured by her pedantic and somewhat conceited air.

Dr. Cramer by Mrs. Bennet's most cordial request joined the Bennets for dinner that evening, and found a willing audience and eager interlocutor in Mary as he spoke about the concept of *agape* in the *Summa Theologiae* of Thomas Aquinas.*

---

* The *Summa Theologiae* was a manual compiling theological teachings, written from 1265-74 by (Saint) Thomas Aquinas (1225-1274, canonized 1324), a great philosopher and theologian of the Catholic Church. *Agape* is a Greek word for charitable as opposed to sexual or erotic love. –Ed.

The following evening by Mrs. Bennet's invitation he returned for whist and supper, and when his attention was not fully required for the game he conversed with an entranced Mary about the concept of love of wisdom, *philosophia*, in the teachings of Socrates. He informed the Bennets, that he had postponed his departure from Hertfordshire for a week in order to continue his researches into the local records.

On Wednesday evening he met the Bennets at the Gouldings' for dinner. The guests were no doubt greatly edified by his disquisition on the implications for domestic politics and religious observance of Mary Tudor's marriage to Philip of Spain, and Mary contributed several reflections of her own on the subject.

On Thursday evening he joined a party at Mr. and Mrs. Phillips' house in Meryton. To a small group of listeners, of whom Mary was the principal, he spoke of the Stoic philosophy of Seneca reflected in his *Epistulae Morales*,[*] in particular the phrase *alteri vivas oportet, si vis tibi vivere*,[**] and of Seneca's devoted wife Paulina, who had refused to continue her life when Seneca ended his.

On Friday morning he sent a short letter to Mary praising her quick comprehension of the finer points of Seneca's philosophy; and enclosing a copy of the *Aeneid*[***] as a gift. Citing her interest in history he made a few observations on Dido's speech in Book IV predicting the Carthaginian Wars. Mary immediately sat down with her Latin dictionary to read Book IV, and had made a little progress through it when Dr. Cramer came to take tea with her and her mother that afternoon.

On Saturday he paid a morning call on Mrs. and Miss Bennet, and spoke most learnedly about the concept of *caritas*[****] in St. Paul's first epistle to the Corinthians. Mary sat beside him with flushed cheeks and from time to time interjected pertinent thoughts that she was forming.

On Sunday he joined the Bennets in their pew at morning service in the parish church at Longbourn, and following the service he took the opportunity to mention to Mary a few of his ideas for a forthcoming sermon on chapter seven of the first epistle to the Corinthians, taking as his text verse four. Mary listened with bright eyes and a swelling heart.

On Monday he paid a farewell morning call on the Bennets, and departed from Hertfordshire.

---

* Lucius Annaeus Seneca, *Epistulae morales ad Lucilium* (Moral letters to Lucilius), written in the first half of the 1st century AD. –Ed.

** Latin. "You must live for another, if you wish to live for yourself." –Ed.

*** Vergil, The Aeneid, written in the first century BC, c. 29-19 BC. In Book IV, Dido, Queen of Carthage, falls in love with the hero Aeneas; and when he rejects her she kills herself. –Ed.

**** *Caritas* is the Latin equivalent of the Greek *agape*. –Ed.

"Good gracious!" said Mrs. Bennet in great vexation. "What did he mean by coming here and eating all those meals? I made sure he would offer for Mary and now he's gone without a by-your-leave."

"You keep too good a table, Mrs. Bennet," said her husband. "It must have been appetite rather than love that drew him here."

Mary shut herself up in her room and with intense concentration laboured over a translation of the lines in Book IV of the *Aeneid* concerning Dido's death at her own hand by Aeneas's sword and the pyre.

On Tuesday a letter came to Mrs. Bennet thanking her for her hospitality and praising her board. She was so thoroughly exasperated that she dropped the letter on the coals in the breakfast-room fireplace and stirred the shrivelling paper viciously with the poker.

On Thursday a letter arrived for Mr. Bennet.

> The Rectory
> —, Cambridgeshire
> April –, 1814
>
> My dear sir,
> On my recent visit to Sir William and Lady Lucas you must have marked my attentions to your daughter Mary. I now wish to ask formally for her hand in marriage. Although there is an age difference between us—indeed both of my daughters are her elders—I feel that she is of a turn of mind and temperament that would fit her well for a husband of more mature years. I believe Miss Bennet has shown a preference for me that will make this proposal not unwelcome, although of course I leave the actual decision to you as her father.
>
> In the matter of settlements, I have endowed property on each of my daughters on their marriages and they will not be greatly prejudiced by my taking of a new wife. I would propose to settle 2500 pounds on my wife and any children we may have and a matching sum from her own family would ensure a reasonable degree of comfort in the event of my death. The rectory of course I do not own and possess no other real property at this time.
>
> If you agree to my proposal I will write immediately to Miss Bennet and acquaint her with my wishes and your consent.
>
> I remain, sir, your servant,
> Tho. Cramer

Chapter Thirty-Seven

[April 1814, London]

"Darcy, I have had such an odd letter from my father this morning," said Elizabeth. "He writes that Mary is going to marry an old man and air his flannel waistcoats in front of the fire and rub ointment on his rheumatic joints. What do you suppose is the meaning of this?"

"Your father's letters tend towards the eccentric—as well as the infrequent—but usually contain some kernel of news," said Darcy. "I conjecture this to be an announcement of Mary's engagement."

"But who can it be? He has not given himself the trouble of mentioning a name. Mary has written nothing to me about any gentleman, although I have not had a letter from her for more than four weeks. Can she have met a man and become engaged to him in such a short time?"

The mystery was solved the following day when a letter arrived from Mary herself.

> Longbourn House, Herts
> April –, 1814
>
> My dear sister,
> The first bond of society is marriage. I must ask for your good wishes as I have with our father's consent engaged myself to marry Dr. Thomas Cramer of —, Cambridgeshire. Dr. Cramer is some years our father's senior, but he is hale and his intellect is very vigorous.
>
> I believe the greatest likelihood of happiness in marriage arises where a husband can through his understanding of moral philosophy be his wife's guide to leading a virtuous life, and where he can compel her obedience not only as a duty but by reason of the true respect

he inspires. Dr. Cramer is a most learned man who has studied both the classics and Christian theology and is the author of fifteen books, and who therefore naturally has sought in a companion of his bosom one who is equipped also to be a companion of his mind. We will make our home at —, Cambridgeshire, where I will hope to receive your letters.
Your sister,
Mary Bennet

Despite the absence of close feeling between Mary and herself, Elizabeth was distressed by this letter.

"Not a single word of affection," she said to her husband. "Nothing but respect. Do you believe a happy marriage may be founded on respect alone?"

"Your sister certainly appears to think so, and love may come in time. Speaking for myself, however, and acknowledging your almost unbounded respect for me, my dearest Elizabeth, I hope that it is tempered by some more tender emotion, at least on occasion."

"Indeed I am quite filled with love, which I date from my first seeing your beautiful grounds at Pemberley."

An entreaty that she would be serious, however, soon produced the desired effect, and she satisfied him with solemn assurances of her affection, supported by a warm embrace.

Chapter Thirty-Eight

[May 1814, London and Wiltshire]

First Lady Catherine's life, and then her reason, were despaired of by her household after she received tidings of Colonel Fitzwilliam's treachery, but in a strikingly short time she recovered sufficiently to put pen to paper.

> Rosings Park, Kent
> May –, 1814
>
> Fitzwilliam,
> I write to you in heaviness of heart. I was scarcely able to credit a report of which I was made aware a fortnight ago that you intended to unite yourself to Miss Catherine Bennet, or indeed to comprehend the existence of such a report when all arrangements had been made for your marriage to my daughter. I had given every possible encouragement and was entirely prepared to devote myself to all matters of practical import related to the marriage, and of this you were undoubtedly aware. All that was lacking was the formality of your offer to Anne, which was of trifling moment. However I surmise that you look upon this deficiency as adequate justification for your actions, and that you trust that in the eyes of the world you have not committed breach of promise or otherwise injured your reputation. I do not speak of astonishment, amazement, or incredulity when I heard the report, but rather of the familiarity of a great blow. Once more the arts and allurements of a Bennet girl have infatuated a nephew and caused him to forget what he owes to his own family. I will refrain from speaking of Miss Bennet herself—other than to point out that she has no money nor do you, therefore you will starve

together—for I know that to do so would have no more effect on you than it did upon Darcy; and to speak of the defects of her family is quite futile now that her sister is Darcy's wife and the mother of his heir. I am an old woman, scorned and held in contempt. I will live out my few remaining days at Rosings, without expectation of notice from the family whose interests I have always held so dear to my bosom.
C. de Bourgh

Colonel Fitzwilliam promptly replied as follows:

London
May –, 1814

Dear Lady Catherine,
I am most abjectly apologetic that the news of my engagement to Miss Bennet came to you from a source other than myself, and I sincerely beg your pardon. However I do not consider it a formality that I never asked my cousin for her hand, indeed I see it as absolutely the essential point. I should be quite distraught to think of you moldering away to dust at Rosings, and beg you to reconsider your resolve.
Your affectionate nephew,
J Fitzwilliam

Having repelled the first attack, Fitzwilliam readied himself for further skirmishes from within the family. The next was not long in coming, for a letter from his brother Viscount Fitzwilliam summoned him to his estate in Wiltshire.

Fitzwilliam departed from London for the interview with resignation and when he arrived at his brother's house was shown up to the room where his brother and sister were sitting. Viscount Fitzwilliam, his senior by two years, shared with him a similarity of features that was at the moment distorted by unaffected annoyance. His wife put down her needlework when Fitzwilliam entered and rose to greet him, for she was fond of him and was sorry to see him the object of her husband's wrath. Lady Fitzwilliam had a large fortune and impeccable connections, and was of distinguished birth, but she was not robust of constitution, her figure was thin and angular and she was rather plain; and the couple's three little girls resembled her to a remarkable degree.

The Viscount cut short his wife's affectionate words of welcome. "James, what the devil do you think you are doing?"

"Pleasing myself. Not father, not Lady Catherine, and neither you nor anyone else."

"Damn it, what business do you have pleasing yourself? You have an old and honourable name to uphold. If you wish to take up with some common girl, for heaven's sake do it discreetly and decently and make her your mistress. Look at father—he never created such a turmoil when a woman caught his fancy, his conduct has been exemplary."

"Fitz, you are speaking about the lady whom I engaged to marry, and if you keep this up I am going to punch you in the nose."

"James, this is ridiculous. *You* are being ridiculous. There is yet time to extricate yourself from this foolish engagement without damage to your reputation or the girl's. Darcy will be reasonable about the matter and he will persuade the girl and her family to be reasonable as well."

"You believe that Darcy will acknowledge that it is acceptable for him to take a wife from the Bennet family, but that I am so far superior to him in rank that it would disgrace me?"

"You are an earl's son."

"An earl's younger son, and Darcy is an earl's grandson, and I am scarcely more likely than he ever to be a peer. Look, Fitz, you are just splitting hairs about this. Darcy will not help you to separate me from Miss Bennet. You will have to conceive a different design. Why do you not tell our father to disinherit me and cast me off?"

"You are perfectly aware that he has no control over your income, and nothing to leave you on his death."

"And neither do you. Nor do you have any control over my conduct, if only you had the sense to concede it. Wait—here is another plan for you. Offer me a large sum of money to leave the country."

"James, if you reflect upon it you cannot possibly wish to marry this girl. At least take time to consider your decision. Leave England and travel for several months. Go to the Continent."

"Fitz, if you continue in this vein I shall go to America, and take Miss Bennet with me. As my wife."

Lord Fitzwilliam was aghast. "James I sincerely hope that is an idle menace. What would you do in that uncouth country? Although from what I hear at least no one there would be shocked by your *mésalliance*. Soldiers and traders take bush wives from among the Indian women, and abandon them when they return to their homes."

"You are testing my patience, Fitz. America would be too merciful a destination for you. We shall go to Canada instead."

Lady Fitzwilliam's countenance grew paler as Fitzwilliam's threats accumulated.

"Canada! There is nothing there at all! What did that Frenchman call it, '*quelques arpents de neige*'?* You would freeze and perish of hunger—even the French did not want to go there, no matter how rich the furs. King Louis had to round up prostitutes and send them over as companions for the deluded men who agreed to settle in the snow. Well—a girl would not long survive the travails and you could return a free man."

"Fitz, you have gone too far! My wife and I will not go either to America or to Canada, we shall go to Australia!"

"Oh!" cried Lady Fitzwilliam in horror, darting from her seat with a white face, and sitting down again suddenly, unable to support herself. Fitzwilliam quitted the room and left the Viscount tending to his wife, calling to the servant to bring wine for her present relief, and unable to pursue his brother for such further converse as he might have desired.

---

* Voltaire, *Candide* (1758), Chapter 23, although he made similar references in numerous other works. –Ed.

Chapter Thirty-Nine

[May 1814, Castle Tyrconnell]

Colonel Fitzwilliam was sensible of a deep attachment to his father and was sorry to grieve him through a marriage that the family considered unsuitable. When he was summoned to Ireland, he went with regret but also with a determination not to be swayed by injured affection.

Upon his arrival at Castle Tyrconnell he found the Earl sitting in his library, behind a large desk, with papers spread out before him. "Well, James," he said, looking up from them as his son came into the room.

"Hello, Father. It is good to see you."

"Is it? Not afraid of anything I am going to say to you?"

"No sir. The title goes to the heir, and the property is all entailed—you see our family has carefully arranged to put no weapons into the hands of the fathers against the sons."

Colonel Fitzwilliam came and sat on the edge of the desk, and smiled warmly at the Earl. His father smiled back at him, a little conspiratorially.

"I've had several letters from Fitz, each one more apopleptic than the last. And a singularly pitiable one from my sister Catherine. They want me to lay down the law to you."

"Consider it laid down then, and we can turn to more pleasant topics. Have you finished that drainage project yet?"

"I am thinking of leaving it as a legacy to the next Earl. James, are you quite certain about what you are doing?"

"Yes, Father, I am."

"But you will not object to explaining it all to me, I take it?"

"Not in the least."

"Well, go ahead then. I understand that a reasonable number of young ladies of good birth and some wealth have been paraded before you and you have turned your nose up at all of them. What does this young lady have to offer?"

"It is quite simple. I love her, and I did not love any of the other ladies and saw no prospect of doing so in the future."

The Earl looked thoughtful. "You must know, James, that love is not an important consideration in marriage within our rank. Marriage is about political and economic alliances, and about maintaining or improving the situation of the family."

"I shall become Darcy's brother-in-law—is that of assistance?"

"Not particularly, since you are already his first cousin. James, I realize that Darcy has previously breached the wall, so to speak, between our family and this Bennet family, but there is a difference of position. By all accounts—except those of my sister Catherine—Darcy's wife is a lady—and a very pretty one at that—and sufficiently fitted for carrying out her duty. But you are an Earl's son—"

"Just the younger son of an Irish Earl," interjected Fitzwilliam blithely.

"An Earl's son," said the Earl firmly. "Is this girl really suitable to become your wife?"

"The long and the short of it is, Father, that I love her, and I believe she is just exactly suited to become my wife, whoever I may be."

The Earl sighed. "Do you not know that Fitz and Catherine are going to make an infernal nuisance of themselves if you marry her?"

"Burn their letters without reading them, and sport the oak if they come to visit," suggested Fitzwilliam.

"I have already thought of that." He tapped his fingers on the desk.

"Do you care to hear something about your future daughter?"

"I have heard a great deal already."

"From Fitz and my aunt. You might like her better if you were to hear about her from a more favourable source."

"As you wish, James."

"She is young, just twenty. I've had enough boys under my command and watched them grow up into soldiers to know that she will be a brave, spirited woman who will not shirk responsibility. She has an excellent seat on a horse."

"You are thinking of turning her into a soldier then?"

"She'd make a fine one, but my present plan is only to turn her into a wife."

"Is she pretty?"

"Very. She is tall and slender, with a fair complexion, and dark hair and fine dark eyes. She is amiable, without being subservient or placatory. She plays the pianoforte and sings—pleasingly but not excellently—, speaks very bad French, and prefers to draw livestock over flowers. Her manners are perfectly natural and unaffected."

The Earl nodded. "She sounds restful. Your mother was a fine woman, and she played the role of my Countess without a mis-step, but she could not have been called restful."

"No," agreed Fitzwilliam. "She was always and ever the countess, and a countess is not a particularly restful sort of thing to be."

"Catherine admired and approved of her."

"*That's* an encomium."

The Earl rose and began to pace around the library. "Would it surprise you, James, to know that I once had my eye on a girl something like your Miss Bennet?"

"No, Father, it would not surprise me, for I am quite certain that you and my mother were not especially well-suited to each other as a man and a woman."

"I was visiting friends in England, near the town of Allington. This was before I was married of course, or had been introduced to your mother. I met a young lady, her name was Margaret, and we fell deeply in love. We spent the whole summer together, it was endless delight. And then my father sent for me and informed me that everything had been arranged for me to marry your mother. I protested, but no thought could be given to Margaret at all—everything that was important to me about her, her joy, her sweetness of temper, her humour, her beauty—counted for nothing with my father or the family. She was a girl beneath our station, with no money and no connections. They gave no more thought to her than they would to a hunter that was to be sold or destroyed. Less, probably. I left Margaret to see my father and was not allowed to return. Perhaps I did not want to, for I did not have the courage to look at her when I told her I was about to marry another woman."

"And what became of her?" asked Fitzwilliam.

"I believe I broke her heart," said the Earl. "I heard from my friends that she was very ill for several months. At last she recovered, but she never married. I was told that she said that she had loved me and would always love me, but that she would never see or speak to me again even if I came to her. And I did. I did," he repeated, his air gloomy. "After your mother died I went to see her. She refused to receive me."

"Father, you never told me anything of this."

"I never told anyone, James. My behaviour was no credit to me. And it is usually best kept a secret that one loved another woman the whole length of one's marriage."

"I am very sorry, Father."

"No need to be sorry, James. There are many stories like mine I expect. Men and women who could not marry as they pleased. They married for duty and the family carried on."

"And—having told me this story—do you believe that I should marry for duty too? Will you order me to marry for duty?"

"No. I am not going to order you, I am not going to interfere. And I have no property to give you to support a family. So you may look upon me as a neutral power."

"May I bring Miss Bennet to meet you after we are married?"

"Fitz and Catherine would absolutely forbid such a proceeding."

"Very well for Fitz and my aunt, but what do you say?"

The Earl paused and thought for a moment. "Yes, James, I will meet her."

Chapter Forty

[May 1814, London]

A week after Fitzwilliam returned to London from Ireland, as he and Kitty and Georgiana were sitting together in the Darcys' townhouse, their attention was drawn to the window by the sound of a conveyance, and they perceived a carriage driving up to the front door. It was too early in the morning for visitors. They then saw that the chaise and the livery of the servant who preceded it were familiar; it was Lady Catherine de Bourgh. Their astonishment was great. "We had better form ranks," said Fitzwilliam.

Lady Catherine descended from her carriage and, pausing only to remark that the brass door fittings in the hall required polishing, ordered the servant to bring her directly to Colonel Fitzwilliam. She entered the room with an air more than usually ungracious, made no other reply to Georgiana's diffident salutation than a slight inclination of the head, ignored Kitty completely, sat down, and fixed her nephew with her eye.

"Well, Fitzwilliam."

"How do you do, ma'am."

"I am most unhappy, Fitzwilliam. That is how I do. I have been crossed first by Darcy and now by you, and my daughter has twice been publicly slighted. I am at a loss to understand what allurements the Bennet females have practised to make both of my nephews forget what they owe to themselves and their family."

"Madam, I must ask you to recollect that you are in the presence of Miss Bennet."

"Fitzwilliam, do not interrupt me. I will not be interrupted. Hear what I wish to say. You and Darcy believe your actions must escape my censure. However I have not been in the habit of brooking disappointment and I must insist on my right to speak frankly. Your conscience must tell you to submit to hearing me."

"In fact it does not, ma'am. I regret that my cousin's feelings have been injured, but otherwise my conscience is quite clear in all respects."

"Hear me in silence," said Lady Catherine peremptorily. "You have chosen, both you and Darcy—"

"And I also regret that he not with us to hear his share of this."

"Silence! You have both chosen to spurn your own family for young women of inferior birth and no importance in the world, despite the wishes of your nearest relations—" "'A little more than kin and less than kind,'" murmured Fitzwilliam, but Lady Catherine ignored this interjection and proceeded. "You have fallen to the arts of upstart sisters without family, connection or fortune. You have shown no regard for your own honour." She paused ostentatiously. "Now I have spoken my opinion frankly. I will make no effort to interfere with your marriage to Miss Bennet. But you know without a doubt where I stand on the subject. I take my leave of you."

Darcy and Elizabeth had been informed by a servant of Lady Catherine's arrival and were duly astounded. "What can she be doing here?" was a wonder which led to one or two suppositions, and as they passed through the hall intending to meet her, she herself descended the stairs towards them. Husband and wife gazed at each other in increased astonishment. "Has she come all this distance, only to leave immediately? What can she be about?"

Darcy advanced to her. "Lady Catherine, I beg pardon that we were not at hand to receive you, but we were quite unaware that you intended travelling up to town."

"I came upon particular business, and I have concluded it; now I will take my departure."

"You must not go now. Can not anything be said or done on my part that will detain you here?"

"No, Darcy," she said bitterly. "It gives me no pleasure to remain in a house where duty and honour are scorned. Respect and gratitude are bygone things, and selfishness must rule the world. It is time for me to entomb myself at Rosings, held in contempt and forgotten by all, to await the end."

Had Darcy really believed that his aunt was facing imminent demise he would have been much distressed, for despite her arrogance he felt a real attachment for her that those who were not intimate with him might well not have credited. However he thought it doubtful that anyone in a truly moribund condition could look as fresh after the early journey from Hunsford to London as Lady Catherine did. Elizabeth now joined them, and she and Darcy set themselves to persuade her to stop with them for a few days.

Lady Catherine's self-importance had suffered greatly at the hands of her nephews, but in truth that was the only vital part that was damaged; great as the pain was that had been inflicted on her, the injury was very unlikely to prove fatal. Her motive in undertaking the journey, were she to search her heart, had been less to reprimand Colonel Fitzwilliam than to remind her nephews that she was still a force to be dealt with. To lose all opportunity to dictate to her family and interfere in their affairs might indeed have caused her to decline into senescence and decay. Therefore although she upheld her dignity by putting up a strong resistance to their pleas, she at length permitted herself to be convinced of the necessity of remaining there for at least one day and night.

Having ceded the point, she did not long postpone making her presence felt further within confines of the house. She requested that Kitty be sent to her in a private sitting room and she addressed her in these terms:

"Miss Bennet, if you were sensible of your own good, you would not wish to quit the sphere in which you were brought up. I think you do not yet understand what a great step it is for you to become the wife of an Earl's son. Your new rank will give you responsibilities that I do not believe you are fitted for." Lady Catherine paused a moment, and then added with what she considered extravagant condescension, "As yet." She continued. "I am told that you have not ceased to ride by yourself at times, without even a servant in attendance. That must stop at once. It is not done. I will speak to Fitzwilliam about it. You will need wedding clothes. What I have seen you wearing is neither fashionable nor well cut. I will give you the name of a dressmaker who is familiar with the needs of ladies of rank."

Lady Catherine was never in need of encouragement to talk, and continued in the same style for several minutes, while Kitty gave all the appearance of being a very attentive listener, regarding her with wide eyes and an expression of great concentration. It was a look she had perfected while listening to her French master extol the beauty of Racine's verse, and it had frequently been useful in permitting her to think about horses, or about Colonel Fitzwilliam, or about horses and Colonel Fitzwilliam, while appearing to hang on every word issuing from the mouth of the speaker. The discourse, not being absorbed by Kitty to any degree at all, did not interfere with her natural train of thought.

"I will tell Fitzwilliam that you must be married at St. George's. You will be married by special licence of course. Then you must be presented at St. James's on your marriage, and I shall act as your sponsor. You will require full court dress, and you must learn the proper deportment. A dancing master here in London must be engaged to teach you how to walk and curtsey."

The reference to a master penetrated Kitty's ear and she was moved to respond, "I already know how to walk and curtsey, Lady Catherine."

"Do not be impertinent to me. You do not know a court curtsey, or how to approach and move away from Their Royal Highnesses. As I said, you are not ready to be the wife of an Earl's son."

After half an hour, as there seemed danger of Lady Catherine engrossing Kitty until dinner, Elizabeth came into the room and rescued her sister by requiring her presence elsewhere on important business. Kitty rose from her seat with an activity which took Lady Catherine quite by surprise and hurried off almost as if, Lady Catherine observed sharply to Elizabeth, she was eager to escape.

It cannot be said that Lady Catherine's reconciliation with her family produced so happy an effect as to make her thereafter amiable and complaisant; however this was perhaps fortunate, for they might have been at a loss how to deal with her in such an altered state. For the remainder of her visit, which was extended from one night to a week, she presented herself to them much in her usual form, overbearing and arrogant, to Darcy's unspoken relief.

Chapter Forty-One

[May 1814, Cambridgeshire]

Mary and Dr. Cramer were wed in the parish church at Longbourn, and set off from the church door for Cambridgeshire. "The last of my daughters," wept Mrs. Bennet to Lady Lucas in an outpouring of maternal grief. But as Mrs. Bennet had always felt more vexation at Mary's peculiarities than any other emotion towards her, it is to be supposed that she was soon able to bear up under the burden of her departure.

The newly wed couple arrived at their home in —, Cambridgeshire that evening, and were greeted with considerable curiosity by Dr. Cramer's servants. Mary, vain of her new status of wife and mistress of a house, acknowledged each of them with a rather conceited air. Dr. Cramer after dismissing them said to his wife with affection, "My dear Mary, I wish you welcome to our home, and I pray sincerely for our happiness here."

"To be happy at home is the ultimate ambition, and the end of every enterprise," said Mary. She added, "My dearest husband, I do not doubt that we shall know conjugal felicity in our abode."

"Ah—yes," said Dr. Cramer.

A cold meal had been laid out in the dining room and Mary presided proudly over the table.

"I confess myself uncertain what appellation to bestow upon you," said Mary. "I have been accustomed to addressing you as Dr. Cramer, but now we are husband and wife."

"Mary, my dearest, I think you may continue to call me Dr. Cramer. Given the difference in our ages it would not seem appropriate for you to call me anything more informal, do you not agree?"

"Yes, if that is your wish," said Mary, a little disconcerted. "My dear husband," she added consciously.

Dr. Cramer smiled. "'She that is married careth for the things of the world, how she may please her husband.'" But I am afraid, my dear, that as a husband I may not be pleasing my wife. It is not possible for me to take any more time from my work at the moment, and I hope that you will forgive me for the lack of a wedding tour. I will try to find some way to make it up to you."

"I do not repine. I am fully aware that your work must take precedence, and I am prepared to commence immediately."

"Commence, my dear? What is it that you will commence?"

"Assisting you in writing your book, naturally. What do you require of me? I have read Foxe's *Book of Martyrs*, and you will tell me with what other volumes I ought to familiarize myself so that you may benefit from my reflections on the thesis and proofs of your work in our diurnal conferences. I can also extract facts and verify quotations, and organize your notes. I am certain there are other means by which I will be able to provide aid to you as well. You need only direct me."

"Mary—ah—I have not formed any design for you to assist me in writing the book."

"You have been so pressed between your work and our marriage, of course you have not had a proper opportunity to contemplate our relationship. You must have a little time, and I will not press you. But in the interval there must be tasks that I can perform."

"Yes—well—perhaps. I have draft chapters that have to be copied out in a fair hand."

"I write with great clarity and will undertake that duty most willingly. It will allow me to acquaint myself with the work you have done to this point. As to what I ought to read, if you will disclose on what texts you are relying I shall peruse them."

"How will you have the time to read all of these books and copy the chapters, and manage the household and fulfill your duties within the parish?"

"It does not take a great deal of time to direct a household if the servants are properly trained and instructed. I will speak to them tomorrow. As for the parish, I have no vocation to visit the elderly and infirm. There are surely others who can perform those services."

"Mary, the servants have all been with me for many years. I must ask you to tread very lightly in speaking to them. They will be offended if you question their competence."

"If they have long been here and given you satisfaction then there will be no necessity for me to supervise them. I shall be quite at liberty to join you at work."

"We will discuss this further in a few days. Perhaps today we may allow ourselves a holiday from our labours and celebrate our marriage?"

To this proposition Mary acquiesced and the newlywed couple turned their attention to the delicacies that had been laid out for the bridal feast.

Dr. Cramer's daughters had not attended their father's wedding, but soon hastened to pay their respects to—and examine—their new stepmother upon her arrival at their father's home. The daughters were handsome young women of seven-and-twenty and five-and-twenty, each with a family and busy household of her own. Mrs. Ridley, the elder, lived in Cambridge, and Mrs. Latimer, the younger, lived a few miles outside of town. They met in front of the Rectory to make the morning call, each lady emerging from her carriage.

"Do you think Father has taken leave of his senses?" inquired Mrs. Ridley.

"Naturally he misses Mama and is lonely," said Mrs. Latimer. "I think we are to blame for leaving him by himself too much. If we had come to see him more often, he would not have had to take this step."

"But Emma, how do you imagine we can care for our husbands and our children and our own households, and act in place of Mama as well? It is not possible."

"It would certainly be difficult," granted Mrs. Ridley. "But we could at least have guided his attention to a more suitable lady. I mean one closer to him in years. There is Mrs. Casaubon, who has been quite attentive to him since her husband died."

"Well, it is too late for Mrs. Casaubon or anyone else, he has chosen for himself. Are you ready to go in now?"

"Yes, pull the bell."

A servant appeared and welcomed them.

"Good morning, Nellie, I hope all is well with Father?" said Mrs. Ridley.

"Well enough," said Nellie. "You can put your minds at ease, Miss Emma and Miss Marianne. The new mistress is a far cry from your mother but she is a lady and gives no trouble, and the master is very fond of her."

"I am glad to hear it, but we would like to have a look at her for ourselves. We will wait for her in the breakfast room, Nellie, I hope you have a good fire in there? There is still a chill in the air."

Nellie assured them of the adequacy of the fire, and went to find her mistress.

Mary had been watching Dr. Cramer's daughters arrive from an upper window and came down immediately. The ladies curtsied politely to each other.

Mrs. Ridley and Mrs. Latimer looked at Mary and then at one another.

"My dear," said Mrs. Ridley returning her gaze to Mary, "I shall call you Mary and you must call me Emma and my sister Marianne. Father tells us that you are just one-and-twenty, is that correct?"

Mary gravely responded, "Surely you do not aver that the only matter of importance in conjugal matters is a female's age? Virtue must always be of greater importance. Then account must be taken of a woman's abilities, whether she is clever, and to what extent she has improved her mind by study. Dr. Cramer has greater interest in my accomplishments than my age, for we are both alike dedicated to erudition."

Mrs. Ridley and Mrs. Latimer looked at one another again. Mrs. Ridley's raised eyebrows repeated her earlier inquiry whether their father had taken leave of his senses. "But naturally," she said, "you will not neglect his physical well-being, Mary, as the mind cannot function without food and sleep and domestic order."

"Do not give yourselves concern, for his corporeal needs will be met. The servants are efficient at their tasks."

This did not quite satisfy Mrs. Ridley's concerns for her father, and she conceived that some gentle instruction was indicated.

"Dear Mama was so solicitous of him—she never thought of herself until she had first assured herself of his comfort and happiness. She made certain that the servants never disturbed him, but that they were always ready to do whatever he required on the slightest notice. Indeed, she herself was constantly watching to see if she could anticipate his wants. But, my dear Mary, our father is not a tyrant—his wants are really quite few and simple. He needs to be protected from distraction when he is working, and to have a good meal ready when he is hungry, and someone to listen to him when he wants to speak of his work. Often he would sit with Mama in the evening and take his tea and talk out some problem he was having with a book or a sermon. She would do her needlework and listen and nod. She always said it quite relaxed her after a long day just to hear him!"

"Dear Mama," echoed Mrs. Latimer with poignant affection. "We miss her so. She was a true example of a Christian wife and mother. She lived for her husband and children, and was very modest in her requests of others."

"I am collaborating with Dr. Cramer on his book," announced Mary.

"Are you, my dear Mary?" said Mrs. Ridley. "In what way?"

"I will assist him with his researches and writing. I will take down his notes and organize them, and look up references for him, and copy out his manuscript in a fair hand. I will serve as his amanuensis."

Mrs. Ridley and Mrs. Latimer exchanged yet another look. "Well, perhaps our father is ready for a little change in his habits," said Mrs. Latimer diplomatically. "But dear Mary, you must make sure to run the household so that he is kept contented; that must be your first care before you help with his work. You will do that, will you not?"

"Of course, the household must be ordered so that we may work undisturbed. I shall ensure the comprehension of all the servants."

"Once you have a child you may find it difficult to attend to your duties and assist our father as well," said Mrs. Ridley. Mary's countenance grew a little pale, and she lowered her eyes. "But once you have a child you may not have the same interest in notes and references! I am sure everything will work out for the best, dear Mary. We will be very happy and pleased with you as long as you take good care of our father, in whatever way suits him."

"Now," said Mrs. Latimer, "will you ring for refreshment or shall I do it?"

Recovering herself Mary said, "As I am mistress here, I shall do it, naturally."

Dr. Cramer's daughters were singularly mystified by their father's new wife but supposed that she would soon settle into her conjugal role and abandon her odd notions about assisting him to write books. Their father had been writing books for as long as they could recall, and it seemed to them a dull and laborious process. That a young wife should wish to engage in such an activity and spurn more agreeable domestic pursuits seemed remarkably peculiar.

Mrs. Ridley and Mrs. Latimer declined to interrupt their father's work to visit with him, but asked that Mary convey to him their love and best wishes. After the ladies had partaken of cake and fruit preserves they parted with civil professions of regard, and Mary's promise to wait upon her husband's daughters shortly.

Chapter Forty-Two

[June 1814, Cambridgeshire]

Newly wed husbands, being exceedingly sensible of their domestic comfort, are apt to wish to defer argument with their wives for the longest period possible. However Mary, ever a hard worker and eager to display her abilities, produced the fair copy of the manuscript chapters considerably more rapidly than her husband had anticipated.

"Dr. Cramer, here are the chapters inscribed in a fair hand. I am prepared to undertake the next task. And you have not yet informed me what books I am to read."

"Mary—really—I do not expect you to read my books about Tudor history and the religious crises. They are difficult and often tedious works."

"I do not object to that at all. In point of fact, I am quite accustomed to reading difficult works and making extracts from them."

"Mary, I think you fail to comprehend me. The proper role of a woman is not that of a scholar or a secretary, but of a wife and mother."

Mary fixed her eyes on her husband, and an uncomfortable silence arose between them, which after a moment she broke. "I am endeavouring to be a good *wife* to you, Dr. Cramer, by assisting you with your work. A virtuous wife works willingly and the heart of her husband safely trusts in her."

"Mary, the way in which you can be a good wife to me is to pour me my tea at breakfast, and sit with me in the evening, and supervise the servants and ensure that the household runs properly so that I am not disturbed. And it is time for you to take up your duties in the parish, as is expected of the Rector's wife."

She looked at him with incredulous astonishment. However she was mistress enough of herself to say, "Dr. Cramer, you cannot intend to assert that you do not wish my assistance."

"You did not misapprehend me, my dear."

"But my dear husband, any female can pour tea! You chose me for your wife because you admire my abilities as a scholar and wish me to be the companion of your labours."

Dr. Cramer gazed at Mary with an expression of mingled affection and pity. "Mary, my dearest, I chose you because you are a lovely young lady, womanly and warm, and interested in *me*—not in my work. But in any event you are not fitted to assist me. You do not have sufficient education even to enter a university, if you were a young man, and when I look for an assistant I look among those who have received a degree."

Mary was inexpressibly shocked. "Not fitted? But I have studied for years. I was the most accomplished young woman in the neighbourhood in Hertfordshire. And you—and you complimented me on my understanding."

"Your understanding of matters of the intellect is excellent for one of your sex, but it is irrelevant to your role as my wife."

"But Dr. Cramer, my role as your wife is to be your partner in cerebration and share your life—"

"Mary, you are a very important part of my life."

"I do not allude to drinking tea and sitting by the fire in the evening."

"I have no desire to share my intellectual existence with my wife. I have sufficient of it in my study the entire day."

"Previously you engaged in discourse with me about matters which were the subject of your cogitations—St. Paul, and Seneca, and Virgil. Why are we not to continue in a like manner?"

Dr. Cramer, being a cleric and a faithful husband of thirty years, had not had a ready supply of amorous discourse to see him through his courtship of Mary, and had therefore been forced to make use of what resources he could summon. Having won her and made her his wife, he had no further need to speak to her of love under the guise of philosophy and theology. "Because, my dear, I do not have the time to go on in such a way now that we are married. When I have an inclination to discuss my work with you, I will do so. But your duty is to run the household."

"But my pursuits heretofore have always been scholarly ones, not domestic."

"If you do not find your household and wifely duties sufficient, then your next duty is to work in the parish. We have parishioners who require visiting and comforting, and the poor are always in need of a basket of potatoes or onions. There is also work to be done in the church—cleaning the altar silver, arranging flowers, embroidering linen altar cloths and so on." An appalled expression suffused Mary's features. "You may also help in the parish school. You can teach needlework to the girls, or some other feminine art."

"I detest needlework," said Mary almost fiercely.

"Well then, a little music if you wish. Although they have no need of it in their station in life."

"I do not wish to teach feminine arts!" cried Mary. "I wish to share your interests, and converse with you, and offer my accomplishments in your service! If in your estimation my knowledge does not suffice, then you must instruct me. My comprehension is remarkable for its velocity."

"Mary, I am not a tutor. I have a great deal of work, and I cannot add to it teaching a young woman. And I do not wish you to be any better educated, I do not want to render you unfit to be my wife, and the mother of my children."

Mary turned her head away. Then she said in a low voice, "Will I ever be a mother to your children?"

"Mary!" said Dr. Cramer in amazement. "I did not think to hear you reproach me in such a way!" He gazed at her for a moment, and then moved toward his desk. "I must ask you to leave me now as I have much to do. We shall speak again of this in the evening, if you feel it necessary."

Mary was about to protest her dismissal, but turning her eyes to her husband she saw that he was very pale. She was immediately contrite for arguing with him. "Are you in discomfort?" she asked. "Do your legs pain you?"

"I am a little fatigued," said Dr. Cramer, sitting down carefully behind the desk.

"You scarcely slumbered last night, I know."

"I am sorry I disturbed you, my dear. I did not intend to wake you."

She went to him and knelt beside him, and looked up into his face. "I would rather keep vigil with you when you cannot find repose. Perhaps I could have palliated your distress by chafing your limbs."

"No, my dear, chafing them does not help."

"Should not the apothecary come and examine you?"

"I have already been examined by a physician in Cambridge."

"Were his ministrations ineffective?"

"He gave me a preparation to dull the pain, however I find it also dulls the senses and interferes with my work, so I prefer to endure the pain."

"Your daughters informed me, that you were habituated to walking several miles each day. Yet you ambulate rarely now. Perhaps taking more exercise would be beneficial?"

"Unfortunately, my dear, I find that exercise increases rather than reduces the discomfort. Mary, my dearest, leave me now and let me proceed with my work. I will see you when tea is served. In the meantime try to remember that you have taken a vow of obedience to me, and that both as your husband and one considerably your elder I must discern what is best for you. I am very well aware, that you desire to engage with me in learned pursuits, but you must accept that such a desire is not proper in a young wife. There are duties that you are expected to perform, and although they may not be to your taste you must nonetheless perform them. We are none of us our own masters in this world, you know," he said affectionately, and stroked her hair. "To submit to authority is a difficult lesson to learn, but St. Paul reminds us that the husband is the head of the wife, even as Christ is the head of the church. Rise up, now, dearest, and go about your own tasks."

Mary complied with his command, but she left her husband with feelings scarcely to be defined. She was troubled about his health, but far more was she shaken and angered by his assessment of her capabilities, and injured in her vanity. Astonishment filled her. Not well enough educated to assist him! She discredited this opinion entirely. In a perturbed state of mind she walked about the house, with thoughts that could rest on no one thing for more than a moment. It would inconceivable to her that Dr. Cramer considered her ignorant. Collecting herself as well as she could she enumerated her accomplishments. In the Latin language, the five declensions withheld no secrets from her, and she could conjugate even the most irregular verb into the farthest reaches of the pluperfect subjunctive. She could translate from the French. She had boxes of extracts in proof of her extensive reading. She could produce with greatest celerity an apt quotation, whether scholarly or moral, on a great variety of subjects. She understood thorough-bass perfectly and could play a passage of many bars.

She reflected deeply. Perhaps she had not sufficiently exhibited herself to her husband. Their courtship had been of short duration and they had naturally spoken more of his work and interests than of hers. He had simply not seen the full evidence of her intellectual pursuits and accomplishments, and once she had produced it his estimation of her abilities would of course be greatly altered and ameliorated.

The following morning therefore, after her husband had retired to his study, she knocked gently on the door and entered. Dr. Cramer looked up. "Is there something you wish to speak to me about, dearest?"

"No, my dear husband, I am seeking a book to read. Please do not let me disturb you."

"Which book is it you would like?"

"I thought perhaps an exegesis on St. John."

"Mary, if you are interested in St. John I believe you would do better to read his Gospel. All the spiritual food you require you may take directly from him. It will only confuse you to read any of the commentaries."

"I would not be confused. I have drawn much edification in the past from commentaries on the gospels."

"Mary dearest, I must ask you refrain from reading any of the exegetes. There is a Bible in our bedroom. If you wish it, we will read St. John together this evening."

"Then do you have any of Descartes' writings? I will not read biblical commentary if you desire me not to."

"Mary, there are no books in my library that are suitable for you to read. Dearest, I must ask that you respect my wishes and take up your own duties. I have arranged for a lady of the parish, Mrs. Vincy, to call upon you this morning and acquaint you with what it is requisite for you to know. Therefore you may go and prepare yourself to receive a visitor."

"But Dr. Cramer, if only you will permit me to display to you—"

"Mary, if you please. This discussion confers no benefit on either of us. You may tell me what you have learned from Mrs. Vincy when we take our tea. And now I must have the room to myself for I am in the midst of writing a rather difficult sermon."

Mary could not oppose such a direct command, and she withdrew. But her vanity told her that the battle was not yet lost. She could not have access to her husband's library to show him her abilities, but she had a library of her own. That day, following the visit from Mrs. Vincy and a tour of the parish church and visits to some of the poor and afflicted who lived within easy walking distance of the Rectory, she wrote to Mrs. Hill, the housekeeper at Longbourn, and asked her to pack up all of her books and notes and send them to her. Then she awaited their arrival.

When the boxes were delivered she made a show of unpacking them, that Dr. Cramer could not fail to notice. "I see that you have received some materials from your father's house."

"Yes, my books and notes. I must have books, and you do not wish me to take them from your library."

"I could forbid you to read them, Mary, for I am greatly concerned what effect they have had and will have on your mind. But I will not take that step, I will only ask you to consider my wishes as your husband, with which I believe you are now well acquainted. And I must insist that you carry out your duties each day before you turn to the books. They must not take precedence over your domestic and parochial work."

Mary was silent.

"Dearest, do you understand that I am speaking to you out of love and not as you may suppose out of petty-mindedness? Your fulfillment does not lie in the dry pages of those volumes. If you will make a true effort to obey me because I know what is best for you, you will come to understand my meaning. Will you make that effort, my dear?"

"You are my husband and I must keep my vow of obedience to you."

"Strive to do so with a glad heart, dear Mary. Obedience given willingly is much more susceptible of reward."

"I will make the endeavour," said Mary, attempting to sound cheerful. But she was overcome with despondency and went away to her room, where with earnest self-pity she wondered whether anyone would ever again be impressed by the rapidity of her understanding or the solidity of her reflections; or what admiration and praise she could hope to purchase by directing servants in their cleaning and cooking, or visiting the poor.

Chapter Forty-Three

[June 1814, Pemberley, Longbourn and Castle Tyrconnell]

"What is your opinion?" asked Elizabeth. She and Kitty were standing in the portrait gallery at Pemberley, examining a painting of a lovely young woman clad in a low-necked white silk dress, with pearls around her neck and in her ears. The artist had exactly caught the colour and shape of the subject's fine dark eyes, and their expresssion.

"You look very nice," said Kitty. "Is Darcy pleased with it?"

"Yes, very pleased. I conjecture that I am no longer here on approval, and liable to be turned away for unbecoming behaviour."

"I cannot imagine Darcy ever turning you away."

"I was thinking of Lady Catherine, I suppose."

"She is going to be very cross when Fitzwilliam and I do not appear at Rosings for our wedding. But Elizabeth, I really could not do it, even for the sake of peace within the family. James agrees."

"Shall you still be presented at Court?"

"I do not think I can escape it. James says it is proper and that I must go."

The wedding accordingly took place at Pemberley and the Honourable Mr. and Mrs. Fitzwilliam departed to Ireland for their wedding tour. At Longbourn Mrs. Bennet entertained her neighbours with the greatest satisfaction.

"Lady Lucas, have you seen The Times or the Courier? Kitty's wedding you know. I have the announcement here. 'On 21st June, at Pemberley House, Derby, The Honourable James Fitzwilliam, second son of the Earl of Tyrconnell, to Miss Catherine Bennet, daughter of J. Bennet, Esq. of Longbourn House, Herts.' And she is to be presented at Court. I do not recollect if you take the Court Circular? I will lend you mine when the announcement is made. They have gone to Ireland just now to visit the Earl.

At Castle Tyrconnell you know." Mrs. Bennet seemed incapable of fatigue when embarked upon such an animating subject, and Lady Lucas was soon yawning and thinking with regret of time past when everyone had considered the Bennets the unluckiest family in the world because of Lydia's elopement, and was at length even driven by irritability to begin refining her calculations how many years longer Mr. Bennet was likely to live and keep her daughter Charlotte out of Longbourn. "I said, did I not, that the girls were sure to be thrown into the way of other rich men once Jane and Elizabeth married rich," finished Mrs. Bennet with complacency.

"He is a second son," said Lady Lucas waspishly. "He cannot be so very rich."

"Oh, fiddlestick. These prosperous men cry poor when they do not own the moon. Kitty will do very well with him I am sure."

The Fitzwilliams made the sea crossing to Kingstown near Dublin and set out by carriage for Castle Tyrconnell. The Castle, which was approached through a large park with fine trees, was a square building erected around a medieval hall, with crenellated towers at the corners, and had once been surrounded by a moat that was now a verdant ditch. The Earl warmly received his son and new daughter-in-law in the Oak Room, and was delighted with Kitty when she expressed a disinclination to retire to her chamber to repose after the fatigue of the journey, preferring to make an immediate visit to the stables. He was even more delighted with her when not only did she admire a chestnut stallion that had done very well at Bellewstown, and for whom the Earl had high hopes at the Curragh,* but demonstrated a sound knowledge of the line of the Darley Arabian in general and of the stallion's great-grandsire Eclipse.** "Eclipse first, the rest nowhere,"*** cried the Earl, enchanted. His own wife the Countess had taken no interest in horses, beyond expecting her coach-and-four to look elegant.

The visit passed very pleasantly, which must have vexed Viscount Fitzwilliam and Lady Catherine had they known. And Georgiana would have been horrified had she learned that Kitty had engaged Fitzwilliam in an *impromptu* steeplechase. One morning when they were riding out, Kitty inquired, looking into the distance, how far a steeple was, whose upper portion was visible above a rise in the land. Fitzwilliam replied that it was about four miles away, and Kitty then gave it as her opinion that she could

* Bellewstown (County Meath) and the Curragh (County Kildare) were famous racetracks. –Ed.

** Eclipse, 1764-1789, named for the eclipse of the sun that occurred at the time he was foaled. He could cover four miles in six minutes and was never defeated in a race. Today almost ninety per cent of thoroughbreds are descended from him. All thoroughbreds are descended from one of three horses brought into Europe in the 17th or 18th century: the Byerley Turk, the Darley Arabian, and the Godolphin Arabian –Ed.

*** A remark made by Denis O'Kelly (later Eclipse's owner) after Eclipse's first race, in 1769, at Epsom. –Ed.

reach it before he. When Fitzwilliam pronounced himself extremely dubious of her claim, she immediately gathered up her reins and kicked her horse into a gallop, and arrived, indeed, at the church two lengths ahead of her husband. Fitzwilliam complained indignantly that since she rode some four stone lighter than he, and had enjoyed an advantage of at least three lengths at the commencement of the race, he in fact had won it. Kitty remained quite untroubled, however.

After a fortnight they parted from the Earl with expressions of great mutual affection, leaving him to write belated replies to the agitated correspondence from his sister and son demanding that he in no way distinguish Kitty upon her marriage by receiving her into the Castle.

Chapter Forty-Four

[July 1814, Ulverston]

Elizabeth's much anticipated trip to the Lakes had been prodigiously delayed, in the first year by Mr. Gardiner's business concerns, and in the second by Elizabeth's situation. But it finally was undertaken, and the Darcys and the Gardiners set off from Pemberley in quest of novelty and pleasure, their satisfaction assured at least in part by the companions' suitableness, comprehending affection and intelligence, good health, cheerfulness to enhance every pleasure, and temper to bear every inconvenience. Two weeks' rambling brought them nearly to the end of their tour and to the town of Ulverston.

"I hope I have learned my lesson," said Elizabeth to Mrs. Gardiner as they sat in the parlour of their inn in the evening, returning to a subject that had been frequently canvassed among the travellers, that is, the marriage of Colonel Fitzwilliam and Kitty. "I thought I was displaying such a quantity of good sense and reason when I told Kitty that she must have nothing to do with Fitzwilliam, and instead I was acting exactly like Lady Catherine when she came to Longbourn and forbade me to marry Darcy."

"I must apply for my share of the blame," said Mrs. Gardiner, "for I thought exactly the same when I warned you last year that they were growing too close."

"I at any rate was fortunate that Lady Catherine's resentment was too great for her to communicate with me after Darcy told her of our engagement. She is quite persecuting Kitty with advice about how to behave in her new rank. Kitty threatens to run away if she receives another letter or if Lady Catherine calls upon her again. I think she may never recover from Lady Catherine's officious role in her presentation at Court."

"There is little you or anyone can do to intervene," remarked Mrs. Gardiner, who even though she had never had the honour of an introduction to Lady Catherine was perfectly acquainted with her character.

"No, indeed. But in any event, I must now do something that may have a useful effect, which is to write a letter to Jane. If I defer writing it any longer we will be back at Pemberley before she receives it."

Bradyll's Arms, Ulverston*
July –, 1814

Dearest Jane,
I would have written before, as I ought to have done, with minutest particulars of our tour; but we have been moving about too much to devote the time to a letter that you deserve. I hardly know where to begin to tell you about this country. I cannot relate all in this letter or I should be writing it for several days, but I will give you my impressions—and rest assured that, when I next see you I will take you captive and show you on a map all the places we have been with a very detailed description of what we observed in each.

The weather is naturally much on a traveller's mind, and we had heard before we set out that twice as much rain falls here as in the rest of England! However by happy chance there have been very few days when the landscape was obscured by drizzle. Several times there has been a good strong rain, but it has always been followed by clear weather, with the added charm that afterwards the brooks sing loudly and the waterfalls roar. Other days we have watched showers darting from hill to hill, the sky brightening and darkening from moment to moment, and have only come under the dampening influence ourselves for a short time. On certain mornings there have been mists lying by turns upon the lakes and on the mountain heights, softening the summits, but on bright days the peaks have been brushed by clouds, sometimes lingering, sometimes rushing out of sight. (One day the mist lay also on the road, so that one could not see ten feet ahead, and we were obliged to put off our departure for two or three hours until it lifted; and then the sky was bright.) Two or three evenings there has been a sunset such as I have never seen before, with clouds behind the western ridges turned blazing red or yellow. The light is ever changing, brightness and shadow constantly playing over the features of the landscape and altering them by the minute. One could remain

* Elizabeth's letter undoubtedly owes a debt to William Wordsworth's *A Guide Through the District of the Lakes,* first published in 1810, a copy of which she quite likely took with her on her tour. –Ed.

stationary and watch the landscape for an hour or two together, and almost feel that one had been journeying the whole time!

The mountains are many and no two are alike, standing in ranks like the waves of the sea, some towering, others floating below them. Their colours are varied, for although they are generally rich and green, in some places the grey rock is laid bare, especially on the heights. The sides of many mountains are scarred by ravines from the torrents of water that flow down from the rains, from a distance forming letters to be read by the passing traveller, V and W and Y in particular. Some mountainsides are adorned by trees, but they are intermixed with fields delineated by stone walls, so that there is a complex beauty of wildness and domestication.

The vallies are long and winding, with spacious floors decorated by hills and large rocks arising like islands, as well as by the low stone walls that mark the fields. Villages cling to these islands, or climb up the sides of the mountains, but the natural beauty of a valley is often enhanced by the presence of a single white cottage lying on its verdant bosom. ("A quiet treeless nook, with two green fields,/a liquid pool that glitters in the sun,/And one bare Dwelling; one Abode, no more!")

As you can imagine, our interest in houses was most greatly aroused by Dove Cottage. Mr. Wordsworth* no longer lives there, for he and his family have removed to a larger house nearby, but it is let to a man named Quincey** (a friend of Mr. Wordsworth and a writer of some kind), and he very civilly allowed us to look through it. It is so small, that I can scarcely conjecture how its many inhabitants dwelt there! Mr. Wordsworth and his sister and his wife—and her sister as well—and three children! Upstairs is the room that Mr. Wordsworth used as his study, with a view over meadows to Lake Grasmere. I wonder if that is the meadow where the daffodils danced along the lake, ten thousand in the breeze? How I long to be here in spring to find out! I know that once I had seen them for myself they would "flash upon my inner eye"; then surely I would declare with the poet that, "my heart with pleasure fills/and dances with the daffodils."

The lakes flow through the vallies, and are mirrors to the sky and hills when not agitated by the wind or currents, reflecting the

---

* William Wordsworth, 1770-1850, the great Romantic poet, lived most of his life in the Lake District, and resided at Dove Cottage from 1799 to 1808. At the time of Elizabeth's visit, Wordworth and his family were living at Mount Rydal, a few miles to the south. –Ed.

** Thomas de Quincey, 1785 to 1859, English author and poet. His acquaintance with William Wordsworth led him to settle at Dove Cottage for a number of years from 1809. –Ed.

mountains and the clouds, and taking part in the play of changing light. At the outlet of a lake one may see a stream noisily escaping from the stillness among the rocks that have fallen from the precipices. Many brooks flow into the lakes; and also waterfalls, which the local people called "forces"—some slender and ribbon-like, others very grand, in particular Aira Force on Ullswater, where we stood a long time at the bottom looking up towards the arched bridge that crosses high over its top. At Grasmere the innkeeper had a boat, and we went out on the water there, which as in the other lakes, was of such crystal clarity that looking down into the depths we felt suspended in air rather than gliding on water! Another kind of small lake called a tarn is found on the mountains, and occasionally in the vallies. Near Grasmere we visited such a one, Loughrigg Tarn, surrounded by green meadows and rocky woods, with reeds and water lilies along its margins, and a few cottages that are reflected on its face. The mountain tarns are difficult to reach, but we are told they often lie in a barren place at the foot of a steep mountainside with huge broken rocks scattered around, appearing black and forbidding when in shadow. There is an affecting story about a tarn deep within the Helvellyn range, a desolate place, where a young traveller perished by falling while attempting to cross westwards. His remains were found only because his faithful dog did not leave him, lingering there with his body for some three months.

There are fewer traces of man than one might expect. The Druids were here of old, and have left a few circles of stones. We walked about one outside Keswick called Castlerigg, and it was an excessively strange sight! We came there late in the day and the stones cast exceedingly eerie shadows. No one knows what the stones' purpose was, although something to do with their rites of worship is supposed, and after walking around and between the stones for half an hour we are unable to shed any light on the matter either. Darcy has seen Stonehenge outside Salisbury and says this is nothing in comparison, although the setting here is more dramatic. The Romans were here also, and we examined their traces at Hard Knott Pass where they had a camp. How lonely the soldiers must have felt up here, so far from home. Furness Abbey forms quite a contrast to the Druid circle and Roman fort, for it lies in magnificent ruins, situated in a dell that hides it from the surrounding countryside, with graceful windows and arches opening into the empty air, and great blocks of stone lying on the green lawn like tombstones. There are stories of ghosts who haunt the site, some of them quite ordinary-sounding spirits like the White Lady who walks there waiting for her lover, and the headless monk on horseback; however the one that we all agreed was worthy of the Abbey is the murdered monk who is seen leaning upon a banister, attempting to drag himself up the shattered staircase—a picture that, like the murdered Abbey itself, rests in one's mind.

You must recollect how exceedingly disappointed I was when the plan for a tour of the Lakes with our aunt and uncle Gardiner was abandoned two years ago; however the delay in undertaking it has merely served to increase my pleasure, for now I am able to share my delight at seeing them with Darcy as well as with our aunt and uncle. When we return to the Lakes, you and Bingley must come with us.

Your affectionate sister,
E. Darcy

Chapter Forty-Five

[July 1814, Clifford Priory]

The Wickhams' manner of living became greatly unsettled after Wickham resigned his commission upon the restoration of peace. They continually moved from place to place in quest of a cheap situation, for Wickham's small income, under the direction of two people who were both extravagant in their present wants and heedless of the future, was quite insufficient to support them. Lydia was occasionally a visitor at Pemberley, when her husband was gone to enjoy himself in London or Bath (for Darcy would never receive *him* at Pemberley), and whenever they changed their quarters Lydia was sure to apply to either Elizabeth or Jane for assistance in discharging their bills, in terms such as these: "I do not mind that we are moving from our present lodgings for our landlady has been horrid unpleasant to me and the fireplaces did not draw properly, and we have found new lodgings that are much better. However we have a few bills that must be paid before we go, and as we are a little short of money I hope you will think of us. It is a great comfort that you are so rich. Twenty pounds should be enough." Elizabeth shook her head over such letters, and replied enclosing small sums of money, that she had collected through economy in her own private expenses.

The Wickhams frequently stayed with the Bingleys, as a saving measure, for so long that Bingley's good humour was almost overcome. Even Jane, who was ordinarily blind to the follies of others, and whose character it was to say nothing of the bad in anyone but to take the good and make it better, was distressed by their conduct; for as time passed their civility in address as well as their affection for each other seemed to diminish.

"Wickham, do you not think that Lieutenant Bertram is handsome?" said Lydia as they took tea in the afternoon during a summer visit at Clifford Priory.

"Yes, a veritable Apollo."

"*I* think he is very good looking. So does Mrs. Marsh, for we were talking about him outside the circulating library one day, and who should come around the corner but him, together with Dean and Winter. She turned red as a beet, for she was afraid he might have heard us. How I laughed at her! I thought it would have been good fun if he *had* heard what we were saying, for then it might have been him who turned red. What about Captain Osborne?"

"What about him?"

"Do you think he is handsome?"

"Lydia, my love, I fear that I do not go about all day looking at other men to see if they are handsome."

"No, you go about looking at women to see if they are pretty."

"You will certainly have better luck asking me if a woman is pretty than if a man is handsome."

"I do not think that the maid at the inn is pretty at all."

"Do you not? Then do not look at her if she doesn't please you."

Jane listened to their exchange with astonishment and concern, and when left alone with Bingley said to him, "I do not wish to hasten to censure anyone, but I would that Lydia and Wickham had more self-command, for they can have no idea of the pain they give me by speaking in such a way. I have never seen such manners. I am glad, at least, that my family are not witness to this display."

"Nay, their conduct deserves to be censured, for they are both thoughtless and indiscreet."

Jane then immediately wished to defend them, supposing that there were extenuating circumstances for their behaviour, presently unknown to the Bingleys, and she pleaded for allowances.

"I would not be so forgiving as you, for a kingdom," replied Bingley. "I wish for their credit and our benefit they would be less disagreeable, but I fear their misery is secured, as will be ours if they remain here much longer."

"We must be willing to hope for the best," she urged. Despite her words, however, she felt a little fearful of her sister's happiness. Her fear was only increased by the young couple's conversation at breakfast a few days later.

"Wickham, you must have come to bed very late last night, and got up very early, for I did not hear you come or go," said Lydia sweetly. "How fatigued you must be this morning! To look at the bed, one would think you were hardly in it at all."

"I slept in the dressing room, I did not wish to disturb you, my dearest Lydia."

"And what kept you up so late? Were you playing billiards with Bingley all that time?"

Bingley looked a little uncomfortable, but Wickham was perfectly at his ease. "We played a game or two."

"And then perhaps you took a little walk outside and forgot the time?"

"I might have done."

"Perhaps you walked as far as the village?"

"Dearest Lydia, I really do not recall where I walked."

"I wonder if the maid at the inn might recall where you walked."

"Lydia!" said Jane in admonition.

"Ah Jane, do you think the servants do not know already? I daresay they talk about it all the time in the servants' hall." But she did not pursue the conversation with Wickham further in Jane's hearing.

"One does not know what to believe," said Jane to Bingley when Lydia, Wickham and the servants had all withdrawn from the breakfast room. "I cannot think so ill of him as Lydia suggests. I most sincerely desire their happiness, and I comfort myself that he would not have married her if he had not a real regard for her."

"We must give them a hint to leave," said Bingley with a firm voice.

"But they are our brother and sister!"

"They have been here for a fortnight, and they were here for nigh on a month at Easter, and they came to us in London for a se'nnight in the winter. They come because they live in lodgings too small for them, and because we keep a good cook at no expense to them."

"Bingley, we cannot ask them to go!"

He did not press the point, and they sat silent for a few moments. At length Jane sighed and said, "Happy shall I be, when their visit is over!"

Chapter Forty-Six

[September 1814, Pemberley]

Sir Hugh Mallinger being neither a young man nor a well one, his death excited no surprise. Sir Henry Mallinger and the new Lady Mallinger entered their elevated rank with composure, and their serene acceptance of condolences on Sir Hugh's passing was much admired by the fashionable world. When the couple's period of full mourning (which Sir Henry, who found such customs tedious, insisted be no longer than four weeks, to the scandal of the dowager Lady Mallinger) ended, the Darcys invited Sir Henry and Lady Mallinger, together with Mr. and Mrs. Bingley and Mr. and Mrs. Hurst to Pemberley for a week's visit.

The journey down from London had by its latter stages produced in Lady Mallinger a violent headache and an uncertain temper consequent upon it. When the Mallingers' carriage drove up to the door of Pemberley, Elizabeth was just come there, returning from a walk. She looked remarkably well, for the exercise had given brilliancy to her complexion and brightened her fine dark eyes. She greeted the Mallingers civilly, and Sir Henry bowed over her hand. Lady Mallinger said, "Mrs. Eliza Darcy, I see that you are still an excellent walker! I shall never forget your appearance when you came to Netherfield that day to visit Jane. I believe your petticoat was six inches deep in mud."

"Very likely," laughed Elizabeth, "I remember that it had been exceedingly wet, and my father wanted the horses on the farm so I could not have the carriage."

"It must have been three or four miles, and you were quite alone. I recall commenting to Darcy and Louisa that it showed a most country-town indifference to respectability."

"I would have walked much farther to see Jane, and in deeper mud. Come in, and we shall find Darcy."

Lady Mallinger soon discovered that her headache required her to retire to her room, where Mrs. Hurst attended her when she and Mr. Hurst arrived at Pemberley a few hours later. Lady Mallinger was not equal to much conversation and certainly was not well enough to rise from her bed. Mrs. Hurst remained with her until five o'clock, and then left to dress for dinner. On joining the Darcys and the other guests Mrs. Hurst assured them that her sister was not seriously ill. Sir Henry remarked that it was a bore to have a headache, and evidently felt that he had discharged his duty towards his wife by asking after her. Mr. Hurst said nothing, for his thoughts were entirely on his dinner. Bingley was uncomfortable about her, but it was left to Elizabeth and Jane to wait on Lady Mallinger, and to bring her a draught prepared by the housekeeper Mrs. Reynolds.

Mrs. Hurst, with renewed tenderness, returned to her sister's room after dinner to wait until the gentlemen removed from the table and she was summoned to coffee. "How long do you intend remaining shut up in this room, Caroline?" she asked impatiently. As Lady Mallinger was too ill to reply other than by a look of irritation, she continued, "It is insupportable to pass an evening in such society without you. The insipidity! I scarcely recognize Darcy since his marriage. Not a stricture on anyone! And Sir Henry is quite engrossed by Mrs. Eliza and Jane. I recommend that your headache improve directly." However after supper Mrs. Hurst was tolerably able to solace her ill humour by duets with Georgiana.

The following day, the gentlemen being out shooting and Lady Mallinger able to talk a little, Mrs. Hurst did not quit her sister's room, and Elizabeth, Georgiana or Jane joined her there from time to time to see to the sick lady's needs. Lady Mallinger continued to mend through the day and was so much recovered by the evening that she made one of the party in the drawing room after dinner. Sir Henry showed her the correct amount of solicitude, and then departed with Mr. Hurst to play billiards. Mr. Hurst would have preferred cards, but no tables had been placed out and his petition for a game of loo was rejected by common accord. Sir Henry found the drawing room too wearisome to permit Mr. Hurst to stretch out on a sofa and sleep, as he would otherwise have done.

Lady Mallinger was welcomed, however, by Darcy and Elizabeth with expressions of concern, and settled by them near the fire where she should be guarded from any chill, and Darcy inquired if she would like a book to read. As a book was rarely her first choice of entertainment, and as she did not wish to be left alone to read while the others engaged in conversation, she greeted the suggestion with enthusiasm.

"How I delight in the Pemberley library!" she cried. "It must be one of the finest in the country. You are always buying books."

"I do not neglect the family library, certainly."

"I know it has been the work of many generations. Charles, you must begin your own library at Clifford immediately."

"I shall, once I have dealt with some trifling issues of crumbling brickwork and mold. I told you, Caroline, that I was more likely to get Pemberley by purchase than by imitation."

"Pemberley is Pemberley only through constant maintenance," said Darcy.

"I declare, I sometimes long to be a tenant at Netherfield again, for the owner had to maintain the property, and I was idle."

"And it was a convenient distance from Meryton, as well as from London," said Lady Mallinger. "You might have purchased it, Charles."

"Yes," said Mrs. Hurst laughing merrily, "and you would have had an excellent attorney at hand to assist with the purchase." These remarks were as close as Bingley's sisters dared come at the moment to offensive allusions to Elizabeth's and Jane's vulgar relations.

Bingley had frequently heard his sisters ridicule Jane's family and immediately sought to avert further witticisms on their part. To turn the conversation he remarked that the last time they had all been together at Netherfield was three years ago. "It is amazing to me, that we should meet again now, with Jane and I, and Darcy and Elizabeth wed."

"It is an oddity, to be sure," said Mrs. Hurst drily. "I was far from expecting such an abundance of domestic felicity to arise from the occasion."

Bingley looked at Jane. "We are very happy, Louisa, I assure you, and I believe that Darcy and Elizabeth are also, although Darcy may speak for himself. I wish with all my heart that you and Caroline are as happy in matrimony as we."

"I am quite happy, when I have a cook who can make a ragout, and a party large enough to make up a card table."

"That will not do. You speak of *Hurst's* felicity," cried Bingley. "What of your own?"

"My felicity must depend upon his, for upon my word, I can have no peace if Mr. Hurst has eaten a bad dinner."

"You speak in jest, Louisa, but I am asking seriously."

"Oh!" said Mrs. Hurst. "For happiness I must look to my milliner and my jeweler. What a peculiar notion, that I should look to my husband!"

"Tell me if this is how all wives think, Jane? Am I second to your milliner in your affections?"

"Bingley, you know you are not," said Jane with a smile of sweet complacency, for theirs was a marriage of true affection, with all the attendant contentment which such a marriage could bestow. "And Louisa *is* speaking only in jest. A woman would not marry an husband if she had not a real regard for him, and if she did not anticipate compatibility of temper and kindness."

Lady Mallinger responded impatiently, "A woman *must* marry, however uncertain of providing happiness marriage may be. For the many it is the only means of preservation from want, and for the fortunate few it is the procuration of a suitable rank in society, or the amelioration of the one she has; for a woman cannot acquire greater importance in the world except through marriage—just as she may lose her existing position through marriage to one beneath her station. In these circumstances how can every woman expect to find what you call happiness in marriage?"

Jane would never willingly have believed in such a surfeit of discontent as Lady Mallinger was proposing and she instantly said with great concern, "Surely you do not suppose, Caroline, that there are many women who are unhappy with their husbands?"

Lady Mallinger had never met with anybody who was so possessed by naivety as her brother's wife, and she directed her eyes towards Mrs. Hurst with an expressive look of contempt, but did not answer.

"Jane," cried Elizabeth, "you are too ready to overlook the follies of others. Think of Charlotte Collins. You cannot believe that there was compatibility of temper there! Charlotte married with the sole object of gaining through her husband an establishment."

"I do not see the folly in Charlotte's choice that you do. It was a good match and she seems perfectly happy with Mr. Collins, and he with her."

"She takes care that he should be. Yet you cannot conjecture that *her* happiness arises out of Mr. Collins' character. If she is happy, her happiness lies in her child, her house and her poultry."

"And what of you, Mrs. Eliza?" asked Lady Mallinger with a slight sneer. "*Your* happiness must have been increased to an infinite extent by the possession of a great house with many servants, and fine carriages and elegant muslins and silks, for you had none of these things previous to your alliance with Darcy."

"I was quite unaware of the deprivation that I was suffering," laughed Elizabeth, caring not at all for Lady Mallinger's scorn. "But I would not have taken Darcy, for all the material advantages he offered, if I had not loved him."

"That is easily said, once the desirable event has taken place."

"Elizabeth is speaking the truth," said Darcy. "I am quite certain, for I gave it a trial. She did not love me when I first asked her, and she rejected my suit in the strongest terms."

Wishing to end the discourse between Elizabeth and Lady Mallinger, he then applied to the ladies for the indulgence of some music. Mrs. Hurst too had wearied of the conversation, and she moved with alacrity to the piano. She was succeeded at the instrument by Georgiana, and then by Elizabeth.

As they listened to Elizabeth play, Lady Mallinger said to Darcy in a low voice, "I recollect that you and I once spoke of that which makes a woman accomplished. You comprehended a great deal in your idea; you believed that an accomplished woman must have a thorough knowledge of music, singing, dancing, drawing, and the modern languages, and a mind improved by reading, as well a superior elegance in her air and address."

"I recall that discussion."

"You claimed not to know more than half-a-dozen really accomplished women in the whole range of your acquaintance."

"That is very likely still true, for the word accomplished is applied to many a woman who does not deserve it."

"I have heard you say that you consider Eliza one of the handsomest women of your acquaintance," she continued. "Is she also one of the half-a-dozen accomplished women?"

Darcy fixed his eyes on Lady Mallinger and smiled slightly. "The recollection of my manners and expressions at the time our discussion occurred is painful to me. I was conceited and overbearing, and thought meanly of all outside my circle. But a little time thereafter I learned that my pretensions were insufficient to please a woman worthy of being pleased; and now experience has taught me that the happiness of a man with a woman is not dependent at all on her accomplishments. I know very well, in the present instance, that Elizabeth does not play with the greatest of skill, in comparison to my sister or yours; yet I listen to her with greater pleasure."

Lady Mallinger was disconcerted by this reply, and made no rejoinder. Fortunately for the comfort of the party she regained her civility in direct proportion to her recovered health, and though she remained somewhat caustic of temper she made no further comments on Elizabeth—to anyone other than Mrs. Hurst—for the remainder of the visit. Yet as the Darcys saw Sir Henry and Lady Mallinger into their coach at week's end, Elizabeth, reflecting on the Mallingers' conduct towards each other and Lady Mallinger's remarks about conjugal happiness, wondered whether importance in the world may sometimes be purchased too dearly.

Chapter Forty-Seven

[September 1814, Pemberley]

Dr. Cramer was puzzled and disturbed by the alteration in his wife's demeanour soon after their marriage. As instructed she carried out her household duties, visited the poor and gathered flowers for the church altar, but with such an air of dejection that he scarcely recognized in her the young woman he had wed. In his solicitude for her, he conferred with his elder daughter, who gave it as her opinion that Mary would recover her spirits once she had a child. As he did not find this to be advice of great practical application, he determined to write privately to Mary's family, after some consideration settling upon Mrs. Bingley rather than Mr. or Mrs. Bennet as the person to whom he ought most properly to address himself. Jane immediately consulted with Elizabeth and it was agreed between them that Mary should be invited to Pemberley, where the liveliness of the household, and the presence of other guests, might go some way towards relieving her despondency.

When Mary received Elizabeth's letter of invitation, to her husband she professed herself unwilling to undertake the fatigue of a journey to Derbyshire. Nevertheless at his insistence she went. Elizabeth on receiving her was amazed by the change in her sister, but trusted (having no other idea) that different scenery and society might raise her low spirits. The Darcys were already entertaining a number of visitors, chiefly gentlemen of political connection, and neither Elizabeth nor Georgiana had much leisure to devote herself to Mary, but they made such efforts as they could to see that she had all requisite comforts. To Elizabeth's astonishment, Mary displayed no interest in Pemberley's extensive library, nor, having been introduced to Will, did she wish to return to the nursery a second time. When Mr. Wilberforce arrived for a short stay with his wife and his secretary Adam Kendall, Elizabeth seized somewhat desperately on Kendall, recalling that Mary had met him in London and shown an interest in his exploits involving horses and carters. Kendall soon found himself separated from his employer and carried off by Elizabeth to the far end of the drawing room where Mary was seated, at a little distance from some ladies who were engaged in lively conversation.

"I believe you have met my sister before, prior to her marriage. She is now Mrs. Thomas Cramer."

"How do you do, Mrs. Cramer, I am glad to see you again," said Kendall politely. He thought he remembered her as a rather spirited girl, but this young woman was pale and drooping like a flower that has been picked and then carelessly left in a dry jar.

Mary nodded to him indifferently. The evening they had met, which had made such an impression on her at the time, seemed remote.

Elizabeth's hope that Mary and Kendall would engage in discussion was disappointed, for Mary showed no desire to speak to him, nor he to make the heroic effort to converse with one who clearly preferred silence and solitude. Shortly after Elizabeth left him, he made his way back to Mr. Wilberforce and pursuits more congenial.

Yet every so often Kendall's eyes would turn to Mary. She rebuffed all efforts of the other ladies at conversation with her, and took no tea or coffee. She reminded him of something, and at last he placed it—a horse that has been ridden too hard, and stands exhausted and trembling in its stall, unable to eat or drink. His heart, attuned to the suffering of animals, began to be touched by Mary's obvious misery. If she had been an animal his thought would have been to bring her water. Though it was not at all in character for him to approach a young woman, he was at last drawn by imperceptible degrees towards Mary until he was standing beside her again.

"Mrs. Cramer," he said to her, as gently as he would speak to a creature in distress, "may I bring you a cup of tea? I think you have taken nothing this evening."

"No thank you," she said, without looking up. Kendall took a chair and placed it near Mary, and he began to speak to her quietly. "I can see you are not happy."

"I am well, thank you."

"Nay, I can see that you are not. Is there something that I may do to ease your spirit?"

Almost in spite of herself Mary replied. "No, I do not think so. I do not think anyone can. I have been mistaken about my—about someone—something, and I must learn to live with my error."

"Sometimes a mistake may be corrected."

"This one is not capable of correction. But it is so hard!" she added almost with a sob. "I did not do it out of any wrong intention. I only wanted to be useful."

"No, there is no wrong motive in wanting to be useful," agreed Kendall. "All hands are needed to do God's work."

After a moment, Mary asked without looking at him, "Is that what you and Mr. Wilberforce believe you are doing?"

"We, and Mr. Martin, and Reverend Broome and Reverend Bonner, and many others, both men and women. The evil of slavery is engaging Mr. Wilberforce much at present, but he has many interests, including shielding cattle and other domestic animals from abuse, which is a particular concern of mine. There are those of us who are working toward the passage of a law that would protect animals from overwork, beatings and neglect. We are often ridiculed, but I believe that the day will come soon when we will prevail and such a law will be passed."

Mary turned her eyes upon Kendall. "Why are you ridiculed?"

"Why indeed? What is ridiculous about thinking and saying that bull-baiting is a barbarous pastime? Or protesting the condition of post-horses, who suffer grievously from the over-loading of coaches with excess passengers, suffer even to death itself by the outrageous excess of labour they must perform merely so that a traveller not be disobliged—or rather, that the innkeeper not lose custom to another establishment by turning travellers away? Or condemning those who buy up horses past their strength from age or disease and working them until they sink and die under their loads, or those who buy them for slaughter but do not kill them at once but rather leave them to starve to death? I need not go on, I am sure you have seen an ass laden beyond its strength and whipped and kicked on its way, or an ox beaten until it is striped in blood. There is nothing ridiculous in wanting to show mercy to these beasts."

"Blessed are the merciful, for they shall obtain mercy," said Mary slowly.

"Man shows so little mercy who needs so much," responded Kendall with a smile. "William Cowper. Have you read 'The Task'?"

"No."

"You must. Cowper speaks far more eloquently than can I on this subject."

For the first time in many weeks, Mary felt a stirring of interest, and a design began to form in her mind. "You told me when we met in London that you had prevented a carter from beating a horse. Is that the nature of the work that you do always?"

"Each of us follows his own conscience in acting, but it is not uncommon for any one of us to intervene to protect a horse, or an ox, a dog, or even a cat. But that is not our chief undertaking. We are constantly talking to men inside and outside government in order to promote passage of new laws that recognize the right of domestic beasts to lead lives that are free of suffering. It is a great deal of work to persuade people to accept this idea."

"Does one need—particular education to work for passage of this law? Must one have been at a university?"

"No, not at all. Many of the men attended Oxford or Cambridge or Trinity, but there is no requirement of a university degree, or of any special knowledge at all. What is necessary is in one's heart at least as much as in one's head."

Mary turned this information over in her mind. Perhaps this was something that she could undertake. It would not be like delivering potatoes to the poor or teaching needlepoint or a few notes of music to labourers' daughters. She might go among the gentry with a new idea, engaging in argument with men and women of her own rank. There would be difficulties in convincing others, no doubt, but work that required no effort would provide no stage for her abilities. If it were difficult all the better, for when she succeeded the respect and esteem bestowed upon her would be so much the greater. She saw herself speaking to the magistrates, soliciting them to exercise their authority, and to the labourers, remonstrating with them over their brutish behaviour. People would wonder at her at first, for the cause was novel, but soon they would come to acknowledge that her activities merited commendation, and she would be much talked of. And surely Dr. Cramer could not object to work of this kind, for it was Christian charity to protect the weak and helpless. He could not tell her that she was unqualified by education to perform it, or excluded from performing it by her sex. She could not recollect at the moment any Biblical passages about animals but she would look them up and have them ready for quotation. Perhaps there were some notes on the matter in her compilation of extracts. She would look them up also, and if she had taken none yet she would go back to her texts and make more extracts.

She lifted her pale face to the young man, a little colour rising into her cheeks. "Mr. Kendall, do you think your work is work that a female could do? That I could do?"

"Yes, I believe so, if you wish to do it."

"Then will you disclose to me how I may go about it?"

"Willingly."

When Elizabeth next looked towards her sister, she was surprised and gratified to see Mary and Adam Kendall sitting with their heads close together, in deep discussion.

Chapter Forty-Eight

[October 1814, Cambridgeshire]

Within two days of her return from Pemberley, Mary received a package in the post. It was small and light, the size of a little book, and when she unwrapped it she discovered inside a volume of poetry—William Cowper's 'The Task'. A piece of notepaper peeped over the top edge, and she opened to the place that the note marked: Book VI, The Winter Walk at Noon. The note was from Adam Kendall.

> London
> October –, 1814
>
> Dear Mrs. Cramer,
> I take the liberty of sending you this little book of Cowper's since you were interested in the lines I quoted to you when we met in Derbyshire. I hope you will let me know your impressions after you have read it.
> Yours faithfully,
> A. Kendall, Esq.
> P.S. You may also wish to read Mr. Jeremy Bentham's Introduction to the Principles of Morals and Legislation, in particular Chapter 17.

She laid aside the note and took up the book and began to read.

> There is in souls a sympathy with sounds,
> And as the mind is pitched the ear is pleased
> With melting airs or martial, brisk or grave;
> Some chord in unison with what we hear

Is touched within us, and the heart replies.
How soft the music of those village bells
Falling at intervals upon the ear
In cadence sweet, now dying all away,
Now pealing loud again, and louder still,
Clear and sonorous as the gale comes on.
With easy force it opens all the cells
Where memory slept.

The poet's thoughts soon turned from the sound of the village church bells to regrets about his life to the wintry weather. Then some lines caught Mary's eye—

Knowledge and wisdom, far from being one,
Have ofttimes no connection. Knowledge dwells
In heads replete with thoughts of other men;
Wisdom in minds attentive to their own.

She looked around mechanically for pen and paper to make an extract of the lines, but seeing none at hand, in a manner somewhat uncharacteristic she stopped and thought closely about the words she was reading.

She had ever believed that she was *seeking wisdom*, but was it possible she had been *acquiring* only *knowledge*, with her books and her boxes full of extracts? Her knowledge was slight compared to her husband's, and it seemed that she had few means of acquiring more. And in truth, how much of real esteem had her knowledge brought her yet?

After musing thus for a time she began to read once more. The poet spoke of the happiness of life in the Garden of Eden

Wondering stood
The new-made monarch, while before him passed,
All happy and all perfect in their kind,
The creatures, summoned from their various haunts
To see their sovereign, and confess his sway.
Vast was his empire, absolute his power,
Or bounded only by a law whose force
'Twas his sublimest privilege to feel
And own, the law of universal love.
He ruled with meekness, they obeyed with joy.
No cruel purpose lurked within his heart,
And no distrust of his intent in theirs.

Then the Fall of Man—

Thus harmony and family accord
Were driven from Paradise; and in that hour
The seeds of cruelty, that since have swelled
To such gigantic and enormous growth,
Were sown in human nature's fruitful soil.
Hence date the persecution and the pain
That man inflicts on all inferior kinds,
Regardless of their plaints. To make him sport,
To gratify the frenzy of his wrath,
Or his base gluttony, are causes good
And just in his account, why bird and beast
Should suffer torture, and the streams be dyed
With blood of their inhabitants impaled.
Earth groans beneath the burden of a war
Waged with defenceless innocence, while he,
Not satisfied to prey on all around,
Adds tenfold bitterness to death by pangs
Needless, and first torments ere he devours.

Mary conjectured that Mr. Kendall must feel as Mr. Cowper did, otherwise he would not fight with carters, and she wondered whether she herself had courage enough to fight with them. She unluckily recalled then how Kendall had been struck by the carter's whip, and that gave her a moment's qualms. She reminded herself, though, that she was a lady and the wife of the Rector of St. —, and tried to assure herself that her station in life would protect her from physical violence and abusive language. But, she thought with determination, even if it did not she would not shrink from a blow. She imagined Adam Kendall's admiration and praise if some brute were to raise a hand to her and she yet stood her ground, and did not cease to call upon him to take pity on the dumb beast that he had dared to mistreat in her presence. A flush of excitement warmed her.

She read the entire poem through, and read again Kendall's note. Then she went to her husband's study. "Dr. Cramer, I wish to I borrow a book from your library, with your permission."

Dr. Cramer was somewhat startled. He had thought this argument decisively won, for it was months since Mary had shown interest in any book at all. Yet his victory had been a Pyrrhic one, for she had simultaneously lost her animation, and almost all interest in her own concerns and his. He could not compel himself to deny her request when it seemed to accompany reviving spirits. "Which book, my dear?"

"Mr. Bentham's *Introduction to the Principles of Morals and Legislation*."

He hesitated, but only for a moment. "You will find it on the third shelf, in the case beside the window."

"Thank you," said Mary.

Dr. Cramer sat for some time with pen in hand after his wife had left the room, ruminating over the incident, before he returned to his writing.

Chapter Forty-Nine

[November 1814, Clifford Priory]

Wickham's affection for Lydia had soon after their marriage sunk into indifference, and although hers for him lasted a little longer, it too in time withered and died. They were very frequently apart, and Lydia often came to Clifford or the Bingleys' London townhouse without her husband; him they saw almost nothing of.

Lydia had been staying in Nottinghamshire for the chief of the month of November when Jane and Bingley, riding in Clifford Wood, encountered a young man in an officer's uniform, riding slowly along the avenue. He looked startled at their approach. Bingley, reining in, spoke to him civilly. "Good morning, sir. Have you lost your way? This road leads to Clifford Priory."

"Oh, ah, does it? Clifford Priory. Yes, that is the name—that is where I am going."

"My name is Bingley, I am the owner of the estate. Were you intending to call on me?"

"Mr. Bingley, how do you do. I, ah, was in fact was calling on an acquaintance of mine, Mrs. Wickham, who I believe is staying here."

"Mrs. Wickham is staying with us. She is our sister."

"My name is Osborne, sir. Mr. Wickham and I were in the same regiment in the regulars."

"She is in the house, if you wish to see her."

Osborne touched his hat, and rode slowly past them.

Jane looked back at him. "Bingley, Lydia did not tell me that anyone was calling on her."

"I cannot explain the matter; however he did not seem to be moving very rapidly. It rather looked as though he were dawdling about, waiting here in the Wood."

"Waiting? For what?"

"Perhaps for Lydia?" He paused a little. "She drove out in the phaeton yesterday by herself."

"Bingley! You would not think—you would not have *me* think—so ill of my sister? Can you believe her so lost to everything as to consent to—to—receive the attentions of this man?"

"Jane, of whom do you ever think ill? All the world are good in your eyes."

Jane now sought earnestly to prove to Bingley that he was in error, and to clear Lydia and the young officer of any wrongdoing. He heard her in silence, but then said, "You know as well as I what your sister's former conduct was, yet you would not think her capable of *this* until it were conclusively proved against her."

"The horror of what you are proposing almost deprives me of my senses. It cannot be true. His coming here may surely be perfectly innocent."

"I wish it may. I shall have some inquiries made in the village, and do you see Lydia and let her speak for herself."

On their return to the house, the servant told them that no one had called, but that Mrs. Wickham had gone out walking alone. Bingley's inquiries sent to the village of Clifford produced the information that Captain Osborne was staying at the inn, and had been there several days. He rode out each day for hours, sometimes in the direction of Clifford Priory, but at other times in the opposite direction.

What a stroke was this for Jane! Bingley had the greatest difficulty consoling her for the discovery. "I am sure you are incapable of triumphing over me, Bingley," she said at length, "but my confidence in my sister was more natural than your suspicion. This is almost past belief."

When the ladies went upstairs to dress for dinner, Jane followed her sister to her room, and, dismissing Lydia's maid and closing the door behind her, gave her to understand that she had a matter of importance to discuss with her.

"Bingley and I met Mr. Osborne when we were out riding this morning," she then began.

"He said he met you in the Wood. Did you not think him handsome?" replied Lydia instantly, without exhibiting the slightest confusion.

Jane was indescribably shocked that Lydia did not even endeavour to deny that she had met the young man.

"Lydia! I did not think about it one way or the other. But what is he doing here?"

"Good Lord! It is none of my business what he is doing here. He may come and go as he chooses."

"But it is excessively strange that he should come and go in the very corner of Nottinghamshire where you are staying."

"He is a friend of Wickham's, perhaps Wickham told him where I was."

"That does not explain why he would follow you here."

"Followed me! Of course he has not followed me. I dare say he is passing through on his way somewhere."

"Bingley has found out he is staying in the village."

"Well, that is more than I know. He does not need my leave to stay in the village, or in any other village."

"Lydia, he must not come here again, and you must not meet him."

"La, you are so strange! I, meet him! He is nothing to me."

With this exchange Jane was forced to be satisfied, for Lydia never listened to anyone for more than half a minute; and it was clear that her easy assurance had not been disturbed by Jane's questions, and that she would not admit any fault on her own part, or any scheme between the two of them.

Jane and Bingley then conferred together, and Jane repeated to him what Lydia had said. "If I did not fear judging without full proof, I would almost be disposed to say that there is an appearance of willful deceit in this matter," said Jane, much perturbed.

"Jane, I do not believe I have ever before heard you voice such a harsh sentiment," said Bingley.

Bingley determined to have the groundskeeper informed that the gentleman was to be sent on his way as a trespasser should he be found on the estate again. Jane thought that she perhaps detected Lydia watching or waiting for his reappearance, but they soon learned that Osborne had departed from the village inn. Lydia stayed with them through the Christmas and returned to her home at the new year, and during that time there was no further mention among them of the young officer. "She is perhaps sorry for what she has done," said Jane to Bingley after Lydia had gone; "and she will be anxious to guard her reputation more carefully in the future." Bingley did not find it advisable to make any answer to this remark.

Chapter Fifty

[November 1814, Cambridgeshire]

Mary, having determined to join in the work of Adam Kendall and the animal protectionists, was not long in finding an opportunity of initiating herself. As she was being driven to make a morning call upon a neighbour she observed a ploughman in a field by the roadside, beating an ox with a stick. There was no one else about, and although she could not help wishing for more spectators than her coachman, at the same time she thought it perhaps prudent to undertake the first exhibition with only a small audience. She tapped for the coachman to stop.

"What is it, Ma'am?"

"Stop the horses, at once. I wish to descend."

Much astonished, he complied. Mary got out of the carriage, entered the field and approached the ploughman.

The man looked at her, as astonished as the coachman. He had never seen a lady walk through a muddy field. "What do you want, mistress?"

"I have come to command you to cease hitting that unfortunate animal."

The man's astonishment increased. "What is it to you? Am I your servant? Is this your ox?"

"You are not my servant and this is not my ox, but I tell you to cease hitting it in the name of Christian charity," said Mary more firmly. "God has given you the right to use that animal but not to abuse it."

"Damn your eyes for an interfering hussy!" cried the man.

Mary experienced some alarm at his language but stoutly responded, "A righteous man regardeth the life of his beast: but the tender mercies of the wicked are cruel."

Glaring at her he brought the stick down on the animal's back again. "Get away before I take this rod to you!"

Mary's resolve gave way under the man's fierce look, and perceiving there was little to be gained by further discourse with him she turned back to the carriage with her knees trembling under her. The coachman looked at her with disapproval and muttered under his breath as he handed her back in, her gown three inches deep in mud.

"What did you say?" she said in as collected a voice as she could find.

"Nothing, ma'am," he replied. "Am I to drive on now?"

"Yes, drive on." She felt a little weak, but then she felt elated. She had publicly reprimanded a brute. She did not think she had made any impression on him, however this was but her first attempt, and the next time she would not retreat so precipitately. She would stand her ground until she had attained her objective.

"Mary, what is this I have heard today?" said Dr. Cramer when he joined her for tea that afternoon in the parlour. "Mr. Lydgate was here. He told me that you interfered with his servant who was ploughing a field."

"He was beating an animal. I required him to desist."

"What, in God's name, led you to act in this way? What knowledge have you of oxen and ploughing?"

"He was treating the animal cruelly."

"Sometimes animals must be whipped to make them obedient."

"He was hurting it out of anger, not to make it obedient."

"Mary, I am filled with amazement by this occurrence. Why have you taken it upon yourself to intervene in matters that do not concern you?"

"Cruelty is a very common failing, to which human nature is particularly prone, and must concern all virtuous men."

"But it was not your animal, or your servant or your field. What right had you to interfere?"

"The right of a Christian female to protect an innocent beast."

Dr. Cramer fixed his eyes on her with incredulity. These proceedings were beyond both his experience and his conjecture.

"Mary, you must know that God gave man dominion over the animals. If a man owns an animal he may use it as he wants."

"But animals were created by God, as was man. They see, and hear, and feel, and think, and they sense pain."

"They were created by God, but not as deserving protection against man. They must be useful to man, and obedient to his desires. Did not Our Lord curse the barren fig tree so that it withered away? Did He not send the unclean spirits into a herd of swine so that they ran violently down into the sea and were drowned?"

"I do not believe He would have beaten an animal," said Mary obstinately. "I have read that as well as pride and prejudice, misrepresentations of God and religion contribute to harden the heart against natural feelings of compassion."[*]

Dr. Cramer was not a cruel or unfeeling man, and although he could quote Scripture in support of man's right to harm an animal, he would not have harmed one himself, and he recognized the want of Christian charity in his position even as he made it. He wanted to please his young wife, who seemed unhappy in her new home. Therefore he took her affectionately by the hand and said, "Dearest Mary, you believed you were acting for the good, and I cannot reprove you for that. But henceforth if you see an animal that you think is being harmed, you must not interfere directly. You must come and tell me, and if I judge that the man is at fault, I will speak to him or his master. It is unseemly for my wife to involve herself in such matters. It is the law that a man may beat his ox or his horse or any other animal of his. I would not have you obstructing anyone who is going about his lawful business."

"The law is defective in morality. Why does it refuse its protection to sensitive beings?" said Mary with spirit.

"They are animals. They do not have the faculty of reason."

"Why should the question be, Can they reason? Why is the question not, Can they suffer? For they do suffer. Anyone can see it."

"You are quoting Mr. Bentham, I think," said Dr. Cramer. "When you asked to borrow the book I did not know what use you intended to make of it." With a sigh he released her hand. "Mary, let us speak no more about this now. I would be very much obliged if you would pour me a cup of tea."

Mary was nettled, for she would purchase no praise if her husband, not she, were the agent of rebuke. But she was young lady of deep reflection, and she soon perceived that she had achieved her first success in her endeavours. Dr. Cramer had not absolutely forbidden her to pursue her planned course, and she flattered herself moreover that she had persuaded him of the merit of her position. If she could next persuade him to take action against the perpetrators of abuse, it could not fail soon to get abroad that it was Mary herself who was directing his actions. She therefore reconciled herself to her husband's orders and determined to wait for some fair prospect to arise.

It was but a few days later that Mary was in the village making some small purchases, and came upon a not-uncommon scene. Three young boys were throwing stones at a thin dog, whose efforts to escape were prevented by a stone wall and the accuracy of the boys' aim. A few loiterers had gathered to watch, and Mary, forgetting her husband's injunction not to interfere directly, instantly seized the chance. She walked quickly towards the boys, calling to them to cease. At first they gave her no attention, until one, turning

---

* Rev. Humphry Primatt, *A Dissertation on the Duty of Mercy and the Sin of Cruelty to Brute Animals*, London: 1776, p. 31. –Ed.

with a stone in his hand with the intention of throwing it at her instead of the dog, recognized the Rector's wife. He immediately dropped it.

"Make the other boys stop," commanded Mary. He wavered for a moment, and then called to them, "Leave off." Looking at Mary but speaking to the other boys he added, "We can go to Featherstone farm. They have kittens there they are going to drown today." The three boys ran away. The dog, an avenue of escape having opened to it, squeezed through a hedge by the wall and vanished.

Mary was exceedingly pleased with the success of her efforts, the moreso as several villagers now stood gawping at her. She turned on them roundly. "You observed the activities of those youths. Why did you not charge them to let the dog be?"

One of the men looked at her in bewilderment. "The lads were doing no harm."

"Doing no harm! They were throwing stones at it."

"It is nobody's dog, it is a stray mongrel. It was skulking about the inn for a scrap of food. The inn-keeper wants to be rid of it."

Mary would have been exceedingly gratified to preach the doctrine of animal protection to the inhabitants of the village, but belatedly recalling that she was to refer all occurrences of abuse to her husband, she contented herself with inquiring who the boys were, and having received an answer she proceeded to carry out her purchases. Upon returning home she immediately went to her husband's study and told him that she must speak with him.

"Can it not wait, my dear? I must finish my sermon this afternoon."

"This is a matter of some importance. Three boys were tormenting a dog in the village. One is the smith's son, the other two were children of a cottager. You promised you would remonstrate with anyone who was harming an animal. You must go to their fathers."

"What were they doing?" asked Dr. Cramer in mild alarm.

"Casting stones at it."

"Casting stones!" he cried. "Mary, boys have thrown stones at dogs from time immemorial. I doubt it is possible to stop them from doing so."

"But it is unchristian!"

"The parish will think I have taken leave of my senses if I endeavour to halt the amusements of children. There is no sin committed here."

"One of the youths would have propelled a missile at me, and abstained only when he recognized me. If it be no sin to cast stones at a dog, will they think it no sin also to stone a mendicant? Did not our Lord say, whatever you have done to the least of my brothers you have done to me?"

Dr. Cramer was ensnared. He had promised his wife that if she would refrain from intervening he would do so, and although he would not willingly have taken action if the boys' only object had been the dog, he could not ignore a threat to injure his wife. He therefore made a visit to the families of the boys, and in mutual amazement he and the boys' fathers discussed the immorality of inflicting suffering on living creatures. Dr. Cramer was very well respected by his parishioners and though the parents privately regarded his interference as not only officious but incomprehensible, they gave civil pledges to curb their sons' baser instincts.

The story of Mrs. Cramer's reprimand to the boys and her husband's subsequent admonishment of their families was quickly retailed through the neighbourhood, and caused much comment. Although puzzlement was the prevailing sentiment, Lord Chettam paused to speak to Dr. Cramer after service on the following Sunday and congratulated him on his effort to inculcate in the lower orders forbearance and compassion towards animals. Dr. Cramer replied that he had been moved to do so by the petition of his wife, and Lord Chettam responded that he would ask Lady Chettam to call upon Mrs. Cramer without delay.

After the passage of a few weeks Mary, cherishing a feeling of self-complacency on the score of her activities, wrote a vain letter to Adam Kendall in which she detailed her triumphs in her encounters with the local populace. "My husband has graciously bestowed praise upon what he calls my 'little sermons' (predicationiculae)," she continued, "and avows that should he find himself unable to preach I am fitted to occupy the pulpit. The vicar of T—, who dined with us Thursday last, gave it as his opinion that if all ladies could express themselves as well as I then he and his clerical brethren must look to their livings! These are pleasantries of the gentlemen, yet my husband's curate is not listened to with half so much attention at the third service, and he is the possessor of a Cambridge degree. I believe indeed that my husband and I have stemmed the tide of brutality in our parish; and one of the magistrates averred to Dr. Cramer that my benevolent activities have so terrorized the neighbourhood that every man is afraid to kick a cat out of his path lest the Rector's wife descend upon him like an avenging Fury." She concluded, "I think it no sacrifice to exert myself in this cause, though it removes me from my household and parish duties, for the usual pursuits of females have few charms for me; however I am mindful that a female cannot be too much guarded in her behaviour in a public forum, for one false step can cause grievous injury to her reputation."

Kendall replied with praise of her actions, and asking what steps she had taken for the animals. This inquiry very much puzzled Mary, for she had given no thought at all to the beaten ox or the starving dog or any other beast. What would he have had her do for them? She could make little sense of the matter, and soon decided to give it no further thought; and when she responded to his letter she did not supply an answer on this subject.

Chapter Fifty-One

[January 1815, Pemberley; and letters]

The Darcy family in accordance with custom spent the Christmas at Pemberley, and were joined by the Bingleys and Fitzwilliams, and the visit was marked by the pleasure that the members of the party took in one another's society as well as the usual gaieties of the season. But hardly had the New Year turned than Colonel Fitzwilliam received an express that his father had died after a short illness. Fitzwilliam had been deeply attached to him and he set off immediately for Ireland, and although Kitty begged to be allowed to accompany him, he would not permit it. The weather was cold and wet, and the passage from Holyhead to Kingstown would be rough, he said, and he feared that Kitty's health might suffer. He was gone within two hours of receiving the express.

News of the Earl's death led to the writing of two letters in Kent. The first was from Lady Catherine DeBourgh to her nephew Robert Fitzwilliam, now Earl of Tyrconnell.

Rosings, Kent
January –, 1815

My dear Lord Tyrconnell,
My daughter Anne and I are most deeply affected by the death of the Earl my brother. However you know that I always speak my mind, and I have lately been disappointed by him not once but twice. Let me be understood. Knowing that I am not to be trifled with or my judgement controverted he nevertheless declined to interfere in the marriage of your cousin Darcy to Miss Elizabeth Bennet, and then actually acceded to the marriage of your brother to Miss Catherine

Bennet. Was nothing due to me on the score of these alliances? His mind perhaps was affected by age or living in Ireland but he disregarded what he owed to himself and his family. The claims of duty and honour he spurned, he acted against the inclinations of his nearest relations in the world, and the noble line has been adulterated.

I do not overlook that Darcy's wife has performed her duty very promptly in providing to him a healthy heir, a duty that your own wife has so far neglected—unfeeling, selfish woman!—although I have advised her most strenuously to see to it. There can in general be no occasion for entailing estates away from the female line, and it was not thought necessary in Sir Lewis de Bourgh's family, despite the fact that daughters are never of so much consequence to a father; however the entail of the Tyrconnell estate is an unalterable thing, and the earldom of course cannot descend to a female. Is it to be endured that the family's land and title should pass to an offspring of the Bennets! It must not, shall not be. I therefore charge you not to neglect on any account your obligations in this respect. In a cause of such moment as this there can be no hesitation or scruple, or reason for delay. If you do not contrive to accomplish this duty you will be acting contrary to the desire of all and without regard for the honour of the family. I shall be most gratified, I assure you, when I hear that you have attended to this matter and accomplished my wishes.

Yours,
C. DeBourgh

The second letter was from Mr. Collins to Mr. Fitzwilliam Darcy.

Hunsford Parsonage, Kent
January –, 1815

Dear Sir,
Having been so fortunate as to be distinguished by your attention as a correspondent, I am compelled by our relationship and the duties of my station to condole with you on the present distress which your family is suffering, and of which we have been informed by my illustrious patroness Lady Catherine de Bourgh. You are grievously to be pitied for your loss of one of the highest personages in the kingdom. Be assured my dear sir that Mrs. Collins and myself most sincerely commiserate, although at the same time I consider it a point of duty to counsel resignation to inevitable evils. Having offered you our sympathy on this affliction, let me now tender our congratulations on a happy event that we understand is to take place

in the spring, of which Mrs. Collins has received intelligence from my amiable cousin Elizabeth. How wonderfully these sorts of things occur! Although cautious of appearing forward and precipitate I flatter myself that I may be able to persuade Lady Catherine to look upon this event as an offered olive-branch. I shall now take the liberty of wishing health and happiness to my cousin Catherine and Colonel Fitzwilliam, as well as to yourself and my cousin Elizabeth. When I do myself the honour of next writing to you I hope to have more satisfactory intelligence to share with you.

Your well wisher and friend,
Wm Collins

Chapter Fifty-Two

[February 1815, Cambridgeshire]

Adam Kendall was not behindhand in replying to Mary's letter, and an active correspondence arose between them. It consisted at first largely of Mary recounting her own exploits and Kendall mildly urging her to take thought for the welfare of the beasts as well as the sins of the abusers, but gradually it came to encompass other matters of mutual interest, and brought considerable satisfaction to both of them. After a period of some months he proposed to visit her and her husband when he should be in the vicinity of Cambridge, and a day was appointed. He was received on arrival by Mary with civility mingled with vanity, but she was distracted from her prepared speech of welcome by the sight of a small squirming animal in the crook of his arm.

"Why Mr. Kendall, what are you carrying?"

"A dog, Mrs. Cramer. A puppy. She was the only survivor of the litter. An inn I passed through has a bitch to keep down vermin, and one of the stable lads was killing the puppies, for the innkeeper does not want another dog about. I took this one from him before he could dash her brains out against the wall."

"But Mr. Kendall, what do you intend doing with this animal? You travel such a great deal for Mr. Wilberforce—how can you tend it?"

"I cannot, as much as I wish to. Therefore I have brought her to you to keep."

"To me? But I have no knowledge of canines."

The puppy squirmed in Kendall's arm and gave several high pitched yelps. "She is hungry," said Kendall. "Do you have some warm milk, and a little bit of meat ground up fine?"

"I—I have not the least idea. I will ring for a servant to remove it to the kitchen."

"Mrs. Cramer, it was my hope that *you* would take her to the kitchen and feed her yourself."

"I? Give sustenance to a canine?"

"Yes."

"But I have never performed such an act."

"It is most easily done. If you will permit me I will show you."

"You wish us to go to the kitchen?"

"Yes."

"At this moment? I am most desirous to show you a letter from one of our magistrates. He writes that I have quite convinced him of the justice of the cause of protecting cattle from cruel usage."

"Mrs. Cramer," said Kendall gently, "the letter is inanimate. It may wait without suffering harm. But this little dog is hungry now, and it would be cruel to delay feeding her."

Mary was excessively disappointed, for the letter was very complimentary to her, and since its receipt, only a day after Kendall had written to inform her of his intention to visit the Rectory while passing through Cambridge, she had often imagined showing it to him and thereby exciting his approval and respect. Kendall continued to look at her with a gentle gaze, while he stroked the puppy to quiet her. "Very well, I will take you to the kitchen, if you wish it. Come this way," she said rather ungraciously.

Kendall smiled at her, and to her astonishment he had in his eyes the very look of approval, that she had expected the letter to produce. Yet feeding a puppy could scarcely be a difficult task or one likely to elicit praise and admiration, nothing in comparison to confronting a surly brute with a whip, or arguing for reform of the law with Lord Cadwallader, who when riding raked his horses with his spurs until their sides bled!

She led the way to the back of the house and down the stairs. The cook stared in surprise at the unaccustomed sight of her mistress, for Mary rarely descended to the kitchen. "Mrs. Pritchard, we require some warm milk, with a little bit of meat ground up, for Mr. Kendall's dog."

"The poor wee mite," said the cook, and immediately poured a saucer of milk and set it down on the floor.

"Now I will show you how to feed your dog," said Kendall with another smile. He set the little animal down in front of the saucer and she immediately began lapping up the milk. "Do you see? Nothing could be more simple." He stroked the puppy as she drank. "Now it is your turn." Mary reached out hesitantly and rubbed the top of the little head.

"Very good," said Kendall, "you will make an excellent mistress for the dog, I can clearly see."

"You really intend leaving it here?"

"I do. And I will come back often to see what good care you are taking of her."

"You believe I can care for it—for her—well?"

"I am sure of it. You will teach her to follow you everywhere, and sit down beside you for a bite of muffin, and roll over for her chest to be tickled. Each time I come I will expect to see a new trick you have taught her."

"I, teach her tricks?"

"Yes, Mrs. Cramer. And as soon as you have named her, I expect to receive a letter from you telling me her name."

"I must name her? Have not you done so?"

"No, of course not. She is your dog, you must name her."

"But I—this is an occurrence of an unexpected nature, Mr. Kendall. I am unsure—I am not prepared—"

"You are perfectly prepared, I think. All you need do, every time you behold her, is remember that I am relying on you to look after her. I will be thinking about her often—about both of you."

Some time later Dr. Cramer sent for a servant to inquire where his wife and his guest might be. Upon being informed that they were in the kitchen and had been there for the space of half an hour, Dr. Cramer, much astonished, told the servant to acquaint them that he was in the drawing room waiting for them. The servant returned shortly with an invitation from Mary for Dr. Cramer to join them below stairs. Dr. Cramer had not yet ceased to wonder at his wife's activities, or to feel uneasy at each new manifestation of them. With a slow step, for his legs were giving him considerable pain, he descended to a realm he had never visited in his life. There he found Mary and Adam Kendall kneeling on the stone floor watching the puppy contort its body in a variety of capers and frisks, and laughing together.

"My dear Mary! What are you doing down here? What is that?"

"My puppy," said Mary happily. "Dr. Cramer, I think Mr. Kendall has not yet been introduced to you."

Kendall rose and bowed, not in the least embarrassed to be found by his host rolling about on the ground in the servants' domain. "How do you do, sir? You and Mrs. Cramer are performing a very great service in this parish, and it is an honour to make your acquaintance."

"You are welcome to my home, Mr. Kendall, but perhaps I may persuade you and my wife to join me in the drawing room."

"Oh no," said Mary, "let us stay here with the puppy. Mr. Kendall says I must name her myself. I have never named a dog, or any animal. You must help me, Dr. Cramer."

"Mary, dearest, I must ask you and Mr. Kendall to come upstairs at once. This is no way to receive our guest. Where did that dog come from?"

"The Boar's Head inn," said Kendall. "A stable lad was about to kill her and I intervened."

"Sir, I thank you for bringing it to show to my wife, you have obviously given her great pleasure. But—I—you will of course be taking it away with you when you depart."

"No, she is mine," said Mary. "She is no longer Mr. Kendall's. What do you think of Brownie for a name?"

"A brave first attempt but I am sure you can improve on that effort," said Kendall gravely.

"Really, Mr. Kendall, I must ask you to take this animal away with you. We cannot have a dog in this house," said Dr. Cramer, a frown creasing his brow.

"Whyever not?" said Mary. "She will be no trouble and I will look after her."

"I must apologize, sir," said Kendall, "but it is out of my control to remove the dog, for she belongs to Mrs. Cramer now. It is her decision whether to part with her."

"Oh, I cannot," said Mary. "I am to take care of her and teach her tricks."

With some further effort Dr. Cramer induced his wife and guest to go upstairs with him, and Mary told the cook she would return later to see the puppy. When they had assembled in the drawing room Kendall said, "Mrs. Cramer, I believe you had a letter you wanted to show me?"

"Oh! I had forgotten about it. It is here somewhere. Oh, here it is. It is just from one of the magistrates."

Kendall read it with a smile. "Very good," he said.

"I hope Mr. Wilberforce receives satisfaction from our efforts. Have you communicated to him what we are undertaking?"

"Oh yes, I have—I mentioned your work to him."

"And what response did he make?"

"I am afraid you will not be pleased with what he said."

"He does not approve?"

"Well, he said that it appeared to him to be proceedings unsuited to the female character as delineated in Scripture."

"Oh!" said Mary, her vanity wounded.

"I could not agree with him more," said Dr. Cramer.

"Ah, sir, I am afraid I must beg to differ with both you and Mr. Wilberforce. There must be Marthas, but there must also be Marys, who bathed our Lord's feet when he was weary, and rubbed costly liniment upon them, and dried them with her own hair."

"Sir!" said Dr. Cramer, affronted. "That is a most improper comment to make in the presence of my wife."

"I apologize, sir, if I have offended you, but I also believe there is no part of the Gospel that cannot be read by a lady and spoken of between the sexes."

"Mary, dearest," said Dr. Cramer, "I wish to speak to Mr. Kendall alone. Would you be good enough to leave us for a few moments."

"If you wish, my husband. I will rejoin you presently."

When Mary had left, Dr. Cramer fixed his eyes on Kendall. "My wife is a sensitive and impressionable young woman. She should not be exposed to the cruelty and especially not to the language and conduct of the owners of cattle, or of their servants."

"She cannot help being exposed, the cruelty is there for everyone to see, day after day. What would you have her do, pass by on the other side of the road each time, and say nothing and do nothing?"

"I would not have her walking on the road at all, and I would certainly not have her reprimanding or entering into arguments with carters, and drovers and farmers. It is not behaviour befitting the wife of the Rector of this parish, nor befitting a lady."

"Surely any behaviour that is Christian is behaviour befitting a lady, and especially a lady who is the wife of a clergyman?"

"She is carrying matters too far. Soon she will be forbidding the servants to kill the blackbeetles and moths."

Kendall smiled. "'I would not enter on my list of friends/Though graced with polished manners, the man/Who heedlessly sets foot on a worm.'"

"That is precisely the kind of nonsense of which I am apprehensive."

His guest, appearing undisturbed, continued, "'We are held/accountable and God some future day/will reckon with us roundly for the abuse/of what he deems no trivial trust.' Dr. Cramer, I have only one question to ask you: do you want your wife to be happy?"

"Of course I wish her happiness."

"Was she happy before? Is she happy now?"

Dr. Cramer had by nature and education no aversion to argument, or even to a dispute; but his health had grown over the past months very indifferent, and there were times when he could scarcely endure talking at all. But further, he did truly wish Mary's happiness, and his conscience pricked him that by his own actions he had been the author of her recent despondency. He turned silently away from Kendall; and after a moment he conceded with a sigh that he could not prevent Mary acting as she wished in this matter. And so he yielded, although without conviction.

For several days after Kendall's visit, from Mary's thoughts the question of what to call the little dog was never absent. She was in all perplexity about the matter, never having been called upon previously to perform such a duty. One evening as she walked about the house re-considering the events that had brought the puppy to her, the lines from Cowper's poem came into her mind—

> Knowledge dwells
> In heads replete with thoughts of other men;
> Wisdom in minds attentive to their own.

A happy idea struck her, and she smiled at the rapidity and ease with which her dilemma was solved; and the following day she wrote to Adam Kendall that she had named the dog Sophia.

Chapter Fifty-Three

[March 1815, Pemberley]

Napoleon Buonaparte, having exercised considerable influence over the European nations for a score of years, was not of a mind to renounce it if other opportunities presented themselves, and on the 26th of February 1815 after escaping from his imprisonment on the island of Elba he returned to France, the army and populace rallying to him as he proceeded north. On the 13th of March, the European powers at the Congress of Vienna declared him an outlaw, and but four days later Great Britain, the Netherlands, Russia, Austria and Prussia agreed to put one hundred and fifty thousand men into the field against him. He entered Paris in triumph on the 20th of March, and the king of one year, Louis XVIII, not by coincidence immediately quitted the country for Belgium.

Colonel Fitzwilliam received early news of these events at Pemberley, where he was staying with Kitty, who was close to her time of confinement, and informed his wife and the Darcys that he would very shortly have to return to his regiment, and that he expected to be on the Continent within the month. However his preparations for departure had not yet been concluded when an express arrived. The family party was at dinner, and a footman carried it to Fitzwilliam at table.

"What is Buonaparte up to now?" asked Darcy as they observed Fitzwilliam open the packet.

"No good, as usual, I suspect," said Fitzwilliam. He read the letter and turned white.

"What is it, James?" said Kitty anxiously.

Fitzwilliam took a moment to respond. "It's Fitz."

"What does he write to you?" asked Darcy. "It is bad news?"

"No—that is, he does not write. There has been an accident in Ireland. Fitz has been killed."

The others exclaimed all together in horror. Kitty went instantly to her husband, and stood beside him. "Darcy, read this," said Fitzwilliam, holding out the letter. "I can hardly understand it." Darcy took the letter and perused it, and while he did so Fitzwilliam appeared to recover a little from the shock he had received. "I must go to my sister the Countess. And I will need to make arrangements with the steward at the Castle."

"How I wish I could come with you James!"

"I hope to return before you are delivered; I must go quickly. There is little you would be able to do even were you not with child." Very shortly he was gone, kissing Kitty and mounting his horse to set out once more for Holyhead.

Elizabeth's head quite spun with the rapidity of events, but as she was much engaged in comforting Kitty over her husband's hasty and untimely departure she did not have an opportunity to speak privately to Darcy until late in the evening. "What did the letter say? What has happened?"

"My cousin was riding a point-to-point—a match race with a neighbour."

"Oh no!" She reflected in silence for a time. "Georgiana was so anxious that Fitzwilliam would kill himself steeplechasing, but now it seems her concern was for the wrong brother. And his wife! And his little girls! How great their distress must be."

"It is excessively unfortunate. Fitz was not yet five-and-thirty, and the eldest of his daughters is but seven years old."

The agitation that Elizabeth felt was great, for she could not prevent herself from thinking how it would be if Darcy suffered such a fate, and left her a widow with a fatherless child; but it was a little relieved by tears. Darcy took her hand and watched her in compassionate silence, and when she was calmer asked if she would take a glass of wine. She refused it, and Darcy did not press her. Endeavouring to recover herself she smiled faintly and said, "I am well, there is nothing really the matter with me. But Darcy, what does this mean? I had not thought of it before—is Fitzwilliam now the Earl?"

"No, he is not—or rather it is yet to be determined whether he is the Earl."

"I do not understand you."

"The letter was from the Earl's steward. He wrote that the Countess is with child. If she is delivered of a boy, then the child is the Earl. If she miscarries, or the child is a girl, then Fitzwilliam is the Earl." Elizabeth was deeply affected by this new intelligence, for she herself expected to be confined within two months; commiseration for the Countess swallowed her up and for a few minutes she could not speak. Darcy sat by her with contracted brow, wishing to offer her consolation but not knowing how.

At length Elizabeth said, "Does the steward say when the child is expected?"

"Yes, in November."

"Poor woman! What she must endure, and what a wretched beginning to the child's life! We must offer her every assistance in our power, Darcy."

With this Darcy concurred, and they spent some time conjecturing what the Countess would now do and determining what actions they ought to take for her comfort and assistance.

Chapter Fifty-Four

[May 1815, London]

Jane Bingley's steady sense and sweetness of temper exactly adapted her for attending to children in every way—teaching them, playing with them, and loving them. She had always been a general favourite of the Gardiners' children, the eldest a little girl now of eleven and the youngest a little boy of five, and her aunt and uncle Gardiner had never hesitated to leave them under Jane's particular care; and she always took great delight on her visits to Pemberley, in spending time with her little nephew Will. After more than two years of marriage, however, Jane did not have a child of her own, and her radiant happiness began to be marred. She struggled to support her spirits, and although Elizabeth with all tender solicitude was most desirous to bring her consolation, it was out of her power to do a great deal; the relief of preaching patience was even denied to her, for Jane had so much already. Elizabeth examined each of her sister's letters with concern. They never contained a complaint, or a communication of suffering; for Jane's feelings, although intense, were little displayed; but there was in all of them a want of her characteristic cheerfulness. Elizabeth saw that her sister's mind, habitually serene, was now clouded. She looked forward to each meeting with her, that would enable her to contribute to the solace of her spirit, by all that affection could do.

She had written to Jane in trepidation of the suffering it would cause her with the news that she had conceived a second child, and had sent word to her of the delivery of Kitty's and Fitzwilliam's son, in March, and of her own daughter in May, almost with sorrow. Jane replied each time with heartfelt congratulations that did nothing to quiet Elizabeth's mind.

Added to her unease about Jane was her anxiety about the unborn and fatherless child of Lady Tyrconnell, and her sympathy for Kitty, who was the constant object of Lady Catherine's letters and visits, all intended to address and rectify Kitty's numerous imperfections. Lady Catherine's apprehension that Lady Tyrconnell would be delivered of another girl was causing her to be more than usually attentive to her nephew and niece, and in particular to the latter, much to Kitty's torment.

To these concerns were lately united fears, for Fitzwilliam had gone to the Continent; and Wickham also, for when the French once again threatened the peace of the nations he had with Darcy's help purchased a lieutenant's commission in the regulars. They were both in Belgium, where large forces of the British and Prussian armies were massing to prepare an invasion of France; and like many officers' wives Lydia had accompanied Wickham there. Each day Elizabeth, Kitty and Georgiana were in the habit of intently studying the newspapers for reports of the movements of Napoleon's army as it made its way to the northeastern border of France, for the Emperor hoped to destroy his enemies before they could attempt the invasion.

Soon after her confinement at the Darcys' London townhouse, Elizabeth had the pleasure of receiving a visit from her aunt Gardiner, which she hoped would be of material service in dispelling her agitation. After Mrs. Gardiner had seen baby Anne, Elizabeth unburdened herself. Mrs. Gardiner listened with compassion. Of her eldest niece she said, "Poor Jane! I am indeed sorry for her. And it is surely hard for her to see that you and Kitty have so easily borne children. But these things happen so often! She is still young, though, and she may yet conceive, and carry a child. Let us take it in the most hopeful light, for there is nothing else we are able to do."

Mrs. Gardiner was at this time much preoccupied with her husband's business affairs, for he had entered into a speculation with John Thorn, to whom he had been introduced through Darcy, that could prove injurious to his family's prosperity if it did not succeed, and she was incapable of giving Elizabeth all of the attention that she had hoped to gain. It soon became Elizabeth's turn to listen, and she heard her aunt with professions of concern and attempts to allay *her* fears.

"Well, I believe I have now told you every thing," said Mrs. Gardiner at length. She then changed the conversation to one more gratifying, that of Darcy's political career, for he seemed to be in a fair way to ascend through the ranks of the Tory party to positions of increasing responsibility. "He has all, in addition to wealth and rank, that will make him a fine politician. His understanding is excellent and his behaviour pleasing, and you have taught him that little more liveliness he was wanting. And the prudence of his marriage is now evident, for he gained in you a partner and hostess exactly suited to further his ambitions."

Elizabeth thanked her for her kindness, and assured her of the great pleasure it would always give her and Darcy to see her and uncle Gardiner, whether in London or at Pemberley, and so they parted, to await the outcome of events.

Chapter Fifty-Five

[June 1815, letters from Brussels; and at Pemberley]

Lydia had never ceased to maintain an occasional correspondence with Kitty, from the time of her visit to Brighton prior to her elopement with George Wickham, which Kitty had not often shared with her elder sisters as the letters were generally much too full of lines under the words to be made public. Lydia now wrote to her exuberantly from Brussels, and Kitty read each succeeding letter with increasing disquiet.

Brussels, Belgium
5 June, 1815

Dear Kitty,
You can't think what fun it is here! Wickham has taken lodgings for us near the Place Royale, and Osborne is in the same house. If I had known what it is like to come to the Continent, I would have begged and teased papa until he brought us. And to think I once thought how fine it would be to go to Brighton! How I wish you could join us. Do tell Colonel Fitzwilliam to send for you here. I would like it of all things! You must be quite out of spirits at Pemberley without him, for I am sure Lizzy is dull company. It would be the most shameful thing in the world if you cannot come. I think everyone in the world is here—London must be empty, there are so many English, people of fashion, lords and ladies. And there are soldiers everywhere! In the morning the bugles wake us and at night we go to bed with the fife and drum, and the bands of the regiments play at all hours. In the afternoons we go sightseeing, to a picture-gallery or a church or the Hotel de Ville, or we have a ride in one of the parks.

Wickham has hired a carriage for me, and he and Osborne go on horseback. However Wickham does not always come with us. Or we go to the flower market. Osborne bought me the most beautiful bouquet yesterday. There is a theatre, and we sometimes go there in the evening; or to the Opera. There are such dinners! And dancing! Everyone here is dancing the waltz, although in England it is considered quite scandalous. The gentleman holds the lady very close—his arm is about her, holding her tight to him! And then they go spinning around until everyone is quite out of breath—oh, what fun it is! How I laugh when I waltz with Osborne. There is a great deal of gambling too, but of course I do not gamble. Wickham does, and sometimes Osborne. The other night we were at a party given by the Brigadier-General and we were up nearly all night. Kitty, do write and say you will come, and we will go out in my carriage every day.
Your affectionate sister
Lydia Wickham

Brussels, Belgium
16 June, 1815

Dear Kitty,
When we were in the park today we met a group of officers on horseback. One of them was rather handsome although a little old and I could see he was looking at me. What do you think, Kitty? He was a general! Then he called Osborne over, and later Osborne told me he had asked my name! Is that not capital? I can hardly write for laughing. Osborne was horrid unpleasant the rest of the afternoon, and I do believe he is jealous. Wickham did not come with us today. I was a little vexed with him but perhaps it turned out as well. Osborne has bought me some laces, and a pretty jewel. Wickham says he does not mind, as he does not have much money, and if I am to have laces and jewels he supposes someone must buy them. He has bought me nothing himself, although I told him very particularly that I had seen a parasol that I liked beyond anything! There is a milliner's near our lodgings and I have bought two or three bonnets there. The shops are much more fashionable here than in Newcastle. Do come, Kitty! It will be such a delicious scheme. I know you will like to waltz with Colonel Fitzwilliam!
Your affectionate sister
Lydia Wickham

Brussels,
18 June, 1815

Dear Kitty,
Last night there was a ball given by the Duchess of R–. Everyone in Brussels was desperate to go, and it would have been quite a shame if we had not got in. But by great luck we managed to get invitations. The famous Mrs. Crawley was there. She arrived very late. But what a throng of officers there was wanting to dance the waltz with her! I declare there must have been fifty of them. However she danced very little. Everyone says she is beautiful, but I think she is only <u>tolerably pretty</u>. Her gown was so delicious though it made me quite wild, I looked at it very particularly and shall have my dressmaker try to copy it. The Duke of Wellington was there also, he arrived just before Mrs. Crawley, after the dancing had started. He did not dance at all, but express after express arrived for him, and aides continually rushed up to him out of breath, I quite laughed to see it. But imagine what happened! An ensign came up to me and handed me a nosegay and said I had dropped it. <u>But I never had a nosegay!</u> I was about to tell him so when I noticed that there was <u>a little note</u> tucked in among the blossoms. So I thanked him very prettily. I did not look at the note right away, for I did not want anyone who might be watching to think that I cared a fig if I received a note; but later on, when I was sitting down and Osborne had gone to bring me a glass of punch, I slipped the note out. It was from General A***! <u>He asks for the honour of being introduced to me, and would like me to join him for a private supper!</u> What impertinence! Of course I hid the note so that Wickham or Osborne would not see it, and then when I was dancing I looked around a little and saw the General gazing at me. I did not nod or smile, as you can imagine, <u>but a little later he had an officer introduce him to me and asked me for a waltz</u>. I could not say no of course for that might have caused some difficulty for Wickham or Osborne. The General held me <u>very tight</u>. He is a capital dancer. He whispered to me about the supper! Of course I will not go. But he is a handsome man, although not so handsome as Wickham or Osborne. But he <u>is</u> a general, and perhaps he is rich. I think it all very good fun, don't you?

Just past midnight we suddenly heard the drums beating to arms and the trumpets sounding, and the music and dancing stopped at once and everyone was asking everyone else what was happening. Everyone rushed out into the street, and we heard that the French had come near and our troops were ordered to march out of the city, to go to a town nearby called Waterloo. We made out way back to our lodgings—although it was horrid difficult with so many people in the streets! and Wickham and Osborne prepared themselves and left for the assembly in Place Royale. Major O'Dowd's wife and I went down a little after them to see all the fun. There were soldiers everywhere, even some sleeping on packs of straw, although I do not know how they could sleep with such a din all about, with people shouting and horses and wagons and guns all clattering about and bugles sounding. Then what do you think happened? The carts began to come in to market from the country, filled with potatoes and cabbages, and the silly old women in the carts were gaping so at the soldiers. Lord, how I laughed to see them! About four o'clock the regiments began to march out and then we came back to our lodgings. I could not sleep for all the excitement so I have written this letter to you. Now how tired I am! I shall sleep all day. Mrs. O'Dowd just came to tell me that some of the English are beginning to leave town, they are afraid we might be defeated. That cannot be, with Wickham and Osborne and General A*** fighting them. I am sure the French will run away!

Your affectionate sister

Lydia Wickham

Kitty was much struck by the thoughtlessness of this letter, which she received after news had reached England of the victory at Waterloo, and of the great loss of life on both sides, and after she had also had word that Colonel Fitzwilliam was safe. What a letter, to be written at such a moment! when her husband was going into the greatest danger. She waited for another, telling of Lydia's reunion with Wickham; but it did not arrive. There came instead a letter for Darcy.

Brussels, Belgium

26 June, 1815

Dear Sir,

I ask that you pardon my writing a letter to you without previous introduction, however Mrs. George Wickham has given me your name and direction. I have been requested by General A*** to escort Mrs. Wickham back to England to her family. Lieutenant George Wickham was wounded in battle on Sunday June 18 under French fire, and died five days later in Brussels. Mrs. Wickham is presently alone here, where it is not safe or desirable for her to remain. With your permission, I shall accompany her to Derbyshire. Although

> travel arrangements are somewhat difficult between Belgium and England at this time, I expect that we will arrive within one week.
> Your obedient servant,
> Capt. Thomas Westove

When intelligence of Wickham's passing was carried abroad, it aroused little grief among those who had known him. His parents were dead, and he had no other living relatives. His fellow officers regretted *his* among the deaths of others, but many of them wondered who was now to pay his debts of honour. Lydia's family, while taken aback by the abruptness of his death, recollected for the most part that he was a man who had had all the appearance of goodness but none of the substance; Mr. Bennet however expressed sorrow at the loss of his (so he said) favourite son-in-law. He wrote to Elizabeth, "I was prodigiously proud of him, for he was as fine a fellow as I ever saw, smiling and smirking and making love to us all, and I fear that Sir William Lucas now must take the honours over me. However I am optimistic that Lydia will exercise her excellent judgment and provide a replacement whom I can hold in equally high regard."

Yet there were three hearts that were troubled. Mrs. Younge, in her London boarding house, sighed when she heard the news, and thought of his handsome young face, his gentle manner, and his generosity when he was in funds. Mrs. Reynolds, walking through the rooms of Pemberley, thought of the boy who had been brought up there, and educated at her late master's expense, and had against all hope and expectation turned out very wild. And Georgiana crept into her father's room and took down Wickham's miniature from over the mantelpiece; and carried it with her to her bedroom, where she cried herself to sleep on that night and many succeeding ones.

Chapter Fifty-Six

[June-July 1815, Pemberley]

Lydia had been exceedingly shocked by the death of Wickham. At nineteen, boisterous, untamed, unabashed, wild, noisy, and fearless, she had never yet suffered the loss of a close relative or friend, and had prior to the moment been almost unable to compass the death of someone of importance in her life. As affection had sunk into indifference soon after their marriage, the grief she felt was not for loss of a beloved husband but for her position as the wife of an officer, and all the parties and flirting that were attendant thereon. However she consoled herself that Osborne would soon come for her, and they would marry, and she would be restored to that desirable situation. It was therefore very soon after her arrival at Pemberley that she regained her spirits.

"Good Lord, how old and ugly I looked in this horrid black!" she said to Elizabeth. "Must I wear it all the time?"

"Really, Lydia, you puzzle me exceedingly. But you shall decide for yourself. If upon mature deliberation you find that the misery of wearing black is more than equivalent to the satisfaction of performing this last obligation to your husband, then by all means do not wear it. But your respectability in the world must be seriously affected by public notice of your disdain of convention. You will be censured wherever you are known."

"*I* don't give three straws about what people will say. I suppose I may take it off when I marry?"

"Heavens! I begin to believe that your character is beyond the reach of amendment!"

"It does not much signify what I wear. Weeping and looking ugly will not bring Wickham back. I am sure he would not want me to look like this. And when I marry again, my husband will want me to look pretty."

"Whom, pray tell, are you intending to marry?"

"Why Osborne of course. He will come for me as soon as he can."

As Osborne, however, showed no indication of arriving at Pemberley, or of communicating with Lydia or anyone else there, Lydia determined to make enquiries of Captain Westove, who had remained in the north of England, and made as frequent visits to his late fellow-officer's widow as his duties permitted. Westove was a tall well-made man with regular, somewhat stern features, and a balding brow. He was rather reserved and not quick to initiate discourse, although he was a conversible companion if it were begun by another.

"Captain Westove, have you heard anything from Captain Osborne? I cannot think why he has not written to me yet, or come to me."

"Mrs. Wickham, Osborne is not coming to you. I am sorry to be the one to tell you this."

"Oh, *that* is quite impossible. His coming is delayed, that is all. He has some duty with the regiment that he must attend to."

"Ma'am, you are mistaken. No duty is delaying him."

"I am not mistaken. It is you who do not know what you are talking about." Lydia, always unguarded and often uncivil, turned away from him in a temper.

"Mrs. Wickham, I can see that you will not believe me unless you know the entire truth, and so I will tell it to you now."

"What truth? What do you mean? What can you know of Osborne's plans to come to me?"

"A great deal more than you, ma'am, it would seem. Perhaps you would like to sit down while I tell you?"

"I do not need to sit down to listen to such an absurd story. Well, what do you wish to say?"

"I will make it short. General A*** sent for me when he learned that Lieutenant Wickham had been grievously injured, and gave orders that I was to take responsibility for returning you to England. He was concerned for your safety in Brussels with your husband unable to protect you and so many of the English having left the city. I knew that you and your husband had been staying in the same house with Osborne, and had been going about the city together, so I immediately went to him, and asked him for assistance in informing you of your husband's situation and in helping you to remove from the city. He refused. He said he would not see you again."

"That is a lie!"

"It is not a lie, ma'am. If you knew me, or if you knew my reputation, you would not impute a falsehood to me, even though," he added more softly, "I know that you do it because my words have caused you pain. I am sorry for that, for I would not hurt you for all the world."

"You tell me you would not lie, but what you have said cannot be the truth! Osborne would never say he would not see me again."

"Ma'am, I would that you would believe me and not press me further in this matter."

"I will not believe you. You do not know what Osborne and I have been to each other."

"But I do know."

Lydia turned and stared at him.

"Osborne himself told me," Captain Westove continued. "He told me that you have been his mistress for nearly a year, and that he had been cuckolding Wickham under his very nose."

Lydia grew pale.

"I asked you not to press me, ma'am, but you would not believe me without hearing everything. Osborne said that once Wickham was dead you would certainly expect him to marry you, and so he was going to take to his heels. His very words ma'am. He is a blackguard, and you are well rid of him, in my opinion."

"But he loves me," said Lydia in a faint voice. "I love him. He would not …."

"He has." After a moment—"Let there be an end to your thoughts of him, Mrs. Wickham."

If Lydia had been shocked by Wickham's death, she was rendered almost insensible by Osborne's betrayal. Now at last she assumed the appearance of a new-made widow, and remained in her bedroom pale, silent and sleepless for a score of nights. Elizabeth, who had in all of Lydia's life never seen her anything other than wild and loud, scarcely knew what to do with her, or what comfort to offer her. Captain Westove told her and Darcy the entire story; and although they were not in the least surprised by it, it materially increased their confusion about how to treat Lydia or consider her future life. Captain Westove, however, did not share their confusion and concern. "Mrs. Wickham," he said, "would make a cannon-ball falter. She has had the wind knocked out of her, that is all. That young lady's liveliness runs right through to the bone. It would take more than the death of Lieutenant Wickham, who was a bounder, and the desertion of Captain Osborne, who is a cad, to cast her down to the ground."

"Captain Westove, I take it you admire my sister," said Darcy.

"Sir, I am a frank man and I like to come to the point and not beat around the bushes. I do admire Mrs. Wickham. Many a time have I looked at her with her husband or with Osborne and wondered what she would be like with a man who was actually worthy of her."

"I fear you may be mistaking my sister's temperament a little," said Elizabeth. "Excuse me, for I must speak plainly to you. She has been a determined flirt since she was fifteen years old, empty-headed, vain and wilful, and nothing I have seen in her behaviour since makes me think it likely she will change."

"Mrs. Darcy, I would say to you then, do not judge the woman she will become by the girl she has been. She has not been tested yet to see what she is made of."

"I am afraid she has been tested considerably, with very similar result each time," said Darcy. "There is in every disposition a tendency to some natural defect, which is not easily overcome."

"I do not agree with your opinion of Mrs. Wickham. You look at her and see an empty-headed flirt. I look at her and I see a young woman with strength, energy and good humour, and a pretty face and a womanly figure that are not often matched. There is too much of her for the life she was brought up to."

"What other kind of life is she likely to find?"

"You will perhaps find it presumptuous in me to say this, but *I* could offer your sister another kind of life."

Darcy and Elizabeth looked at him in astonishment. After a moment Darcy said, "Captain Westove, before we proceed on this subject, allow me to say that the British army has been my sister's undoing. It would be most inadvisable for her to marry another soldier."

"Will you hear me out?"

"Most willingly."

"The war is over, and I intend to resign my commission shortly. I was posted to Fort York* in 1812, and as an officer I am now entitled to an allotment of land, a few hundred acres, in Upper Canada. I have made up my mind to take up my grant, for I believe life there will suit me. It will not be an easy one, it is hard work to clear ground and plant a first crop, to build a house; it is cold in the winter and hot in the summer. But there is good soil, game a-plenty, great personal liberty, and a host of opportunities for a man with a quick mind and strong back. I am not a rich man, and my family before me were not rich either. I am not used to a delicate life, and I know something about farming. I believe I can make a success of myself. And if I could take with me the right wife, I believe that she and I could be happy in our new home and our work, and could raise sturdy children and leave them a legacy. But the hardships of a settler's life are felt most greatly by the women, and few who are used to the refinements of life here in England would willingly give them up. Only some urgent reason would make them leave. A fine lady would suffer from the conditions we would meet at first, but a lady like Mrs. Wickham, with her youth and vigour, might even take pleasure in what we would find there." He added as an afterthought, "Outside of the larger towns in Canada such as York

* The town and military post of York were established in 1793, becoming the City of Toronto in 1834 (now Toronto, Ontario). –Ed.

and Quebec and Halifax, there are very few officers to create a—distraction for Mrs. Wickham. The population indeed is quite sparse."

Darcy and Elizabeth exchanged a glance. "We can perceive that you have an attachment to *her*—but what do you know of *her* sentiments? Do you believe her to be wishing or expecting your addresses?" asked Darcy.

"On the contrary, I think her indifferent to me at the moment. But I will be direct with you once more. Your sister has a claim to reputation that will not easily be overlooked by any gentleman who is presently acquainted with her. It will be difficult for her to find another husband in England whom her family would think fitting."

"I am far from disagreeing with you in your estimation of her chances of a suitable marriage," said Darcy gravely, "but I am very much in doubt of Mrs. Wickham's inclination to leave English society. I think you must abandon the plan."

"You are perhaps unaware," said Westove, "that it is British officers and their families who are populating Canada, for half-pay officers of every rank are accepting land grants there. There is an enforced period of residence, which not many men would undertake without the comfort of their families; and so come into the colony men and women who are civilized, and often of respectable descent."

"Darcy," said Elizabeth, who was ready to allow that the suggested arrangement might be a wise and desirable measure for both parties, and felt persuaded of her sister's acquiescence if the design were presented to her in the most favourable light, "I think we must give leave to Captain Westove to try his fortune with Lydia. I believe his plan is an eligible one, and I am not convinced that Lydia has such a strong attachment to this country and to her family, that she would reject his proposal."

Darcy was doubtful but did not oppose her wishes. "Perhaps, Captain Westove, you may bring about a happier conclusion to Lydia's affairs than there is at present reason to hope. We will speak further of this matter."

With this Captain Westove was content, and he left Pemberley that day and returned to the inn at Lambton revolving plans in his head that were tolerably satisfying to him.

A day or two after this conversation, Lydia received a letter. She did not quite recognize the hand, yet it struck her as familiar for some reason.

> London
> July –, 1815
>
> Dear Mrs. Wickham,
> I ask you to pardon my intrusion upon your grief, and offer as my excuse a most sincere concern for your health and happiness. The

loss of a husband for one so young as yourself is a particularly hard blow, yet at the same time the recuperative powers of youth may soon lead you to restored equanimity of spirits. As you are now deprived of the guidance and care of your husband, and are set adrift in the world, I wish to offer you my protection. If you will accept it you have my assurance of steady affection, and provision of suitable accommodation and income. I await your response.

Your most obedient servant,
General A***

Although Lydia was considered thoughtless and empty headed by most of her family, she was not in fact slow to credit what was to her immediate advantage, or to think slightingly of material pleasures in the form of a house and servants, fine clothes, jewels and pin-money, carriages and outings to the theatre or other places of pleasure, and the company of admiring army officers. Nor did she disparage the admiration of a single officer, especially one in the highest ranks. She did not devote an excessive amount of time to weighing life as a respectable widow, making her home quietly at Longbourn or Clifford Priory or Pemberley, against life as the darling of General A*** with her own home and (as she perceived) continual excitement and luxury. As a widow under the guidance of her family she would have to wait at the very least a full year—an unimaginably long period of time!—to remarry, and the likelihood of finding an officer as handsome as Wickham or Osborne for her husband, now that the war was over and the camps disbanded, seemed small. She did not address in her own mind the effect that her reputation might have on her marital opportunities, for her natural self-consequence and assurance, and her past successes, told her that her person and manners would be sure to captivate any man who caught her fancy.

Lydia took the first opportunity of communicating her plans to Elizabeth, announcing that she intended to travel to London soon.

"Why do you wish to go up to London?" asked Elizabeth in surprise.

"I am going to see General A***."

"General A***! What possible reason do you have to call on General A***?"

"He has written that he wishes to take care of me, and I think I should like it."

Elizabeth's astonishment was almost boundless. "That would be a delightful scheme indeed! Lydia, this is quite impossible. Become the… the…*companion* of General A***!"

"Well, it is a better scheme than being buried here at Pemberley, or at Clifford or Longbourn, dressed in black as if I were as dead as Wickham! Think what a miserable life else I shall have!"

In vain did Elizabeth attempt to make her sister reasonable, representing to her the detestable impropriety of such a scheme, and at length she was reduced to saying to her, "Lydia, you will not be permitted to go to General A***. You will be locked up before you ever set foot out of Pemberley."

"I'm sure I shall break my heart if I must remain here!" cried Lydia. "You are so disagreeable."

"I am perfectly serious in my refusal to allow you to go to General A***, whether your heart break or not. The matter may be considered as finally settled. But if you wish to remarry as soon as possible, there does lie an alternative before you."

"What is that?"

"To wed Captain Westove. He admires you, and has spoken to Darcy and me of you. I think it not impossible that you would suit each other."

"Good Lord!" exclaimed Lydia boisterously. "How can you tell such a story! He is sour as turned milk whenever he comes here."

"I speak nothing but the truth; I never saw a more promising inclination in a man. You may apply to Darcy if you do not believe me."

"Captain Westove?" said Lydia doubtfully. "He is not especially handsome." She reflected for a few moments. "However I think he *is* in love with me. And he is quite tall, and his shoulders are broad. I thought the other day how well he looked in his red coat."

"The one objection that might have material weight is that he is shortly emigrating to Canada."

"Canada! What is in Canada? I do not think there would be any fun in it."

"There would be a new life. Darcy would give you a dowry so that you would have the means to set yourselves up. I think you must choose between an union with Captain Westove and a widow's life in *respectable* mourning."

Lydia took very little more time to consider this proposition than she had General A***'s. With the creative eye of fancy, infinitely aided by an uninformed mind, she saw herself flirting with handsome Indian braves and French woodsmen, who laid rich fur pelts at her feet; and garnering the admiring glances of women dressed in shapeless gowns of homespun wool as she passed before them in an elegant bonnet.

"Very well then," she said, "if he will ask me himself. It would be much better to marry him than to be a widow, if I cannot go to General A***. But what about the baby?"

The letter that Elizabeth wrote to her sister Jane on this occasion will prove the variety of her feelings.

Pemberley
July –, 1815

Dearest Jane,
What do you think has happened? Captain Thomas Westove, the officer, you will recall, who brought Lydia back from Brussels, has made an offer for her, and wishes to take her with him as his wife to Upper Canada, where he is determined to emigrate. This of course occasioned much conversation, both among him and Darcy and me, and then between Lydia and me, and Lydia was brought to look positively upon the match. Darcy and I are in agreement that it would be to the benefit of all to secure and expedite such a marriage (whether or not this might be considered proper for the generality of widows) and also to remove Lydia to a place where she may be able to re-establish her character with more credit. Captain Westove believes that life in Canada (amid the forests and snow), with plenty of fresh air, and work to keep her occupied, will bring forth her more laudable qualities. The connection would certainly be a prudent one on the lady's side, although I cannot help having some doubts about its prudence on the gentleman's. Nevertheless I am ready to allow it a wise and desirable measure for both. There is more, however. No sooner had Lydia been persuaded to turn a friendly eye on the alliance than she asked, "But what about the baby?" As I wrote you, Lydia will be confined in August, and it is not to be expected that Captain Westove would wish to enter the married state burdened with the child of another man; and Lydia herself does not seem pleased at the prospect of its arrival and expresses no tenderness for it. Further, I feel a wholly justifiable concern at carrying so young an infant across the ocean to a land where there may be many hardships. What we are to do now I am at a loss to imagine! The circumstances seem hopeless of remedy. Kitty and small James Fitzwilliam are well, and his parents are wondering already how soon they may be able to mount him on a pony. Kitty bids me tell you she will write to you herself very soon. All Darcy's and my love to you and Bingley, and Lydia sends affectionate greetings.
Your sister,
E. Darcy

Jane read Elizabeth's letter with astonishment; but all surprise was shortly lost in other emotions. The thought of the child, of Lydia's apparent indifference to it, and the possibility of it having to endure pain or privation of any kind, were enough to interest all her tender feelings. She could reflect with certainty on only one point—that the child would suffer if it went to Canada, first by the voyage and then by the roughness of travel and any trials that Lydia and her husband might have to undergo once there. Jane's imagination was very swift; it jumped from concern to affection and from affection to motherhood, all in a moment. It had required all her good sense and attention to the feelings of her husband and family to check the indulgence of regrets arising from her own inability to bear a child, and now with clear sight she envisioned the remedy of her own unhappiness and of Lydia's predicament. Nothing remained therefore to be done except speak to Bingley, and she went to him without a moment's loss of time.

"Bingley," she exclaimed, "something has occurred of a most unexpected nature, relating to Lydia. This letter is from Lizzy, and what it contains has surprised me a great deal."

"Let me hear the particulars."

"I will read it to you."

Bingley listened attentively, and when she had concluded he said "Come, Jane. What is in your mind?"

"I will have no reserves from you. Lydia seems to have no strong attachment to the child, and to take one so young on the voyage to Canada would surely be perilous. No one of common humanity would not wish to guard it from hurt. Bingley—what if we were to offer to take the child and raise it as our own?"

The rapidity of her husband's thought was not equal to Jane's on this occasion and he paused. "Jane," he said after a moment's deliberation, "I should think it possible that this child is illegitimate, that its father was not Wickham."

Jane could not assert this to be altogether impossible, but she replied, "If indeed that is true, I cannot help blaming Lydia, for she was very wrong. Yet I pity her also because her present feelings must be quite different; she must feel that she acted wrong. But the child ought not be made to suffer for the fault of its parents."

"Should we make Elizabeth and Darcy understand the matter?"

"Surely there can be no occasion; we do not know beyond all possible doubt that the father is not Wickham, and if we were to expose Lydia we would thereby injure the child. It seems unjustifiable. What is your view?"

"That we shall not undeceive anyone, now, or ever, as to our suspicions concerning Lydia's conduct or the child's parentage."

"We must endeavour to forget all that has passed," said Jane with increasing cheerfulness. "I hope and trust Lydia and Captain Westove will be happy. Their mutual affection will steady her; and they will settle quietly in Canada, and live in a rational a manner. In time her past imprudence will be forgotten by all. And Bingley—we shall take the child, shall we not?"

Bingley was a sweet-tempered and amiable man, who was not only desirous of procuring the happiness of his wife but also of raising a family of his own. He replied with a smile, "With all my heart, Jane. Write to Elizabeth without delay."

Jane's anxiety under the suspense of waiting for Elizabeth's reply was painful, but a letter from Pemberley arrived very shortly, and answered every wish of her heart. Lydia was exceedingly pleased with the proposal, Elizabeth wrote, and nothing could give herself and Darcy more delight than to have the Bingleys take the child. Jane went immediately to Bingley with a glow of such happy expression as amply marked her joy, and instantly embracing him declared that she was the most fortunate being that ever existed. "How happy Lydia has made me!" she cried.

Jane then had to listen to all Bingley had to say of his own happiness, which he did with words so sincere and warm that every sentence was a fresh source of delight to her. They sat together and engaged in earnest conversation about the prospect of their new duties and their expectations of felicity; and in an hour's conference they managed to say no more than half that they wished to say to each other.

Chapter Fifty-Seven

[August-September 1815, Longbourn]

Mrs. Bennet fell into an exceedingly spiritless condition at the idea that her youngest daughter was to leave England for the colonies. It had been a severe disappointment to her when Lydia had settled in the North upon her marriage to Wickham, just when she had most expected to have pleasure and pride in the company of her first-married daughter, and now she was marrying a new husband who wanted to carry her very much farther away. "But why must they go to Canada? I made sure that when Wickham died she would come back to Longbourn, at least until Jane and Bingley or Lizzy and Darcy could find her a new husband in a year or so. It was so sudden that she agreed to marry Captain Westove, and now she is talking of crossing the ocean! They would have no trouble finding a place to live in Hertfordshire. There is the great house at Stoke, I should not mind them living there even though the drawing-room is very small. I should not even mind them living at Ashworth, though it is ten miles away."

"His Majesty, in his wisdom, has not seen fit to offer Captain Westove five hundred acres of land in Hertfordshire, as he has in Upper Canada, Mrs. Bennet," said her husband.

"And she will be leaving the regiment where she was acquainted with everybody! There were several young men that she liked very much, I believe. Where will she find such friends in Canada?"

"If she and Captain Westove are fortunate, she shall not."

"It is quite shocking to send her away like this! I do not even know when we shall meet again. Perhaps not for four or five years."

"I do not intend making any plans to visit Canada, my dear, and it is likely that once Westove and Lydia arrive there their residence will be of some duration."

"Ah, then if she leaves England I may never see her more! And she is such a bad writer, except to Kitty. Mr. Bennet, this is exceedingly hard. I shall be quite forlorn without her."

"My dear Mrs. Bennet, I urge you to console yourself. From what I understand, there is a grave possibility that if Lydia *remain* in England you will never see her more."

In due course Mr. and Mrs. Bennet received the news that Lydia had been delivered of a girl, whom she named Cassandra, and that the baby had been taken away by Jane and Bingley. Jane wrote to her mother most blissfully of the child's beauty and sunny disposition, adding that Lydia had not seemed distressed to part with her but had been anxious for the Bingleys to take her. "The child reminds her too much of Wickham, I suppose," said Mrs. Bennet, "and of the happy time that she spent with him. Perhaps it is best for her to forget him now that she will have another husband."

"It is perhaps best for all of us to forget Wickham," said Mr. Bennet drily.

A few weeks later the Bennets received a farewell letter from Lydia.

> Pemberley House, Derby
> September –, 1815
>
> Dear mamma and papa,
> I am sorry you could not come to Derbyshire to see my new husband before we go off to Canada. It was good luck to marry again so quickly for I did not at all like being a widow. Captain Westove was married in a blue coat, which made me think of my wedding to Wickham, although you would not find Westove as handsome. He is a little bald. We shall not come to Hertfordshire as we have a great many things to do before the ship sails from Greenock in Scotland. When we are settled I shall send you my direction and you and my sisters may write to me, and I shall write to you if I have leisure. Westove thinks we will be exceedingly busy, however. Darcy and Lizzy have given us a handsome wedding present that they say we are to use to buy a better piece of land if we do not like what the King has chosen. It appears that there is not much else to buy there anyway, and no dressmakers to speak of, and I shall have to make do with the clothes I bring with me for quite a long time. However I daresay that I shall be more fashionably dressed than the other ladies, so that is something. I am taking several pretty bonnets with me and I suppose I can trim them new myself if I cannot find a milliner. Captain Westove says that it will be more important to have a warm cloak than a pretty bonnet, but as you can see he knows very

little about women yet. Do not worry about me going so far away for I will like it there of all things I am sure.
Your affectionate daughter,
Lydia Westove

Chapter Fifty-Eight

[November 1815, Damson Hall]

"Have you seen this, Sir Henry?" asked Lady Mallinger of her husband as she entered his library at Damson Hall. "One of my acquaintances sent it to me, with a charming little note inquiring whether it is an ode to an unnamed friend of yours. She wonders if the lady in question might also be an *inamorata* of Lord Byron, who penned the lines this year."

"As far as I know Byron has never met Leonora," said Mallinger carelessly. "Let me see them."

She walks in beauty, like the night
Of cloudless climes and starry skies,
And all that's best of dark and bright
Meets in her aspect and her eyes;
Thus mellow'd to that tender light
Which Heaven to gaudy day denies.

One shade the more, one ray the less,
Had half impair'd the nameless grace
Which waves in every raven tress
Or softly lightens o'er her face,
Where thoughts serenely sweet express
How pure, how dear their dwelling-place.

And on that cheek and o'er that brow
So soft, so calm, yet eloquent,
The smiles that win, the tints that glow
But tell of days in goodness spent,—

A mind at peace with all below,
A heart whose love is innocent.

"Ha! That describes Leonora very well."

"I thought the last three lines particularly *à propos* of your beloved," said Lady Mallinger with singular irony.

"I am certain those lines describe *you* much better, Caroline. When we are apart I often think of the purity of your love for me and the sweetness of your temper. Do you have in mind any little journeys to the North while I am gone to Venice?"

"Do not be impertinent. Comments of that nature become you remarkably ill."

"I met Byron the other day at my club, he was asking me about Venice. I suspect England is becoming too hot for him—his activities begin to make me look like a bishop. I am grateful to him, however, for as long as he is about tongues will scarcely bother to wag about our arrangements."

"I cannot pretend that I shall regret *your* departure for Italy, whatever plans Lord Byron may form. When do you intend leaving?"

Sir Henry, fatigued with his wife's disagreeable manner, replied, "Shortly. The sky grows cold and gloomy as your regard for me, it is time to be away. Now if you have finished your communication, I shall be glad to be left alone."

Lady Mallinger although provoked by his words knew better than to quarrel seriously with her husband, and she withdrew in silence.

Chapter Fifty-Nine

[November 1815, Cambridgeshire]

In October Dr. Cramer's health had begun to fail precipitously. He suffered greatly in his illness and Mary was incapable of the relief of his affliction, more than affectionate care and words could procure; however he underwent his ordeal with Christian patience and resignation.

When Dr. Cramer had fallen ill, Mary had written of it to Adam Kendall. She had counted the days till she might reasonably hope to hear from him, but her impatience was as well rewarded as impatience generally is. Four weeks passed away and she saw and heard nothing of him; not a note nor a line did she receive. As she sat by her husband's bedside, her thoughts were as often on Kendall as her husband, for she could not prevent herself from indulging in reflection on him. One evening, with a solemn countenance, she sat by her husband's bedside striving to determine her feelings towards the young man. She respected him for his principles and courage. She was grateful to him for giving her work which brought her esteem, and for taking an interest in her welfare. But she felt that there was within her another motive that heightened respect and gratitude. Because she had never even fancied herself in love before she had met him, and in spite of her many years' study in books, it took her an inordinate time to make out the composition of her sentiments: with mingled astonishment and dismay she came to the realization that she cherished a tender affection for him. The discovery could not have made a stronger impression on her mind, and struck her too forcibly for refutation. From herself to Kendall, from Kendall to Dr. Cramer, her thoughts moved in a line which soon brought to her an overpowering sense of shame. "How despicably I have been acting!" she thought in misery. "I who have prided myself on my virtue! Loss of virtue in a female is irretrievable, and one false step may involve her in endless ruin." She could hardly keep her seat. It was exceedingly painful to her to know that she had been so unguarded in her feelings, and she grieved heartily over her infidelity to her husband. "What must Dr. Cramer think of me?" she asked herself, deeply ashamed. "And what do others say of me? A woman's reputation is no less brittle than it is beautiful." Her colour heightened with a bitter sense of disgrace. How degrading was this discovery!

Without a long interval that evening, another discovery, scarcely less mortifying, succeeded. Mary had learned from Kendall, that she could more easily win *his* praise and approval by caring for a puppy than by disputing with the local landowners and magistrates. Now as she tended her husband she elicited more of commendation and gratefulness from him by bringing a glass of wine to his lips or holding his hand than ever she had by parading her learning before him. She had prided herself beyond measure on her accomplishments, and attempted to gratify her vanity by exhibiting her abilities on every propitious occasion; but her pride and her vanity had been folly, and her accomplishments had had but little efficacy in purchasing the admiration that she sought with all her heart. Although Dr. Cramer had been dismissive of her knowledge that had been acquired with such hard work, in his final days he often spoke lovingly to Mary of his gratitude for her constant presence and ministrations.

"I have been blinded by vanity," she thought in humiliation. "I, who have studied human nature with such application. Vanity is a very common failing, indeed. I have been complacent about my accomplishments, and have expected others to praise them. However it has been giving food to a puppy or bathing my husband's brow that have brought me true regard and approval. Until now, I never comprehended this!" She could not help remembering what Dr. Cramer's opinion had always been, and now she could not deny the justice of it. However her husband's affectionate looks and words, although grateful to her feelings, were hardly capable of consoling her, and the evening as it passed seemed infinitely long.

Mary's sense of shame now led her to rejoice at Kendall's silence. She declared to herself that she was convinced of his indifference and was henceforth free from the offense of his further notice; but all of her intentions to deny her attachment were powerless, and she still yearned for an answer to her letter or a visit from him. Every day she devised a new excuse for him, but as day after day passed away without bringing any word, she gave way to distress. She strove not to regret the loss of his society or to wish for a renewal of his acquaintance, and determined to put herself on her guard against any feelings for him that lingered in her breast, but she could not prevent sorrow frequently occurring. She was very unhappy. If he had cared about her, he must have visited her or written to her, long ago. Her attachment to him must have escaped his observation, and any regard she perceived in him had been no more than an error of fancy on her side. She had nothing to reproach *him* with therefore, for she had been deceived here as well by her vanity!

When Dr. Cramer died, in her shame she considered herself justly punished by the loss of her husband as well as of Kendall's society. Surely one who had conducted herself with such impropriety as she deserved to be solitary! She struggled to check the indulgence of grief and regrets, and to support her spirits, but having no one by her to contribute to their recovery (for she had declined invitations from her sisters Elizabeth and Jane, and from her step-daughters, to come to them), she often experienced dejection. Seeking in her extracts for words that would comfort her, she found them instead cold and lifeless, and she turned with additional dependence to the steady attachment of her little dog Sophia.

She was sitting one morning in the breakfast parlour with her work, with Sophia at her feet, when the servant announced a caller, and she saw to her utter amazement Adam Kendall enter the room. On the gentleman's appearing, her colour increased and then as quickly fled from her face, and her eyes were fixed on him with the most painful sensations. Her heart beat quickly to see him—yet she considered his coming to visit her the most ill-judged thing in the world. It might seem as if she had an understanding with him, to meet after her husband's death! In what a disgraceful light might it not strike the servants and the neighbours! Therefore although she could not help her pleasure, all sense of it was lost in shame and vexation. However she forced a smile and strove to receive him with a decorum free of any symptom either of resentment or of satisfaction at his coming.

She resolutely kept her place and continued her work, anxious that no difference should be perceived in her—endeavouring to be composed, and resolved to repress such reflections as must make her unfit for ordinary conversation. But she could not overcome the discomfiture which must attend their meeting, and *his* embarrassment was plainly conveyed also. He expressed his condolences on the loss of her husband. She inquired after Mr. Wilberforce, and about Kendall's own work in animal protection. Thereafter several minutes passed without the sound of his voice or hers, and when she was unable to resist looking at him she found his eyes on the ground or the window. Every glance convinced her of what she dreaded, that he had no partiality for her. "Could it be otherwise?" she asked herself in frustration and sadness. " But—Oh! why did he come?"

It was evident that he had no enjoyment in the meeting, and after a short time he rose to go away. "Forgive me for having taken up your time," he said, "and I offer you my sympathy, and my best wishes for your health."

As soon as he was gone, Mary walked about the room in a futile effort to recover her spirits. "Why did he come here to be so silent and ill at ease?" she said aloud. She could find no answer to her question, and made a resolution to think of him no more, which was as instantly broken, and she continued her reflections on him for several minutes more; until she was suddenly roused from them by the sound of the door-bell, and a moment later Kendall walked into the room again.

Her astonishment at his return was even greater than what she had known on first seeing him that day. However his behaviour was strangely altered, for she saw him still looking embarrassed and awkward but now also exhibiting purpose and animation.

"I beg you to accept my apologies, Mrs. Cramer," he said immediately, "but I could not leave until I said to you what I came here to say. I have striven to contain my feelings, but I find that I cannot. I am not ashamed of them. I have returned to tell you that I—I admire you—no, that is not it—that I love you."

Mary's astonishment was now beyond expression. The colour which had been driven from her face by his reappearance returned with additional radiance, and she looked almost handsome. Whatever of her own vanity she had not yet been able to reason away was highly gratified, but almost immediately her severe sense of shame recalled her to propriety.

"It is impossible for me to do other than remonstrate with you over such language," she cried. "I am widowed only these four weeks, and it is reprehensible for you to speak to me in such a manner. I must require you to leave this house instantaneously and not return."

"I perfectly comprehend your feelings," he said with a composure uncommon in a gentleman who has just been ordered by a lady to depart from her dwelling. "They are natural and just. But—I believe they are not all that you feel."

Mary could find no words, and now silent and pale lowered her head. Kendall continued earnestly, looking sometimes at her and sometimes away from her. "Have you ever seen a runaway horse?"

"Assuredly," said Mary looking up, surprised and mystified.

"If a young untrained animal is frightened or unruly, we think no ill of the rider or driver. We may be alarmed if he falls off; or amused, if he is not hurt; or admiring if he guides it to a safe halt. But we do not think him at fault."

Mary pondered his words. At last she said, "What if the horse strikes one who is standing by?"

"That is a very bad case, but even then if the rider did all he could to stop the animal, we do not blame him. But—do you believe that anyone has been struck?"

"How can you make that inquiry? I was a consort, who owed all her affection to her husband!"

"Mrs. Cramer—Mary—you have conducted yourself without any impropriety; if you injured your husband in any way by your feelings, which you could not regulate, you did not by your actions, which were under your regulation."

Mary now began to revive a little, and was able to look at Kendall as he spoke.

"I felt it wrong," he continued, "to correspond or visit while your husband was suffering—dying; it would have been wrong of me to take pleasure in his wife's companionship—and perhaps to—to give her pleasure in mine—at such a time. I did not mean to injure your feelings, but not to communicate with you seemed the lesser breach of morality." He paused and gave her a very serious look. "I will go now, and hope that you do not think too ill of me for speaking to you as I have done; and that you will one day forgive me, and allow me to call upon you again. And to—and to make my addresses to you." He bowed and turned to leave.

Mary felt a sudden alarm to see him going and said quickly, "But I do not know where I shall be in the future! I must soon leave the Rectory, for the new incumbent will now have the use of it."

Kendall turned back in haste. "But where will you go? I do not wish you to be taken away to a new home, without my knowing where you may be gone!"

"Mr. Kendall," said Mary, laughing suddenly, "I believe you look upon me as a sort of canine or feline that has lost its master and is in peril of being turned out into the streets to perish of inanition!"

Kendall looked a little embarrassed at this reflection, and then smiled awkwardly. "I do not want to lose you," he said. "You will not leave without telling me where I may find you thereafter?"

Mary's joy burst forth. "Naturally I shall not depart without communicating my destination!" she said. "And now—do you wish to see the new tricks I have taught to Sophia?"

Chapter Sixty

[November-December 1815, letters received from Canada]

Lydia's last letter from Scotland had informed her family that her husband had found a ship, and had paid fifteen pounds apiece for their passage to Montreal, in Lower Canada. The family now waited eagerly for news from the other side of the ocean. They received them sooner than they had expected, knowing that Lydia was at best a dilatory correspondent, particularly if there was no flirting to boast of to Kitty, for Elizabeth and Darcy had a letter just seven weeks after Lydia's ship sailed from Greenock. It had been written in the Gulf of the St. Lawrence River, where a ship bound for England had met Lydia's and had taken off any letters that the passengers wished to give them. Lydia wrote that they had had very favourable winds and had sighted Newfoundland in less than four weeks, and although this was considered a very quick time for making the crossing she had very rapidly tired of the voyage, for she had had nothing to do but sit on a bench on the deck when the weather was fine, or walk about the deck with her husband, or go below the deck to their cabin when it rained. The only events of interest that occurred during the crossing were the sightings as they drew nearer to land of large numbers of seabirds, a whale, three porpoises, and a party of seals, and she had been in raptures when they finally came within view of the bleak and rocky coast of Newfoundland. The second letter arrived little more than three weeks later. It had been written from a hotel in Montreal, where they had disembarked from their ship. She had been much struck by the scenery as they travelled up the river, after a month at sea, especially by the interminable forest on both sides, although it was very beautiful at this time of year, with leaves of almost every hue imaginable; and by Quebec and its fortress situated on a cliff looking over the river which was a mile wide at that point, where they took on for the first time since they had left Scotland fresh provisions. Montreal was very different in appearance from Quebec, being situated on lower ground, with the royal mountain above it, and when they were ferried from their ship (for Montreal had no wharfs) she found the lower town dark and dull in appearance, with narrow ill-paved streets. However they were received very civilly at their hotel, and the company was agreeable, consisting mainly of other emigrants like themselves and some French people, and an older gentleman who had been a settler in Canada for many years. Lydia had expressed enthusiasm for the idea of a log house, and asked if it were true that one could be put up in a single day. "You can raise the walls within a day," he had replied, "but that hardly means the house is finished. If you go into the backwoods, you will have no choice but a log house, for you will be hard put to find a sawmill." One of the men staying at the hotel was an English officer who had taken up his grant of land, and was now returning home. He had come down with the ague,* however that was but one of his objections to the country. He said the woods were supposed to be filled with game, but he had never been able to find anything to shoot, and the roads were nothing but tracks filled with mudholes, though the mudholes were sometimes covered by something he called corduroy that he said was designed to dislocate the bones with jolting. In the inns there was no privacy but everyone must take a vermin-filled bed in a public sleeping room, and there was nothing to eat but greasy pork. When he arrived at his lot of wild land, he lived for two months in a wretched shed in which one would not put a cow or a pig in England, trying to plant a crop among the tree stumps, and eaten alive by musquitoes. Lydia was alarmed by his stories, and exceedingly relieved that Darcy had spared them the necessity of settling wild land and that they were to look for a farm that had already been established. They were to take a coach the following day to Lachine (rapids above Montreal preventing water travel to that town) where they would again board a boat that would carry them up the river and along the shore of Lake Ontario to the town of Amherst.**

In December, the Darcys received a third letter from Lydia.

Smith's Creek,*** Upper Canada
November –, 1815

Dear Lizzy and Darcy,
After hearing the officer in Montreal find fault with this country, you can imagine how closely I watched the shore as we travelled towards

---

* Malaria. –Ed.

** Now part of the town of Cobourg, Ontario, which received the name it bears today in 1819. – Ed.

*** Now the town of Port Hope, Ontario, so re-named in 1819. – Ed.

Amherst! The further we went up the river the more cleared land we saw, and there were some log farm houses, surrounded by fields and orchards (although there is still a very great deal of forest!); now that I see the log houses I do not like them at all. Also there are horrid ugly fences of split wood that zig-zag back and forth, and nothing pretty like a hedge row to separate the fields, or even a stone wall. There was a woman on the boat I spoke with, who had lived in Canada a long while, and she said that fifteen years ago the land we were passing was wild and used by nobody but the Indians, for hunting. In the Ontario there are impressive hills on the north shore, covered of course with woods, which have now lost their leaves. When we arrived in Amherst we found a pleasant little village, with stores and mills, and quite a few English families from the army and navy. The woods are cut down for some distance around and the village is surrounded by fields and orchards and pastures with grazing cattle, and log farm houses. The manners of some of the people we have met here in Upper Canada are very strange, for the lower classes, as soon as they arrive, whether from England or Scotland or Ireland or America, become presumptuous. There was a Scotch man in Amherst, who was offensive in his conduct to Westove, and when Westove reprimanded him the man replied that he considered himself equal to a gentleman! But Westove gave him quite a setdown and said that his proposition was worth nothing unless he could persuade a gentleman to agree with it. And there was a maidservant in the inn, who coming upon me sitting in the parlour, said she did not see why I should sit about all day when she had to work, as if I were better than she! And when I told her to hold her tongue, she said she hoped she would see me on my knees scrubbing floors one day! I hope that our servants will not take any ideas from these people.

Westove talked to the innkeeper and the merchants in Amherst about buying a farm, and several urged us to go a little further west to Smith's Creek, and look for a property in Hope township. We therefore travelled here by wagon, a journey of a few hours, and came to the inn from which I write. We were able to obtain a room of our own—it is very small but at least we are not in the public sleeping room! The other day an officer to whom Westove had received an introduction invited us to dinner at his house near the village, and in the morning I told Sally to take a gown out of my trunk and hang it up to take out the creases. I went out and when I returned the gown had disappeared. Sally knew nothing of it, so I went to the Mrs. Moodie the innkeeper's wife. "Oh!" she said cool as can be, "I showed it to Miss Traill the dressmaker, and she borrowed it to get the pattern. She will return it tomorrow." Well, it did not come back the next day, and I wanted it back, so I went to see Miss Traill. It would not have done to anger her, in case she is a good dressmaker, so I asked very civilly for the return of the dress, and she said she should only want it another two or three days! Can you imagine that? When we went to dinner, Captain Strickland laughed to hear this story and said I would come to know the Loyalists better if we stayed, and that they think that we English emigrants are sheep to be fleeced, especially if we show them our pretty manners. It was only the next day that a young woman who is a friend of Mrs. Moodie asked to borrow my bonnet! I declined lending it to her of course. But then what should I see not an hour later but this person sitting in the inn parlour with my bonnet upon her head. I did not want to acquire a reputation as a lady who could be imposed upon, so I went up to her and said I believed she was wearing my bonnet. "I have only borrowed it," she said, "as I particularly wished to wear it this evening, but I will return it to you tomorrow." Her cloak was lying on a chair nearby, so I picked it up and said to her, "You are very welcome to my bonnet for the evening, and I have a particular wish to borrow your cloak; so when you give my bonnet back to me I will give your cloak back to you." The autumn rains have begun now and the weather was quite cold (although only a few days ago it was very warm and the sky such a blue as you hardly ever see in England—Westove said it put him in mind of the sky over Italy), so she looked very surprised and vexed, and then when I turned to go she called me back. "Miss, I wouldn't have done your bonnet harm, but I need my cloak because of the chill. So take your bonnet and give me my cloak." We made the exchange, with Mrs. Moodie watching, and I hope she has taken the hint and will not make free with my belongings any more.

What a great long letter this is turning out to be! I did not think I could write so much and never mention a ball or a party once. However there has not been much to do in the day except write something to you. Westove has been talking to men and going about to look at properties, and he has now made a purchase, a farm of five hundred acres for four hundred pounds, on the Front, as the local people call the lake shore. The house is log, but it has been covered on the outside with boards that run up and down, so it is not quite so ugly as other log houses. I think it will look quite pretty when it is painted white, and some flowers are planted around it, and the view to the lake is very fine. It belonged to a Loyalist who had got into debt. Only a hundred acres of it are cleared, but there is

a good young orchard, and a beautiful spring that runs into a stone basin behind the house. Westove says the soil is fertile, and he will send back to England for equipment he wants. We are to move there in two weeks, and Westove was very firm that he would not hand over a penny more than ten pounds until we are in possession of the place. The owner was angry over this, which only made us think that he would have taken the money and then announced he was going to borrow the farm back for a few years! Westove and I are most grateful for Darcy's gift, as we would not at all have liked to live in a shed in the woods, but I am sure we will do very well here now. You may write me in care of the inn in Smith's Creek, and tell me all your news. How is Cassandra, and how are Will and Anne? Has Lady Tyrconnell's baby been born yet, and is it a boy? Do not be concerned about me for Westove makes a very good husband.
Your affectionate sister,
Lydia Westove

"I believe indeed that they *will* do very well, and I begin to feel sure of their happiness together," said Darcy when he had finished reading the letter.

"Now that I have her direction I shall write to her," said Elizabeth, "and tell her how much delight Cassandra gives to Jane and Bingley, and of their expectation that she will have a little brother or sister in the spring."

Chapter Sixty-One

[December 1815, London and Longbourn]

One morning Kitty was sitting in the parlour of the Fitzwilliams' London lodgings dejectedly reading a letter from her habitual correspondent Lady Catherine de Bourgh. Her ladyship was inquiring minutely into the Fitzwilliams' domestic concerns, for she believed herself entitled to know them all, and indeed direct them, and from experience Kitty was aware that an early and detailed reply was expected. Kitty sighed. "A report reached me yesterday that Miss Metcalf is on the point of becoming engaged," wrote Lady Catherine, proceeding to another subject. "The marriage might or might not be advantageous to her, but I have not been consulted by her mother Lady Metcalf, and I insist on being satisfied of the eligibility of the young man. I am resolved on calling on Lady Metcalf to make my sentiments known to her, for she appears to be paying no regard to the wishes of her friends. If I am not persuaded of the suitability of his connections and fortune, and find that he is presumptuous to aspire to an union with Miss Metcalf, I shall know how to act, and she should not expect to be noticed by me if the marriage take place. As Lady Metcalf is a person with whom it is proper for you to be acquainted, you shall accompany me when I make this call and I shall introduce you to her." Kitty sighed yet more deeply, for of the many disagreeable aspects that Lady Catherine presented, benefactress to her niece counted perhaps as the worst.

As Kitty was preparing to console herself for the prospect of a morning call with Lady Catherine, by a visit to the nursery, her husband entered the room hurriedly.

"Kitty," he said without preamble, "I have some very distressing news for you. I must ask you to prepare yourself."

"Oh James!" cried Kitty in consternation. "What is wrong! Has something happened to my sisters? Or my father or mother? We have had so much bad news this year."

"No, I am afraid it is much worse than that." Kitty exclaimed, much distressed. "I have heard from Marjorie's brother. She has been safely delivered of a child, a girl, and they are both well."

"But that is good news!—Oh. ... Oh James, oh no. You are teazing me, are you not?"

"I regret to say that I am not, Lady Tyrconnell."

"Oh James, this is perfectly horrid!"

"You are undoubtedly the only person in the United Kingdom who would see the inheritance of an earldom as an unmitigated tragedy. But Kitty, I am now the Earl, therefore you must be the Countess and you will simply have to put up with it. No repining, and you absolutely may not leave me and go and live in destitution under a hedge."

"Must you be the Earl? Can you not decline it?"

"Kitty, for better, for worse, you remember."

"Yes, but I did not think of anything as bad as becoming a countess."

"You must endeavour to compose yourself. This will be a permanent condition, you will have to become resigned to it, and you might as well do it sooner as later."

"Lady Catherine has been quite bad enough while you were only presumptive heir to the title, now she will be thoroughly impossible."

"It is done. Now Kitty, we do not have to be at Court. We do not even have to be in England. We can live in Ireland and breed horses."

"Does Lady Catherine suffer from seasickness?"

"I do not know. However she visited my father exceedingly rarely, so there is hope that it is now too late for her to begin making the journey."

"Will you promise me that we do not have to invite her to Ireland?"

"Well—yes, I will promise you that. I cannot however promise to turn her away if she arrives without warning. We could perhaps flood the moat around the Castle and dig some pits, if that would relieve you of your apprehensions. And you may feed her letters to the cows if you wish."

Despite Lord Tyrconnell's assurances, it was some time before Lady Tyrconnell was able to reconcile herself to her new position; and considerably longer before Lady Catherine did so.

It had been the business of Mrs. Bennet's life to get her daughters well married, and upon first hearing from her husband the news of Kitty's elevation to the peerage, she sat quite still, unable to move or utter a word, for many minutes, scarcely able to comprehend what she had been told. At length she got up and began to walk about her husband's room with an erratic step, and to speak distractedly in a flood of joy. "Lord bless me! Kitty a countess? The other girls are nothing to this, nothing at all. Good gracious! Is it really true? I shall go distracted!"

"Ah Mr. Bennet," she continued in spirits oppressively high, "did I not tell you that it was a fine thing for our girls when Mr. Bingley took Netherfield Park?"

Mr. Bennet had sufficiently witnessed his wife's elation and he replied, "You did, Mrs. Bennet, and you have proved in the event to have shown some greatness of mind. But now if you will permit me the sole occupation of my library…."

Mrs. Bennet withdrew, to go and tell the housekeeper and the housemaids of her daughter's remarkable good fortune, and Mr. Bennet, left in privacy, contemplated with some astonishment the satisfactory accomplishment of his wife's desire to establish all of her children.

EPILOGUE

A decent veil must be drawn over Lady Catherine's reaction when it was made known to her that Kitty had become Countess of Tyrconnell. For a time she went into seclusion, abased by her matrimonial defeats at the hands of her nephews. However it was not long before she rebounded and was again writing letters to the Earl and Countess instructing them how to conduct their lives. Kitty was by then so far resigned to her fate that she did not feed these letters to the cows; yet she rejoiced that Lady Catherine did not offer to promote the welfare of her niece and nephew by making the sea journey to Dublin.

Mrs. Bennet's maternal ambitions were more than fulfilled by the disposition of her five daughters, and she talked to her neighbours with delighted pride of all of them—but especially of Lady Tyrconnell—and looked forward to the visits of the four who remained on her side of the Atlantic Ocean, and to the occasional letters of Lydia. Although she anticipated the event daily, Mr. Bennet did not expire and she remained mistress of Longbourn.

Mr. Bennet had never supposed that his children could be provided for by marriage with so little inconvenience to himself and such trifling exertion on his part, for his wish had always been to have the least trouble in the business as possible; and it had been a very welcome surprise that his indolence in failing to lay by a sum for their dowries or provision after his death had been so generously rewarded. When the last of his daughters had been provided with a deserving husband, he continued all his former inactivity which was, however, punctuated by unpredictable visits to Pemberley, Clifford Priory and Castle Tyrconnell.

Mr. and Mrs. Collins were forced by circumstance to remain at Hunsford Parsonage, where they were able to make themselves useful to Lady Catherine by taking dinner at Rosings twice a week and listening to her grievances related to her daughter's matrimonial misadventures. Charlotte Collins continued to encourage her husband's healthful outdoor exercise as much as possible and grew extremely adept at making fires smoke.

Darcy was a stalwart member of the Tory party, and becoming a trusted associate of the Prime Minister was given positions of increasing responsibility. Elizabeth became a renowned political hostess. Their children were introduced to the political life at an early age; though none of them was able to match the precocity of William Pitt the Younger who in 1783 had become Prime Minister of England at the age of four-and-twenty.

Georgiana retained a tender regard for Wickham to the end of her life.

Jane's tranquillity and cheerfulness of temper were re-established by the advent of Cassandra at Clifford Priory, and enhanced by the birth of little Charles Bingley in the spring of 1816. The two events completely restored to her her privilege of universal good-will, much to the disgust of her sister Lady Mallinger. Cassandra and Charles were followed by several more children, delighting Jane and Bingley beyond measure.

Mr. Gardiner's business venture with John Thorn succeeded past all expectation, and with the profit he purchased an estate in Yorkshire, in order to be closer to the manufacturing centres of England; where, in addition to every other source of happiness, the Gardiners and Darcys and Bingleys were within thirty miles of each other.

If Lady Mallinger did not love Sir Henry Mallinger, or if she continued to love John Thorn, she disclosed neither feeling by her demeanour, which was always highly esteemed by fashionable society. Sir Henry persisted in dividing his time between England and Venice, and was followed to that aqueous city in 1816 by Lord Byron, who occasionally entertained Sir Henry and Signora Giovanese at his *palazzo* on the Grand Canal.

John Thorn's advice concerning roads and railroads and other modernizations was greatly valued by ministers of the Government, and he was within a short time made a baronet.

Mrs. Hurst did not again try her hand at matchmaking.

The Earl and Countess of Tyrconnell established a famous stud in Ireland, and their horses regularly won at the Curragh. The Countess wrote an anonymous monograph on the treatment of leg injuries in horses which was well received by horsemen. Their children, if not quite born in the saddle, all learned to ride fearlessly before the age of five. Kitty became a hunting countess, reasoning that as Miss Bennet of Longbourn for her to hunt would have been the height of indecorum, but as an Irish countess it was mere eccentricity. Lady Catherine de Bourgh's frequently expressed disapprobation failed to alter either her opinion or her activities.

Mary Cramer and Adam Kendall married, and worked tirelessly for the cause of animal protection. I wish I could affirm that this marriage of affection had the pleasing consequence of relieving Mary of all of her conceitedness, but if truth be told she remained a little vain and was always impatient for display. She was in the visitors' gallery of the House of Commons when the Ill-treatment of Cattle Bill (Richard Martin's Act) was passed on July 24, 1822, and was also in attendance at Old Slaughter's Coffee House on June 16, 1824 when the Society for the Prevention of Cruelty to Animals was formed by a committee consisting of Sir Jas. Mackintosh MP, A. Warre Esqr. MP, Wm. Wilberforce Esqr. MP, Basil Montagu Esqr., Reverend Arthur Broome, Reverend G. Bonner, Reverend G. A. Hatch, A.E. Kendal Esqr., Lewis Gompertz Esqr., Wm. Mudford Esqr., and Dr. Henderson.* Mary was her children's first Latin tutor.

Lydia's high spirits were brought under regulation by the lack of eligible officers to flirt with in Upper Canada. Although the occasional redcoat (and once even a full troop of soldiers) came to the village near the Westoves' farm, none ever stayed long. The comparative isolation and harshness of life in the new world required husband and wife to have the firmest reliance on one another, and Lydia after a time became deeply attached to Westove. Several children also took up much of her attention. The hard work of being a farmer's wife in the new world suited her, and she became almost as pleased over a new crop of vegetables or a row of jars of preserved fruit as she had ever been over a new bonnet. Thomas Westove proved to be an astute man of business and he prospered, and built for his wife and family the finest brick house for many miles around.

---

* The SPCA was granted royal status by Queen Victoria in 1840, becoming the Royal Society for the Prevention of Cruelty to Animals (RSPCA). –Ed.

This book is dedicated to
Abby, Bill, Heidi and Oz

With affection and gratitude to J.

Cover photo of author by Zdenka Darula

LaVergne, TN USA
25 March 2011
221665LV00004B/77/P

9 780986 778902